A World Dying

On the giant world called Helliconia, where one year lasts two and a half thousand earth years and winter is seven centuries long, the temperature is dropping as the skies darken. War, pestilence, and the inexorable cycle of change holds the planet in an increasingly icy grip. Faced with the total destruction of their culture and environment, the inhabitants of Helliconia must use all their wit and courage in an attempt to avoid the ultimate Death.

Brian Aldiss's *Helliconia* Trilogy—already hailed as his greatest achievement and possibly the greatest science fiction epic of our time—comes to a spectacular conclusion in *Helliconia Winter*.

"The superior finale to an awesome and fascinating spectacle."
—*Kirkus Reviews*

COLLIER NUCLEUS
FANTASY & SCIENCE FICTION

Consulting Editor, James Frenkel

HELLICONIA
WINTER

Brian W. Aldiss

COLLIER BOOKS
Macmillan Publishing Company
New York

Maxwell Macmillan International
New York   Oxford   Singapore   Sydney

Collier Books
Macmillan Publishing Company
866 Third Avenue
New York, NY 10022

Macmillan Publishing Company is part of the
Maxwell Communication Group of Companies.

Library of Congress Cataloging-in-Publication Data
Aldiss, Brian Wilson, 1925–
    Helliconia winter/Brian W. Aldiss.—1st Collier Books ed.
      p.   cm.
    ISBN 0-02-016092-5
    I. Title.
    PR6051.L3H46 1993   92–30921   CIP
    823'.914—dc20

Map by Margaret Aldiss

First Collier Books Edition 1993

10 9 8 7 6 5 4 3 2 1

Printed in the United States of America

In the first place, since the elements of which we see the world composed—solid earth and moisture, the light breaths of air and torrid fire—all consist of bodies that are neither birthless nor deathless, we must believe the same of the Earth as a whole, and of its populations. . . . And whatever earth contributes to feed the growth of others is restored to it. It is an observed fact that the Universal Mother is also the common grave. Earth, therefore, is whittled away and renewed with fresh increment.

Lucretius: *De Rerum Natura*
55 BC

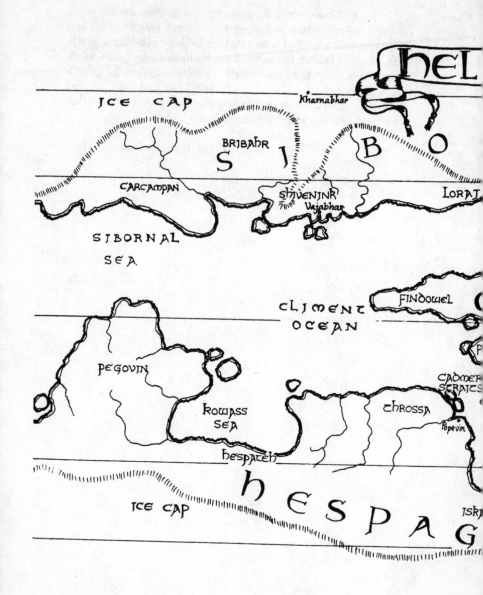

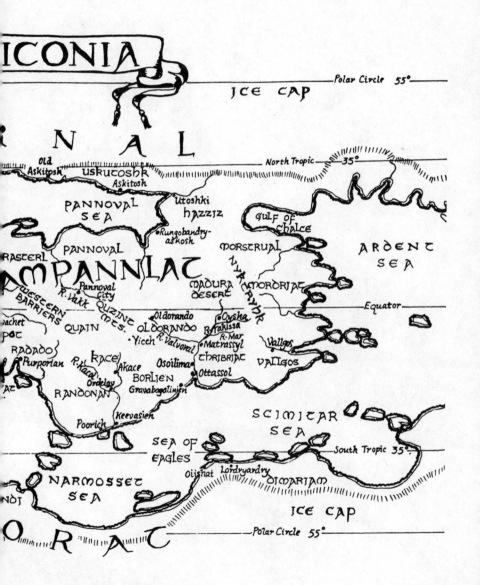

ICONIA

ICE CAP

Polar Circle 55°

N A L

North Tropic 35°

old
Askitosh   USRUTOSHR
   Askitosh
                 Utoshki
PANNOVAL   HAZZIZ
   SEA   GULF OF
            •Rungobandry-   CHALCE
PANNOVAL   askosh
                    MORSTRUAL   ARDENT
AMPANNLAT   MADURA   SEA
RASTERL   Pannoval DESERT   MORDRIAT
         •city   Equator
    WESTERN R. Vakk QUZINT MTS.
    BARRIERS QUAIN   Oldorando •Oysha
rachet   OLDORANDO R.Takissa
POT   •Yicch R. Valvoral R. Mar
RADADO   •Matrassyl   Vallgos
•Purporian   RACE   THRIBRIAT   VALLGOS
         R. Kaca Akace Osoilima
AT   Ordelay BORLIEN Ottassol
      RANDONAN Gravabagalinien
                                 SCIMITAR
         Poorich Keevasien   SEA
                                        South Tropic 35°
              SEA OF
NOT   EAGLES
      NARMOSSET   Oiishat Lordryardry
         SEA   OIMARIAM
                                 ICE CAP
ORAT   Polar Circle 55°

CONTENTS

Helliconia Winter

PRELUDE

Luterin had recovered. He was free of the mysterious illness. He was allowed out again. The couch by the window, the immobility, the grey schoolmaster who came every day—they were done with. He was alive to fill his lungs with the brisk airs of outdoors.

The cold blew down from Mount Shivenink, sharp enough to peel the bark from the north side of trees.

The fresh wind brought out his defiance. It drew the blood to his cheeks, it made his limbs move with the beast which carried him across his father's land. Letting out a yell, he spurred the hoxney into a gallop. He headed it away from the incarcerating mansion with its tolling bell, away along the avenue traversing the fields they still called the Vineyard. The movement, the air, the uproar of his own blood in his arteries, intoxicated him.

Around him lay his father's territory, a dominion triumphing over latitude, a small world of moor, mountain, valley, plunging stream, cloud, snow, forest, waterfall—but he kept his thought from the waterfall. Endless game roved here, springing up plenteously even as his father hunted it down. Roving phagors. Birds whose migrations darkened the sky.

Soon he would be hunting again, following the example of his father. Life had been somehow stayed, was somehow renewed. He must rejoice and force away the blackness hovering on the edges of his mind.

He galloped past bare-chested slaves who exercised yelk about the Vineyard, clinging to their snaffles. The hoofs of the animals scattered mounds of earth sent up by moles.

Luterin Shokerandit spared a sympathetic thought for the moles. They could ignore the extravagances of the two suns. Moles could hunt and rut in any season. When they died, their bodies were devoured by other moles. For moles, life was an endless tunnel through which the males quested for food and mates. He had forgotten them, lying abed.

"Moledom!" he shouted, bouncing in the saddle, rising up in the stirrups. The spare flesh on his body made its own movements under his arang jacket.

He goaded the hoxney on. Exercise was what was needed to bring him back into fighting shape. The spare fat was falling away from him even on this, his first ride out for more than a small year. His twelfth birthday had been wasted flat on his back. For over four hundred days he had lain like that—for a considerable period unable to move or speak. He had been entombed in his bed, in his room, in his parents' mansion, in the great grave House of the Keeper. Now that episode was finished.

Strength flowed back to his muscles, arriving from the animal beneath him, from the air, from the trunks of trees as they flashed by, from his own inner being. Some destructive force whose nature he did not comprehend had wiped him out of the world; now he was back and determined to make a mark upon that flashing stage.

One of the double entrance gates was opened for him by a slave before he reached it. He galloped through without pause or sideways glance.

The wind yelped in his unaccustomed ear like a hound. He lost the familiar note of the bell of the house behind him. The small bells on his harness jingled as the ground responded to his advance.

Both Batalix and Freyr were low in the southern sky. They flitted among the tree trunks like gongs, the big sun and the small. Luterin turned his back on them as he reached the village road. Year by year, Freyr was sinking lower in the skies of Sibornal. Its sinking called forth fury in the human spirit. The world was about to change.

The sweat that formed on his chest cooled instantly. He was whole again, determined to make up for lost time by rutting and hunting like the moles. The hoxney could carry him to the verge of the trackless caspiarn forests, those forests which fell away and away into the deepest recesses of the mountain ranges. One day soon, he planned to fade into the embrace of those forests, to fade and be lost, relishing his own dangerousness like an animal among animals. But first ue would be lost in the embrace of Insil Esikananzi.

Luterin gave a laugh. "Yes, you have a wild side, boy," his father had once said, staring down at Luterin after some misdemeanour or other—staring down with that friendless look of his, while placing a hand on the boy's shoulder as if estimating the amount of wildness per bone.

And Luterin had gazed downwards, unable to meet that stare. How could his father love him as he loved his father when he was so mute in the great man's presence?

The distant grey roofs of the monasteries showed through the naked trees. Close lay the gates of the Esikananzi estate. He let the brown hoxney slow to a trot, sensing its lack of stamina. The species was preparing for hibernation. Soon all hoxneys would be useless for riding. This was the season for training up the recalcitrant but more powerful yelk. When a slave opened the Esikananzi gate, the hoxney turned in at walking pace. The distinctive Esikananzi bell sounded ahead, chiming randomly as the wind took its vane.

He prayed to God the Azoiaxic that his father knew nothing of his activities with Ondod females, that wickedness he had fallen into shortly before paralysis had overcome him. The Ondods gave what Insil so far refused him.

He must resist those inhuman females now. He was a man. There were sleazy shacks by the edge of the forest where he and his school friends—including Umat Esikananzi—went to meet those shameless eight-fingered bitches. Bitches, witches, who came out of the woods, out of the very roots of the woods . . . And it was said that they consorted with male phagors too. Well, that would not happen again. It was in the past, like his brother's death. And like his brother's death, best forgotten.

It was not beautiful, the mansion of the Esikananzis. Brutality was the predominant feature of its architecture; it was constructed to withstand the brutal onslaughts of a northern climate. A row of blind arches formed the base of it. Narrow windows, heavily shuttered, began only on the second floor. The whole structure resembled a decapitated pyramid. The bell in its belfry made a slatey sound, as if ringing from the adamantine heart of the building.

Luterin dismounted, climbed the steps, and pulled the doorbell.

He was a broad-shouldered youth, already lofty in the Sibornalese manner, with a round face seemingly built naturally for merriment: although, at this moment, awaiting sight of Insil, his brows were knit, his lips compressed. The tension of his expression caused him to resemble his father, but his eyes were of a clear grey, very different from his father's dark, in-dwelling pupils.

His hair, curling riotously about his head and the nape of his neck, was light brown, and formed a contrast to the neat dark head of the girl into whose presence he was ushered.

Insil Esikananzi had the airs of one born into a powerful family. She could be sharp and dismissive. She teased. She lied. She cultivated a helpless manner; or, if it suited her better, a look of command. Her smiles were wintery, more a concession to politeness than an expression of her spirit. Her violet eyes looked out of a face she kept as blank as possible.

She was carrying a jug of water through the hall, clasped in both hands. As she came towards Luterin she lifted her chin slightly into the air, in a kind of mute exasperated enquiry. To Luterin, Insil was intensely desirable, and no less desirable for her capriciousness.

This was the girl he was to marry, according to the arrangement drawn up between his father and hers at Insil's birth, to cement the accord between the two most powerful men of the district.

Directly he was in her presence, Luterin was caught up once more into their old conspiracy, into that intricate teasing web of complaint which she wove about herself.

"I see, Luterin, you are on your two feet again. How excellent. And like a dutiful husband-to-be, you have perfumed yourself with sweat and hoxney before presuming to call and present your compliments. You have certainly grown while in bed—at least in the region of your waist-line."

She fended off an embrace with the jug of water. He put an arm about her slender waist as she led him up the immense staircase, made more gloomy by dark portraits from which dead Esikananzis stared as if in tether, shrunken by art and time.

"Don't be provoking, Sil. I'll soon be slim again. It's wonderful to have my health back."

Her personal bell uttered its light clap on every stair.

"My mother's so sickly. Always sickly. My slimness is illness, not health. You are lucky to call when my tedious parents and my equally tedious brothers, including your friend Umat, are all attending a boring ceremony elsewhere. So you can expect to take advantage of me, can't you? Of course, you suspect that I have been had by stable boys while you were in your year's hibernation. Giving myself in the hay to sons of slaves."

She guided him along a corridor where the boards creaked under their worn Madi carpets. She was close, phantasmal in the little light that filtered here through shuttered windows.

"Why do you punish my heart, Insil, when it is yours?"

"It's not your heart I want, but your soul." She laughed. "Have more spirit. Hit me, as my father does. Why not? Isn't punishment the essence of things?"

He said heatedly, "Punishment? Listen, we'll be married and I'll make you happy. You can hunt with me. We'll never be apart. We'll explore the forests—"

"You know I'm more interested in rooms than forests." She paused with a hand on a door latch, smiling provocatively, projecting her shallow breasts toward him under their linens and laces.

"People are better outside, Sil. Don't grin. Why pretend I'm a fool? I know as much about suffering as you. That whole small year spent prostrate—wasn't that about the worst punishment anyone could imagine?"

Insil put a finger on his chin and slid it up to his lip. "That clever paralysis allowed you to escape from a greater punishment—having to live here under our repressive parents, in this repressive community— where you for instance were driven to cohabit with non-humans for relief . . ."

She smiled as he blushed, but continued in her sweetest voice. "Have you no insight into your own suffering? You often accused me of not loving you, and that may be so, but don't I pay you better attention than you pay yourself?"

"What do you mean, Insil?" How her conversation tormented him.

"Is your father at home or away on the hunt?"

"He's at home."

"As I recall, he had returned from the hunt not more than two days before your brother committed suicide. Why did Favin commit suicide? I suspect that he knew something you refuse to know."

Without taking her dark gaze from his eyes, she opened the door behind her, pushing it so that it opened to allow sunshine to bathe them as they stood, conspiratorial yet opposed, on the threshold. He clutched her, tremulous to discover that she was as necessary to him as ever, and as ever full of riddles.

"What did Favin know? What am I supposed to know?" The mark of her power over him was that he was always questioning her.

"Whatever your brother knew, it was that which sent you escaping into your paralysis—not his actual death, as everyone pretends." She was twelve years and a tenner, not much more than a child: yet a tension in her gestures made her seem much older. She raised an eyebrow at his puzzlement.

He followed her into the room, wishing to ask her more, yet tonguetied. "How do you know these things, Insil? You invent them to make yourself mysterious. Always locked in these rooms . . ."

She set the jug of water down on a table beside a bunch of white flowers which she had picked earlier. The flowers lay scattered on the polished surface, their faces reflected as in a misted mirror.

As though to herself, she said, "I try to train you not to grow up like the rest of the men here . . ."

She walked over to the window, framed in heavy brown curtains which hung from ceiling to floor. Although she stood with her back to him, he sensed that she was not looking out. The dual sunlight, shining in from two different directions, dissolved her as if it were liquid, so that her shadow on the tiled floor appeared more substantial than she. Insil was demonstrating once more her elusive nature.

It was a room he had not entered before, a typical Esikananzi room, loaded with heavy furniture. It held a tantalising scent, in part repugnant. Perhaps its only purpose was to hoard furniture, most of it wooden, against the day when the Weyr-Winter came and no more furniture would be made. There was a green couch with carved scrollwork, and a massive wardrobe which dominated the chamber. All the furniture had been imported; he saw that by its style.

He shut the door, remaining there contemplating her. As if he did not exist, she began arranging her flowers in a vase, pouring water from the jug into the vase, shuffling the stems peremptorily with her long fingers.

He sighed. "My mother is always sickly, too, poor thing. Every day of her life she goes into pauk and communes with her dead parents."

Insil looked up sharply at him. "And you—while you were lying flat on your back—I suppose you've fallen into the habit of pauk too?"

"No. You're mistaken. My father forbad me . . . besides, it's not just that . . ."

Insil put fingers to her temples. "Pauk is what the common people do. It's so superstitious. To go into a trance and descend into that awful underworld, where bodies rot and those ghastly corpses are still spitting the dregs of life . . . oh, it's disgusting. You're *sure* you don't do it?"

"Never. I imagine my mother's sickness comes from pauk."

"Well, sherb you, *I* do it every day. I kiss my grandmother's corpse-lips and taste the maggots . . ." Then she burst into laughter. "Don't look so silly. I'm joking. I hate the thought of those things underground and I'm glad you don't go near them."

She lowered her gaze to the flowers.

"These snowflowers are tokens of the world's death, don't you think? There are only white flowers now, to go with the snow. Once, so the histories say, brightly coloured flowers bloomed in Kharnabhar."

She pushed the vase resignedly from her. Down in the throats of the pale blossoms, a touch of gold remained, turning to a speck of intense red at the ovary, like an emblem of the vanishing sun.

He sauntered across to her, over the patterned tiles. "Come and sit on the couch with me and talk of happier things."

"You must be referring to the climate—declining so rapidly that our grandchildren, if we live to have any, will spend their lives in near darkness, wrapped in animal skins. Probably making animal noises . . . That sounds a promising topic."

"What nonsense you talk!" Laughing, he jumped forward and grasped her. She let him drag her down on the couch as he uttered fevered endearments.

"Of course you can't make love to me, Luterin. You may feel me as you have before, but no lovemaking. I don't think I shall ever take kindly to lovemaking—but in any case, were I to permit it, you would lose your interest in me, your lust being satisfied."

"It's a lie, a lie."

"It had best stand as the truth, if we are to have any marital happiness at all. I am not marrying a sated man."

"I could never have enough of you." As he spoke, his hand was foraging up her clothes.

"The invading armies . . ." Insil sighed, but she kissed him and put the point of her tongue in his mouth.

At which moment, the door of the wardrobe burst open. Out jumped a young man of Insil's dark colouration, but as frenzied as his sister was passive. It was Umat, brandishing a sword, shouting.

"Sister, sister! Help is at hand! Here's your brave rescuer, to save you and the family from dishonour! Who's this beast? Isn't a year in bed enough for him, that he must rise immediately to seek the nearest couch? Varlet! Rapist!"

"You rat in the skirting!" Luterin shouted. He rushed at Umat in a rage, the wooden sword fell to the floor, and they wrestled furiously. After his long confinement, Luterin had lost some of his strength. His friend threw him to the floor. As he picked himself up, he saw that Insil had flitted away.

He ran to the door. She had vanished into the dark recesses of the house. In the scuffle, her flowers had been spilt and the jug broken on the tiled floor.

Only as he made his way disconsolately back to the village road, letting the hoxney carry him at walking pace, did it occur to Luterin that possibly Insil had staged Umat's interruption. Instead of going home, he turned right at the Esikananzi gate, and rode into the village to drink at the Icen Inn.

Batalix was close to setting when he followed the mournful Shoke-randit bell home. Snow was falling. No one was about in the grey world. At the inn, the talk consisted mainly of jokes and complaints concerning the new regulations being introduced by the Oligarch, such as curfew. The regulations were intended to strengthen communities throughout Sibornal for ordeals to come.

Most of the talk was cheap, and Luterin despised it. His father would never speak of such things—or not in his one remaining son's hearing.

The gaslights were burning in the long hall of his home. As Luterin was unbuckling his personal bell, a slave came up, bowed, and announced that his father's secretary wished to see him.

"Where is my father?" Luterin demanded.

"Keeper Shokerandit has left, sir."

Angrily Luterin ran up the stairs and threw open the door into the secretary's room. The secretary was a permanent member of the Shokerandit household. With his beaklike nose, his straight line of eyebrow, his shallow forehead, and the quiff of hair which protruded over that forehead, the secretary resembled a crow. This narrow wooden room, its pigeonholes stuffed with secret documents, was the crow's nest. From here, it surveyed many secret prospects beyond Luterin's ken.

"Your father is off on a hunt, Master Luterin," announced this wily bird now, in a tone mingling deference with reproach. "Since you were nowhere to be found, he had to leave without bidding you farewell."

"Why didn't he let me accompany him? He knows I love the hunt. Perhaps I can catch him up. Which way did his entourage go?"

"He entrusted me with this epistle for you. You would perhaps be advised to read it before dashing off."

The secretary handed over a large envelope. Luterin snatched it from his talons. He ripped open the cover and read what was set down on the enclosed sheet in his father's large and careful hand:

Son Luterin,

There is a prospect in the days to come that you will be appointed Keeper of the Wheel in my place. That role, as you are aware, combines both secular and religious duties.

When you were born, you were taken to Rivenjk to be blessed by the Priest-Supreme of the Church of the Formidable Peace. I believe this to have fortified the godly side of your nature. You have proved a submissive son in whom I am satisfied.

Now it is time to fortify the secular side of your nature. Your late brother was commissioned to the army, as is the tradition with elder sons. It is fitting that you should take up a similar office, especially as in the wider world (of which you so far know nothing), Sibornal's affairs are moving towards a point of decision.

Accordingly, I have left a sum of money with my secretary. He will hand it over to you. You will proceed to Askitosh, chief city of our proud continent, and there enroll yourself as a soldier, with a commissioned rank of lieutenant ensign. Report to Archpriest-Militant Asperamanka, who will be familiar with your situation.

I have instructed that a masque shall be held in your honour, to celebrate your departure.

You are to leave without delay and gather esteem to the family name.

Your father

A blush spread over Luterin's face as he read his father's rare word of praise. That his father should be satisfied with him despite all his failings!—satisfied enough to declare a masque in his honour!

His glow of happiness faded when he realised that his father would himself not be present at the masque. No matter. He would become a soldier and do anything asked of him. He would make his father proud of him.

Perhaps even Insil would warm to the name of glory. . . .

The masque was performed in the banqueting hall of the Shokerandit mansion on the eve of Luterin's departure south.

Stately personages in grand costume enacted preordained roles. A solemn music played. A familiar story was performed telling of innocence and villainy, of the lust to possess, and of the convoluted role of faith in the lives of men. To some characters harm was allotted, to some good. All came under a law greater than their own jurisdiction. The musicians, bent over their strings, emphasised the mathematics which prevailed over relationships.

The harmonies evoked by the musicians suggested a cadence of stern compassion, inviting a view of human affairs far beyond the normal acceptances of optimism or pessimism. In the leitmotifs for the woman forced to give herself to a ruler she hated and for the man unable to control his baser passions, musical members of the audience could detect a fatality, a sense that even the most individual characters were indissolubly functions of their environment, just as individual notes formed part of the greater harmony. The stylised acting of the performers reinforced this interpretation.

Some entrances were politely applauded by the audience, others observed without especial pleasure. The actors were well rehearsed in their roles, but not all by any means commanded the same presence as the principals.

Figures of state, figures of noble families, figures of the church, allegorical figures representing phagors and monsters, together with the various humours of Love, Hatred, Evil, Passion, Fear, and Purity, played their parts on the boards and were gone.

The stage emptied. Darkness fell. The music died.

But Luterin Shokerandit's drama was just beginning.

I

THE LAST BATTLE

S uch was the nature of grass that it continued to grow despite the wind. It bowed to the wind. Its roots spread under the soil, anchoring it, leaving no room for other plants to find lodgement. The grass had always been there. It was the wind which was more recent—and the bite in it.

The great exhalations from the north carried with them a fast-moving sky, comprising a patchwork of black and grey cloud. Over distant high ground the clouds spilled rain and snow. Here, across the steppelands of Chalce, they purveyed nothing worse than a neutral obscurity. That ~utrality found an echo in the monotony of the terrain.

A series of shallow valleys opened one into the next, without definite feature. The only movement to be seen was among the grasses. Some tufts bore insignificant yellow flowers which rippled in the wind like the fur of a supine animal. The sole landmarks were occasional stone pillars marking land-octaves. The south-facing sides of these stones sometimes bore lichens, yellow and grey.

Only keen eyes could have discerned minute trails in the grass, used by creatures which appeared at night or during dimday, when only one of the two suns was above the horizon. Solitary hawks, patrolling the sky on motionless wings, explained the lack of daytime activity. The widest trail through the grasslands was carved by a river which flowed southwards towards the distant sea. Deep and sluggish in movement, its waters appeared partly congealed. The river took its colour from the tatterdemalion sky.

From the north of this inhospitable country came a flock of arang. These long-legged members of the goat family loosely followed the tedious bends of the river. Curly-horned dogs kept the arang closely grouped. These hardworking asokins were in turn controlled by six men on hoxney-back. The six sat or stood in their saddles to vary their journey. All were dressed in skins lashed about their bodies with thongs.

The men frequently looked back over their shoulders, as if afraid of pursuit. Keeping up a steady pace, they communicated with their asokins by whoops and whistles. These encouraging signals rang through the hollow spaces round about, clear above the bleat of the arang. However often the men glanced back, the drab northern horizon remained empty.

The ruins of a place of habitation appeared ahead, nestling in an elbow of the river. Scattered stone huts stood roofless. A larger building was no more than a shell. Ragged plants, taking advantage of the windbreak, grew about the stones, peering from the blank window sockets.

The arangherds gave the place a wide berth, fearing plague. A few miles farther on, the river, taking a leisurely curve, served as a boundary which had been in dispute for centuries, perhaps for as long as there had been men in the land. Here began the region once known as Hazziz, northernmost land of the North Campannlatian Plain. The dogs channelled the arang along beside the river, where a path had been worn. The arang spread into a fast-moving line, face to tail.

They came in time to a broad and durable bridge. It threw its two arches across the wind-troubled face of the water. The men whistled shrilly, the asokins marshalled the arang into a bunch, preventing them crossing the bridge. A mile or two away, lying against the northern bank of the river, was a settlement built in the shape of a wheel. The name of the settlement was Isturiacha.

A bugle sounded from the settlement, telling the arangherds that they had been sighted. Armed men and black Sibornalese cannon guarded the perimeter.

"Welcome!" shouted the guards. "What did you see to the north? Did you see the army?"

The arangherds drove their animals into pens already awaiting them.

The stone farmhouses and barns of the settlement had been built as a fortification along its perimeter. The farms, where cereals and livestock were raised, lay in the middle. At the hub of the circle, a ring of barracklike offices surrounded a tall church. There was continual coming and going in Isturiacha, which increased as the herdsmen were taken into one of the central buildings to refresh themselves after their journey across the steppes.

On the south side of the bridge, the plain was more varied in contour. Isolated trees betokened increased rainfall. The ground was stippled with fragments of a white substance, which from a distance resembled crumbling stone. On closer inspection the fragments proved to be bone. Few pieces measured more than six inches in length. Occasionally a tooth or wedge of jawbone revealed the remains to be those of men and phagors. These testimonies to past battles stretched across miles of plain.

Over the immobility of this doleful place rode a man on yelk-back, approaching the bridge from the south. Some way behind him followed two more men. All three wore uniform and were equipped for war.

The leading rider, a small and sharp-featured man, halted well before he reached the bridge, and dismounted. He led his animal down into a dip and secured it to the trunk of a flat-topped briar tree before climbing to the level, where he stood peering through a spyglass at the enemy settlement ahead.

The other two men presently joined him. They also dismounted and tied their yelk to the roots of a dead rajabaral. Being of senior rank, they stood apart from the scout.

"Isturiacha," said the scout, pointing. But the officers spoke only to each other. They too scrutinised Isturiacha through a spyglass, conferring together in low tones. A cursory reconnaissance was made.

One officer—an artillery expert—remained on watch where he was. His brother officer galloped back with the scout to pass information to an army which advanced from the south.

As the day passed, the plain became broken by lines of men—some mounted, many more on foot—interspersed by wagons, cannon, and the impedimenta of war. The wagons were drawn by yelk or the less sturdy hoxney. There were columns of soldiers marching in good order, contrasting with baggage trains and women and camp followers in no order at all. Above a number of the marching columns waved the banners of Pannoval, the city under the mountains, and other flags of religious import.

Further back came ambulances and more carts, some carrying field kitchens and provisions, many more loaded with fodder for the animals involved in this punitive expedition.

Although these hundreds and thousands of people functioned like cogs in the war machine, nevertheless each underwent incidents peculiar to his or her self, and each experienced the adventure through his or her limited perceptions.

One such incident occurred to the artillery officer who waited with his mount by the shattered rajabaral tree. He lay silent, watching his front, when the whinnying of his yelk made him turn his head. Four small men, none coming higher than his chest, were advancing on the tethered mount. They evidently had not observed the officer as they emerged from a hole in the ground at the base of the ruined tree.

The creatures were humanoid in general outline, with thin legs and long arms. Their bodies were covered in a tawny pelt, which grew long about their wrists, half concealing eight-fingered hands. The muzzles of their faces made them resemble dogs or Others.

"Nondads!" the officer exclaimed. He recognised them immediately, although he had seen them only in captivity. The yelk plunged about in terror. As the two leading Nondads threw themselves at its throat, he drew his double-barrelled pistol, then paused.

Another head thrust itself up between the ancient roots, struggled to get its shoulders free, and then rose, shaking soil from its thick coat and snorting.

The phagor dominated the Nondads. Its immense box-head was crowned by two slender horns sweeping backwards. As the bulk of it emerged from the Nondad hole, it swung its morose bull face between its shoulders, and its eyes lit on the crouching officer. Just for a moment, it paused without movement. An ear flicked. Then it charged at the man, head down.

The artillery officer rolled onto his back, steadied the pistol with both hands, and fired both barrels into the belly of the brute. An irregular golden star of blood spread across its pelt, but the creature still came on. The ugly mouth opened, showing spadelike yellow teeth set in yellow gums. As the officer jumped to his feet, the phagor struck him full force. Coarse three-fingered hands closed round his body.

He struck out again and again, hammering the butt of his gun against the thick skull.

The grip relaxed. The barrel body fell to one side. The face struck the ground. With an enormous effort, the creature managed to regain its feet. It bellowed. Then it fell dead, and the earth shook.

Gasping, choking on the thick milky stench of the ancipital, the officer pulled himself to his knees. He had to steady himself with a hand on the phagor's shoulder. In amid the thick coat of the body, ticks flicked hither and thither, undergoing a crisis of their own. Some climbed onto the officer's sleeve.

He managed to stagger to his feet. He trembled. His mount trembled nearby, bleeding from lacerations at its throat. Of the Nondads there was no sign; they had retreated into their underground warrens, into the domain they knew as the Eighty Darknesses. After a while, the artillery officer was sufficiently master of himself to climb into the saddle. He had heard of the liaison between phagors and Nondads, but

had never expected to confront an example of it. There could be more
of the brutes beneath his feet . . .

Still choking, he rode back to find his unit.

The expedition mounted from Pannoval, to which the officer belonged, had been operating in the field for some while. It was engaged
in wiping out Sibornalese settlements established on what Pannoval
claimed as its own territory. Starting at Roonsmoor, it had carried out
a series of successful forays. As each enemy settlement was crushed, the
expedition moved farther north. Only Isturiacha remained to be destroyed. It was now a matter of timing before the small summer was
over.

The settlements, with their siege mentality, rarely assisted each
other. Some were supported by one Sibornalese nation, some by another. So they fell victims to their destroyers one by one.

The dispersed Pannovalan units had little more to fear than occasional phagors, appearing in even greater numbers as the temperatures
on the plains declined. The experience of the artillery officer was not
untypical.

As the officer rejoined his fellows, a watery sun emerged from scud-
ding cloud to set in the west amid a dramatic display of colour. When
it was quenched by the horizon, the world was not plunged into darkness. A second sun, Freyr, burned low in the south. When the cloud
formations parted about it, it threw shadows of men like pointed
fingers to the north.

Slowly, two traditional enemies were preparing to do battle. Far
behind the figures toiling on the plain, to the southwest, was the great
city of Pannoval, from which the will to fight issued. Pannoval lay hidden within the limestone range of mountains called the Quzints. The
Quzints formed the backbone of the tropical continent of Campannlat.

Of the many nations of Campannlat, several owed allegiance through
dynastic or religious ties with Pannoval. Coherence, however, was always temporary, peace always fragile; the nations warred with each
other. Hence the name by which Campannlat was known to its external enemy: the Savage Continent.

Campannlat's external enemy was the northern continent of Sibornal.
Under the pressure of its extreme climate, the nations of Sibornal preserved a close unity. The rivalries under the surface were generally
suppressed. Throughout history, the Sibornalese nations pressed southwards, across the land-bridge of Chalce, to the more productive mead-
ows of the Savage Continent.

There was a third continent, the southern one of Hespagorat. The
continents were divided, or almost divided, by seas occupying the tem-
perate zones. These seas and continents comprised the planet of

Helliconia, or Hrl-Ichor Yhar, to use the name bestowed on it by its elder race, the ancipitals.

At this period, when the forces of Campannlat and Sibornal were preparing for a last battle at Isturiacha, Helliconia was moving towards the nadir of its year.

As a planet of a binary system, Helliconia revolved about its parent sun, Batalix, once every 480 days. But Batalix itself revolved about a common axis with a much larger sun, Freyr, the major component of the system. Batalix was now carrying Helliconia on its extended orbit away from the greater star. Over the last two centuries, the autumn—that long decline from summer—had intensified. Now Helliconia was poised on the brink of the winter of another Great Year. Darkness, cold, silence, waited in the centuries ahead.

Even the lowest peasant was aware that the climate grew steadily worse. If the weather did not tell him as much, there were other signs. Once more the plague known as the Fat Death was spreading. The ancipitals, commonly referred to as phagors, scented the approach of those seasons when they were most comfortable, when conditions returned most closely to what they once had been. Throughout the spring and summer, those ill-fated creatures had suffered under the supremacy of man: now, at the chill end of the Great Year, as the numbers of mankind began to dwindle, the phagors would seize their chance to rule again—unless humankind united to stop them.

There were powerful wills on the planet, wills which might move the mass of people into action. One such will sat in Pannoval, another, even harsher, in the Sibornalese capital of Askitosh. But at present those wills were most preoccupied with confounding each other.

So the Sibornalese settlers in Isturiacha prepared for siege, while looking anxiously to see if reinforcement would come from the north. So the guns from Pannoval and her allies were wheeled into position to aim at Isturiacha.

Some confusion reigned both at the front and the rear of the mixed Pannovalan force. The elderly Chief Marshal in charge of the advance was powerless to stop units who had looted other Sibornalese settlements from heading back to Pannoval with their spoils. Other units were summoned forward to replace them. Meanwhile, the artillery situated inside the walls of the settlement began to bombard the Pannovalan lines.

Bruum. Bruum. The short-lived explosions burst among the contingent from Randonan, which had come from the south of the Savage Continent.

Many nations were represented in the ranks of the Pannovalan expeditionary army. There were ferocious skirmishers from Kace, who marched, slept, and fought with their dehorned phagors; tall stone-faced men of Brasterl, who came kilted from the Western Barriers;

tribes from Mordriat, with their lively timoroon mascots; together with a strong battalion from Borldoran, the Oldorando-Borlien Joint Monarchy—Pannoval's strongest ally. A few amid their number presented the squat shape of those who had suffered the Fat Death and lived.

The Borldoranians had crossed the Quzint Mountains by high and windy passes to fight beside their fellows. Some had fallen ill and turned for home. The remaining force, fatigued, now discovered their access to the river blocked by units which had arrived earlier, so that they were unable to water their mounts.

The argument grew hot while shells from Isturiacha exploded nearby. The commandant of the Borldoranian battalion strode off to make complaint to the Chief Marshal. This commandant was a jaunty man, young to command, with a military moustache and a concave back, by name Bandal Eith Lahl.

With Bandal Eith Lahl went his pretty young wife, Toress Lahl. She was a doctor, and also had a complaint for the old Chief Marshal— a complaint about the poor standards of hygiene. She walked discreetly behind her husband, behind that rigid back, letting her skirts trail on the ground.

They presented themselves at the Marshal's tent. An aide-de-camp emerged, looking apologetic.

"The Marshal is indisposed, sir. He regrets that he is unable to see you, and hopes to listen to your complaint another day."

" 'Another day'!" exclaimed Toress Lahl. "Is that an expression a soldier should use in the field?"

"Tell the Marshal that if he thinks like that," Bandal Eith Lahl said, "our forces may not live to see another day."

He made a bold attempt to tug off his moustache before turning on his heel. His wife followed him back to their lines—to find the Borldoranians also under fire from Isturiacha. Toress Lahl was not alone in noticing the ominous birds already beginning to gather above the plain.

The peoples of Campannlat never planned as efficiently as those of Sibornal. Nor were they ever as disciplined. Nevertheless, their expedition had been well organized. Officers and men had set out cheerfully, conscious of their just cause. The northern army had to be driven from the southern continent.

Now they were less buoyant in mood. Some men, having women with them, were making love in case this was their last opportunity for that pleasure. Others were drinking heavily. The officers, too, were losing their appetites for just causes. Isturiacha was not like a city, worth the taking: it would hold little except slaves, heavy-bodied women, and agricultural implements.

The higher command also was depressed. The Chief Marshal had received word that wild phagors were now coming down from the High Nyktryhk—that great aggregate of mountain ranges—to invade the plains; the Chief Marshal suffered a fit of coughing as a result.

The general feeling was that Isturiacha should be destroyed as soon as possible, and with as little risk as possible. Then all could return quickly to the safety of home.

So much for the general feeling. The fainter of the suns, Batalix, rose again, to reveal a sinister addition to the scene.

A Sibornalese army was approaching from the north.

Bandal Eith Lahl jumped onto a cart to peer through a spyglass at the distant lines of the enemy, indistinct in the light of a new day.

He called to a messenger.

"Go immediately to the Chief Marshal. Rouse him at all costs. Instruct him that our entire army must wipe out Isturiacha immediately, before their relieving army arrives."

The settlement of Isturiacha marked the southern end of the great Isthmus of Chalce, which connected the equatorial continent of Campannlat with the northern continent of Sibornal. Chalce's mountainous backbone lay along its eastern edge. Progress back or forth from one continent to the other entailed a journey through dry steppeland, which extended in the rain shadow of the eastern mountains from Koriantura in the north, safe in Sibornal, all the way down to perilous Isturiacha.

The kind of mixed agriculture practised by the Campannlatians had no place in the grasslands, and consequently their gods no foothold. Whatever emerged from that chill region was bad for the Savage Continent.

As fresh morning wind dispersed the mist, columns of men could be counted. They were moving over the undulant hills north of the settlement by the river tracks along which the arangherds had come the previous day. The soaring birds above the Pannovalan force could, with the merest adjustment of their wingtips, be hovering above the new arrivals in a few minutes.

The sick Pannovalan Marshal was helped from his tent and his gaze directed northwards. The cold wind brought tears to his eyes; he mopped absently at them while regarding the advancing foe. His orders were given in a husky whisper to his grim-faced aide-de-camp.

The hallmark of the advancing foe was an orderliness not to be found among the armies of the Savage Continent. Sibornalese cavalry moved at an even pace, protecting the infantry. Straining animal teams dragged artillery pieces forward. Ammunition trains struggled to keep up with the artillery. In the rear rattled baggage carts and field kitchens. More and more columns filled the dull landscape, winding southwards as if in imitation of the sluggish river. No one among the alarmed forces of Campannlat could doubt where the columns came from or what they intended.

The old Marshal's aide-de-camp issued the first order. Troops and auxiliaries, irrespective of creed, were to pray for the victory of Campannlat in the forthcoming engagement. Four minutes were to be dedicated to the task.

Pannoval had once been not merely a great nation but a great religious power, whose C'Sarr's word held sway over much of the continent and whose neighbouring states had sometimes been reduced to satrapy under the sway of Pannovalan ideology. Four hundred and seventy-eight years before the confrontation at Isturiacha, however, the Great God Akhanaba had been destroyed in a now legendary duel. The God had departed from the world in a pillar of flame, taking with him both the then King of Oldorando and the last C'Sarr, Kilandar IX.

Religious belief subsequently splintered into a maze of small creeds. Pannoval, in this present year of 1308, according to the Sibornalese calendar, was known as the Country of a Thousand Cults. As a result, life for its inhabitants had become more uncomfortable, more uncertain. All the minor deities were called upon in this hour of crisis, and every man prayed for his own survival.

Tots of fiery liquor were issued. Officers began to goad their men into action.

"Battle Stations" sounded raggedly from bugles all over the southern plain. Orders went out to attack the settlement of Isturiacha immediately and to overwhelm it before the relieving force arrived. Whereupon a rifle brigade began almost at once to cross the bridge in a businesslike way, ignoring shellfire from the settlement.

Among the conscripts of Campannlat, whole families clustered together. Men with rifles were accompanied by women with kettles, and the women by children with teething troubles. Along with the military chink of bayonet and chain went the clank of dishpans—as later the shrieks of the newly weaned would merge with the cries of the injured. Grass and bone were trampled underfoot.

Those who prayed went into action along with those who scorned prayer. The moment was come. They were tense. They would fight. They feared to die this day—yet life had been given them by chance, and luck might yet save that life. Luck and cunning.

Meanwhile the army from the north was hastening its progress southwards. A strictly disciplined army, with well-paid officers and trained subordinates. Bugle calls sounded, the snare drum set the pace of advance. The banners of the various countries of Sibornal were displayed.

Here came troops from Loraj and Bribahr; tribes from Carcampan and primitive Upper Hazziz, who kept the orifices of their bodies plugged on the march, so that evil spirits from the steppes should not enter them; a holy brigade from Shivenink; shaggy highlanders from Kuj-Juvec; and of course many units from Uskutoshk. All were banded together under the dark-browed, dark-visaged Archpriest-Militant, famed Devit Asperamanka, who in his office united Church and State.

Among these nations trudged phagor troops, sturdy, sullen, grouped into platoons, corniculate, bearing arms.

In all, the Sibornalese force numbered some eleven thousand. The force had moved down from Sibornal, travelling across the steppelands which lay as a rumpled doormat before Campannlat. Its orders from Askitosh were to support what remained of the chain of settlements and strike a heavy blow against the old southern enemy; to this end, scarce resources had been assembled, and the latest artillery.

A small year had passed while the punitive force gathered. Although Sibornal presented a united face to the world, there were dissentions within the system, rivalries between nations, and suppressions on the highest level. Even in the choosing of a commander, indecision had made itself felt. Several officers had come and gone before Asperamanka was appointed—some said by no less than the Oligarch himself. During this period, settlements which the expedition had been designed to relieve had fallen to Pannovalan onslaught.

The vanguard of the Sibornalese army was still a mile or so from the circular walls of Isturiacha when the first wave of Pannovalan infantry went in. The settlement was too poor to employ a garrison of soldiers; its farmers had to defend themselves as best they could. A quick victory for Campannlat seemed certain. Unfortunately for the attacking force, there was the matter of the bridge first.

Turmoil broke out on the southern bank. Two rival units and a Randonanese cavalry squadron all tried to cross the bridge at the same time. Questions of precedence arose. There was a scuffle. A yelk slipped with its rider from the bank and fell into the river. Kaci claymores clashed with Randonanese broadswords. Shots were fired.

Other troops attempted to cross the waters by ropeline, but were defeated by the depth of the water and its surly force.

A conflict of mind descended on everyone involved in the confusion at the bridge—except possibly for the Kaci, who regarded battles as an opportunity to consume huge libations of pabowr, their treacherous national drink. This general uncertainty caused isolated misadventures. A cannon exploded, killing two gunners. A yelk was wounded and ran amok, injuring a lieutenant from Matrassyl. An artillery officer plunged from his steed into the river, and was found, when dragged out, to exhibit symptoms of illness which none could mistake.

"The plague!" The news went round. "The Fat Death."

To everyone involved in the operations, these terrors were real, these situations fresh. Yet all had been enacted before, on this very sector of the North Campannlat plain.

As on earlier occasions, nothing went exactly as planned. Isturiacha did not fall to its attackers as punctually as was expected. The allied members of the southern army quarrelled among themselves. Those who attacked the settlement found themselves attacked; an ill-organised running battle took place, with bullets flying and bayonets flashing.

Nor were the advancing Sibornalese able to retain the military organisation for which they were renowned. The young bloods decided to dash forward to relieve Isturiacha at all costs. The artillery, dragged over two hundred miles in order to bombard Pannovalan towns, was now abandoned, shelling being as likely to kill friendly as enemy troops.

Savage engagements took place. The wind blew, the hours passed, men died, yelk and biyelk slipped in their own blood. Slaughter mounted. Then a unit of Sibornalese cavalry managed to break through the melee and capture the bridge, cutting off those of the enemy attacking Isturiacha.

Among the Sibornalese moving forward at that time were three national units: the powerful Uskuti, a contingent from Shivenink, and a well-known infantry unit from Bribahr. All three units were reinforced by phagors.

Riding with the forward Uskuti force went Archpriest-Militant Asperamanka. The supreme commander cut a distinguished figure. He was clad in a suit of blue leather with heavy collar and belt, and his feet were shod in black leather turnover boots, calf-high. Asperamanka was a tall, rather ungainly man, known to be soft-spoken and even sly when not issuing commands. He was greatly feared.

Some said of Asperamanka that he was an ugly man. True, he had a large square head, in which was set a remarkably rectangular face, as if his parents had had their geometries at cross purposes. But what gave him distinction was a permanent cloud of anger which appeared to hover between the brows, the bridge of the nose, and the lids, which shielded a pair of dark eyes ever on the watch. This anger, like a spice, flavoured Asperamanka's least remark. There were those who mistook it for the anger of God.

On Asperamanka's head was an ample black hat and, above the hat, the flag of the Church and of God the Azoiaxic.

The Shiveninki and the Bribahr infantry poured forward to do battle with the enemy. Judging that the day was already turning in Sibornal's favour, the Archpriest-Militant beckoned his Uskuti field commander to one side.

"Just allow ten minutes until you go in," he said.

The field commander protested impatiently, but was overruled.

"Hold back your force," said Asperamanka. He indicated with a black glove the Bribahr infantry, firing steadily as they advanced. "Let them bleed a little."

Bribahr was currently challenging Uskutoshk for supremacy among the northern nations. Its infantry now became involved in a desperate hand-to-hand engagement. Many men lost their lives. The Uskuti force still held back.

The Shiveninki detachment went in. Underpopulated Shivenink was reputed the most peaceable of the northern nations. It was the home of the Great Wheel of Kharnabhar, a holy place; its honours in battle were few.

A mixed squadron of Shiveninki cavalry and phagor troops was now commanded by Luterin Shokerandit. He bore himself nobly, a conspicuous figure, even among many flamboyant characters.

Shokerandit was by now thirteen years and three tenners old. More than a year had passed since he had said good-bye to his bride-to-be, Insil, on leaving Kharnabhar for military duties in Askitosh.

Army training had helped remove from his body the last traces of the weight he had gained during his period of prostration. He was as slender as he was upright, generally carrying himself with a mixture of swagger and apology. Those two elements were never far from his manner, betokening an insecurity he sought to hide.

There were some who claimed that the young Shokerandit had attained his rank of lieutenant ensign only because his father was Keeper of the Wheel. Even his friend Umat Esikananzi, another ensign, had wondered aloud how Luterin would conduct himself in battle. There remained something in Luterin's manner—perhaps an aftereffect of that eclipse which had followed his brother's death—which could distance him from his friends. But in the saddle of his yelk he was the picture of assurance.

His hair grew long. His face was now thin, hawklike, his eye clear. He rode his half-shaven yelk more like a countryman than a soldier. As he urged his squadron forward, the excitement tightening his expression made him a leader to follow.

Driving his beast forward to the disputed bridge, Luterin rode close enough to Asperamanka to hear the commander's words—"Let them bleed a little."

The treachery of it pierced him more than the shrilling bugle. Forcing through the press, spurring on, he raised a gloved fist.

"Charge!" he called.

He waved his own squadron forward. Their lily-white banner bore the great hierogram of the Wheel, its inner and outer circles connected by wavy lines. It flew with them, unfurled above their heads as they surged towards the foe.

Later, when the struggle was over, this charge by Shokerandit's squadron was reckoned one of its pivotal moments.

As yet, however, the fight was far from won. A day passed, and still the fighting continued. The Pannovalan artillery got itself marshalled at last and began a steady bombardment on the Sibornalese rear, causing much damage. Their fire prevented the Sibornalese guns from pulling forward. Another artilleryman went down with the plague, and another.

Not all the settlers in Isturiacha had been employed shooting down Pannovalans. The wives and daughters, every bit as hardy as their menfolk, were dismantling a barn and ripping out its planking.

By next Batalix-rise, they had built two stout platforms, which were thrown across the river. A cheer rose from the Sibornalese. With thunderous sound, metal-shod yelk of the northern cavalry crossed the new bridges and burst among the ranks of Pannoval. Camp followers who, an hour before, had considered themselves safe were shot down as they fled.

The northerners spread out across the plain, widening their front as they went. Piles of dead and dying marked their progress.

When Batalix sank once more, the fight was still undecided. Freyr was below the horizon, and three hours of darkness ensued. Despite attempts by officers of both camps to continue the fighting, the soldiery sank to the ground and slept where they were, sometimes no more than a spear's throw from their opponents.

Torches burned here and there over the disputed ground, their sparks carried away into the night. Many of the wounded gave up the ghost, their last breath taken by the chill wind rolling over them. Nondads crept from their burrows to steal garments from the dead. Rodents scavenged over the spilt flesh. Beetles dragged gobbets of intestine into their holes to provide unexpected banquets for their larvae.

The local sun rose again. Women and orderlies were about, taking food and drink to the warriors, offering words of courage as they went. Even the unwounded were pale of face. They spoke in low voices. Everyone understood that this day's fighting would be decisive. Only the phagors stood apart, scratching themselves, their cerise eyes turned towards the rising sun; for them was neither hope nor trepidation.

A foul smell hung over the battlefield. Filth unnamed squelched underfoot as fresh lines of battle were drawn up. Advantage was taken of every dip in the land, every hummock, every spindly tree. Sniping began again. The fighting recommenced, wearily, without the previous day's will. Where human blood was voided it was red, where phagor, gold.

Three main engagements took place that day. The attack on the Isturiachan perimeters continued, with the Pannovalan invaders managing to occupy and defend a quarter of the settlement against both the settlers and a detachment from Loraj. A manoeuvre by Uskuti forces, eager to make amends for their previous delay, was held south of the bridge, and involved sections of either army; long lines of men were crawling and sniping at each other before engaging in hand-to-hand fighting. Third, there were prolonged and desperate skirmishes taking place in the Campannlatian rear, among the supply wagons. Here Luterin Shokerandit's force again set the pace.

In Shokerandit's contingent, phagors stood side by side with humans. Both stalluns and gillots—the latter often with their offspring in attendance—fought, and male and female died together.

Luterin was gathering honour to his family's name. Battle lust made him secure from caution and, seemingly, injury. Those who fought with him, including his friends, recognised this fearful enchantment and took heart from it. They cut into the Pannovalan enemy without fear or mercy, and the enemy gave way—at first with stubborn resistance, then in a rush. The Shiveninki pursued, on foot or in the saddle. They cut down the defeated as they ran, until their arms were weary of thrusting and stained to the shoulder with blood.

This was the beginning of the rout of the Savage Continent.

Before the forces from Pannoval itself began to retreat, Pannoval's doubtful allies cast about for a safe way home. The battalion from Borldoran had the misfortune to straggle across the path of Shokerandit, and came under attack. Bandal Eith Lahl, their commander, valiantly called on his men to fight. This the Borldoranians did, taking refuge behind their wagons. A gun battle ensued.

The attackers set fire to the wagons. Many Borldoranians were slain. There came a lull in the firing, during which the noise of other encounters reached the ears of the protagonists. Smoke floated over the field, to be whipped away by the wind.

Luterin Shokerandit saw his moment. Calling to the squadron, he dashed forward, Umat Esikananzi at his side, throwing himself at the Borldoranian position.

In the wilds of his homeland, Luterin was accustomed to hunting alone, lost to the world. The intense empathy between hunter and hunted was familiar to him from early childhood. He knew the moment when his mind became the mind of the deer, or of the fierce-horned mountain goat, the most difficult of quarries.

He knew the moment of triumph when the arrow flew home—and, when the beast died, that mixture of joy and remorse, harsh as orgasm, which wounded the heart.

How much greater that perverted victory when the quarry was human! Leaping a barricade of corpses, Luterin came face to face with Bandal Eith Lahl. Their gazes met. Again that moment of identity! Luterin fired first. The Borldoranian leader threw up his arms, dropping

his gun, doubling forward to clutch his intestines as they burst outwards. He fell dead.

With the death of their commander, the Borldoranian opposition
collapsed. Lahl's young wife was taken captive by Luterin, together
with valuable booty and equipment. Umat and other companions embraced him and cheered before seizing what loot they could gather.

Much of the booty the Shiveninki gathered was in the form of supplies, including hay for the animals, to ease the return of the contingent
to their distant home in the Shivenink Chain.

On all quarters of the field, the forces of the south suffered mounting defeat. Many fought on when wounded, and continued to fight
when hope had gone. It was not courage they lacked, but the favour of
their countless gods.

Behind the Pannovalan defeat lay a history of unrest extending over
long periods. During the slow deterioration of climate, as life became
harder, the Country of a Thousand Cults was increasingly at odds with
itself, with one cult opposed to another.

Only the fanatical corps of Takers had the power to maintain order in
Pannoval City. This sworn brotherhood of men lived inside the re-
motest recesses of the Quzint Mountains. It still clung to the ancient
god Akhanaba.

The Takers and their rigid discipline had become a byword over the
centuries; their presence on the field might have turned the tide of
defeat. But in these troublous times, the Iron Formations judged it best
to remain close to home.

At the end of that dire day, wind still blew, artillery still boomed,
men still fought. Groups of deserters wended their way southwards,
towards the sanctuary of the Quzints. Some were peasants who had
never held a gun before. The forces of Sibornal were too exhausted to
pursue defeated foes. They lit camp fires and sank down into the daze
of battle slumber.

The night was filled with isolated cries, and with the creak of carts
making their way to safety. Yet even for those who retreated to distant
Pannoval, there remained other dangers, fresh afflictions.

Enmeshed in their own affairs, the human beings had no perception
of the plain as other than an arena on which they made war. They
did not see the place as a network of interrelated forces involved in the
continual slow mechanisms of change, its present form being merely
the representative of a forgotten series of plains stretching into the
remote past. Approximately six hundred species of grass clothed the
North Pannovalan flatlands; they were either spreading or in retreat
under the dictates of climate; and with the success of any one kind of

grass was bound up the fate of the animal and insect chains which fed
on it.

The high silica content of the grasses demanded teeth clad in strongly
resistant enamel. Impoverished as the plain looked to a casual human
glance, the seeds of the grass represented highly nutritious packages—
nutritious enough to support numerous rodents and other small mammals. Those mammals formed the prey of larger predators. At the top
of that food chain was a creature whose omnivorous capabilities had
once made it lord of the planet. Phagors ate anything, flesh or grass.

Now that the climate was more propitious to them, free phagors
were moving into lower ground. To the east of the equatorial continent
stood the mass of the High Nyktryhk. The Nyktryhk was far more than
a barrier between the central plains and the horizons of the Ardent
Sea: its series of plateaux, building upwards like steps of a giant staircase, its complex hierarchies of gorge and mountain, constituted a
world in itself. Timber gave way to tundralike uplands, and those to
barren canyons, excoriated by glaciers. The whole was crowned nine
miles above sea level by a dominating plateau, a scalp on nodding terms
with the stratosphere.

Ancipital components who had lived the long centuries of summer
in the high grasslands secure from man's depredations were descending
to more abundant slopes as their refuges were assailed by the furies of
oncoming winter. Their populations were building up in the labyrinthine
Nyktryhk foothills.

Some phagor communities were already venturing into territories
traversed by mankind.

Into the area of battle, under cover of darkness, rode a company of
phagors, stalluns, gillots, and their offspring, in all sixteen strong. They
were mounted on russet kaidaws, their runts clinging tight against their
parents, half smothered in their rough pelages. The adults carried
spears in their primitive hands. Some of the stalluns had entwined
brambles between their horns. Above them, riding the chilly night air,
flew attendant cowbirds.

This group of marauders was the first to venture among the weary
battle lines. Others were not far behind.

One of the carts creaking towards Pannoval through the darkness had
stuck. Its driver had attempted to drive it straight through an uct, a
winding strip of vegetation which broke the plain in an east–west
direction. Although much reduced from its summer splendour, the uct
still represented a palisade of growth, and the cart was wedged with
saplings between both axles.

The driver stood cursing, attempting by blows to make his hoxneys
budge.

The occupants of the carts comprised eleven ordinary soldiers, six of them wounded, a hoxney-corporal, and two rough young women who served as cooks, or in any other capacity required. A phagor slave, dehorned, chained, marched behind the vehicle. So overcome by fatigue and illnesses was this company that they fell asleep one on top of the other, either beside the cart or in it. The luckless hoxneys were left to stand between the shafts.

The kaidaw-phagor component came out of the night, moving in single file along the straggling line of the uct. On reaching the cart, they bunched closer together. The cowbirds landed in the grass, stepping delicately together, making noises deep in their throats, as if anxiously awaiting events.

The events were sudden. The huddled band of humans knew nothing until the massive shapes were on them. Some phagors dismounted, others struck from their saddles with their spears.

"Help!" screamed one of the doxies, to be immediately silenced with a thrust to the throat. Two men lying half under the cart woke and attempted to run. They were clubbed from behind. The dehorned phagor slave began to plead in Native Ancipital. It too was despatched without ceremony. One of the wounded men managed to discharge a pistol before he was killed.

The raiders picked up a metal pot and a sack of rations from the cart. They secured the hoxneys on trailing leads. One of them bit out the throat of the groom-corporal, who was still living. They spurred their massive beasts on into the expanses of the plain.

Although there were many who heard the shot and the cries, none on that vast battlefield would come to the aid of those on the cart. Rather, they thanked whatever deity was theirs that they themselves were not in danger, before sinking back into the phantasms of battle slumber.

In the morning by dim first light, when cooking fires were started and the murders discovered, it was different. Then there was a hue and cry. The marauders were far away by that time, but the torn throat of the groom-corporal told its own tale. The word went round. Once more that ancient figure of dread—horned ancipital riding horned kaidaw—was loose in the land. No doubt of it: winter was coming, old terror-legends were stirring.

And there was another dread figure, just as ancient, even more feared. It did not depart from the battlefield. Indeed, it thrived on the conditions, as if gunpowder and excreta were its nectar. Victims of the Fat Death were already showing their horrifying symptoms. The plague was back, kissing with its fevered lips the lips of battlewounds.

Yet this was the dawn of a day of victory.

II

A SILENT PRESENCE

In Luterin Shokerandit's mind, the sense of victory was mingled with many other emotions. Pride like a shrill of trumpets moved in him when he reflected that he was now a man, a hero, his courage proved beyond everyone's doubt but his own. And there was the excitement of knowing that he now had within his clutches a beautiful and powerless woman. Yet not entirely silenced was the continual unease of his thoughts, a flow so familiar that it was part of him. The flow brought before him continually the question of his duty to his parents, the obligations and restrictions at home, the loss of his brother—still painfully unexplained—the reminder that he had lost a year in prostrating illness. Doubt, in short, which even the sense of victory would not entirely still. That was Luterin's perceptual universe at thirteen years; he carried about with him an uncertainty which the scent, the voice, of Toress Lahl by turn soothed and aroused. Since he had no one in whom he could confide, his strategy was to suppress, to behave as if all were well.

So at first light, he threw himself gladly back into action. He had discovered that danger was a sedative.

"One last assault," said Archpriest-Militant Asperamanka. "Then the day will be ours." His face of anger moved among the thousand other grim faces, dry of lip, again preparing to fight.

Orders were shouted, phagors mustered. Yelk were watered. Men spat as they swung themselves again into the saddle. The plain lightened with Batalix-dawn and human suffering again took on movement. The rise of the greater luminary was a more gradual event: weakening Freyr could not climb far above the horizon.

"Forward!" In went the cavalry at walking pace, infantry behind. Bullets flew. Men staggered and fell.

The Sibornalese attack lasted a little under the hour. Pannovalan morale was sinking fast. One by one, its units fell into retreat. The Shiveninki force under Luterin Shokerandit moved off in pursuit, but was recalled; Asperamanka had no wish to see this young lieutenant acquire yet more glory. The army of the north withdrew to the northern side of the river. Its wounded were taken to Isturiacha, to a field ambulance established in some barns. Tenderly, the broken men were laid to bleed on straw.

As the opponents withdrew from the plain, the cost of battle could clearly be seen. As if in a gigantic shipwreck, pallid bodies lay strewn upon their last shore. Here and there, an overturned wagon burned, its smoke carrying thin across the soiled ground.

Figures moved among the dead. A Pannovalan artillery officer was one of them, scarcely recognisable. Sniffing at a corpse like a dog, he wrenched at its jacket until the sleeve came off. He commenced to chew at the arm. He ate in snatches, face distorted, raising his head to look about as he chewed each mouthful.

He continued to chew and stare even when a rifleman approached. The latter raised his weapon and fired at short range. The artillery officer was blown backwards, to lie motionless with arms outspread. The rifleman, with others similarly detailed, moved slowly about the death-field, shooting the devourers of corpses. These were the unfortunates who had contracted the Fat Death and, in the throes of bulimia, were driven to feast on the dead. Plague victims were reported on both sides.

As the main body of the Pannovalan army made its untidy retreat, it left behind a detail of monumental masons.

The masons had no victory to celebrate. Nevertheless, their trade had to be exercised. Back in Pannoval, the defeated commanders would be bound to claim a victory. Here, at the limits of their territory, the lie had to be reinforced in stone.

Although the plain offered no quarries, the masons found a ruinous monument near at hand. They demolished it and carried its separate stones nearer to the bridge by the sullen river.

These guildsmen took pride in their craft. With practised care, they reerected the monument almost stone for stone on its new site. The master-mason carved upon the base of the monument the name of the place and the date, and, in grander lettering, the name of the old Chief Marshal.

All stood back and regarded the stonework with pride before returning to their wagon. None who executed this act of practical piety realised that he had demolished a monument commemorating a similar battle fought here eons ago.

The gaunt Sibornalese watched with satisfaction as the defeated enemy withdrew southwards. They had sustained heavy losses, and it was clear there was nothing to be gained by pressing on farther as had once been planned; their other settlements had been wiped out, as refugees in Isturiacha reported.

Those who survived the battle felt relief that the challenge was behind them. Yet there was also a sense in some quarters that the engagement had been a dishonourable thing—dishonourable and even paltry, after the months of training and preparation which had preceded it. For what had it been fought? For ground that would now have to be conceded? For honour?

To quell such doubts, Asperamanka announced a feast to be held that evening in celebration of the Sibornalese victory. Some arang, newly arrived in Isturiacha, would be slaughtered; they and supplies captured from the enemy would provide the fare. The army rations, needed for the journey home, would not be touched.

Preparations for this celebration went forward even while the dead were being buried in nearby consecrated ground. The graves lay in a great shallow vale, open to the wide skies, where aromas of cooking wafted over the corpses.

While the settlers were busy, the army was content to rest. Their trained phagors sprawled with them. It was a day for grateful sleep. For binding of wounds. For repairs to uniforms, boots, harness. Soon they would have to be on the move again. They could not remain in Isturiacha. There was not enough food to support an idle army.

Towards the end of the day, the smells of woodsmoke and roasting meats overcame the lingering stench of the battlefield. Hymns of thanksgiving were offered up to God the Azoiaxic. The men's voices, and the ring of sincerity in them, brought tears to the eyes of some women settlers, whose lives had been saved by these same hymn singers. Rape and captivity would have been their lot after a Pannovalan invasion.

Children who had been locked in the church of the Formidable Peace while danger threatened were now released. Their cries of delight brightened the evening. They clambered among the soldiery, chuckling at the attempts of the men to get drunk on weak Isturiachan beer.

The feast began according to the omens, as dimday snared the world. The roast arang were attacked until nothing but the stained cages of their ribs remained. It was another memorable victory.

Afterwards, three solemn elders of the settlement council approached the Archpriest-Militant and bowed to him. No hand touching took place since Sibornalese of high caste disapproved of physical contact with others.

The elders thanked Asperamanka for preserving the safety of Isturiacha, and the senior among them said formally, "Revered sire, you understand our situation here is that of the last and southernmost settlement of Sibornal. Once there were/continued other settlements farther into Campannlat, even as far as Roonsmoor. All have been overwhelmed by the denizens of the Savage Continent. Before your army will/must retire to our home continent, we beseech you on behalf of all in Isturiacha to leave a strong garrison with us, that we may not/avoidance suffer the same fate as our neighbours."

Their hairs were grey and sparse. Their noses shone in the light of the oil lamps. They spoke in a high dialect larded with slippery tenses, past continuous, future compulsive, avoidance-subjunctive, and the Priest-Militant responded in similar terms, while his gaze evaded theirs.

"Honoured gentlemen, I doubt if you can/will/could support the extra mouths you request. Although this is the summer of the small year, and the weather is clement, yet your crops are poor, as I perceive, and your cattle appear starved." The thundercloud was dark about Asperamanka's brow as he spoke.

The elders regarded each other. Then all three spoke simultaneously.

"The might of Pannoval will return against us."

"We pray/praying every day for better climates as before."

"Without a garrison we die/will/unavoidable."

Perhaps it was the use of the archaic fatalistic future which made Asperamanka scowl. His rectangular face seemed to narrow; he stared down at the table with pursed lips, nodding his head as if making some sly pact with himself.

It was by Asperamanka's command that young Lieutenant Shokerandit sat next to him in a place of honour, so that some of the latter's glory might be deflected to his commander. Asperamanka turned his head to Shokerandit and asked, "Luterin, what reply would/dare you give these elders to their request—in high dialect or otherwise?"

Shokerandit was aware of the danger lurking in the question.

"Since the request comes not from three mouthpieces but from all the mouths in Isturiacha, sire, it is too large for me to answer. Only your experience can discover the fit reply."

The Priest-Militant cast his gaze upwards, to the rafters and their long shadows, and scratched his chin.

"Yes, it could be said that the decision is mine, to speak for the Oligarchy. On the other hand, it could be said that God has already decided. The Azoiaxic tells me that it is no longer possible to maintain this settlement, or the ones to the north of it."

"Sire—"

He raised one triangular eyebrow in his rectangular face as he addressed the elders.

"The crops fail year by year despite all prayer can do. That's a matter of common record. Once these southern settlements of ours grew vines. Now you are hard put to it to raise barley and mouldy potatoes. Isturiacha is no longer our pride but our liability. It is best that the settlement be abandoned. Everyone ˉhould leave when the army leaves, two days from now. In no other way can you escape eventual starvation or subjection to Pannoval."

Two of the leaders had to prop up the third. Consternation broke out among all who overheard this conversation. A woman rushed to the Priest-Militant and clasped his stained boots. She cried that she had been born in Isturiacha, together with her sisters; they could not contemplate leaving their home.

Asperamanka rose to his feet and rapped on the table for attention. Silence fell.

"Let me make this matter clear to you all. Remember that my rank entitles me—no, forces me—to speak on behalf of both Church and State. We must be under no illusions. We are a practical people, so I know that you will accept what I say. Our Lord who existed before life, and round whom all life revolves, has set this generation's steps on a stoney path. So be it. We must tread it gladly because it is his will.

"This gallant army who celebrates with you tonight, these brave representatives from all our illustrious nations, must start almost immediately northwards again. If the army is not on the move, it will starve from lack of fodder. If it remains here in Isturiacha, it will starve you with it. As farmers you understand the case. These are laws of God and nature. Our first intention was to press on to conquer Pannoval; such was our charge from the Oligarch. Instead, I must start my men homewards in two days, neither more nor less."

One of the elders asked, "Why such a sudden change of plan, Priest-Militant, when yours was the victory?"

The rectangular face managed a horizontal smile. He looked about at the greasy faces, lit by firelight, hanging on his words, while he timed his utterance with the instinct of a preacher.

"Yes, ours was the victory, thanks be to the Azoiaxic, but the future is not ours. History stands against us. The settlements to the south where we hoped we might find support and supplies are wiped out, destroyed by a savage enemy. The climate deteriorates faster than we judged—you see how Freyr scarce rises from his bed these days. My judgement is that Pannoval, that heathen hole, lies too far for victory, and near enough only for defeat. If we continued there, none of us would return here.

"The Fat Death spreads from the south. We have it among us. The most courageous warrior fears the Fat Death. Nobody goes into battle with such a companion by his side.

"So we bow to nature and return home to report our victory to the Oligarchy in Askitosh. We leave, as I have said, in fifty hours. Use that time, settlers, use it well. At the end of that period, those of you who have decided to return to Sibornal with your families will be welcome to come north with us, under the army's protection.

"Those who decide to stay may do so—and die in Isturiacha. Sibornal will not, cannot return here. Whatever you decide, you have fifty hours to do it in, and God bless you all."

Of the two thousand men, women, and children in the settlement, most had been born there. They knew only the harsh life of the open fields or—in the case of the more privileged men—of the hunt. They feared leaving their homes, they dreaded the journey to Sibornal across the steppes, they even misdoubted the sort of reception they might receive at the frontier.

Nevertheless, when the case was put to them by the elders at a meeting in the church, most settlers decided to leave. For longer than anyone could recall, the climate had been worsening, year by small year, with few remissions. Year by year, connections with the northern homeland had become more tenuous, and the threat from the south greater.

Tears and lamentations filled the camp. It was the end of all things. All that they had worked for was to be abandoned.

As soon as Batalix rose, slaves were sent off into the fields to gather in all the crops they could, while the households packed their worldly goods. Scuffles broke out between those who intended to leave and a smaller group who intended to stay at all costs; the latter shouted that the crops should be preserved.

Three kinds of slaves were driven out to labour in the fields. There were the phagors, dehorned, who served as something between a slave proper and a beast of burden. Then there were the human slaves. Lastly there were slaves of non-human stock, Madis, or, more rarely, Driats. Both humans and non-humans were regarded as dishonoured persons, male or female. They were the socially dead.

It counted as a sign of rank to keep slaves; the more slaves, the higher the ranking. The many Sibornalese who did not keep slaves looked with envy on those who did, and aspired to own at least a phagor. In easier times, slaves in the cities of Sibornal had often been maintained in idleness, almost as if they were pets; in the settlements, slaves and owners worked side by side. As times grew harsher, the attitudes of the owners changed. Slaves became drudges, except in rare cases. The slaves of the settlement, when they returned from the fields, were now put to building carts, and given other tasks beyond their competence.

When the Priest-Militant's stipulated two days were up, bugles were sounded and everyone had to assemble outside the confines of the settlement.

The quartermasters of the Sibornalese army had set up field kitchens and baked bread for the start of the homeward trek. Rations were going to be short. After a conference, the chiefs of staff announced that the settlers heading north must shoot their slaves or set them free, in order to cut down the number of mouths to be fed. From this order, ancipitals were spared, on the grounds that they could double as beasts of burden and were able to forage for their own food.

"Mercy!" cried both slaves and masters. The phagors stood motionless.

"Kill off the phagors," some men said, with bitterness.

Others, remembering old history, replied, "They were once our masters . . ."

The settlers were now under military law. Protests were of no avail. Without their slaves, householders would be unable to transport many of their goods; still the slaves had to go. Their usefulness had expired.

Over a thousand slaves were massacred in an old riverbed near the settlement. The corpses were given casual burial by phagors, while hordes of carrion birds descended, perching on nearby fences in silence, awaiting their chance. And the wind blew as before.

After the wailing a terrible silence fell.

Asperamanka stood watching the ceremony. As one of the women of the settlement passed near him, weeping, he was moved by compassion and placed a hand on her shoulder.

"Bless you, my daughter. Do not grieve."

She looked up at him without anger, her face blotched by crying. "I loved my slave Yuli. Is it not human to grieve?"

Despite the edict, many slaves were spared by their owners, especially those who were sexually used. They were concealed or disguised, and assembled with the families for the journey. Luterin Shokerandit protected his own captive, Toress Lahl, giving her trousers and a fur cap to wear as a disguise. Without a word, she tucked her long chestnut hair into the confines of the cap and went to hold Luterin's yelk by its bridle.

The marching columns began to form up.

While this bustle was afoot and carts were being overloaded and arrangements were being made for the wounded, six arangherds left slyly, climbing the perimeter, and made off over the plain with their dogs. Theirs was the wild free life.

Asperamanka stood alone by his black yelk, thinking his dark thoughts. He called an orderly to fetch Lieutenant Shokerandit to him.

Luterin arrived, looking, in his unease, very immature.

"Have you two reliable men on reliable mounts, Lieutenant Shokerandit? Two men who would travel fast? I wish news of our victory to

get to the Oligarch by the fastest means. Before he hears from other
sources."

"I could find two such men, yes. We from Kharnabhar are great
riders."

Asperamanka frowned, as if this news displeased him. He produced a
leather wallet, which he then tucked under one arm.

"This message must be taken by your reliable men to the frontier
town of Koriantura. It is there to be delivered to an agent of mine, and
he will deliver it in person to the Oligarch. Your reliable men's re-
sponsibility ends at Koriantura, you understand? Report to me when
all is ready."

"Sire, I will."

The wallet was pulled from under the arm and held out towards
Shokerandit in a blue-gloved hand. It was sealed with the Archpriest-
Militant's seal and addressed to the Supreme Oligarch of Sibornal,
Torkerkanzlag II, in Askitosh, Capital City of Uskutoshk.

Shokerandit chose two reliable youths, well-known to him and like
brothers back in Shivenink. They left their comrades and their fighting
phagors and mounted two shorn yelk, with nothing more than packs of
provisions and water at their backs. Within the hour they were off
across the grasslands, riding northwards with the message for the dread
Oligarch.

But the Oligarch of Sibornal, ruling over his vast bleak continent, had
spies everywhere. Already a trusted man of his, placed close to the Archpriest-Militant Asperamanka, had ridden off with the news of the
engagement, for one particular interest of the Oligarch's was the progress
of the plague northwards.

It was the time for farewells. The trek northwards began in some
disorder. Each unit started off with its carts, supply animals, phagors,
and guns. Their noise filled the shallow landscape. They jostled for the
course they had traversed only a few days earlier. The settlers leaving
Isturiacha, many for the first time in their lives, went in greatest dis-
arrary, clutching children and precious possessions which had found no
place on their overloaded carts.

Tearful good-byes were called to those individuals who had made the
decision to remain behind. Those exiles stood outside the perimeter,
stiff and upright, hands upraised. In their bearing was a consciousness of
playing the honourable role, of defying fate—a consciousness, too, of the
elemental forces slowly mounting against them. From now on, only the
Azoiaxic and their own competence would be their defence.

Luterin Shokerandit sat at the head of the Shivenink force, aware
of how his status had changed since last he passed this way. He was
now a hero. His captive, Toress Lahl, disguised in her cap and breeches,

was forced to ride behind him on his yelk, clinging to his belt. The death of her husband still burned inside her, so that she spoke no word.

In her pain, Toress Lahl showed no fear of the yelk, a creature of mild habits but ferocious aspect. Its horns curled about its shaggy head. Its eyes, shielded by furry lids, gave the beast a watchful look. The curl of its heavy underlip suggested that it despised all that it saw of human history.

The settlement fell away behind the procession. A succession of wearyingly similar valleys began to unfold ahead. The wind blew. The grass rustled.

Silence closed over the procession. But one of the elders who had elected to leave Isturiacha was a garrulous old man who enjoyed the sound of his own voice; he urged his mount over until he was riding beside Shokerandit and his lieutenants, and tried to pass the time of day with him. Shokerandit had little to say. His mind was on the immediate future and the long journey back to his father's house.

"I suppose it really was the Supreme Oligarch who ordered Isturiacha to be closed," he said.

No response. He tried again. "They say the Oligarch is a great despot, and that his hand is harsh over all Sibornal."

"Winter will be harsher," said one of the lieutenants, laughing.

After another mile, the elder said confidentially, "I fancy you young men do not see eye-to-eye with Asperamanka . . . I fancy that in his position you would have ordered a garrison to stay and defend us."

"The decision was not mine to make," Shokerandit said.

The elder smiled and nodded, revealing his few remaining teeth. "Ah, but I saw the expression on your face when he announced his ruling, and I thought to myself—in fact, I said it to the others—'Now there's a young man with a measure of mercy in him . . . a saint,' I said . . ."

"Go away, old man. Save your breath for the ride."

"But to break up a fine settlement just like that. In the old days, we used to send our food surplus back to Uskutoshk. Then to break it up . . . You'd think the Oligarch would be grateful. We're all Sibornalese, are we not? You can't argue against that, can you?"

When Shokerandit had been given, and failed to take, his chance to argue against it, the elder wiped his mouth with the back of his hand and said, "Do you think I was wise to leave, young sir? It was my home, after all. Perhaps we should all have stayed. Perhaps another of the Oligarch's armies—one with more generous impulses towards its compatriots—will be coming this way again in a year or two . . . Well, this is a bitter day for us, that's all I will say."

He was turning his steed's head and about to ride off when Shokerandit reached out suddenly and grasped the collar of his coat, almost unseating the old man.

"You must know nothing of the world if you can't see the truth of the situation more clearly than that! What I think of the Priest-Militant is immaterial. He gave the only judgement possible. Work it out for yourself instead of airing your grievances. You see what a multitude we are? By dimday, we shall have spread out until we stretch from one horizon to the other. Feet, steeds, mouths to be fed . . . the weather becoming more bleak . . . Work it out for yourself, old man."

He gestured over the moving multitude, gestured towards all the grey, black, and russet backs of the soldiers, each back burdened with a pack containing a three-day ration of hardtack, plus unspent ammunition, each back turned towards the south and the pallid sun. The multitude spread wider and wider, to allow the creaking carts more room. It moved with a dull entombed sound which the low hills returned.

Among the men riding went others on foot, often clinging to a saddlestrap. Some carts were piled with equipment, others with wounded, who suffered at every jog of the axle. Loaded phagors trudged by their masters, backs bent, eyes to the ground; the ancipital fighting corps marched slightly apart with their strange jointless stride.

The halt that night was a confused affair. Not all the shouted orders and bugle calls could discipline it. Units settled where they would, pitching tents or not as the case was, to the inconvenience of other units seeking a better site. Animals had to be fed and watered. The watering entailed sending water carts off into the gloom to one side or the other, to seek out streams in the hills. The mutter of men's voices, the restless movement of animals, were never absent during the brief night.

The clouds parted. It grew colder.

The Shivenink contingent formed a close group. Being young, most of them clustered about Luterin Shokerandit, preparing to drink the night away. Their canteens contained the spirit they called yadahl, fermented from seaweed, ruby red in colour. In yadahl they celebrated their recent victory, Luterin's heroism, and the excitement of being on the plains rather than in the familiar mountains of home—and the pleasure of simply being alive, and anything else that entered their heads. Soon they were singing, despite outcries from groups of would-be sleepers.

But the yadahl did not inspire Luterin Shokerandit to sing. He moved apart from his companions from Kharnabhar, his thoughts dwelling on his fair captive. Though she had been married, he doubted if she was as old as he, despite her assured manner; the women of the Savage Continent married young.

He longed to possess her. And yet his parents had committed him to marry in Kharnabhar. Why should that make a difference to what he did here, in the wilds of Chalce? His friends would laugh at his scruples.

His memories returned to the night before the Sibornalese army had left the frontier town of Koriantura to head south. His contingent had been given leave. His friend Umat had tried to persuade him to come on the rampage, but no, he had hung back like a fool.

While the rest of them had gone drinking and whoring, Luterin had walked the cobbled streets alone. He had entered a deuteroscopist's shop, set in a square next to an old theatre.

The deuteroscopist had shown him many curious things, including a small object like a bracelet, said to come from another world, and a tapeworm in a jar one hundred inches long, which the deuteroscopist had charmed from the entrails of a lady of quality (by using a small silver flute which he was prepared to sell at a price).

"Have I the courage for battle?" Luterin had asked the diviner.

Whereupon the old man had become busy on Luterin's skull with calipers and other measuring devices before saying finally, "You are either a saint or a sinner, young master."

"That was not my question. My question was, am I hero or coward?"

"It's the same question. It needs courage to be a saint."

"And none to be a sinner?" He thought of how he had not dared to join his friends.

Much nodding of the hairy old head. "That needs courage too. Everything needs courage. Even that tapeworm needed courage. Would you care to pass your life imprisoned in someone's entrails? Even the entrails of a beautiful lady? If I told you that such a fate lay in your future, would you be happy?"

Impatient with his procrastination, Luterin said, "Are you going to give me an answer to my question?"

"You will answer it yourself very soon. All I will say is that you will display great courage . . ."

"But?"

A smile that pleaded forgiveness. "Because of your nature, young man. You will find yourself both sinner and saint. You will be a hero, but I think I see that you will behave like a scoundrel."

He had recalled that conversation—and the tapeworm—all the way down to Isturiacha. Now he had become a hero, could he dare to be a scoundrel?

As he sat there, drinking but not singing, Umat Esikananzi grabbed him by the boot and pulled him forcibly nearer the fire.

"Don't be glum, old lad. We're still alive, we've played the hero—you especially—and soon we'll be back home." Umat had a big puddingy face rather like his father's, but it beamed now. "The world's a horribly empty place; that's why we're singing—to fill it up with noise. But you've got other things on your mind."

"Umat, your voice is the most melodious I ever heard, including a vulture's, but I'm going to sleep."

Umat waved an admonitory finger. "Ah, I thought as much. That fair captive of yours! Give her hell from me. And I promise not to tell Insil."

He kicked Umat on the shin, "How Insil had the rotten luck to get a brother like you I'll never know."

Taking another swig of yadahl, Umat said cheerfully, "She's a girl, is Insil. Come to think of it, she might be grateful to me if I took you by the scruff of your neck and made you get a bit of practice in."

The whole group roared with laughter.

Shokerandit staggered to his feet and bid them good night. With an effort, he made for his own pitch, close by a cart. Despite the stars overhead, it seemed very dark. There was no aurora in these latitudes as there so often was in Kharnabhar.

Clutching his canteen, he half fell against the bulk of his yelk, which was staked to the ground by the tether burnt through its left ear. He went down on his knees and crawled to where the woman was.

Toress Lahl lay curled up small, hands grasping her knees. She stared up at him without speaking. Her face was pale in the obscurity. Her eyes reflected minutely the litter of stars in the sky above them.

He caught hold of her upper arm and thrust the canteen at her.

"Drink some yadahl."

Mutely she shook her head, a small decisive movement.

He clouted her over the side of the head and thrust the leather bottle in her face. "Drink this, you bitch, I said. It'll put heart in you."

Again the shake of head, but he took her arm and twisted it till she cried out. Then she grasped the canteen and took a swallow of the fiery liquor.

"It's good for you. Drink more."

She coughed and spluttered over it, so that her spittle lighted on his cheek. Shokerandit kissed her forcibly on the lips.

"Have mercy, I beg you. You are not a barbarian." She spoke Sibish well enough, but with a heavy accent, not unpleasant to his ear.

"You are my prisoner, woman. No fine airs from you. Whoever you were, you are mine now, part of my victory. Even the Archpriest would do with you as I intend, were he in my boots . . ." He gulped at the liquid himself, heaved a sigh, slumped heavily beside her.

She lay tense; then, sensing his inertia, spoke. When not crying out, Toress Lahl had a voice with a low liquid quality, as if there were a small brook at the back of her throat. She said, "That elder who came to you this afternoon. He saw himself going into slavery, as I see myself. What did you mean when you said to him that your Archpriest gave the only judgement possible?"

Shokerandit lay silent, struggling with his drunken self, struggling with the question, struggling with his impulse to strike the girl for so blatantly trying to turn the channel of his desires. In that silence, up from his consciousness rose an awareness darker than his wish to violate her, the awareness of an immutable fate. He threw down more liquor and the awareness rose closer.

He rolled over, the better to force his words on her.

"Judgement, you say, woman? Judgement is delivered by the Azoiaxic, or else by the Oligarch—not by some biwacking holy man who would see his own troops bleed to serve his ends." He pointed to his friends carousing by the camp fire. "See those buffoons there? Like me, they come from Shivenink, a good part of the round globe away. It's two hundred miles just to the frontiers of Uskutoshk. Lumbered with all our equipment, with the necessity for foraging for food, we cannot cover more than ten miles a day. How do you think we feed our stomachs in this season, madam?"

He shook her till her teeth rattled and she clung to him, saying in terror, "You feed, don't you? I see your wagons carry supplies and your animals can graze, can't they?"

He laughed. "Oh, we just feed, do we? On what, exactly? How many people do you think we have spread across the face of this land? The answer is something like ten thousand humans and ahumans, together with seven thousand yelk and whatever, including cavalry mounts. Each of those men needs two pounds of bread a day, with an extra one pound of other provisions, including a ration of yadahl. That adds up to thirteen and a half tons every day.

"You can starve men. Our stomachs are hollow. But you must feed animals or they sicken. A yelk needs twenty pounds of fodder every day; which for seven thousand head comes to sixty-two odd tons a day. That makes some seventy-five tons to be carried or procured, but we can only transport nine tons . . ."

He lay silent, as if trying to convert the whole prospect in his mind into figures.

"How do we make up the shortfall? We have to make it up on the move. We can requisition it from villages on our route—only there aren't any villages in Chalce. We have to live off the land. The bread problem alone . . . You need twenty-four ounces of flour to bake a two-pound loaf. That means six and a half tons of flour to be found every day.

"But that's nothing to what the animals eat. You need an acre of green fodder to feed fifty yelk and hoxneys—"

Toress Lahl began to weep. Shokerandit propped himself on an elbow and gazed across the encampment as he spoke. Little sparks glowed in the dark here and there over a wide area, constantly obscured as bodies moved unseen between him and them. Some men sang; others abased themselves and communicated with the dead.

"Suppose we take twenty days to reach Koriantura at the frontier, then our mounts will need to consume two thousand eight hundred acres of fodder. Your dead husband must have had to do similar sums, didn't he?

"Every day an army marches, it spends more time in quest of food than it does in moving forward. We have to mill our own grain—and there's precious little of anything but wild grasses and shoatapraxi in these regions. We have to make expeditions to fell trees and gather wood for the bakeries. We have to set up field bakeries. We have to graze and water the yelk. . . . Perhaps you begin to see why Isturiacha had to be left? History is against it."

"Well, I just don't care," she said. "Am I an animal that you tell me how much these animals eat? You can all starve, the lot of you, for all I care. You got drunk on killing and now you're drunk on yadahl."

In a low voice, he said, "They didn't think I would be any good in battle, so at Koriantura I was put in charge of animal fodder. There's an insult for a man whose father is Keeper of the Wheel! I had to learn those figures, woman, but I saw the sense in them. I grasped their meaning. Year by year, the growing season is getting shorter—just a day at either end. This summer is a disappointment to farmers. The Isthmus of Chalce is famine-stricken. You'll see. All this Asperamanka knows. Whatever you think of him, he's no fool. An expedition such as this, which set out with over eleven thousand men, cannot be launched ever again."

"So my unfortunate continent is safe at last from your hateful Sibish interference."

He laughed. "Peace at a price. An army marching through the land is like a plague of locusts—and the locusts die when there's no food in their path. That settlement will soon be entirely cut off. It's doomed.

"The world is becoming more hostile, woman. And we waste what resources we have. . . ."

Luterin lay against her rigid body, burying his face in his arms. But before sleep and drink overpowered him, he heaved himself up again to ask how old she was. She refused to say. He struck her hard across the face. She sobbed and admitted to thirteen plus one tenner. She was his junior by two tenners.

"Young to be a widow," he said with relish. "And—don't think you'll get off lightly tomorrow night. I'm not the animal fodder officer anymore. No talk tomorrow night, woman."

Toress Lahl made no reply. She remained awake, unstirring, gazing miserably up at the stars overhead. Clouds veiled the sky as Batalix-dawn drew near. Groans of the dying reached her ears. There were twelve more deaths from the plague during the night.

But in the morning those who survived rose as usual, stretched their limbs, and were blithe, joking with friends of this and that as they queued for their rations at the bread wagons. A two-pound loaf each, she remembered bitterly.

There was no soldier on that long trail homeward who would admit to enjoying himself. Yet it was probable that everyone took some pleasure in the routine of making and breaking camp, in the camaraderie, in the feeling that progress was being made, and in the chance of being in a different place each day. There was simple pleasure in leaving behind the ashes of an old fire and pleasure in building a new one, in watching the young flames take hold of twigs and grass.

Such activities, with the enjoyments they generated, were as old as mankind itself. Indeed, some activities were older, for human consciousness had flickered upward—like young flames taking hold—amid the challenges of mankind's first long peregrination eastwards from Hespagorat, when forsaking the protection of the ancipital race and the status of domesticated animal.

The wind might blow chill from the north, from the Circumpolar Regions of Sibornal, yet to the soldiers returning home the air tasted good in their lungs, the ground felt good beneath their feet.

The officers were less lighthearted than their men. For the general soldiery, it was enough to have survived the battle and to be returning home to whatever welcome awaited them. For those who thought more deeply, the matter was more complex. There was the question of the increasingly severe regime within the frontiers of Sibornal. There was also the question of their success.

Although the officers, from Asperamanka downwards, talked repeatedly of victory, nevertheless, under that terrible enantiodromia which gripped the world, under that inevitable and incessant turning of all things into their opposites, the victory came to feel more and more like a defeat—a defeat from which they were retreating with little to show but scars, a list of the dead, and extra mouths to feed.

And always, to heighten this oppressive sense of failure, the Fat Death was among them, keeping pace easily with the fastest troops.

In the spring of the Great Year was the bone fever, cutting down human populations, pruning the survivors to mere skeletons. In the autumn of the Year was the Fat Death, again cutting down human populations, this time melding them into new, more compact shape. So much and more was well enough understood, and accepted with fatalism. But fear still sprang up at the very word "plague." And at such times, everyone mistrusted his neighbour.

On the fourth day, the forward units came across one of the two messengers whom Shokerandit had sent ahead. His body lay face down in a gully. The torso had been gnawed as if by a wild animal.

The soldiers preserved a wide circle about the corpse, but seemed unable to stop looking at it. When Asperamanka was summoned, he too looked long at the dreadful sight. Then he said to Shokerandit, "That silent presence travels with us. There is no doubt that the terrible scourge is carried by the phagors, and is the Azoiaxic's punishment upon us for associating with them. The only way to make restitution is to slay all ancipitals who are on the march with us."

"Haven't we had slaughter enough, Archpriest? Could we not just drive the ancipitals away into the wilds?"

"And let them breed and grow strong against us? My young hero, leave me to deal with what is my business." His narrow face wrinkled into severe lines, and he said, "It is more necessary than ever to get word swiftly to the Oligarch. We must be met and given assistance as soon as possible. I charge you now, personally, to go with a trusted companion and bear my message to Koriantura for onward transmission to the Oligarch. You will do this?"

Luterin cast his gaze on the ground, as he had often done in his father's presence. He was accustomed to obeying orders.

"I can be in the saddle within an hour, sir."

The wrath that seemed always to lurk under Asperamanka's brow, lending heat to his eyes, came into play as he regarded his subordinate.

"Reflect that I may be saving your life by charging you with this commission, Lieutenant Ensign Shokerandit. On the other hand, you may ride and ride, only to discover that the silent presence awaits in Koriantura."

With a gloved finger, he made the Sign of the Wheel on his forehead and turned away.

III

THE RESTRICTIONS
OF PERSONS
IN ABODES ACT

K oriantura was a city of wealth and magnificence. The floors of its
palaces were paved with gold, the domes of its pleasure houses
lined with porcelain.

Its main church of the Formidable Peace, which stood centrally along
the quaysides from which much of the city's wealth came, was furnished
with an exuberant luxury quite foreign to the spirit of an austere god.
"They'd never allow such beauty in Askitosh," the Korianturan congregation was fond of saying.

Even in the shabbier quarters of the city, which stretched back into
the foothills, there were architectural details to catch the eye. A love of
ornamentation defied poverty and broke out in an unexpected archway,
an unpremeditated fountain in a narrow court, a flight of wrought-iron
balconies, capable of lifting the spirits even of the humdrum.

Undeniably, Koriantura suffered from the same divisions of wealth
and outlook to be found elsewhere. This might be observed, if in no
other way, from the welcome given to a rash of posters from the presses
of the Oligarchy at present flooding the cities of Uskutoshk. In the
richer quarters, the latest proclamation might draw forth an "Oh, how

45

wise, what a good idea!"; while, at the other end of town, the same pronouncement would elicit merely an "Eh, look what the biwackers are up to now!"

Most frontier towns are dispiriting places, where the lees of one culture wait upon the dregs of the next. Koriantura was an exception in that respect. Although known at an earlier date in its history as Utoshki, it was never, as the old name implied, a purely Uskutoshk city. Exotic peoples from the east, in particular from Upper Hazziz and from Kuj-Juvec beyond the Gulf of Chalce, had infiltrated it and given it an exuberance which most cities of Sibornal did not possess, stamping that energy into its very architecture and its arts.

"Bread's so expensive in Koriantura," went a saying, "because the opera tickets are so cheap."

Then, too, Koriantura was on an important crossroads. It pointed the way southwards, south to the Savage Continent and—war or no war—its traders sailed easily to such ports as Dorrdal in Pannoval. It also stood at one end of the frequented sea route which led to distant Shivenink and the grainlands of Carcampan and Bribahr.

Then again, Koriantura was ancient and its connections with earlier ages had not been broken. It was still possible to find, in the antiquarian stalls of its back streets, documents and books written in antique languages, detailing lost ways of life. Every lane seemed to lead backwards into time. Koriantura had been spared many of the disasters which afflict frontier towns. Behind it stood, range on range, the foothills of the greater hills which in turn formed a footstool to the Circumpolar Mountains, where the ice cap ground its many teeth in cold fury. Before it lay the sea on one side and, on the other, a steep escarpment up which those must climb who would leave the barren steppes of Chalce and enter the city. No invading Campannlatian armies, having survived the march across the steppes, had ever stormed that escarpment.

Koriantura was easy to defend against everything but the impending winter.

Although many military personnel were stationed in Koriantura, they had not succeeded in downgrading it into a garrison town. Peaceful trade could prosper, and the arts to which trade paid somewhat grudging homage. Which was why the Odim family lived there.

The Odim business ranged along one of the wharfs on Climent Quay. The family house stood not far away, in an area that was neither the smartest nor the shabbiest in town. The day's business done, Eedap Mun Odim, chief support of his large family, saw his employees off the premises, checked that the kilns were safe and the windows bolted, and emerged from a side door with his first mistress.

The first mistress was a vivacious lady by name Besi Besamitikahl. She held various packages for Odim as he fussed over locking the door to his premises. When the task was done to his satisfaction, he turned and gave her his gentle smile.

"Now we go our separate ways, and I will see you at home soon."

"Yes, master."

"Walk fast. Watch out for soldiers on the way."

She had only a short walk, round the corner and into Hill Road. He turned in the other direction, towards the local church.

Eedap Mun Odim kept a straight back against middle age. He tucked his beard inside his suede coat. He had a rather grand walk: more of a strut, which he emphasised despite the wind. He turned in at the church in time for service, as he did every evening after business was done. There, like the good Uskuti round him, he humbled himself before God the Azoiaxic. It was only a short service.

Besi Besamitikahl, meanwhile, had reached the Odim house and knocked to be let in by the watchman.

The Odim mansion was the last in the street leading down to Climent Quay. From its upper windows, good views were obtained of the harbour, with the Pannoval Sea beyond. The house had been built two centuries earlier by prosperous merchants of Kuj-Juveci descent. To avoid high Korianturan ground rents, each floor of the five-storey house was larger than the one below. There was ample room under the roof, where the best views were, and little room on the ground floor for anything but the entrance hall and a lair for a surly watchman with his hound. A narrow staircase twisted up through the building. In the many stuffy rooms of the second, third, and fourth floors, many stuffy Odim relations were housed. The top floor belonged to Odim and his wife and children alone. Eedap Mun Odim was a Kuj-Juveci, despite the fact that he had been born in this very house. About Besi it was more difficult to say.

Besi was an orphan who remembered neither of her parents, although rumour had it that she was the daughter of a slave woman from far Dimariam. Some claimed that this slave woman had been accompanying her master on a pilgrimage to Holy Kharnabhar; he had kicked her out on the streets on discovering that she was about to give birth. Whether true or not (Besi would say cheerfully), the story had a ring of truth. Such things happened.

Besi had survived her childhood by dancing in those same streets into which her mother had been kicked. By that dancing, she had come to the notice of a dignitary on his way to the Oligarch's court in Askitosh. After undergoing a variety of abuses at the hands of this man, Besi managed to escape from the house in which she was imprisoned with other women by hiding in an empty walrus-oil vat.

She was rescued from the vat by a nephew of Eedap Mun Odim's, who traded on his uncle's behalf in Askitosh. She so charmed this impressionable young man, particularly when she played her trump card and danced for him, that he took her in marriage. Their joy, however, was brief. Four tenners after their wedding day, the nephew fell from the loft of one of his uncle's warehouses and broke his neck.

As orphan, ex-dancing girl, slave, other dubious things, and now widow, Besi Besamitikahl had no standing in any respectable Uskuti community.

Odim, however, was a Kuj-Juveci, and a mere trader. He protected Besi—not least from the scorn of her relations by marriage—and so discovered that the girl could think as well as employ her more obvious talents. Since she still had her beauty, he adopted her as first mistress.

Besi was grateful. She became rather plump, tried to look less flighty, and assisted Odim in the countinghouse; in time, she could supervise the complex business of ordering his cargoes and scrutinising bills of lading. The days of the Oligarch's court and the walrus oil were now far behind her.

After a brief exchange with the watchman, she climbed the winding stair to her own room.

She paused at one of the tiny kitchens on the second floor, where an old grandmother was busy preparing supper with a maidservant. The old woman gave Besi a greeting, then turned back to the business of making pastry savrilas.

Lamplight gleamed on pale and honey-coloured forms, the simple shapes of bowls and jugs, plates, spoons and sieves, and on dumpy bags of flour. The pastry was being rolled wafer-thin, as mottled old hands moved above its irregular shape. The young maidservant leaned against a wall, looking on vacantly, pulling at her lower lip. Water in a skillet hissed over a charcoal fire. A pecubea sang in its cage.

What Odim said could not be true: that everyday life in Koriantura was threatened—not while the grandmother's capable hands continued to turn out those perfect half-moon shapes, each with a dimpled straight edge and a twist of pastry at one end. Those little pillows of pleasure spoke of a domestic contentment which could not be shattered. Odim worried too much. Odim always worried. Nothing would happen.

Besides, tonight Besi had someone other than Odim on her mind. There was a mysterious soldier in the house, and she had glimpsed him that morning.

All the lower and less favoured rooms were occupied by Odim's many relatives. They constituted almost a small township. Besi held little communication with any of them except the old grandmother, resenting the way they sponged off Odim's good nature. She patrolled through their rooms with her nose in the air, tilting that organ at an angle which enabled her to see what was happening in those enervating abodes.

Here basked remote female Odims of great age, grown monstrous on sloth; younger female Odims, their figures flowing like loose garments under the impact of bearing multitudinous small Odims; adolescent female Odims, willowy, reeking of zaldal perfume, frugal in all but the spots and pallors of indoor life; and the multitudinous small Odims themselves, clad in bright frocks or frocklets, so that boy could scarcely be distinguished from girl, should anyone wish to do so, scurrying, sicking, scuttling, squabbling, suckling, screaming, sulking, or sleeping.

Scattered here and there like cushions, overwhelmed by the preponderance of femininity, were a few Odim males. Castrated by their dependence on Eedap Mun Odim, they were vainly growing beards or smoking veronikanes or bellowing orders never to be complied with, in an effort to assert the ascendancy of their sex. And all these relations and interrelations, of whatever generation, bore, in their sallow skin colour, their listless eye, their heaviness of jowl, their tendency—if an avalanche may be so termed—towards corpulence, flatulence, and somnolence, such a family resemblance that only loathing prompted Besi to distinguish one odious Odim from the next.

Yet the Odims themselves made clear distinctions. Despite their superabundance, they kept each to their own portion of whatever room they occupied, squabbling luxuriously in corners or lounging on clearly defined patches of carpet. Narrow trails were traced out across each crowded chamber, so that any child venturing onto the territory of a rival, even that of a mother's sister, might expect a clout straight off, no questions asked. At night, brothers slept in perfect and jealously guarded privacy within two feet of their voluptuous sisters-in-law. Their tiny portions of real estate were marked off by ribbons or rugs, or draperies hung from lines of string. Every square yard was guarded with the ferocity normally lavished on kingdoms.

These arrangements Besi viewed with jaundiced eye. She saw how the murals on the walls were becoming besmirched by her master's vast family; the sheer fattiness of the Odims was steaming the delicate tones from the plaster. The murals depicted lands of plenty, ruled over by two golden suns, where deer sported amid tall green trees, and young men and women lay by bushes full of doves, dallying or blowing suggestively on flutes. Those idylls had been painted two centuries ago, when the house was new; they reflected a bygone world, the vanished valleys of Kuj-Juvec in autumn.

Both the paintings and their pending destruction fed Besi's mood of discontent; but what she was chiefly seeking was a place where she could enjoy a little privacy away from her master's eye. As she completed her tour in increasing disgust, she heard the outside door slam and the watchdog give its sharp bark.

She ran to the stairwell and looked down.

Her master, Eedap Mun Odim, was returning from worship, and
setting his foot on the lowest stair. She saw his fur hat, his suede coat,
the shine of his neat boots, all foreshortened. She caught glimpses
of his long nose and his long beard. Unlike all his relations, Eedap
Mun Odim was a slender man, a morsel; work and money worries had
contained his waistline. The sole pleasures he allowed himself were
those of the bedchamber, where—as Besi knew—he kept a cautious
mercantile tally of them and entered them in a little book.

Uncertain what to do, she stood where she was. Odim drew level and
glanced at her. He nodded and gave a slight smile.

"Don't disturb me," he said, as he passed. "I shall not want you
tonight."

"As you please," she said, employing one of her well-worn phrases.
She knew what was worrying him. Eedap Mun Odim was a leading light
in the porcelain trade, and the porcelain trade was in difficulties.

Odim climbed to the top of the house and closed his door. His wife
had a meal prepared; its aromas filtered through the house and down to
those quarters where food was less easily come by.

Besi remained on the landing, in the dusk among the odours of
crowded lives, half-listening to the noises all round her. She could hear,
too, the sound of military boots outside, as soldiers marched along the
Climent Quay. Her fingers, still slender, played a silent tune on the
bannister rail.

So it was that she stood concealed from anyone on the floors below
her. So it was that she saw the old watchman creep from his lair, look
furtively about, and slink out the door. Perhaps he was going to find
out what the Oligarch's soldiery were doing. Although Besi had taken
care to befriend him long ago, she knew the watchman would never
dare let her out of the house without Odim's permission.

After a moment, the door opened again. In came a man of military
bearing, whose wide bar of moustache neatly divided his face along its
horizontal axis. This was the man who had provided the secret motive
for Besi's inspection of her domain. It was Captain Harbin Fashnalgid,
their new lodger.

The watchdog came rushing out of the watchman's lair and began to
bark. But Besi was already moving swiftly down the stairs, as nimbly
as a plump little doe down a steep cliff.

"Hush, hush!" she called. The dog turned to her, swinging its black
jowls around and making a mock charge to the bottom of the stairs. It
thrust out a length of tongue and spread saliva across Besi's hand
without in any way relaxing its menacing scowl.

"Down," she said. "Good boy."

The captain came across the hall and clutched her arm. They stared
into each other's eyes, hers a deep deep brown, his a startling grey. He

was tall and slim, a true pure Uskuti, and unlike the proliferating Odims in every way. Thanks to the Oligarch's troop movements, the captain had been billeted on Odim the previous day, and Odim had reluctantly made room for him among his family on the top floor. When the captain and Besi clapped eyes on each other, Besi—whose survival through a hazardous life had had something to do with her impressionability—had fallen in love with him straight away.

A plan came immediately into her mind.

"Let's have a walk outside," she said. "The watchman's not here."

He held her even more tightly.

"It's cold outside."

All he needed was her slight imperious shake of the head, and then they moved together to the door, looking up furtively into the shadows of the staircase. But Odim was closeted in his room and one woman or another would be playing a binnaduria and singing him songs of forsaken fortresses in Kuj-Juvec, where maidens were betrayed and white gloves, dropped one fateful dimday, were forever treasured.

Captain Fashnalgid put his heavy boot to the chest of the hound—which had shown every sign of following them away from captivity—and whisked Besi Besamitikahl into the outside world. He was a man of decision in the realm of love. Grasping her arm firmly, he led her across the courtyard and out of the gate where the oil lamp burned.

As one they turned to the right, heading up the cobbled street.

"The church," she said. Neither said another word, for the cold wind blew in their faces, coming from the Circumpolar Mountains with ice on its breath.

In the street, winding upwards with it, went a line of pale dogthrush trees, wan between the two enclosing stone cliffs of houses. Their leaves flapped in the wind. A file of soldiers, muffled, heads down, walked on the other side of the road, their boots setting up echoes. The sky was a sludgy grey which spread to everything beneath it.

In the church, lights burned. A congregation cried its evensong. Since the church had a slightly bohemian reputation, Odim never came here. Outside its walls, tall man-high stones stood in rows, more correct than soldiers, commemorating those whose days beneath the sky were done. The furtive lovers picked their way among the memorials and hid against a shadowy sheltered wall. Besi put her arms round the captain's neck.

After they whispered to each other for some while, he slid a hand inside her furs and her dress. She gasped at the cold of his touch. When she reciprocated, he grunted at the chill of her hand. Their flesh seemed ice and fire alternately, as they worked closer together. Besi noticed with approval that the captain was enjoying himself and in no great hurry. Loving was so easy, she thought, and whispered in his ear, "It's so simple . . ." He only burrowed deeper.

When they were united, he held her firmly against the wall. She let her head roll back against the rough stone and gasped his name, so newly learned.

Afterwards, they leaned together against the wall, and Fashnalgid said matter-of-factly, "It was good. Are you happy with your master?"

"Why ask me that?"

"I hope one day to make something of myself. Maybe I could buy you, once this present trouble's over."

She snuggled against him, saying nothing. Life in the army was uncertain. To be a captain's chattel was a steep step down from her present security.

He brought a flask from his pocket and drank deeply. She smelt the tang of spirits and thought, Thank God Odim doesn't booze. Captains are all drinkers . . .

Fashnalgid gasped. "I'm not much catch, I know that. The fact is, girl, I'm worried about this errand I'm on. They've landed me with a real sherber this time, my scab-devouring regiment here. I reckon I'm going mad."

"You're not from Koriantura, are you?"

"I'm from Askitosh. Are you listening to me?"

"It's freezing. We'd better get back."

Grudgingly, he came along, taking her arm in the street, which made her feel like a free woman.

"Have you heard the name of Archpriest-Militant Asperamanka?"

With the wind about her head, she gave him only a nod. He wasn't as romantic as she had hoped. But she had been to listen to the Priest-Militant just a tenner earlier, when he had held an outdoor service in one of the city squares. He had spoken so eloquently. His gestures had been pleasing and she had enjoyed watching. Asperamanka!—what a gift of the gab! Later, she and Odim had watched him lead his army through the city and out by the East Gate. The guns had shaken the ground as they passed. And all those young men marching off . . .

"The Priest-Militant took my oath of fealty to the Oligarchy when I was made captain. That's a while ago." He smoothed his heavy moustache. "Now I'm really in trouble. Abro Hakmo Astab!"

Besi was deeply disgusted to hear this curse spoken in her presence. Only the lowest and most desperate would use it. She tugged her arm from his and quickened her pace down the street.

"That man has won a great victory for us against Pannoval. We heard about it in the mess at Askitosh. But it's being kept secret. Secrets . . . Sibornal lives on sherbing secrets. Why do you think they should do that?"

"Can you tip our watchman so that he doesn't make a fuss to Odim?" She paused as they got to the outer gate. A new poster had been pasted up there. She could not read it in the dark, and did not wish to.

III · R E S T R I C T I O N S   I N   A B O D E S   A C T   53

As Fashnalgid felt in his pocket for money as she requested, he said, in a flat way that seemed characteristic, "I have been posted to Koriantura to help organise a force which will ambush the Priest-Militant's army when it returns from Chalce. Our orders are to kill every last man, including Asperamanka. What do you make of that?"

"It sounds awful," Besi said. "I'd better go in first in case there's trouble."

Next morning, the wind had dropped, and Koriantura was enveloped in a soft brown fog, through which the two suns gleamed intermittently. Besi watched the thin, parched form of Eedap Mun Odim as he ate breakfast. She was allowed to eat only when he had finished. He did not speak, but she knew that he was in his usual resigned good humour. Even while she recollected the pleasures that Captain Fashnalgid could offer, she knew that she was, despite everything, fond of Odim.

As if to test out his humour, he allowed upstairs one of his distant relations, a second cousin who professed to be a poet, to speak to him.

"I have a new poem, cousin, an Ode to History," said the man, bowing, and began to declaim.

> "Whose is my life? Is history
> To be considered property
> Only of those who make it?
> May not my finer fancy take it
> Into my heart's morality
> And shape it just as it shapes me?"

There was more of the same. "Very good," said Odim, rising and wiping his bearded lips on a silken napkin. "Fine sentiments, well displayed. Now I must get down to the office, if you will excuse me—refreshed by your ornamental thoughts."

"Your praise overwhelms me," said the distant cousin, and withdrew.

Odim took another sip of his tea. He never touched alcohol.

He summoned Besi to his side as a servant came forward to help him into his outdoor coat. His progress down the stairs, Besi obediently following, was slow, as he underwent the barrage of his relations, those Odims who squawked like starlings on every stair, cajoling but not quite begging, jostling but not quite pushing, touching but not quite impacting, calling but not quite shrieking, lifting tiny befrocked Odims for inspection but not exactly thrusting them in his face, as he performed his daily spiral downwards.

"Uncle, little Ghufla can do his arithmetic so well . . ."

"Uncle, I am so shamed that I must tell you of yet another infidelity when we are private together."

"Darling Unky, stop a while while I tell you of my terrifying dream in which some terrible shining creature like a dragon came and devoured us all."

"Do you admire my new dress? I could dance in it for you?"

"Have you news from my creditor yet, please?"

"Despite your orders, Kenigg kicks me and pulls my hair and makes my life a misery, Unky. Please let me be your servant and escape him."

"You forget those who love you, darling Eedap. Save us from our poverty, as we have pleaded so often."

"How noble and handsome you look today, Unk Eedap . . ."

The merchant showed neither impatience at the constant supplications nor pleasure at the forced compliments.

He pushed slowly through the thickets of Odim flesh, the odours of Odim sweat and perfume, saying a word here and there, smiling, permitting himself once to squeeze the mangolike breasts proffered by a young great-niece, sometimes even going so far as to press a silver coin into a particularly protruding hand. It was as if he considered—and indeed he did—that life could be got through only by sufferance, dispensing as few advantages to others as possible but nevertheless retaining a general humanity for the sake of one's self-respect.

Only when he was outside, as Besi closed the gate after him, did Odim display emotion. There, pasted to his wall, were two posters. He made a convulsive clutch at his beard.

The first poster warned that the PLAGUE was threatening the lives of the citizens of Uskutoshk. The PLAGUE was particularly active in ports, and most especially in THE RENOWNED AND ANCIENT CITY OF KORIANTURA. Citizens were warned that public meetings were henceforth banned. More than four people gathering together in public places would be subject to severe punishment.

Further regulations designed to restrict the spread of THE FAT DEATH would be introduced shortly. BY ORDER OF THE OLIGARCH.

Odim read this notice through twice, very seriously. Then he turned to the second poster.

THE RESTRICTIONS OF PERSONS IN ABODES ACT. After several clauses in obscurantist language, a bolder clause stood out:

THESE LIMITATIONS as regards houses, demesnes, lodgings, rooms, and other Dwellings apply in particular to any household where the Householder is not of Uskuti blood. Such Persons are shown to be particularly liable to conduct the Spread of the Plague. Their numbers will henceforth be limited to One Person per Two Square Metres floorspace. BY ORDER OF THE OLIGARCH.

The announcement was not unexpected. It was aimed at doing away with the more bohemian quarters of the city, where the Oligarchy found no favour. Odim's friends on the local council had warned him of its coming.

Once more, the Uskuti were demonstrating their racial prejudices—prejudices of which the Oligarchy was quick to take advantage. Phagors had been banned from walking untended in Sibornalese cities long ago.

It made no difference that Odim and his forebears had lived in this city for centuries. The Restrictions of Persons in Abodes Act rendered it impossible for him to protect his family any longer.

Looking quickly about him, Odim tore the poster from the wall, screwed it up, and thrust it under his suede coat.

This action alarmed Besi almost as much as the captain's oath had done the previous evening. She had never seen Odim step outside the law before. His unswerving obedience to what was legal was well-known. She gasped and stared at him with her mouth open.

"The winter is coming," was all he said. His face was drawn into bitter lines.

"Take my arm, girl," he said huskily. "We shall have to do something . . ."

The fog rendered the quayside a place of beauty where a copse of swaying masts floated in the sepia glow. The sea lay entranced. Even the customary slap of rigging against mast was silent.

Odim wasted no time admiring the view, turning in at the substantial arcade above which a sign bore the words ODIM FINEST EXPORT PORCELAINS. Besi followed him past bowing clerks into his inner sanctum.

Odim stopped abruptly.

His office had been invaded. An army officer stood there, warming himself before the lignite fire and picking his teeth with a match. Two armed private soldiers stood close, their faces impervious in usual bodyguard fashion.

By way of greeting, the major spat the match on the floor and tucked his hands behind his back. He was a tall man in a lumpy coat. He had grey in his hair and a lumpish protruding mouth, as if his teeth, imbued with true military spirit, were waiting to burst through his lips and bite a civilian.

"What can I do for you?" asked Odim.

Without answering the question, the major announced himself in a way that exercised his teeth prominently.

"I am Major Gardeterark of the Oligarch's First Guard. Well-known, not liked. From you I will have a list of all times of sailing for ships in which you have an interest. Today and coming week." He spoke in a deep voice, giving each syllable an equal weight, as if words were feet to be firmly planted on a long march.

"I can do that, yes. Will you sit and take some tea?"

The major's teeth moved a little further forward.

"I want that list, nothing else."

"Certainly, sir. Please make yourself comfortable while I get my chief clerk—"

"I am comfortable. Don't delay me. I have waited six minutes for your arrival as it is. The list."

Whatever its disadvantages, the northern continent of Sibornal had reserves of minerals and seams of lignite unmatched elsewhere. It also boasted a variety of clays.

Both china and glass drinking vessels had been in regular use in Koriantura while the little lords of the Savage Continent were still quaffing their rathel from wooden bowls. As early as the spring of the Great Year, potteries as far afield as Carcampan and Uskutoshk were producing porcelains fired in lignite-fuelled kilns at temperatures of 1400° C. Through the centuries, these fine wares were increasingly sought after and collected.

Eedap Mun Odim took little part in porcelain manufacture, though there were auxiliary kilns on his premises. He exported fine china. He exported the local, prized Korianturan porcelain to Shivenink and Bribahr, but mainly to ports in Campannlat, where, as a man of Kuj-Juveci descent, he was more welcome than his Sibornalese competitors. He did not own the ships which carried his wares. He made his business from the entrepreneurial trade, and from banking and financing; he even lent money to his rivals and made a profit.

Most of his wealth came from the Savage Continent, from ports along its northern coastline, from Vaynnwosh, Dorrdal, Dowwel, and from even farther afield, Powachet and Popevin, where his competitors would not trade. It was precisely this adventurous element of Odim's business which made his hand tremble slightly as he handed his sailing timetable over to the major. He knew without being told that foreign names would be bad for the soldier's liver.

The gaze of the major, as brown and foggy as the air outside, travelled down the printed page.

"Your trade goes mainly to alien ports," he said at last, in the leathery voice. "Those ports are all thick with the plague. Our great Oligarch, whom the Azoiaxic preserve, fights to save his peoples from the plague, which has its source in the Savage Continent. There will be no more sailings for any Campannlat port from now on."

"No more sailings? But you can't—"

"I can, and I say no more sailings. Until further notice."

"But my trade, my business, good sir . . ."

"Lives of women and children are more important than your trade. You are a foreigner, aren't you?"

"No. I am not a foreigner. I and my family have lived in Uskutoshk for three generations."

"You're no Uskutoshi. Your looks, your name, tell me that."

"Sir! I am Kuj-Juveci only by distant origins."

IV

AN ARMY CAREER

The Restrictions of Persons in Abodes Act met with the mixed reception customary for proclamations from the Oligarchy. In the more privileged sectors of the city people nodded their heads and said, "How wise—what a good idea." Nearer the docks, they exclaimed, "So that's what the biwackers are up to now!"

Eedap Mun Odim gave no overt expression to his dismay when he returned to his crowded five-storey home. He knew that the police would call soon enough to inform him that he was contravening the new law.

That night, he patted his children, settled his modest anatomy beside the slumbrous bulk of his wife, and prepared his mind for pauk. He had said nothing to his spouse, knowing that her display of anguish, her tears, her undoubted rushing from one end of the room to the other, kissing her three children with huge hydropic kisses en route, would do nothing to resolve the problem. As her breath became as regular as a balmy breeze over the autumn valleys of Kuj-Juvec, Odim gathered together his inner resources and underwent that small death which forms the entrance gate to pauk.

For the poor, the troubled, the persecuted, there was always that refuge: the trance state of pauk. In pauk lay communication with those

59

of the family whose life on earth was ended. Neither State nor Church
had jurisdiction over the region of the dead. That vast dimension of
death placed no restriction on persons; nor did God the Azoiaxic prevail there. Only gossies and the more remote fessups existed in orderly
oblivion, sinking towards the unrisen sun of the Original Beholder,
she who took to her bosom all who lived.

Like a feather, the tremulous soul of Eedap Mun Odim sank down,
to hold what intercourse it might with the gossie of its father, recently
departed the world above.

The father now resembled a kind of ill-made gilt cage. It was difficult
to see it through the obsidian of nonexistence, but Odim's soul made its
obeisances, and the gossie twinkled a little in response. Odim poured
out his troubles.

The gossie listened, expressing consolation in little dreadful gasps of
bright dust. It in its turn communed with the guttering ranks of
ancestors below it. Finally it uttered advice to Odim.

"Gentle and beloved son, your forebears honour you for your tender
duty towards our family. Family must rely upon family, since governments do not comprehend families. Your good brother Odirin Nan
lives distantly from you, but he, like you, shares an abiding fondness for
our poor people. Go to him. Go to Odirin Nan."

The voiceless voice sank away in an eddy. To which Odim faintly
responded that he loved his brother Odirin Nan, but that brother lived
in far Shivenink; might it not be better instead to cross the mountains
and return to a remote branch of the family which still lived in the
vales of Kuj-Juvec?

"These here with me who still can make voice advise no return to
Kuj-Juvec. The way over the mountains becomes more hazardous every
month, as new arrivals here report." The tenuous framework guttered
even as it spoke. "Also, the valleys are becoming stonier, and the cattle
herds grow thin of flank. Sail westwards to your brother, beloved one,
most dutiful of young men. Be advised."

"Father, to hear the melody of your voice is to obey its music."

With tender expressions on either side, the soul of Odim drifted upwards through obsidian, like an ember through a starry void. The ranks
of past generations were lost to view. Then came the pain of finding a
feeble human body lying inert on a mattress, and seeking entry to it.

Odim returned to his mortal body, weakened by the excursion but
strengthened by the wisdom of his father. Beside him, his ample wife
breathed on, undistressed in her sleep. He put an arm about her and
snuggled into her warmth, like a child against its mother.

There were those—lovers of secrecy—who rose almost at the time that
Odim was settling to sleep. There were those—lovers of night—who

liked to be about before dawn, in order to get ahead of their fellow men. There were those—lovers of chill—whose constitutions were such that they found satisfaction in the small hours when human resistance is at its lowest.

At the chime of three in the morning, Major Gardeterark stood in his leather trousers, keeping a watchful eye on his reflection in the mirror while he shaved.

Major Gardeterark would have no nonsense with pauk. He regarded himself as a rationalist. Rationalism was his creed, and his family's. He had no belief in the Azoiaxic—Church Parade was a different matter— and less than a belief in pauk. It would never occur to the major that his thinking had confined him to an *umwelt* of living obsidian, through which no light shone.

At present, with each stroke of his cut-throat razor, he contemplated how to make miserable the lives of the inhabitants of Koriantura, as well as the existence of his under officer, Captain Harbin Fashnalgid. Gardeterark believed he had rational family reasons for hating Fashnalgid, over and above the motive of the latter's inefficiency. And he was a rational man.

A great king had once ruled in Sibornal, before the last Weyr-Winter. His name had come down as King Denniss. King Denniss's court had been held in Old Askitosh, and his retreat had been in the mighty edifices now known as the Autumn Palaces. So legend had it.

To his court, King Dennis had summoned learned men from all quarters of the globe. The great king had fought for Sibornal's survival through the grim centuries of Weyr-Winter, and had launched an invasion force across the seas to attack Pannoval.

The king's scholars had compiled catalogues and encyclopaedias. Everything that lived had been named, listed, categorised. Only the slow-pulsed world of the dead had been excluded, in deference to the Church of the Formidable Peace.

A long period of confusion followed the death of King Denniss. The winter came. Then the great families of the seven Sibornalese nations had joined together to form an Oligarchy, in an attempt to rule the continent on rational and scientific lines, as proposed by King Denniss. They had sent learned men abroad to enlighten the natives of Campannlat, even as far afield as the old cultural centre of Keevasien, in the southwest of Borlien.

The autumn of the present Great Year had witnessed one of the most enlightened of the Oligarchy's decrees. The Oligarchy had altered the Sibornalese calendar. Previously, Sibornalese nations, with the exception of backwaters like Upper Hazziz, had adhered to a "so many years after the coronation of Denniss" formula. The Oligarchy abolished such prescriptions.

Henceforth, the small years were numbered as the astronomers directed, in precedence following the small year in which Helliconia and its feebler luminary, Batalix, were most distant from Freyr: in other words, the year of apastron.

There were 1825 small years, each of 480 days, in a Great Year. The present year, the year of Asperamanka's incursion into Chalce, was 1308 After Apastron. Under this astronomical system, nobody could forget where they stood with regard to the seasons. It was a rational arrangement.

And Major Gardeterark rationally finished shaving, dried his face, and commenced in a rational way to brush his formidable teeth, allowing so many strokes for each tooth in front, so many for each behind.

The innovation of the calendar alarmed the peasantry. But the Oligarchy knew what it was doing. It became secretive; it amassed secrets. It deployed its agents everywhere. Throughout the autumn it developed a secret police force to watch over its interests. Its leader, the Oligarch, gradually became a secret person, a figment, a dark legend hovering over Askitosh, whereas—or so the stories said—King Denniss had been loved by his people and seen everywhere.

All the acts and edicts promulgated by the Oligarchy were backed by rational argument. Rationality was a cruel philosophy when practised by the likes of Gardeterark. Rationality gave him good reason for bullying people. He drank to rationality every evening in the mess, sinking his huge teeth deep over the rim of his glass as the liquor ran down his throat.

Now, having finished his toilet, he allowed his servant to help him into his boots and greatcoat. Rationally clad, he went out into the frosty predawn streets.

His under officer, Captain Harbin Fashnalgid, was not rational, but he drank.

Fashnalgid's drinking had begun as an amiable social habit, indulged in with other young subalterns. As Fashnalgid's hatred of the Oligarch grew, so did his need for drink. Sometimes, the habit got out of hand.

One night, back in the officers' mess in Askitosh, Fashnalgid had been peaceably drinking and reading, ignoring his fellow men. A hearty captain by the name of Naipundeg halted by Fashnalgid's chair and laid his hoxney-crop across the open page of the book.

"Always reading, Harbin, you unsociable dog! Filth, I suppose?"

Closing the volume, Fashnalgid said in his flat voice, "This is not a work you would have come across, Naipundeg. It's a history of sacred architecture through the ages. I picked it up from a stall the other day. It was printed three hundred years ago, and it explains how there are

secrets that we in these later days have forgotten. Secrets of contentment, for example. If you're interested."

"No, I'm not interested, to be frank. It sounds wretchedly dull."

Fashnalgid stood up, tucking the little book into a pocket of his uniform. He raised his glass and drained it dry. "There are such block-
heads in our regiment. I never meet anyone interesting here. You don't
mind me saying that? You're proud of being a blockhead, aren't you?
You'd find any book not about filth dull, wouldn't you?"

He staggered slightly. Naipundeg, himself far gone in drink, began
to bellow with rage.

It was then that Fashnalgid blurted out his hatred of the Oligarchy,
and of the Oligarch's increasing power.

Naipundeg, throwing another tumbler of fiery liquor down his throat,
challenged him to a duel. Seconds were summoned. Supporting their
primaries, they jostled them into the grounds of the mess.

There a fresh quarrel broke out. The two officers drove off their
seconds and blazed away at each other.

Most of the bullets flew wild.

All except one.

That bullet hit Naipundeg's face, shattering the zygomatic bone,
entering the head by way of the left eye, and leaving through the rear
of the skull.

In that casual military society, Fashnalgid was able to pass off the
duel as an affair of honour regarding a lady. The court-martial convened
under Priest-Militant Asperamanka was easily satisfied; Naipundeg, an
officer from Bribahr, had not been popular. Fashnalgid was exonerated
of blame. Only Fashnalgid's conscience remained unappeased; he had
killed a fellow officer. The less his drinking companions blamed him,
the more he judged himself guilty.

He applied for leave of absence and went to visit his father's estates
in the undulating countryside to the north of Askitosh. There he intended to reform, to become less prodigal with women and drink.
Harbin's parents were growing senile, although both still rode daily—
as they had done for the past forty years or more—about their fields and
stands of timber.

Harbin's two younger brothers ran the estate between them, aided by
their wives. The brothers were shrewd, sowing coarser crops when finer
ones failed, selecting strains with more rapid growth periods, planting
cold-resistant caspiarn saplings where gales blew down established trees,
building stout fences to keep out the herds of flambreg which came
marauding from the northern plains. Sullen phagors worked under the
brothers' direction.

The estate had seemed a paradise to Harbin in his childhood. Now
it became a place of misery. He saw how much labour was required to

maintain a status quo threatened by the ever worsening season, and wanted no part of it. Every morning, he endured his father's repetitive conversation rather than join his brothers outdoors. Later, he retired to the library, to leaf moodily through old books which had once enchanted him and to allow himself the occasional little drink.

Harbin Fashnalgid had often grieved that he was ineffectual. He could not exert his will. He was too modest to realise how many people, women especially, liked him for this trait. In a more lenient age, he would have been a great success.

But he was observant. Within two days, he had noticed that his youngest brother had a quarrel with his wife. Perhaps the difference between them was merely temporary. But Fashnalgid began offering the woman sympathy. The more he talked to her, the weaker became his resolve to reform. He worked on her. He spun her exaggerated tales about the glamour of military life, at the same time touching her, smiling at her, and feigning a great sorrow which was only part feigned. So he won her confidence and became her lover. It was absurdly easy.

It was an irrational way to behave.

Even in that rambling two-storey parental house, it was impossible that the affair should remain secret. Intoxicated by love, or something like it, Fashnalgid became incapable of behaving with discretion. He lavished absurd gifts on his new partner—a wicker hammock; a two-headed goat; a doll dressed as a soldier; an ivory chest crammed with manuscript versions of Ponipotan legends; a pair of pecubeas in a gilt cage; a silver figurine of a hoxney with a woman's face; a pack of playing cards in ivory inlaid with mother-of-pearl; polished stones; a clavichord; ribbons; poems; and a fossilized Madi skull with alabaster eyes.

He hired musicians from the village to serenade her.

The woman in her turn, driven to ecstasies by the first man in her life who knew nothing about the planting of potatoes and pellamountain, danced for him on his verandah in the nude, wearing only the bracelets he gave her, and sang the wild zyganke.

It could not last. A lugubrious quality in the countryside could not tolerate such exuberance. One night, Fashnalgid's two brothers rolled up their sleeves, rushed into the love nest, kicked over the clavichord, and bounced Fashnalgid out of the house.

"Abro Hakmo Astab!" roared Fashnalgid. Not even the labourers on the estate were allowed to employ that vile expression aloud.

He picked himself up and dusted himself down in the darkness. The two-headed goat chewed at his trousers.

Fashnalgid stationed himself under his old father's window, to shout insults and supplications. "You and Mother have had a happy life, damn you. You're of the generation which regarded love as a matter of will. 'Will marks us from the animal, and love from lovelessness,' as sayeth the poet. You married equally for life, do you hear, you old fool? Well, things are different now. Will's given way to weather . . .

"You have to grab love when you can now. . . . Didn't you have a parental duty to make me happy? Eh? Reply, you biwacking old loon. If you've been so sherbing happy, why couldn't you have given me a happy disposition? You've given me nothing else. Why should I always be so miserable?"

No answer came from the dark house. A doll dressed as a soldier sailed from one of the windows and struck him on the side of the head.

There was nothing for it but to return to his regiment in Askitosh. But news travelled fast among the landed families. Scandal followed Fashnalgid. As ill fortune would have it, Major Gardeterark was an uncle of the woman he had disgraced, of that very woman who had so recently danced naked on his verandah and sung the wild zyganke. From then on, Harbin Fashnalgid's position in the regiment became one of increasing difficulty.

His money went on obscure books as well as women and drink. He was accumulating a case against the Oligarchy, discovering just how the authoritarian grip on the Northern Continent had increased over the sleepy centuries of autumn. Searching through the rubbish in an antiquarian's attic, he came across a list of entitlements of Uskuti estates of over a certain annual income; the Fashnalgid estate was listed. These estates had "pledged assignments to the Oligarchy." This phrase was not explained.

Fashnalgid fulfilled his military duties while brooding over that phrase. He became convinced that he was himself part of the property assigned.

Between bouts of drinking and wenching, he recalled some of his father's boasts. Had not the old man once claimed to have seen the Oligarch himself? Nobody had seen the Oligarch. There was no portrait of the Oligarch. No vision of the Oligarch existed in Fashnalgid's mind, except possibly a pair of great claws reaching over the lands of Sibornal.

After garrison duties one evening, Fashnalgid ordered his personal servant to saddle up his hoxney and rode furiously out to his father's estate.

His brothers snarled at him like curs. Nor was he allowed as much as a glimpse of his light of love, except for a bare arm disappearing round a door as she was dragged away. He recognised the bracelets on the lovely wrist. How they had rattled when she danced!

His father lay on a day sofa, covered in blankets. The old man was scarcely able to answer his son's questions. He rambled and procrastinated. Sadly, Fashnalgid recognised his own portrait in his father's lies and pretences. The old man still claimed once to have seen Torkerkanzlag II, the Supreme Oligarch. But that had been over forty years ago, when his father was a youth.

"The titles are arbitrary," the old man said. "They are intended to conceal real names. The Oligarchy is secret, and the names of the Members and the Oligarch are kept secret, so that no one knows them. Why, they don't know each other . . . Just as well . . ."

"So you never met the Oligarch?"

"No one ever claimed to have met him. But it was a special occasion, and he was in the next room. The Oligarch himself. So it was said at the time. I know he was there, I've always said so. For all I know, he could be a gigantic lobster with pincers stretching to the sky, but he was certainly there that day—and had I opened the door, I would have seen him, pincers and all . . ."

"Father, what were you doing there, what was this special occasion?"

"Icen Hill, it's called. Icen Hill, as you know. Everyone knows where it is, but even the Members of the Oligarchy don't know each other. Secrecy is important. Remember that, Harbin. Honesty's for boys, chastity's for women, secrecy's for men. . . . You know the old saying my grandfather used to tell me, 'There's more than an arm up a Sibornalese sleeve.' Some truth in that."

"When were you at Icen Hill? Did you assign a tithe of this estate to the Oligarchy? I must know."

"Duties, boy, there are duties. Not just buying women dolls and poems. The estate is entitled to protection if you assign it. Winter's coming, you need to look ahead. I'm getting old. Security . . . There's no need for you to be upset. It was agreed before you were born. I *was* someone then, more than you'll ever—you should be a major by now, son, but from what I hear from the Gardeterarks. . . . That's why I signed the agreement that my firstborn son should serve in the Oligarch's army, in the defence of that state act, when I—"

"You sold me into the army before I was born?" Fashnalgid said.

"Harbin, Harbin, sons go into the army. That's gallantry. And piety. It's piety, Harbin. As taught in church."

"You sold me into the army? What precisely did you get in return?"

"Peace of mind. A sense of duty. Security, as I said, only you weren't listening. Your mother approved. You ask her. It was her idea."

"Beholder . . ." Fashnalgid went and poured himself a drink. As he was throwing the liquid down his throat, his father sat up and said in a distinct voice, "I received a promise."

"What sort of a promise?"

"The future. The safety of our estate. Harbin, I was for many years myself a Member. That's why I signed you over to the army. It's an honour—a good career, fine career. You should cultivate young Gardeterark more. . . ."

"You *sold* me. Father, you sold your son like a slave. . . ." He began to weep and rushed from the house. Without looking back, he galloped away from the place where he had been born.

A few months later, he was posted with his battalion to Koriantura, under his enemy, Major Gardeterark, and ordered to prepare a warm reception for Asperamanka's returning army.

Throughout recorded time, Sibornal had existed more unitedly than had the rabble of nations which comprised Campannlat. The nations of the northern continent had their differences, but remained capable of uniting in the face of an external threat.

In milder centuries, Sibornal was a favoured continent. From early in spring of the Great Year, Freyr rose and never set, permitting the northern lands to develop early. Now that the Year was declining, the Oligarchy was busy tightening the reins of its power—bringing in its own kind of darkness.

Both Oligarchy and common people understood that winter, setting in steadily, could burst society apart like a frozen water pipe. The disruptions of cold, the failure of food supplies, could spell the collapse of civilisation. After Myrkwyr, only a few years away, darkness and ice would be upon the land for three and a half local centuries: that was the Weyr-Winter, when Sibornal became the domain of polar winds.

Campannlat would collapse under the weight of winter. Its nations could not collaborate. Whole peoples would revert to barbarism. Sibornal, under more severe conditions, would survive through rational planning.

Still seeking consolation, Harbin Fashnalgid consorted with priests and holy men. The Church was a reservoir of knowledge. There he discovered the answer to Sibornal's survival. Obsessed as he was with his virtual exile from his father's estates, from those fields and woods where his brothers laboured, the answer had the force of revelation. It was not to the land that Sibornal would turn in extremity.

The huge continent was so largely covered by polar ice that it might best be regarded as a narrow circle of land facing sea. In the seas lay Sibornal's winter salvation. Cold seas held more oxygen than warm ones. Come winter, the seas would swarm with marine life. The durable food chains of the ocean would yield their plenty—even when ice covered those estates of his family from which he had been banished.

The awful working of history gnawed at Fashnalgid. He was used to thinking in periods of days or tenners, not in decades and centuries. He fought his disposition to drink and took to spending as much time with priests as with whores. A Priest-Servitant attached to the military chapel in the Askitosh barracks became his confidant. To this priest, Fashnalgid one day confessed his hatred of the Oligarchy.

"The Church also hates the Oligarchy," said the priest mildly. "Yet we work together. Church and State must never be divided. You resent the Oligarchy because, through its pressures, you had to enter the army. But the flaws in your character under which you labour are yours—not the army's, not the Oligarchy's.

"Praise the Oligarchy for its positive aspects. Praise it for its continuity and benevolent power. It is said that the Oligarchy never sleeps. Rejoice that it watches over our continent."

Fashnalgid kept silent. He took a while to understand why the priest's answer alarmed him. It came to him that "benevolent power" was a contradiction in terms. He was an Uskuti, yet he had been virtually sold into the slavery of the army. As for the Oligarchy not sleeping: anyone who went without sleep was by definition inhuman, and therefore as opposed to humanity as the phagors.

It was a while later that he realised the priest had spoken of the Oligarchy in the same terms he might have used for God the Azoiaxic. The Azoiaxic also was praised for his continuity and his benevolent power. The Azoiaxic also watched over the continent. And was it not claimed that the Church never slept?

From that moment on, Fashnalgid ceased to attend church, and was more confirmed than ever in his opinion that the Oligarchy was monstrous.

The Oligarch's First Guard had escaped being sent with Asperamanka's punitive expedition to Northern Campannlat. Only a few weeks later, however, it received orders to move to Koriantura to man the frontier.

Fashnalgid had dared to question Major Gardeterark on the reasons for the move.

"The Fat Death is spreading," said the major brusquely. "We don't want any rioting in the frontier towns, do we?" His dislike of his junior officer was such that he would look him not in the eyes but in the moustache.

On his last evening in Askitosh, Fashnalgid was with a woman he currently favoured, by name Rostadal. She lived in an attic only a few streets from the barracks.

Fashnalgid liked Rostadal and pitied her. She was a displaced person. She had come from a village in the north. She had nothing. No possessions. No political or religious beliefs. No relations. She still managed to be kind, and made her little rented room homely.

He sat up suddenly in bed and said, "I'll have to go, Rostadal. Get me a drink, will you?"

"What's the matter?"

"Just get me a drink. It's the weight of misery. I can't stay."

Without complaint, she slipped out of bed and brought him a glass of wine. He threw it down his throat.

She looked down at him and said, "Tell me what's worrying you."

"I can't. It's too terrible. The world's full of evil." He began dressing. She slipped into her soiled heedrant, wordless now, wondering if he would pay her. There was only an oil lamp to light the scene.

After lacing up his boots, he collected the book he had set by the bedside and put down some sibs for her. His look was one of misery. He saw her fright but could do nothing to comfort her.

"Will you come back, Harbin?" she asked, clasping her hands together.

He looked up at the cracked ceiling and shook his head. Then he went out.

A spiteful rain fell over Askitosh, setting its gutters foaming. Fashnalgid took no notice. He walked briskly through the deserted streets, trying to wear out his thoughts.

On the previous night, a messenger on an exhausted yelk had ridden through these same streets. He rode to the army headquarters at the top of the hill. Although the incident had been hushed up, the officers' mess soon heard about it. The messenger was an agent of the Oligarch. He brought a report concerning Asperamanka, announcing the victory of the latter's forces against the combined armies of Campannlat, and the relief of Isturiacha. Asperamanka, said the report, was expecting a triumphal reception on his return to Sibornal.

The messenger bearing this letter dismounted in the square and fell flat on his face. He was suffering all the symptoms of the Fat Death. A senior officer shot the man as he lay.

Only an hour or two later, Fashnalgid's mother came to him distraught in a dream, saying, "Brother shall slay brother." He was himself dangling from a hook.

Two days passed and Fashnalgid was posted to Koriantura.

As he took his orders from Major Gardeterark, he saw clearly the plan the Oligarch had devised. There was one factor which would disrupt the scheme for carrying Sibornal through the Weyr-Winter. That factor was more divisive even than the cold: the Fat Death. In the madness the Fat Death carried with it, brother would devour brother.

The death of his midnight messenger warned the Oligarch that the return of Asperamanka's army would bring the plague from the Savage Continent. So a rational decision had been arrived at: the army must not return. The First Guard, of which Fashnalgid was an officer, was in Koriantura for one reason only: to annihilate Asperamanka's army as it approached the frontier. The antiplague regulations, the Restrictions of Persons in Abodes Act, imposed on the city and on Eedap Mun Odim, were moves to make the massacre when it came more acceptable to the population.

These terrible reflections ran through Harbin Fashnalgid's head as he lay in his billet under Odim's roof. Unlike Major Gardeterark, he was not an early riser. But he could not escape into sleep from the vision in his head. The Oligarchy he now saw as a spider, sitting somewhere in the darkness, sustaining itself through the ages at whatever cost to ordinary people.

That was the implication behind his father's remark that he had bought the promise of the future. He had bought it with his son's life. His father had ensured his own safety as an ex-Member of the Oligarchy, at no matter what expense to others.

"I'll do something about it," Fashnalgid said, as he finally dragged himself out of bed. Light was filtering through his small window. All round him, he could hear Odim's vast family beginning to stir.

"I'll do something about it," he said as he dressed. And when, a few hours later, the girl Besi Besamitikahl entered his office, he read in the unconscious gestures of her body a willingness to do his will. In that moment, he saw how he might make use of her and Odim to disrupt the Oligarch's plan and save Asperamanka's army.

The escarpment to the east of Koriantura, which tumbled down to the Isthmus of Chalce, marked the point where the continents of Sibornal and Campannlat joined. The broken land south of the escarpment— through which any army must make its way if approaching Uskutoshk— was bounded to the west by marshes which led eventually to the sea, and was terminated after a few miles by the Ivory Cliffs, standing like sentries before the steppes of Chalce.

Harbin Fashnalgid and the three common soldiers under him reined their yelk at the foot of the Ivory Cliffs and dismounted. They discovered a cave from which to shelter from the stiff breeze, and Fashnalgid ordered one of the men to light a small fire. He himself took a pull from a pocket flask.

He had already made some use of Besi Besamitikahl. She had shown him a way through the back alleys of Koriantura which curved downhill. The route avoided the rest of the First Guard mustering along the ramparts of the escarpment. Fashnalgid was now technically a deserter.

He gave a little misleading information to his detail. They would wait here until Asperamanka's army came from the south. They were in no danger. He had a special message from the Oligarch for Asperamanka himself.

They tethered their yelk in lying positions so that they could crouch against the animals and derive benefit from their body warmth. There they waited for Asperamanka. Fashnalgid read a book of love poetry.

Several hours elapsed. The men began to complain to each other. The fog cleared, the sky became a hazy blue. In the distance, they heard the sound of hoofs. Riders were approaching from the south.

The Ivory Cliffs were the bastions of the inhospitable spine of the highlands which curled about the Gulf of Chalce. They formed canyons through which all travellers must go.

Fashnalgid stuffed the poetry volume into his pocket and jumped up. He felt—as so often in the past—the feebleness of his own will. The hours of waiting, not to mention the languorous tenor of the verse, had sapped his determination to act. Nevertheless, he gave crisp orders to his men to position themselves out of sight and stepped from concealment. He expected to see the vanguard of an army. Instead, two riders appeared.

The riders came on slowly. Both slumped wearily in the saddles of their yelk. They were in army uniform, the yelks were half-shaved, in the military fashion. Fashnalgid ordered them to halt.

One of the riders dismounted and came forward slowly. Although he was little more than a stripling, his face was grey with dust and fatigue. "Are you from Uskutoshk?" he called, in a hoarse voice.

"Yes, from Koriantura. Are you of Asperamanka's army?"

"We're a good three days ahead of the main body. Maybe more."

Fashnalgid considered. If he let them through, the two riders would be stopped by Major Gardeterark's lookouts, and might reveal his whereabouts. He did not consider himself capable of shooting them in cold blood—why, this young fellow was a lieutenant ensign. The only way to halt them was to tell them of the fate which hung over the army, and enlist their cooperation.

He stepped one pace nearer the lieutenant. The latter immediately produced a revolver and braced it against his crooked left arm to aim. As he squinted down the barrel, he said, "Come no nearer. You have other men with you."

Fashnalgid spread wide his hands. "Look, don't do that. We mean you no harm. I want to talk. You look as if you might like a drink."

"We'll both stay where we are." Without ceasing to squint down his gun barrel, the lieutenant called to his companion, "Come and get this man's gun."

Licking his lips nervously, Fashnalgid hoped that his men would come to his rescue; on the other hand, he hoped they would not, since that might lead to his being shot. He watched the second rider dismount. Boots, trousers, cloak, fur hat. Face pale, fine-featured, beardless. Something in her movements told Fashnalgid, an expert in such matters, that this was a woman. She came hesitantly towards him.

As she got to him, Fashnalgid pounced, grasping her outstretched wrist, twisting her arm and swinging her violently about. Using her as a shield between him and the other man, he pulled his own gun from its holster.

"Throw your weapon down, or I'll shoot you both." When his order was obeyed, Fashnalgid called to his men. The soldiers emerged cautiously, looking unwarlike.

The rider, having dropped his gun, stood confronting Fashnalgid. Fashnalgid, still pointing his revolver, reached inside his captive's coat with his left hand, and had a feel of her breasts.

"Who the sherb are you?" He burst out laughing, even as the woman began to weep. "You're evidently a man who likes to ride with his creature comforts . . . and a well-developed creature it is."

"My name is Luterin Shokerandit, Lieutenant. I am on an urgent mission for the Supreme Oligarch, so you'd better let me through."

"Then you're in trouble." He ordered one of his men to collect Shokerandit's pistol, turned the woman about, and removed her hat so that he could get a better look at her. Toress Lahl stood before him, her eyes heavy with anger. He patted her cheek, saying to Shokerandit, "We have no quarrel. Far from it. I have a warning for you. I'll put my gun away and we will shake hands like proper men."

They shook hands warily, looking each other over. Shokerandit took Toress Lahl's arm and drew her beside him, saying nothing. As for Fashnalgid, the feel of breasts had heartened him; he was beginning to congratulate himself on his handling of a difficult situation when one of his men, keeping lookout, called that riders were approaching from the north, from the direction of Koriantura.

A line of mounted men was nearing the Ivory Cliffs, a banner flying in its midst. Fashnalgid whipped a spyglass from his coat pocket and surveyed the advance.

He uttered a curse. Leading the advance was none other than his superior, Major Gardeterark. Fashnalgid's first thought was that Besi had betrayed him. But it was more likely that one of the citizens of Koriantura had seen him leaving the city and reported the fact.

The figures were still some distance away.

He had no doubt what his fate would be if he was caught, but there was still time to act. His manner as much as his words persuaded Shokerandit and the woman that they would be safer joining him than trying to escape—particularly when Fashnalgid offered them two of his fresh yelk to ride. Shouting to his men to stand their ground and tell the major that there was a large body of armed men at the other end of the Cliffs, Fashnalgid flung himself onto his yelk and galloped off at full speed, Shokerandit and Toress Lahl following. He kicked one of the unmounted yelk before him.

Some way along the narrow defile of the Cliffs was a side passage. Fashnalgid drove the unmounted yelk straight forward, but led the other down the defile. He calculated that the sound of the escaping yelk would lead the enemy force to ride straight on.

The defile dwindled to a mere fissure. By setting their mounts determinedly forward, they could scramble up the crumbling slope onto higher ground. They emerged in a confusion of broken rock where small trees and bushes, arched over by the prevailing wind, pointed

southwards. From somewhere below them came the thunder of the
major's troop galloping past.

Fashnalgid wiped the cold sweat from his brow and picked a course
westward among the rocks. Both the suns lay close in the sky, Freyr low
as ever in the southwest, Batalix sinking to the west.

The three riders urged their mounts through a series of eroded buttes
and round a shattered boulder the size of a house, where there were
signs of past human habitation. In the distance, beyond where the land
fell away, was the glint of the sea. Fashnalgid halted and took a drink
from his flask. He offered it to Shokerandit, but the latter shook his
head.

"I've taken you on trust," he said. "But now that we have eluded
your friends, you had better tell me what is on your mind. My job is
to get word to the Oligarch as soon as possible."

"My job is to evade the Oligarch. Let me tell you that if you present
yourself before him, you will probably be shot." He told Shokerandit
of the reception being arranged for Asperamanka. Shokerandit shook
his head.

"The Oligarchy ordered us into Campannlat. If you believe that they
would massacre us on our return, then you are plainly crazed."

"If the Oligarch thinks so little of an individual, he will think no more
of an army."

"No sane man would wipe out one of his own armies."

Fashnalgid started to gesticulate.

"You are younger than I. You have less experience. Sane men do
the most damage. Do you believe that you live in a world where men
behave with reason? What is rationality? Isn't it merely an expectation
that others will behave as we do? You can't have been long in the army
if you believe the mentalities of all men are alike. Frankly, I think my
friends mad. Some were driven mad by the army, some were so mad
they were attracted to that area of idiocy, some simply have a natural
talent for madness. I once heard Priest-Militant Asperamanka preach.
He spoke with such force that I believe him to be a good man. There
are good men . . . But most officers are more like me, I can tell you—
reprobates that only madmen would follow."

There was silence after this outburst, before Shokerandit said coldly,
"I certainly would not trust Asperamanka. He was prepared to let his
own men die."

" 'Wisdom to madness quickly turns, If suffering is all one learns,' "
quoted Fashnalgid, adding, "An army carrying plague. The Oligarchy
would be happy to be rid of it, now there's little danger of an attack
from Campannlat. Also, it suits Askitosh to get rid of the Bribahr
contingent. . . ."

As if there was nothing more to be said, Fashnalgid turned his back
on the other two and took a long swig from his flask. As Batalix

descended towards the strip of distant sea, clouds drew across the sky.

"So what do you propose doing, if we are not to be trapped between armies?" Toress Lahl asked boldly.

Fashnalgid pointed into the distance. "A boat is waiting across the marshes, lady, with a friend of mine in it. That's where I'm going. You are free to come if you wish. If you believe my story, you'll come."

He swung himself up slowly into the saddle, strapped his collar under his chin, smoothed his moustache, and gave a nod of farewell. Then he kicked his beast into action. The yelk lowered its head and started to move down the rocky slope in the direction of the distant glimmering sea.

Luterin Shokerandit called after the disappearing figure, "And where's that boat of yours bound for?"

The wind stirring the low bushes almost drowned the answer that came back.

"Ultimately, Shivenink . . ."

The gaunt figure on its yelk moved down into a maze of marshes which fringed the sea; whereupon birds rose up under the shaggy hoofs of the animal as small amphibians disappeared underneath them. Things hopped in rain-pocked puddles. Everything that could move fled from the man's path.

Captain Harbin Fashnalgid's mood was too bleak for him even to question why mankind's position should remain so isolated in the midst of all other life. Yet that very question—or rather a failure to perceive the correct answer to the problem it posed—had brought into existence a world which moved above the planet in a circumpolar orbit.

The world was an artificial one. Its designation was Earth Observation Station Avernus. Circling the planet 1500 kilometres above the surface, it could be seen from the ground as a bright star of swift passage, to which the inhabitants of the planet had given the name Kaidaw.

On the station, two families supervised the automatic recording of data from Helliconia as it passed below them. They also saw to it that that data—in all its richness, confusion, and overwhelming detail—was transmitted to the planet Earth, a thousand light-years distant. To this end, the EOS had been established. To this end, human beings from Earth had been born to populate it. The Avernus was at this time only a few Earth years short of its four thousandth birthday.

The Avernus was an embodiment, cast in the most advanced technology of its culture, of the failure to perceive the answer to that age-old problem of why mankind was divorced from its environment. It was the ultimate token in that long divorce. It represented nothing less than the peak of achievement of an age when man had tried to conquer space and to enslave nature while remaining himself a slave.

For this reason, the Avernus was dying.

Over the long centuries of its existence, the Avernus had gone through many crises. Its technology had not been at fault; far from it—the great hull of the station, which had a diameter of one thousand metres, was designed as a self-servicing entity, and small servomechanisms scuttled like parasites over its skin, replacing tiles and instruments as required. The servomechanisms moved swiftly, signalling to each other with asymmetrical arms, like crabs on an undiscovered germanium shore, communicating with each other in a language only the WORK computer which controlled them understood. In the course of forty centuries, the servomechanisms continued to serve. The crabs had proved untiring.

Squadrons of auxiliary satellites accompanied the Avernus through space, or dived off in all directions, like sparks from a fire. They crossed and recrossed in their orbits, some no bigger than an eyeball, others complex in shape and design, coming and going about their automatic business, the gathering of information. Their metaphorical throats were parched for an ever flowing stream of data. When one of them malfunctioned, or was silenced by a passing speck of cosmic debris, a replacement floated free from the service hatches of the Avernus and took its place. Like the crabs, the sparklike satellites had proved untiring.

And inside the Avernus. Behind its smooth plastic partitioning lay the equivalent of an endomorphic skeleton or, to use a more suitably dynamic comparison, a nervous system. This nervous system was infinitely more complex than that of any human. It possessed the inorganic equivalent of its own brains, its own kidneys, lungs, bowels. It was to a large extent independent of the body it served. It resolved all problems connected with overheating, overcooling, condensation, microweather, wastes, lighting, intercommunication, illusionism, and hundreds of other factors designed to make life tolerable physiologically for the human beings on the ship. Like the crabs and the satellites, the nervous system had proved untiring.

The human race had tired. Every member of the eight families—later reduced to six, and now reduced to two—was dedicated, through whatever speciality he or she pursued, to one sole aim: to beam as much information about the planet Helliconia as possible back to distant Earth.

The goal was too rarified, too abstract, too divorced from the bloodstream.

Gradually, the families had fallen victim to a sort of neurasthenia of the senses and had lost touch with reality. Earth, the living globe, had ceased to be. There was Earth the Obligation only, a weight on the consciousness, an anchor on the spirit.

Even the planet before their view, the glorious and changing balloon of Helliconia, burning in the light of its two suns and trailing its cone

*of darkness like a wind sock behind it, even Helliconia became an
abstract. Helliconia could not be visited. To visit it meant death. Although the human beings on its surface, scrutinised so devotedly from
above, appeared identical to Earthlings, they were protected from
external contact by a complex virus mechanism as untiring as the
mechanisms of the Avernus. That virus, the helico virus, was lethal to
the inhabitants of the Avernus at all seasons. Some men and women
had gone down to the planet's surface. They had walked there for a
few days, marveling at the experience. And then they had died.*

On the Avernus, a defeated minimalism had long prevailed. The
attenuation of the spirit had been embraced.

With the slow crawl of autumn across the planet below, as Freyr
receded day by day and decade by decade from Helliconia and its sister
planets—as the 236 astronomical units of periastron between Batalix and
Freyr lengthened to the formidable 710 of apastron—the young on the
Observation Station rose up in despair and overthrew their masters.
What though their masters were themselves slaves? The era of asceticism
was gone. The old were slain. Minimalism was slain. Eudaemonism
ruled in its stead. Earth had turned its back on the Avernus. Very well,
then Avernus would turn its back on Helliconia.

At first, blind indulgence in sensuality had been sufficient. Just to
have broken the sterile bonds of duty was glory enough. But—and in that
"but" lies possibly the fate of the human race—hedonism proved in-
sufficient. Promiscuity proved as much of a dead end as abstention.

Cruel perversions grew from the sullied beds of the Avernus. Wound-
ings, slashings, cannibalism, pederasty, paedophilia, intestinal rape,
sadistic penetrations of infants and the ageing became commonplace.
Flayings, public mass fornications, buggery, irrumation, mutilation—
such was the daily diet. Libido waxed, intellect waned.

Everything depraved flourished. The laboratories were encouraged to
bring forth more and more grotesque mutations. Dwarfs with enlarged
sex organs were succeeded by hybrid sex organs imbued with life. These
"pudendolls" moved with legs of their own; later models progressed by
labile or preputial musculature. These reproductive leviathans publicly
aroused and engulfed each other, or overwhelmed the humans thrown
into their path. The organs became more elaborate, more aposematic.
They proliferated, reared and tumbled, sucked, slimed, and reproduced.
Both those forms resembling priapic fungi and those resembling
labyrinthiform ooecia were ceaselessly active, their colours flaring and
fading according to their flaccidity or engorgement. In their later stages
of evolution, these autonomous genitalia grew enormous; a few became
violent, battering like multicoloured slugs at the walls of the glass tanks
wherein they spent their somewhat holobenthic existence.

Several generations of Avernians venerated these strange polymorphs *almost as if they were the gods which had been banished from the station long ago. The next generation would not tolerate them.*

A civil war, a war between generations, broke out. The station became a battleground. The mutated organs broke free; many were destroyed.

The fighting continued over several years and lifetimes. Many people died. The old structure of families, stable for so long, based on patterns of long endurance on Earth, broke down. The two sides became known as the Tans and the Pins, but the labels had little reference to what had once existed.

The Avernus, haven of technology, temple of all that was positive and enquiring in mankind's intellect, was reduced to a tumbled arena, in which savages ran from ambush at intervals to break each other's skulls.

V

A FEW MORE
REGULATIONS

A system of raised dykes covered the marshlands between Koriantura and Chalce like a network of veins. Here and there, the dykes intersected. The intersections were sometimes marked by crude gates, which prevented domestic cattle from wandering. The tops of the dykes were flattened where animals and men had worn paths; the sides of the dykes were covered in rough lush grass that merged into reeds bearding the lips of ditches which ran with black water. The land divided by these features squelched when walked upon. Heavy domestic cattle crossed it with slow deliberation. They paused occasionally to drink from dark open pools.

Luterin Shokerandit and his captive woman were the only human figures to be seen for miles. Their progress occasionally disturbed flocks of birds, which rose up with a clatter, flew low, and suddenly folded up the fan of their winged cloud to sink in unison back to earth.

As the man drew nearer to the sea and the distance between him and the following woman increased, so the little streams which flowed became more subject to the sea and their waters more brackish. The slight babble they made was a pleasant accompaniment to the plod-plod of the yelk's hoofs.

Shokerandit halted and waited for Toress Lahl to catch up. He intended to shout to her, but something stopped him.

He was certain that the strange Captain Fashnalgid was lying about the reception which awaited Asperamanka on the Koriantura ridge. To believe Fashnalgid was to cast doubt on the integrity of the system by which Shokerandit lived. All the same, a certain sincerity about the man made Shokerandit cautious. Shokerandit's duty was to bear Asperamanka's message to Koriantura, to the army headquarters there. It was therefore his duty also to avoid possible ambush. The wisest course seemed to be to pretend to believe Fashnalgid's story, and to escape from Chalce by boat.

The light over the marshes was deceptive. Fashnalgid's figure had disappeared. Shokerandit was not making the progress he wished. Though his mount followed the trail along the top of the dykes, every step seemed sluggish and mired in marsh.

"Keep close to me," he called to Toress Lahl. His voice sounded thickly in his head. He jerked the yelk forward again.

The brownish rain had threatened earlier to turn into a regular Uskuti up-and-downer, as the old phrase had it. Its shawls had now trailed away to the south, leaving confused light patterns over the marshes. To some, the scene might appear dismal; yet even in this marginal land, processes were at work which were vital to the health of those species which contended for the mastery of Helliconia, the ancipitals and the humans.

In the tidal waters which fed the pools to either side of the dykes, marine algae flourished. They were similar to laminaria, and concentrated the iodine in the water in their narrow brown fingers. The algae dissipated this chemical into the air in the form of iodine compounds, notably methyl iodine. As the methyl iodine decomposed back into iodine in the atmosphere, the circulation of the winds carried it to every last corner of the globe.

The ancipitals and humans could not live without iodine. Their thyroid glands harvested it in order to regulate their metabolisms with iodine-bearing hormones.

At this time of the Great Year, after the trigger time of the Seven Eclipses, some of those hormones were ensuring that the human species was more susceptible than usual to the depredations of the helico virus.

As if caught in a maze, his thoughts travelled round and round in familiar patterns. Time and again, he recalled his celebrated exploits at Isturiacha—but no longer with pride. His companions had admired him for his courage; each bullet he had fired, each thrust of his sword which had broken an enemy body now had a legendary glamour attached to

it. Yet he shrank in horror from what he had done, and from the exulta-
tion he had felt while doing it.

And with the woman. On their lonely journey north, he had possessed
Toress Lahl. She had lain unresisting while he had his way. He still
rejoiced in the feel of her flesh, and in his power over it. Yet he thought
with remorse of his intended wife, Insil Esikananzi, waiting back in
Kharnabhar. What would she think if she saw him lying with this
foreign woman from the heart of the Savage Continent?

These thoughts returned in distorted and fugitive shape until his
skull ached. He had a sudden memory of intruding on his mother when
a child. He had run thoughtlessly into her chamber. There stood that
dim figure, closeted so frequently in her own room (and more so since
Favin's death). She was being dressed by her handmaid, watching the
process in her misty silver mirror in which the cluster of her bottles of
perfume and unguents was reflected like the spires and domes of a
distant city.

His mother had turned to confront him, without reproach, without
animation, without—as far as he could remember—a word. She was
being helped into her gown in preparation for some special grand
reception. The gown was one that learned associations of the Wheel
had given her, embroidered all over with a map of Helliconia. The
countries and islands were depicted in silver, the sea in a bright blue.
His mother's hair, as yet undressed, hung down darkly, a waterfall that
flowed from the Northern Pole to the High Nyktryhk and beyond. The
gown buttoned down the back. He noticed as she stood there and
the maid stooped to do up the buttons that the city of Oldorando
in the Savage Continent marked the site of his mother's private parts.
He had always been ashamed of this observation.

He saw the thick clumps of marsh grass underfoot like coarse body
hair. The grass was getting closer in a puzzling way. He saw small
amphibians hop away into hair-fringed clefts, heard the tinkle of water
travelling, watched tiny pied daisies fall beneath the hoofs of the yelk
as if they were stars going into eclipse. The universe came to him. He
was slipping from his saddle.

At the last moment, he managed to pull himself upright and land
on two feet. His legs felt unfamiliar.

"What's the matter with you?" Toress Lahl asked, riding up.

Shokerandit found difficulty in moving his neck to look up at her.
Her eyes were shielded by her hat. Mistrusting her, he reached for his
gun, then remembered it was stashed in his saddle. He fell forward,
burying his face in the wet fur on his yelk's rump. He sank to the
ground and felt himself sliding down the side of the dyke.

A rigidity had seized him. A disconnection between will and ability
had taken place. Yet he heard Toress Lahl dismount and come
squelching down to where he lay sprawled.

He was conscious of her arm about him, of her voice, anxious, seeking out his sense. She was helping him up. His bones ached. He tried to cry out in pain, but no noise emerged. The bone ache, the limb pain, crept into his skull. His body twisted and contorted. He saw the sky swing on a hinge.

"You're ill," Toress Lahl said. She could not bring herself to mention the dread name of the disease.

She dropped him and let him lie in the wet grasses. She stood looking round at the vacancy of the marshes and at the distant bald hills from which they had come. There were still moving banners of rain in the southern sky. Tiny crabs ran in the streamlets at her feet.

She could escape. Her captor lay powerless at her feet. She could shoot him with his own gun as he lay. A return to Campannlat overland would be too perilous, with an army approaching somewhere over the steppe. Koriantura was only a few miles away to the northwest; the escarpment which marked the frontier could be discerned as a smudge on the horizon. But that was enemy territory. The light was fading.

Toress Lahl walked a few paces back and forth in her indecision. Then she returned to the prone figure of Luterin Shokerandit.

"Come on, let's see what can be done," she said.

She managed to get him back in the saddle with a struggle, climbing up behind him and kicking the yelk into action. Her yelk followed in fits and starts, as if preferring company to a night alone on the marshes.

Prompted by anxiety, she urged increased speed out of her animal. As dusk closed in, she caught a glimpse of Fashnalgid ahead, his figure silhouetted against the distant sea. Raising Shokerandit's revolver, she fired it in the air. Birds rose in flocks from the surrounding land, screaming as they escaped.

In another half hour, night or its half-brother lay over the land, although shimmering pools here and there picked up a reflection from the southwestern horizon, just below which Freyr lurked. Fashnalgid could no longer be seen.

She spurred on the yelk, supporting Shokerandit's body against hers.

Water flooded in on either side of the raised path. Its noise was greater now, which Toress Lahl believed indicated that the tide was rising. She had never seen the sea before, and feared it. In the deceptive light, she came on a small jetty before she knew it. A boat was moored there.

The sallow sea lapped with a greedy sound on the mud. Glumaceous grasses and sedges set up a ghostly rustle. Small waves slapped against the side of the dinghy. There was no sign of any human being.

Toress Lahl climbed from the yelk and eased Shokerandit down on a bank. Cautiously she ventured onto the creaking jetty to which the dinghy was moored.

"Got you, then! Hold still!"

She gave a small scream as the shout came from beneath her feet. A man jumped out from under the jetty and pointed his gun at her head.

She smelled the spirits on his breath, saw his luxuriant moustache, and recognised Captain Fashnalgid with relief. He gave a grunt of recognition, expressing not so much pleasure or displeasure as an admission that life was full of tiresome incidents, each demanding to be dealt with.

"Why did you follow? Are you leading Gardeterark after you?"

"Shokerandit is ill. Will you help me?"

He turned and called towards the boat.

"Besi! Come out. It's safe."

Besi Besamitikahl, wrapped in her furs, emerged from under a tarpaulin where she had been sheltering and came forward. She had listened almost without astonishment as the captain, in one of his ranting moods, had outlined his scheme to snatch Asperamanka from the wrath of the Oligarch—as he dramatically put it. He would go such and such a way to meet the Priest-Militant, and would ride with him to the coast, where Besi would have a boat waiting. This boat would be lent by courtesy of Eedap Mun Odim. She must not fail him. Life and honour were at stake.

Odim had listened to this plan, as the girl related it, with delight. Once Fashnalgid became involved in an illegal enterprise, he would be in Odim's power. By all means he should have a little boat, with a boatman to crew her, and Besi should sail round the bay and meet him and his holy companion.

Even while these arrangements had been made, the laws of the Oligarch were pressing down harder on the population. Day by day, street by street, Koriantura was falling under military control. Odim saw all, said nothing, worried for his herd of relations, and made his own plans.

Besi now helped Toress Lahl to carry the stiff body of Luterin Shokerandit into the boat. "Do we have to take these two?" she asked Fashnalgid, staring down with disfavour at the sick man. "They are probably infectious."

"We can't leave them here," Fashnalgid said.

"I suppose you want us to take the yelks too."

The captain ignored this remark and motioned to the boatman to cast off. The yelks stood on the shore, watching them depart. One ventured forward into the mud, slipped, and withdrew. They remained staring at the small boat as it faded away over the water in the direction of Koriantura.

It was cold on the water. While the boatman sat by the tiller, the others crouched below the tarpaulin, out of the wind. Toress Lahl was disinclined to talk, but Besi plied her with questions.

"Where are you from? I can tell by your accent that you're not from here. Is this man your husband?"

Reluctantly, Toress Lahl admitted that she was Shokerandit's slave.

"Well, there are ways out of slavery," said Besi feelingly. "Not many. I'm sorry for you. You could be worse off if your master dies."

"Perhaps I could find a boat in Koriantura which would take me back to Campannlat—once Lieutenant Shokerandit is safe, I mean. Would you help me?"

Fashnalgid said, "Lady, there will be trouble enough for us when we get back to Koriantura, without helping a slave to escape. You're a good-looking woman—you should find a good billet."

Ignoring this last remark, Toress Lahl said, "What kind of trouble?"

"Ah . . . That is up to God, the Oligarch, and a certain Major Gardeterark to devise," said Fashnalgid. He brought out his flask and took a long swig at its contents.

With some reluctance, he offered it round to the women.

From under the tarpaulin, Shokerandit said, slowly but distinctly, "I don't want to go through this again . . ."

Toress Lahl rested a hand on his burning head.

Fashnalgid said, "You'll find that life is essentially a series of repeat performances, my fine lieutenant."

The population of Sibornal was less than forty percent that of its neighbour Campannlat. Yet communications between distant national capitals was generally better than in Campannlat. Roads were good, except in backward areas like Kuj-Juvec; since few centres of population were at a great distance from the coast, seas acted as thoroughfares. It was not a difficult continent to govern, given a strong will in the strongest city, Askitosh.

A street plan of Askitosh revealed a semicircular design, the centre point of which was the gigantic church perched on the waterfront. The light on the spire of this church could be seen for some miles down the coast. But at the rear of the semicircle, a mile or more from the sea, was Icen Hill, upon which granite mound stood a castle housing the strongest will in Askitosh and all Sibornal.

This Will saw to it that the land and sea roads of the continent were busy—busy with military preparation and with that forerunner of military preparation, the poster. Posters appeared in towns and in the smallest hamlets, announcing one new restriction after another. Often the announcements these posters bore came in the guise of concern

for the population: they were for the Prevention of the Spread of Fat
Death, or they were for the Limitation of Famine, or for the Arrest of
Dangerous Elements. But what they all boiled down to was the Cur-
tailment of Individual Liberty.

It was generally supposed by those who worked for the Oligarchy that
the Will behind these edicts regulating the lives of the inhabitants of
the northern continent was that of the Supreme Oligarch, Torkerkanzlag II. No one had ever seen Torkerkanzlag. If he existed, Torkerkanzlag confined himself to a set of chambers within Icen Hill Castle. But
such edicts as were currently being issued were felt to be consistent with
the nature of someone who had so little love for his own liberty that he
locked himself up in a suite of windowless rooms.

Those higher up the scale had their doubts about the Supreme Oligarch, and often maintained that the title was an empty one, and that
government was in the hands of the Inner Chamber of the Oligarchy
itself.

It was a paradoxical situation. At the core of the State was an entity
almost as nebulous as the Azoiaxic One, the entity at the heart of the
Church. Torkerkanzlag was understood to be a name adopted on elec-
tion, and possibly used by more than one person.

Then there were the obiter dicta supposed to filter down from the
very lips—the beak, some claimed—of the Oligarch himself.

"We may debate here in council. But remember that the world is
not a debating chamber. It more closely resembles a torture chamber."

"Do not mind being called wicked. It is the fate of rulers. That the
people want nothing but wickedness you can ascertain by listening at
any street corner."

"Use treachery where possible. It costs less than armies."

"Church and State are brother and sister. One day we will decide
which shall inherit the family fortune."

Such morsels of wisdom passed through the oesophagus of the Inner
Chamber and into the body politic.

As for that Inner Chamber, it might be expected that those who
belonged to it would know the nature of the Will. Such was not the
case. The Members of the Inner Chamber—they were now in session
and came masked—were collectively even less sure of the nature of the
Will than the ignorant citizens living in the damp streets below the
hill. So close to that formidable Will were they that they had to fence
it about with pretence. The masks they wore were but an outer cover
for a barrier of deviousness; these men of power trusted each other so
little that each had developed a posture with regard to the nature of
the Oligarch by which truth could not be distinguished—much like
insects which, if predatory, disguise themselves as something innocuous
whereby to deceive their prey, or, if innocuous, as a poisonous species
to deceive their predators.

Thus it might be that the Member from Braijth, the capital city of Bribahr, was a man who knew the truth about the Will that dominated them. He might admit to his cronies the truth of the matter; or he might tell a guarded half-truth; or he might lie about the matter in one way or another, according to what best suited him.

And in the case of that Member from Braijth, in actual fact, the degree of his deceitfulness could scarcely be judged, since, beneath the imposed continental unity, guaranteed by many a solemn pact, Uskutoshk was at war with Bribahr, and a force from Askitosh was besieging Rattagon (as far as it was possible to besiege that island fortress).

Moreover, other Members feigned to trust the Member from Braijth according to their secret sympathies with his country's policy in daring to challenge the leadership of Uskutoshk. Feigning was all. Their very sincerity was feigned.

No one was secure in his understanding. With this they were collectively content, finding security in believing that their fellow Members were even more deluded than they were themselves.

Thus the soul of the most powerful city on the planet had at its core a profound obfuscation and confusion. It was with this confusion that they chose to meet the challenge of the changing seasons.

The Members were currently discussing the latest edict to descend from the unseen hand of the Oligarch for their ratification. This was the most challenging edict yet. The edict would prohibit the practice of pauk, as being against the principles of the Church.

If the required legislation was passed, it would entail in practice the stationing of soldiery in every hamlet throughout the continent in order to enforce the prohibition. Since the Members considered themselves learned, they approached the subject by leisurely discourse. Their lips moved thinly under their masks.

"The edict brings under consideration our very nature," said the Member for the city of Juthir, the capital of Kuj-Juvec. "We are speaking here of an age-old custom. But what is age-old is not necessarily sacrosanct. On the one hand, we have our irreplaceable Church, the very basis of Sibornalese unity, with its cornerstone God the Azoiaxic. On the other hand, unrecognised by the Church, we have the custom of pauk, by which living persons can sink their selves down into a trance state to commune with their ancestral spirits. Those spirits, as we know, are supposed to be descending to as well as being descended from the Original Beholder, that inscrutable mother figure. On the one hand is our religion, pure, intellectual, scientific; on the other hand is this hazy notion of a female principle.

"It is necessary for us to prepare for the harsher, colder times to come. For that, we must arm ourselves against the female principle in ourselves, and eradicate it from the population. We must strike at this pernicious cult of the Original Beholder. We must banish pauk. I trust that what I say merely elucidates the wisdom behind this fresh and inspired edict of the Will.

"Furthermore, I would go so far as to claim—"

Most of the Members were old, were accustomed to being old, had persisted in being old for a long while. They met in an ancient room in which all items, whether iron or wood, had been polished over the centuries by a host of slaves until they shone. The iron table at which they propped themselves, the bare floor beneath their slippered feet, the elaborately wrought chairs on which they sat, all gleamed at them. The austere iron panelling on the walls threw back distorted reflections of themselves. A fire glowed in the prison of its grate, sending more smoke than flame through the bars; because it did little to remove the chill of the chamber, the Members were well shrouded in felts, like mummers in an ancient play. The one furnishing to relieve this gloomy brightness was a large tapestry which decked one wall. Against a scarlet background, a great wheel was depicted being rowed through the heavens by oarsmen in pale blue garments; each oarsman smiled towards an astonishing maternal figure from whose nostrils, mouth, and breasts spurted the stars in the sky. This ancient fabric lent a touch of grandeur to the room.

While one or other of their number held forth, the Members sipped at pellamountain cordial and stared down at their fingernails or out through the slit windows, which provided glimpses of an Askitosh sliced into small vertical sections.

"Some claim that the myth of the Original Beholder is a poetical image of the self," said the Member from the distant province of Carcampan. "But it has yet to be established whether such an entity as the self exists. If it does, it may not even be, if I may coin a phrase, master in its own house. It may exist outside our selves. That is to say, the self may be a component of Helliconia itself, since our atoms are Helliconia's. In which case, there may be some danger attendant on destroying contact with the Beholder. That I must point out to the Honourable Members."

"Danger or not, the people must bend to the will of the Oligarch, or the Weyr-Winter will destroy them. We must be cured of our self. Only obedience will see us through three and a half centuries of ice. . . ." This platitude came from the other end of the iron table, where reflections and shadows merged.

The view of Askitosh was executed in sepia monochrome. The city was enfolded in one of the famous "silt mists," a thin curtain of cold dry air which descended on the city from the plateaux ranged behind it. To this was added the smoke rising from thousands of chimneys, as the Uskuti endeavoured to keep themselves warm. The city faded under a shadow partly of its own making.

"On the other hand, communication with our ancestors in the pauk state does much to fortify our selves," said one greybeard. "Particularly when in adversity. I mean, I imagine that few of us here have not derived comfort from communication with the gossies."

In a querulous voice, a Member from the Lorajan port of Ijivibir said, "By the by, why have our scientists not discovered how it is that gossies and fessups are now friendly to our souls, whereas—as well-authenticated testaments tell—they were once always hostile? Could it be a seasonal change, do you think—friendly in winter and summer, hostile in spring?"

"The question will be rendered immaterial if we abandon the gossies and fessups to their own devices by promulgating the edict before us," replied the Member from Juthir.

Through the narrow windows could be seen the roofs of the government printing press where, after only a day or two of further discussion, the edict of the Supreme Oligarch Torkerkanzlag II was turned into print. The posters that fell in their thousands from the flatbed presses announced in bold type that hereafter it would be an Offence to Go into Pauk, whether Secretly or in Company with Others. This was explained as another precaution against the Encroaching Plague. Penalty for contravening the law, One Hundred Sibs and, for a Second Offence, Life Imprisonment.

Within Askitosh itself was a rail transport system worked by steam cars which pulled carriages at the rate of ten or twelve miles an hour. The cars were dirty but dependable, and the system was being extended outside the city. These cars took bundles of the posters to distribution points on the fringes of the city, and to the harbour, whence they were distributed by ship to all points of the compass.

Thus bundles soon arrived at Koriantura. Bill stickers ran about the town, pasting up the terms of the new law. One of those posters was stuck to the wall of the house where Eedap Mun Odim's family had lived for two hundred years.

But that house was now empty, abandoned to the mice and rats. The front door had slammed for the last time.

Eedap Mun Odim left the family house behind him with his usual stiff little walk. He had his pride: his face betrayed nothing of the griefs he felt.

On this special morning, he took a circuitous route to Climent Quay, going by way of Rungobandryaskosh Street and South Court. His slave Gagrim followed, carrying his bag.

He was conscious with every step that this was the last time in his life that he would walk the streets of Koriantura. Throughout all the long past years, his Kuj-Juveci background had led him to think of it as a place of exile; only now did he realise how much it had been home.

His preparations for departure had been made to the best of his ability; fortunately, he still had one or two Uskuti friends, fellow merchants, who had helped him.

Rungobandryaskosh Street branched off to the left, the street steep. Odim paused at the turning just before the churchyard and looked back down the road. His old house stood there, narrow at the base, wide at the top, its boxed-in wooden balcony clinging to it like the nest of some exotic bird, the eaves of its steep roof curving outwards until they nearly touched the eaves of the house opposite. Inside, no plentiful Odim family: only light, shadow, emptiness, and the old-fashioned murals on the walls, depicting life as it had once been in a now almost imaginary Kuj-Juvec. He tucked his beard more firmly inside his coat and marched briskly on.

This was an area of small craftsmen—silversmiths, watchmakers, bookbinders, and artists of various kinds. To one side of the street stood a small theatre where extraordinary plays were produced, plays which could not fill the theatres in the centre of town: plays trafficking in magic and science, fantasies dealing with both possible and impossible things (for both sorts were much alike), tragedies dealing with broken teacups, comedies dealing with wholesale slaughter. Also satires. Irony and satire were things the authorities could neither understand nor abide. So the theatre was often closed. It was closed at present, and the street looked the drabber for it.

In South Court lived an old painter who had painted scenery for the theatre and porcelain for the factory whose wares Odim exported. Jheserabhay was old now, but he still had a sure hand with plates and tureens; equally important, he had often given work to the ample Odim family. Odim valued him, despite his sharp tongue, and had brought him a farewell present.

A phagor let Odim into the house. There were many phagors in South Court. Uskuti in general had a marked aversion to the ancipital kind, whereas artistic people seemed to delight in them, perversely enjoying the immobility and sudden movements of the creatures. Odim himself disliked their sickly milky stench, and passed as quickly as possible into the presence of Jheserabhay.

Jheserabhay sat wrapped in an old-fashioned heedrant, feet up on a sofa, close to a portable iron stove. Beside him rested a picture album. He rose slowly to welcome Odim. Odim sat on a velvet chair facing him, and Gagrim stood behind the chair, clutching the bag.

The old painter shook his head gloomily when he heard Odim's news.

"Well, it's a bad time for Koriantura and no mistake. I've never known worse. It's a poor thing, Odim, that you should be forced to leave because things are so difficult. But then, you never really belonged here, did you—you and your family."

Odim made no gesture. He said slowly, without thinking, "Yes, I do belong here, and your words amaze me. I was born here, within this very mile, and my father before me. This is my home as much as yours, Jhessie."

"I thought you were from Kuj-Juvec?"

"Originally my family was from Kuj-Juvec, yes, and proud of it. But I am both a Sibornalese and a Korianturan, first and foremost."

"Why are you leaving then? Where are you going? Don't look so offended. Have a cup of tea. A veronikane?"

Odim soothed his beard. "The new edicts make it impossible to stay. I have a large family, and I must do the best I possibly can for them."

"Oh, yes, yes, so you must. You have a very large family, don't you? I'm against that sort of thing myself. Never married. No relations. Always stuck to my art. I've been my own master."

Narrowing his eyes, Odim said, "It's not only Kuj-Juveci families which get large. We're not primitive, you know."

"My dear old friend, you are sensitive today. I was levelling no accusations. Live and let live. Where are you going?"

"That I would rather not say. News gets about, whispers become shouts."

The artist grunted. "I suppose you're going back to Kuj-Juvec."

"Since I have never in my life been there, I cannot go *back* there."

"Someone was telling me that your house is full of murals of that part of the world. I hear they are rather fine."

"Yes, yes, old but fine. By a great artist who never made a name for himself. But it is my house no more. I had to sell it, lock, stock, and barrel."

"Well then . . . I hope you got a good price?"

Odim had been forced to accept a miserable price, but he rationed himself to one word: "Tolerable."

"I suppose I shall miss you, though I've got out of the habit of seeing people. I hardly ever go over to the theatre now. This north wind gets into my old bones."

"Jhessie, I have enjoyed your friendship over twenty-five years, give or take a tenner. I have also much appreciated your work; maybe I never paid you enough. Although I am only a merchant, nevertheless I appreciate artistry in others, and no one in all Sibornal has depicted birds on porcelain so finely as you. I wish to give you a parting present, something too delicate to travel, which I think you will appreciate. I could have sold it in the auctions but I thought you made a worthy recipient."

Jheserabhay struggled into a sitting position and looked expectant. Odim motioned to his slave to open the bag. Gagrim lifted out an article which he handed to Odim. Odim raised the article and held it temptingly before the artist's eyes.

The clock was of the shape and size of a goose's egg. Its dial showed the twenty-five hours of the day round the outer circle, with the forty minutes of the hour inside, in the traditional way. But on the hour, when striking—and the mechanism could be made to strike at any time by pressing a button—the clock revolved, so that a second, rear, face was briefly revealed. The rear face also had two hands, the outer indicating the week, tenner, and season of the small year, and the inner the season of the Great Year.

The faces were enamel. The egg was of gold. It was clutched, top and bottom, by a figure in jade, the ample figure of the Original Beholder, seated on a bank which formed the base of the clock. To one side of her, wheat grew; to the other, glaciers. The finish of the whole was exquisite, the detail perfect: the toes which peeped from the Beholder's sandals had discernible nails.

Reaching out his old seamed hands, Jheserabhay took the clock and examined it for a long time without speaking. Tears came to his eyes.

"It's a thing of beauty, no less. The workmanship is wonderful. And I can't recognise its provenance. Is it from Kuj-Juvec?"

Odim bridled up immediately. "We barbarians are excellent craftsmen. Didn't you know we live in sherb but spend our life killing people and turning out exquisite artwork? Isn't that the idea you proud Uskuti have of us?"

"I didn't mean to offend you, Odim."

"Well, it is from Juthir, if you must know, our capital city. Take it. It will cause you to remember me for five minutes." As he said this, he turned away and looked out the window. A file of soldiers under a noncommissioned officer were searching a house opposite. As Odim watched, two of them brought a man out into the square. The man hung his head, as if ashamed to be seen in such company.

"I'm really sorry you are going, Odim," said the artist, placatingly.

"Evil is loose in the world. I have to go."

"I don't believe in evil. Mistakes, yes. Not evil."

"Then perhaps you are afraid to believe it exists. It exists wherever men are. It's in this very room. Good-bye, Jhessie."

He left the old man clutching the clock and trying to rise from his dusty chair.

Odim looked round warily before leaving the shelter of the house where Jheserabhar had his apartment. The file of soldiers had disappeared with their prisoner. He stepped briskly in the Court, dismissing the encounter with the artist from his mind. These Uskuti were always hard to deal with, after all. It would be a relief to get away from them.

He was all prepared to go. Everything had been done legally, if hastily. Since Besi Besamitikahl had collected the deserter Captain Fashnalgid in the dinghy, two days earlier, Odim had concentrated on getting his affairs in order. He had sold his house to an unfriendly relation and his export business to a friendly rival. He had purchased a ship with Fashnalgid's aid. He would join his brother in distant Shivenink. It would be a pleasure to see Odirin again; they could help each other now that they were not as young as they had been. . . .

Struggle is the true guise of hope, Odim said to himself, straightening his back and walking a little faster. Don't give up. Life will be easier, winter or no winter. You must cease to think only of money. Your mind is dominated by the mighty sib. This adversity will be good for you. In Shivenink, with Odirin's help, I'll work less hard. I will paint pictures like Jheserabhay. Perhaps I will become famous.

Nourishing similar warming thoughts, he turned onto the quay. His soliloquy was shattered by a steam gun trundling slowly by. It was heading eastwards. Word had spread that a great battle was soon to commence; it was another reason for leaving the city as fast as possible. The gun was so heavy that it shook the ground as it rattled over the cobbles. Its fiendish engine, pistons pumping, belched out smoke. Small boys ran beside it, shouting in delight.

The steam gun followed Odim along Climent Quay, its heavy barrel pointing in his general direction. With a sense of relief, he turned in at ODIM FINEST EXPORT PORCELAINS, Gagrim pressing hard at his heels.

The showroom and warehouse were in confusion, mainly because nobody was doing any work. Hired workers and slaves alike had seized on the opportunity to do nothing. Many of them hung about the door, watching the gun go by. In their reluctance to step aside, they revealed a lack of respect for their ex-boss.

Never mind, he said to himself. We will sail on the afternoon's tide, and then these people can do what they like.

A messenger came up and told him that the new owner of the premises was upstairs and would like to see him. A hint of danger ran through Odim's mind. It seemed unlikely that the new owner should be here, since the hand-over was not officially operative until midnight, according to the terms of the contract. But he told himself not to be anxious, and mounted the stairs with determination. Gagrim followed behind.

The reception room was an elegantly furnished gallery with windows overlooking the harbour. On the walls hung tapestries and a series of miniatures which had belonged to Odim's grandfather. Examples of Odim porcelain services lay about on polished tables. This was where special customers were brought and the firm's most important business transacted.

This morning, only one special customer stood in the low room, and his uniform indicated that his business was unlikely to be pleasurable.

Major Gardeterark stood with his back to the window, head thrust forward, heavy protruding mouth and lips swivelling in the direction of Eedap Mun Odim. Behind him stood a pale Besi Besamitikahl.

"Come in," he said. "Close the door."

Odim stopped so abruptly on the threshold that Gagrim bumped into him. Major Gardeterark was contained within his huge greatcoat, a garment of coarse texture with buttons like flambreg eyes positioned on it at intervals as if on metallic sentry go, and pockets which stuck out like boxes. It was in every way a coat that might go about its master's business if its master were ever posted out of it. Gardeterark, however, was very much on duty, and watched from among his buttons as Odim closed the door as instructed.

What most frightened Odim was not so much the major as the sight of Besi beside him. One look at the girl's pale face told Odim that she had been forced to give away his secrets. His mind flew immediately to the secrets he had been prevailed upon to hide on these premises: Harbin Fashnalgid, officially posted as a deserter; a lieutenant from the army of the enemy, now suffering from the Fat Death; and a Borldoranian girl, a slave, who was nursing the lieutenant. He knew that what to him was simple humanity in Gardeterark's bulging eyes was a fatal list of crimes.

Anger burned in Odim's slender frame. He was frightened but the anger overcame the fear. He had loathed this odious, cold officer ever since the moment when he had found him downstairs, bloated with his own power. The creature could not be allowed to interfere with Odim's plans to take everyone away to safety.

Nodding his head towards Besi, Gardeterark said, "This slave woman tells me that you are harbouring an army deserter, by name Fashnalgid."

"He was here waiting. He forced me—" Besi began. Gardeterark brought up his gloved hand, which featured several buttons, and struck her across the face.

"You are hiding this deserter on the premises," he said. He took a step towards Odim, at no time glancing at the girl, who had subsided against the wall, clutching her mouth.

Gardeterark produced from one of his boxes a pistol, and pointed it at Odim's stomach. "You are under arrest, Odim, you foreign sherb. Take me to where you are concealing Fashnalgid."

Odim clutched his beard. Although the sight of Besi being struck had frightened him with its violence, it had also stiffened his resolve. He gave the major a blank stare.

"I don't know who you mean."

Prominent yellow teeth came into view, framed between lips which immediately squeezed shut again. It was the major's patent way of smiling.

"You know who I mean. He lodged with you. He went on an expedi-

tion into Chalce with this woman of yours, no doubt with your con-
nivance. He is to be arrested for desertion. A wharf hand witnessed him
come in here. Lead me to him or I'll have you taken to headquarters
for questioning."

Odim stepped back.

"I'll take you to him."

At the far end of the gallery was a door into the rear areas of the
building. As Gardeterark followed Odim, he pushed aside one of the
tables obstructing his easy passage. The chinaware fell to the floor and
shattered.

Odim made no sign. He signalled Gagrim forward. "Unlock this
door."

"Your slave can stay behind," Gardeterark said.

"He carries the keys during the day."

The keys were in Gagrim's pocket, secured by a chain to his belt. He
unlocked the door with trembling hand, letting the two men through.

They were in a passage leading to the rear offices. Odim led the way.
They went down the passage and turned left, where four steps led up
to a metal door. Odim gestured to the slave to unlock it. An especially
large key was needed.

Once through it, they emerged on a balcony overlooking a yard.
Most of the yard was occupied by cartloads of wood and two old-
fashioned kilns. The kilns were generally unused; one was at present
being fired to meet an emergency order from the local garrison, for
whom no great finesse was needed. Otherwise, most of the Odim porcelain came from companies situated elsewhere in Koriantura. Four
company phagors stood about, tending the active kiln. It was old and
inefficiently insulated, and the heat and smoke from it filled the yard.

"Well?" Gardeterark prompted as Odim hesitated.

"He's in a loft over there," Odim said, pointing across the yard.
Their balcony was connected to the loft he indicated by a catwalk
which spanned the yard. It was almost as ancient as the kilns below;
its single wooden railing was rickety and sooted up by smoke from
below.

Odim started cautiously across the catwalk. Halfway across, as the
smoke billowed up, he paused, steadying himself with one hand on the
rail. "I'm feeling ill . . . I'd better go back," he said, turning towards
the major. "Look at the kiln."

Eedap Mun Odim was not a violent man. All his life, he had hated
force. Even signs of anger disgusted him—his own anger not least. He
had schooled himself to politeness and obedience, following the example of his parents. Now he threw away his training. He brought his
arms round with a wide swinging movement, hands clasped together,
and as Gardeterark glanced down, caught him on the back of his neck.

"Gagrim!" Odim called. His slave never moved.

Gardeterark staggered with his side against the rail and tried to bring up the gun. Odim kicked him on the knee and butted him in the chest. The officer seemed twice his size, the greatcoat impenetrable.

He heard the rail crack, heard the revolver explode, felt Gardeterark begin to fall, dropped to the catwalk on hands and knees to save himself from going too.

Gardeterark gave a terrible cry as he fell.

Odim watched him go, arms flailing, his animal mouth open. It was not far to fall. He hit the middle of the dual-chamber kiln which was being fired. The roof of the kiln was strewn with loose brick and rubble. Cracks ran across it, widening, flaring red. As the heat came up, Odim pulled himself flat on the catwalk to avoid burning.

Screaming, the major made an attempt to get to his feet. The greatcoat smouldered like an old shed. His leg plunged into one of the cracks in the roof. The arch collapsed. Fire spewed upwards like splashing liquid. The temperature inside the kiln was over eleven hundred degrees. Gardeterark, already burning, plunged down into it.

Afterwards, Odim had no idea how long he lay on the catwalk. It was Besi, with her split mouth, who ventured along the walk and helped him return to the gallery. Gagrim had fled.

She was hugging him and wiping his burnt face with a cloth. He realised that he was saying to her over and over, "I killed a man."

"You saved us all," she said. "You were very brave, my darling. Now we must get into the ship and sail as soon as possible, before anyone discovers what has happened."

"I killed a man, Besi."

"Say rather that he fell, Eedap." She kissed him with her burst lips and began to cry. He clutched her as he never had before in daylight, and she felt his thin, hard body tremble.

So ended the well-organised part of Eedap Mun Odim's life. From now on, existence would be a series of improvisations. Like his father before him, he had attempted to control his small world by keeping accurate accounts, by balancing ledgers, by cheating no one, by being friendly, by conforming in every way he could. At one stroke, all that was gone. The system had collapsed.

Besi Besamitikahl had to assist him across the quayside to the waiting ship. With them went two others, whose lives had been equally disrupted.

Captain Harbin Fashnalgid had seen his own face crudely portrayed on a red poster as he stepped ashore with Besi, after they had sailed the twenty miles from the jetty in the marshlands. The poster was newly arrived from the local printing works commandeered by the army, and still glistened with the bill sticker's glue. For Fashnalgid,

Odim's ship served the purpose, not only of escaping from Uskutoshk, but of staying close to Besi. Fashnalgid had decided that if he were to reform his life, then he needed a courageous, constant woman to look after him. He stepped up the gangplank briskly, longing to be free of the army and its shadow.

Behind him followed Toress Lahl, widow of the great Bandal Eith Lahl, recently killed in battle. Since her husband's death and her capture by Luterin Shokerandit, her life had become quite as disoriented as Odim's or Fashnalgid's. She now found herself in a foreign port, about to sail for another foreign port. And her captor lay already in the ship, tied down while he underwent the agony of the Fat Death. She might elude him; but Toress Lahl knew of no way in which a woman of Oldorando could return home safely from Sibornal. So she remained to tend Shokerandit, hoping to earn his gratitude thereby if he survived the plague.

Of the plague, she had less fear than the others. Back home in Oldorando, she had worked as a doctor. The word that inspired fear and curiosity in her was the name of Shokerandit's homeland, Kharnabhar, a word which embodied legend and romance when spoken from the distance of Borldoran.

To acquire his ship, Odim had worked through intermediaries, local friends who knew useful people in the Priest-Sailors Guild. The money from the sale of his house and company had all gone to purchase the *New Season*. It now lay moored alongside Climent Quay, a two-masted brig of 639 tons, square-rigged on fore- and mainmasts. The vessel had been built twenty years earlier, in Askitosh shipyards.

Loading was complete. The *New Season* contained, besides such provisions as Odim could lay his hands on at short notice, a herd of arang, fine Odim porcelain services, and a sick man bearing the plague, with a slave woman to tend him.

Odim had managed to get clearance from the quaymaster, an old acquaintance of his who had been paid liberally across Odim cargoes for many years. The captain of the vessel was persuaded to compress into the shortest possible time all the ceremonies recommended by deuteroscopists and hieromancers for an auspicious voyage. A cannon was fired to mark the departure of a ship from Sibornal.

A brief hymn was sung on deck to God the Azoiaxic. With tide and wind set fair, a gap widened between ship and Climent Quay. The *New Season* began its voyage for distant Shivenink.

VI

G4PBX / 4582 - 4 - 3

O n the Avernus, fleet Kaidaw of Helliconian skies, the monotony
of barbarism descended. Eedap Mun Odim was rightly proud
of the craftsmanship embodied in the Kuj-Juvecian clock he
presented to Jheserabhay; the very narrowness of societies such as Kuj-
Juvec gives their art a concentrated vitality. But the barbarism prevailing on the Avernus produced nothing but smashed skulls, ambushes,
tribal drumming, simian mirth.

The many generations which had served under Avernian civilisation
had often expressed a longing to escape from the sense of futility, from
a doctrine of minimalism, imposed by the concept of Obligation Earth.
Some had preferred death on Helliconia to a continuation of Avernian
order. They would have said, if asked, that they preferred barbarism to
civilisation.

The boredom of barbarism was infinitely greater than the restraints
of civilisation. The Pins and the Tans had no respite from fear and
deprivation. Surrounded by a technology which was in many respects
self-governing, they were little better off than many of the tribes of
Campannlat, caught between marsh and forest and sea. Barbarism let
loose their fears and curtailed their imaginations.

The sections of the station which had suffered greatest damage were those most intimately connected with human activity, such as the canteens and restaurants, and the protein-processing plants which supplied them. The crop fields dominating the inside of the spherical hull were now battlefields. Man hunted man for food. The great perambulant pudendolls, those genital montrosities created from a perverted genetic inheritance, were also tracked down and eaten.

The automated station continued to flash images on internal screens from the living world below—continued, indeed, to vary the interior weather, so that humanity was not bereft of that eternal stimulus.

The surviving tribes were no longer capable of making the old connections. The images they received of hunters, kings, scholars, traders, slaves, had become divorced from their contexts. They were received as visitants from another world, gods or devils. They brought only wonder into the hearts of those whose forebears had studied them with disdain.

The rebels of the Avernus—a mere dissident handful at the onset—had launched out for greater freedoms than they imagined they enjoyed. They had beached themselves on the shores of a melancholy existence. The rule of the head was taken over by the belly.

But the Avernus had a duty which took precedence over tending its inhabitants. Its first duty was to transmit a continuous signal back to the planet Earth, a thousand light-years away. Over the eventful centuries of the Observation Station's existence, that signal, with its freight of information, had never faltered.

The signal had formed an artery of data, fed back to Earth according to the original plan of a technocratic elite responsible for the grandiose schemes of interstellar exploration. The artery never ran dry, not even when the inhabitants of the Avernus reduced themselves to a state close to savagery.

The artery never ran dry, but somewhere a vein had been cut. Earth did not always respond.

Charon, a distant outpost of the solar system, housed a receiving complex built across the frigid methane surface of the satellite. At this station, on which the nearest approaches to intelligent life were the androids which maintained it, the Helliconia signals were analysed, classified, stored, transmitted to the inner solar system. The outward process was far less complex, consisting merely of a string of acknowledgements, or an order to the Avernus to increase coverage of such and such an area. The news bulletins which had once been sent outwards had long ago ceased, ever since someone pointed out the absurdity of feeding the Avernus with items of news one thousand years old. Avernus knew—and now cared—nothing regarding events on Earth.

As to those events: The crowded nations of Earth spent most of the twenty-first century locked in a series of uncomfortable confrontations: East threatened West, North threatened South, First World helped and cheated Third World. Growing populations, dwindling resources, continuous localised conflicts, slowly transferred the face of the globe into something approaching a pile of rubble. The concept of "terrorist nation" dominated the mid-century; it was at this time that the ancient city of Rome was taken out. Yet, contrary to gloomy expectations, that ultimate Valhalla, nuclear war, was never resorted to. This was in part because the superpowers masked their operations behind manipulated smaller nations, and in part because the exploration of neighbouring space acted as something of a safety valve for aggressive emotions.

Those who lived in the twenty-first century regarded their age as a melancholy one despite exponential developments in technological and electronics systems. They saw that every field and factory producing food was electronically protected or physically patrolled. They felt the increasing regimentation of their life. Yet the structure, the underlying system of civilisation, was maintained. Restrictive though it was, it could be transcended.

Many gifted individuals made the century a brilliant one, at least in retrospect. Men and women arose from nowhere, from the masses, and won enormous fame by their gifts. In their brilliance, their defiance of their underprivileged environment, they lightened the hearts of their audience. When Derek Eric Absalom died, it was said that half the globe wept. But his wonderful improvised songs remained as consolation.

At first, only two of Earth's nations were in competition beyond the confines of the solar system. The number crept up to four and stopped at five. The cost of interstellar travel was too great. No more could play, even in an age when technology had become a religion. Unlike religion, the hope of the poor, technology was a rich man's strategy.

The excitements of interstellar exploration were relayed back to the multitudes of Earth. Many admired intellectually. Many cheered for their own teams. The projects were always presented with great solemnity. Great expenditures, great distances, great prestige: these united to impress the taxpayers back home in their ugly cities.

Occasional automated starships were launched during the heyday of interstellar travel, from approximately 2090 to 3200. These ships carried computer-stored colonists, able to range vacuum continually until habitable worlds were discovered.

The extrasolar planet on which mankind first set foot was solemnly named New Earth. It was one of two moonless bodies orbiting Alpha Centauri C. "Arabia Deserta writ large," said one commentator, but most settled for comfortable awe as the monotonous landscapes of New Earth unrolled.

The planet consisted mainly of sand and tumbled mountain ranges.

Its one ocean covered no more than a fiftieth of the total land area. No life was found on it, apart from some abnormally large worms and a kind of seaweed which grew in the fringes of the salt sea. The air, though breathable, had an extremely low water-vapour content; human throats became parched within a few minutes when breathing it. No rain ever fell on New Earth's dazzling surface. It was a desert world, and had always been so. No viable biosphere could establish itself.

Centuries passed.

A base and rest centre were established on New Earth. The exploration ships moved farther out. Eventually, they covered a sphere of space with a diameter of almost two thousand light-years. This area, though immense in the experience of a species which had only fairly recently tamed the horse, was negligible as a proportion of the galaxy.

Many planets were discovered and explored. None yielded life. Additional mineral resources for Earth, but not life. Down in the gloomy miasmas of a gas giant, writhing things were discovered which came and went in a manner suggesting volition. They even surrounded the submersible which was lowered to investigate them. For sixty years, human explorers tried to communicate with the writhing things—with no success. At this period, the last whale in Earth's polluted oceans became extinct.

On some newly discovered worlds, bases were established and mining carried out. There were accidents—unreported back home. The gigantic planet Wilkins was dismantled; fusion motors, roaring through its atmosphere, converted its hydrogen to iron and heavier metals, and the planet was then broken up. Energy was released as planned—but rather more rapidly than planned. Lethal shortwave radiation killed off all involved in the project. On Orogolak, war broke out between two rival bases, and a short nuclear war was fought which turned the planet into an ice desert.

There were successes, too. Even New Earth was a success. Successful enough, at least, for a resort to be set up on the edge of its chemical-laden sea. Small colonies were established on twenty-nine planets, some of which flourished for several generations.

Although some of these colonies developed interesting legends—which contributed to Earth's rich store—none was large or complex enough to nourish cultural values which diverged from their parent system.

Space-going mankind fell victim to many strange new maladies and mental discomforts. It was a fact rarely acknowledged that every terrestrial population was a reservoir for disease; a considerable proportion of the people of all ethnic groups were unwell for a percentage of their days—for unidentifiable reasons. SUDS (Silent Untreated Disease Syndrome) now clamoured for identification. In gravity-free conditions, SUDS proliferated.

What had been untreated was long to prove incurable. Nervous systems failed, memories developed imaginary life histories, vision became hallucinatory, musculature seized up, stomachs overheated. Space dementia became an everyday event. Shadowy frights passed across the vacuum-going psyche.

Despite its discomforts and disillusions, infiltration of the galaxy continued. Where there is no vision, the people perish—and there was a vision. There was a vision that knowledge, for all its dangers, was to be desired; and the ultimate knowledge lay in an understanding of life and its relationship to the inorganic universe. Without understanding, knowledge was worthless.

A Chinese/American fleet was investigating the dust clouds of the Ophiuchus constellation, seven hundred light-years from Earth. This region contained giant molecular clusters, nonisotropic gravities, accreted planets, and other anomalies. New stars were being created among the palls of inchoate matter.

An astrophysics satellite attached to one of the computerborgoids of the fleet obtained spectrographic readings on an atypical binary system some three hundred light-years distant from the Ophiuchus clouds which revealed at least one attendant planet supporting Earth-like conditions.

The oddity of an ageing G4 yellow star moving about a common axis with a white supergiant no more than eleven million years old had already engaged the interest of the cosmologists attached to the Chinese/American fleet. The spectroanalysis spurred them into active investigation.

The supposedly Earth-like planet of the distant binary system was filed under the appellation G4PBX/4582-4-3. Signals were despatched on their lengthy journey through the dust clouds to Earth.

Berthed inside the flagship of the fleet, then cruising the outer fringes of the Ophiuchus dust clouds, was an automated colonising ship. The ship was programmed and despatched to G4PBX/4582-4-3. The year was 3145.

The colonising ship entered the Freyr-Batalix system in 3600 A.D., to begin immediately the task for which it was programmed, the establishment of an Observation Station.

There was G4PBX/4582-4-3, like something dreamed! Real, but beyond belief, beyond even rejoicing.

As signals from the new station flashed back to Earth, it became more and more clear that the new planet's resemblance to Earth was close. Not only was it stocked with innumerable varieties of life in the prodigal terrestrial manner—and in heartening contrast to previously discovered planets—more, it supported an intriguing cline of semi-intelligent and intelligent species. Among the intelligent species were a humanlike being and a horned being something resembling a rough-coated minotaur.

The signals eventually reached Charon, on the margins of the solar system, where androids fed the data to Earth, only five light-hours distant.

By the middle of the fifth millennium, Earth's Modern Ages were in slow decline. The Age of Apperception was a memory. For all but a few meritocrats in positions of power, galactic exploration had become an abstraction, another burden inflicted by bureaucracy. G4PBX/4582-4-3 changed all that. Ceasing to feature merely as a mysterious body among three sister planets, it took on colour and personality. It became Helliconia, the marvellous planet, the world beyond the veils of darkness where life was.

Helliconia's suns took on symbolic significance. Mystics remarked on the way in which Freyr-Batalix seemed to represent those divisions of the human psyche celebrated in Asian legend long ago:

> Two birds always together in the peach tree:
> One eats the fruit, the other watches it.
> One bird's our individual Self, tasting all the world's gifts:
> The other the universal Self, witnessing all and wondering.

How avidly the first prints of human and phagors, struggling out of a snowbound world, were studied! Inexplicable thankfulness filled human hearts. A link with other intelligent life had been forged at last.

By the time the Avernus was built and established in orbit about Helliconia, by the time it was stocked with the humans reared by surrogate mothers on the colonising ship, the sphere of terrestrial-directed space activity was contracting. The inhabited planets of the solar system were moving towards a centralised form of government, later to evolve into COSA, the Co-System Assemblage; their own byzantine affairs occupied them. Distant colonies were left to fend for themselves, marooned here and there on semihabitable worlds like so many Crusoes on desert islands.

Earth and its neighbouring planets were by this time storehouses of undigested information. While the materials brought back to Earth had been processed, the knowledge had not been absorbed. The enmities which had existed since tribal days, rivalries founded on fear and a lust for possession, remained dormant. The dwindling of space squeezed them into new prominence.

By the year 4901 A.D., all Earth was managed by the one company, COSA. Judicial systems had yielded to profit and loss accounts. Through one chain of command or another, COSA owned every building, every industry, every service, every plant, and the hide of every human on the *planet—even those humans who opposed it. Capitalism had reached its glorious apogee. It made a small percentage on every lungful of oxygen breathed. And it paid out its stockholders in carbon dioxide.*

On Mars, Venus, Mercury, and the moons of Jupiter, human beings were more free—free to found their own petty nations and ruin their own lives their own way. But they formed a sort of second-class citizenry of the solar system. Everything they acquired—and acquisition still played a major part in their lives—they paid for to COSA.

It was in 4901 that this burden became too great, and in 4901 that a statesman on Earth made the mistake of using the old derogatory term "immigrants" about the inhabitants of Mars. And so it was in 4901 that nuclear war broke out among the planets—the War over a Word, as it was called.

Although records of those pre-apocalypse times are scarce, we do know that populations then regarded themselves as too civilized to begin such a war. They had a dread that some lunatic might press a button. In fact the buttons were pressed by sane men, responding to a well-rehearsed chain of command. The fear of total destruction had always been there. Nuclear weapons, once invented, cannot be disinvented. And such are the laws of enantiodromia that the fear became the wish, and missiles sped to targets, and people burned like candles, and silos and cities erupted in an unexpungeable fire.

It was a war between the worlds, as had been predicted. Mars was silenced for ever. The other planets struck back with only a fraction of their total firepower (and so were destroyed). Earth was hit by no more than twelve 10,000-megaton bombs. It was enough.

A great cloud rose above the capital of La Cosa. Dust which comprised fragments of soot, grains of buildings, flakes of bodies, vegetable and mineral, rose to the stratosphere. A hurricane of heat rolled across the continents. Forests, mountains, were consumed by its breath. When the initial fires died, when much of the radioactivity sank to the despoiled ground, the cloud remained.

The cloud was death. It covered all of the northern hemisphere. The sunlight was blotted from the ground. Photosynthesis, the basis of all life, could no longer take place. Everything froze. Plants died, trees died. Even the grass died. The survivors of the strike found themselves straggling through a landscape which came more and more to resemble Greenland. Land temperatures fell rapidly to minus thirty degrees. Nuclear winter had come.

The oceans did not freeze. But the cold, the dirt in the upper atmosphere, spread like discharge over a sheet, poisoning the southern hemisphere as well as the northern. Cold gripped even the favoured lands of the equator. Dark and chill reigned on Earth. It seemed that the cloud was to be mankind's last creative act.

Helliconia was celebrated for its long winters. But those winters were of natural occurrence: not nature's death, but its sleep, from which the planet would reliably arouse itself. The nuclear winter held no promise of spring.

The filthy aftermath of the war merged indistinguishably with another kind of winter. Snow fell on hills which the so-called summer did not disperse; next winter, more snow fell on what remained. The drifts deepened. They became permanent. One permanent bed linked with another. One frozen lake generated another. The ice reservoirs of the far north began to flow southward. The land took the colour of the sky. The Age of Ice returned.

Space travel was forgotten. For Earthmen, it had again become an adventure to travel a mile.

A spirit of adventure grew in the minds of those who sailed in the *New Season*. The brig left the harbour without incident, and soon was sailing westwards along the Sibornalese coast with a fresh northeasterly in her canvas. Captain Fashnalgid found that he was whistling a hornpipe.

Eedap Mun Odim coaxed his portly wife and three children on deck. They stood in a mute line, staring back at Koriantura. The weather had cleared. Freyr wreathed itself in fire low on the southern horizon, Batalix shone almost at zenith. The rigging made complex patterns of shadow on the deck and sails.

Odim excused himself politely, and went over to where Besi Besamitikahl stood alone in the stern. At first he thought she was seasick, until the movements of her head told him she was weeping. He put an arm around her.

"It hurts me to see my precious one waste her tears."

She clung to him. "I feel so guilty, dear master. I brought this trouble on you. . . . Never shall I forget the sight of that man . . . burning. . . . It was all my fault."

He tried to calm her, but she burst out with her story. Now she put the blame on Harbin Fashnalgid. He had sent her out early in the day, when no ordinary people were about, to buy some books, and she had been seized in the street by Major Gardeterark.

"His biwacking books! And he said that that was the last of his money. Fancy wasting the last of your money on books!"

"And the major—what did he do?"

She wept again. "I told him nothing. But he recognised me as one of your possessions. He took me into a room where there were other soldiers. Officers. And he made me . . . made me dance for them. Then he dragged me round to our offices . . . It's me that's to blame. I should never have been fool enough to go out for those books. . . ."

Odim wiped her eyes and made soothing noises. When Besi was

calmer, he asked seriously, "Have you a real affection for this Captain Harbin?"

Again she clutched him. "Not any more."

They stood in silence. Koriantura was sinking in the distance. The *New Season* was sailing past a cluster of broad-beamed herring-coaches. The herring-coaches had their curtain nets out, trawling for fish. Behind the fishermen were salters and coopers, who would gut and preserve the catch as soon as it was hauled aboard.

Amid sniffs, Besi said, "You'll never forget what happened when you —when that man died on the kiln, will you, dear master?"

He stroked her hair. "Life in Koriantura is over. I have put everything that belonged to Koriantura behind me, and would advise you to do the same. Life will begin again when we reach my brother's home in Shivenink."

He kissed her and returned to his wife.

The next morning, Fashnalgid sought Odim out. His tall clumsy figure dominated Odim's slender and tightly parcelled form.

"I'm grateful to you for your kindness in taking me aboard," he said.

"You'll be paid in full when we get to Shivenink, I assure you."

"Don't worry," Odim said, and said no more. He did not know how to deal with this officer, now a deserter, except by his usual method of dealing with people—through politeness. The ship was crowded with people who had begged to be allowed aboard to escape the oligarchic legislation; all had paid Odim. His cabin was stacked with treasures of one sort or another.

"I mean what I say—you will be paid in full," Fashnalgid repeated, looking heavily down at Odim.

"Good, good, yes, thank you," said Odim, and backed away. Out of the corner of his eye, he saw Toress Lahl coming on deck, and went over to her to escape from Fashnalgid's attentions. Besi followed him. She had avoided Fashnalgid's gaze.

"How is your patient?" Odim asked the Borldoranian woman.

Toress Lahl leaned against the rail, closed her eyes, and took a few deep breaths. Her pale, clear features had taken on a translucent quality under strain. The skin below her eyes looked puckered and dirty. She said, without opening her eyes, "He's young and determined. I believe he will live. Such cases generally do."

"You shouldn't have brought a plague case aboard. It endangers all our lives," Besi said. She spoke with a new boldness; she would never have dared speak out previously in front of Odim: but on the voyage all relationships changed.

" 'Plague' is not the scientifically exact term. The plague and the Fat Death are different things, although we use the terms interchangeably. Obscene though the symptoms of the Fat Death are, the majority of young, healthy people who contract it recover."

"It spreads like the plague, doesn't it?"

Without turning her head to reply, Toress Lahl said, "I could not leave Shokerandit to die. I am a doctor."

"If you're a doctor, you should know the dangers involved."

"I do, I do," said Toress Lahl. Shaking her head, she rushed from them and hurried down the companionway below decks.

She paused outside the door of the closet in which she kept Shokerandit. As she rested her head on her arm, she was vouchsafed a glimpse of the turn her life had taken, the misery in which she now lived, and the uncertainty which surrounded all on the ship. What was the reason for this gift of consciousness, which even phagors did not have, this awareness that one was aware, when it was incapable of changing what one did?

She was nursing the man who had taken her husband's lifeblood. And—oh, yes, she felt it—she was already infected with his disease. She knew it could easily leap to everyone else in the confines of this ship; the insanitary conditions on the *New Season* made it a haven for contagion. Why did life happen—and was it possible that, even now, some detached part of her was enjoying life?

She unlocked the door, set her shoulder against its resistance, and entered the closet. There she lived for the next two days, seeing no one, crawling only rarely onto the deck for fresh air.

Besi meanwhile had been given the task of supervising the many relations of Odim who had been stowed in the main hold. Her chief support came from the old grannie who made the delectable pastry savrilas. This aged woman still managed to cook on a small charcoal stove, filling the hold with benevolent aromas, while at the same time soothing the anxieties of the family.

The family lay about on boxes and ottomans and chests, indulging themselves in their customary way even while complaining about the rigours of life at sea. Theatrically, they declaimed to Besi and to anyone who would listen, and was not simultaneously declaiming, of the dangers of sea voyages. But Besi thought, And what of the dangers of plague! If it spreads to this hold, how many of you poor vulnerable bodies will survive? She determined to stay with them whatever happened, and secretly armed herself with a small dagger.

Toress Lahl remained isolated, speaking to no one, even when she crept up on deck.

On the third morning, she saw small icebergs dotting the water. On the third morning, with fever on her, she returned to her vigil as usual. The door was more reluctant than ever to budge.

Luterin Shokerandit was confined in a small irregular area in the bows of the *New Season*. A supporting pillar stood in the middle of the space, leaving enough room only for a bunk to one side of it and a bucket, a bale of hay, a stove, and four frightened fhlebihts, tethered

beneath the small porthole. The porthole admitted light enough for
Toress Lahl to see stains running across the floor and the gross figure
tethered on the lower bunk. She locked the door behind her, rested
against it, and then took a step closer to the prostrate figure.

"Luterin!"

He stirred. Under his left arm, which she had strapped by the wrist
against the supports of the bunk, his head thrust a short way, tortoise-
like, and one eye opened, to regard her through a spike of hair. His
mouth opened, making a croaking noise.

She fetched a ladle of water from a casket standing behind the stove.
He drank.

"More food," he said.

She knew he would recover. These were the first words he had spoken
since they had carried him to this place on the *New Season*. He was
again capable of organized thought. Yet she dare not touch him, although his wrists and ankles were tied securely.

On the top of the stove lay the charred remains of the last fhlebiht
she had killed. She had dismembered it into joints with a cleaver, cooking it as best she could over the charcoal. The corkscrew horns, the
long white fleece of the animal, lay with other rubbish in the corner.

As she threw a joint over to him, Toress Lahl thought for the first
time how good the grilled meat looked. Shokerandit wedged it under
an elbow and commenced to gnaw at the meat. Ever and again he cast
a glance up at her. There was no longer the anger of madness in his
eye. The bulimia had passed.

The thought of his previous savage eating tormented her. She looked
at his naked limbs, gleaming with the sweat of his earlier struggles,
and imagined how it would be to sink her teeth into his flesh. She
snatched the charred meat from the stove.

Chains and manacles lay ready. Toress Lahl fell to her knees and
crawled to them, securing herself to the central post with them. She
locked her wrists together and flung the key clumsily into one corner,
out of reach. The halitus of the place came to her, the stench of the
man's body mingled with the smell of the confined animals and the
odour of their droppings, all flavoured with the fumes from the charcoal. As she choked, a stiffness came on her. She began to stretch as
far as the chains would allow, knees out before her in an ungainly
position, head slowly rolling at the end of its neck. The animal carcass
was cradled under one arm as if it were a child.

The man lay where he was, staring without movement. At last the
woman's name came to his lips and he called to her. Her gaze momentarily met his, but it was the stare of an idiot and her eyeballs continued
to roll.

Jaw hanging open, Shokerandit wriggled to sit up. He was tightly bound to the bunk. The wildest struggles of his delirium, when the helico virus had raged in his hypothalamus, had not sufficed for him to break the leather thongs securing his wrists and ankles.

As he struggled, he found a pair of brass tongs with claws, such as were used for handling lumps of red-hot charcoal, against his side. The implement was useless for cutting his bonds. For a while he slept. Waking, he tried again to set himself free.

He called. Nobody would come. The fear of the Fat Death was too great. The woman lay almost immobile against her pillar. He could prod her with his foot. The animals bleated, turning restlessly on their straw. Their eyes glowed yellow in the half dark.

Shokerandit had been secured so that he lay face down. The stiffness was leaving his joints. He was able to twist his head and look about. He inspected the webbing of the bunk overhead. Halfway down the bed a wooden crossbar was inserted to strengthen the structure. Into the crossbar a long-bladed dagger had been driven.

Minutes passed as he gazed awkwardly up at the dagger. Its handle was not far above him, but he had no hope of grasping it, tied as he was. He was clear in his mind that Toress Lahl had set it there before she succumbed to the disease. But why?

He felt the brass tongs against his flesh. The connection came at once, and with it a revelation of her cleverness. Wriggling, he managed to work the tongs down the bunk until he could grasp them between his knees. Then came an agony of contortion as he rotated his clenched knees and brought them up under the dagger. He worked for an hour, two hours, sweating and groaning in his pain, until at last he had the handle of the dagger secure between the brass claws. Then it was only a matter of time until he worked the dagger free.

It fell against his thighs. Shokerandit rested until he had recovered strength enough to shuffle the blade up the bunk. At last he could take it in his teeth.

There was the painful labour of sawing through one of the leather thongs, but it was done eventually. Once he had one hand free, he was able to cut himself loose. He lay back, panting. At last he climbed from the foetid bunk.

He took a step or two and then collapsed weakly against the wooden pillar. Hands on knees, he contemplated the figure of Toress Lahl, with its slow distorted movements. Although his mind did not feel like his own, he understood her devotion and her thought for him when she felt herself falling to the plague. While under the madness of the fever, he would never have had the coordination to get the dagger and release himself. Without the dagger, he would have been unable to cut himself free when he recovered.

After a rest, he stood up and felt his filthy body. He was changed.

He had survived the Fat Death and was changed. The painful contortions to which he had been subject had served to compress his spine; he was now, he estimated, three or four inches shorter than he had been. His perverted appetite had caused him to put on flesh. In that phase, he would have devoured anything, the blanket on the bunk, his own faeces, rats, had Toress Lahl not fed him cooked meat. He had no knowledge of how many animals he had devoured. His limbs were thicker. He gazed down at his barrel chest in disbelief. He was now a smaller, rounder, more thickset person. His weight had undergone a radical redistribution.

But he lived!

He had come through the eye of the needle and lived!

No matter what was involved, anything was better than death and dissolution. There was a sort of marvellous sense to life, to the unconscious movements of breathing, to the need for nourishment and defecation, to the ease of gesture, to the casual thought—so often not tied to the present moment. It was a sense, a wisdom, that even degradation and discomfort could not deny. Even as he rejoiced in it, feelings of health pervaded him in the stinking closet.

As if a curtain were drawn back, he saw again scenes from his youth in the mountains of Kharnabhar, at the Great Wheel. He recalled his father and mother. He reviewed again his heroism on the field of battle near Isturiacha. It came back clear, washed, as if it had all happened to someone else.

He recalled again striking down Bandal Eith Lahl.

Gratitude filled him that the widow he had taken captive should not have left him to die. Was it because he had not raped and beaten her? Or was the goodness of her action quite independent of anything he had done?

He bent down to look at her, sad to see her so grey, so overcome. He put an arm about her, smelling her sharp, sick stink. Her lolling head came round as if to rest against him. Her dry lips peeled back from her teeth, and she bit his shoulder.

Shokerandit pulled himself away from her. He handed her the meat at her feet. She took a mouthful but could not chew. That would come later, as the full madness developed.

"I'll look after you," he told her. "I'm going up on deck to wash myself and breathe some fresh air." His shoulder was bleeding.

How long had it been? He dragged the door open. The ship was full of creaks, the companion way of shifting shadows.

Rejoicing in the newfound ease of his limbs, he climbed the companionway and looked about. The decks were empty. There was no one at the wheel.

"Hello!" he called. No one answered, yet furtive movement could be heard.

Alarmed, he ran forward, still calling. A body lay half-naked by the mast. He stared down at it. All the flesh of the chest and upper arm had been crudely hacked away and—oh, yes, he could guess it—eaten. . . .

VII

THE YELLOW-STRIPED FLY

I t was not that Icen Hill was impressive as such features go; indeed, compared with many of the hills in Sibornal, it was no more than a pimple. But it dominated its flat surroundings, the outer rings of Askitosh. Icen Hill Castle dominated and almost enveloped the hill.

When the wind from the north brought rain on its breath, the water collected on the roofs, fortifications, and spiteful spires of the castle and flung itself down in gouts upon the population of Askitosh, as if conveying personal greetings from the Oligarch.

One advantage of this exposed position—for the Oligarch and his Inner Chamber if for no one else—was that news could be got rapidly to the castle: not merely by the streams of messengers who laboured up the slippery cobbles of the hill road, but by the tidings flashed by heliograph from other distant eminences. A whole chain of signalling stations was established which girded Sibornal, the main artery of information adhering with fair precision to the line of latitude on which Askitosh lay. Thus was brought to the Oligarch—always assuming he existed—news of the welcome accorded the victorious army returning through Chalce to Koriantura.

That army had halted below the escarpment where Chalce petered out before the brow of Sibornal. It waited there until its stragglers caught up. For two days it waited. Those who died of the plague were buried on the spot. Both men and mounts were more gaunt than when they had set out from Isturiacha, almost half a tenner earlier. But Asperamanka was still in command. Morale was high. The troops cleaned themselves and their equipment, ready for a triumphal entry into Uskutoshk. The military band polished its instruments and practised its marches. Regimental flags were unfurled.

All this was done under the concealed guns of the Oligarch's First Guard.

As soon as Asperamanka's men moved forward, as soon as they were within range, the Oligarch's artillery fired upon them. The steam guns began to pound. Bullets rained down. Grenades exploded.

Down went the brave men. Down went their yelks. Blood in their mouths, faces in the dirt. Those who could scream, screamed. The scene was enveloped in smoke and flying earth. People ran hither and thither, at a loss to understand, rendered senseless by shock. The glittering instruments ceased to play. Asperamanka shouted to his bugler to sound retreat. Not a shot was fired back at their fellow countrymen.

Those who survived this evil surprise lurked like wild beasts in the wilderness. Many became speechless with shock.

"Abro Hakmo Astab!"—that at least they cried, the forbidden Sibish curse which even soldiery hesitated to utter. It was a shout of defiance to fate.

Some survivors climbed into the windswept recesses of the mountains. Some lost their way in the maze of marshland. Some banded together again, determined to recross the grass desert and join forces with those who remained in Isturiacha.

Asperamanka. Using his smooth tongue, he tried to persuade the broken groups to form up in units again. He was foul-mouthed in return. Officers and men alike had lost faith in authority. "Abro Hakmo Astab . . ." They uttered it to his stormy face.

Dire circumstances called forth the ancient curse. Its true meaning was lost in time, like its origins. A polite interpretation was that it recommended befouling both suns. In the northern continent, crouched beneath the chill breath of the Circumpolar Regions, men delivered the curse against the Azoiaxic—and against all other gods remembered or forgotten—as if to call down eternal darkness on the world.

"Abro Hakmo Astab!"—the defilement of the light. Those who hurled the words at Asperamanka then slunk away. Asperamanka made no further command. The thunder gathered below his brow, he tugged his cloak about him, he prepared to look to his own salvation. Yet, as a man of the Church, he felt the ancient curse lie heavy in his mind. He perceived his own defilement.

This much information was carried back by an informer to the Oligarch sitting in his stone hill in Askitosh. Thus the governor of men learned something of the effect of his villainous welcome to Koriantura on Asperamanka's troops.

The Oligarch's next step required little consideration. After the Inner Chamber had deliberated, a poster went out to the farthest corners of the land. It announced that a Plague-ridden Army, intent on spreading Disease and Death throughout the Continent, had been bravely repelled at the Frontier. Let all work harder by way of Celebration.

And the old fisherwomen of Koriantura stood with arms akimbo, reading what was written, and saying, "There you are, always 'work harder'. . . . How are we supposed to work harder than we do?" And they bunched closer and looked askance as units of the First Guard marched by, clattering westward in their noisy boots.

And the remains of that broken army in no-man's-land; it had yet another battle to fight.

Ever since the death of the last C'Sarr of Campannlat, four hundred and seventy-nine years earlier, the phagors had been gathering strength. Even before death-dealing Freyr had expanded to its fullest power and waned again, the components had been growing in numbers. The human will to check them had died in part with the C'Sarr. The more timid ancipitals, who submitted to existence on the plains among the Sons of Freyr, had passed word to the warlike contingents of the High Nyktryhk. The first marauders were out and about earlier in this Helliconian winter.

A group of ancipitals, mounted on kaidaws, could sweep like wind over the grasslands which were so formidable to men. In part this was for a simple reason: stallun, gillot, and kaidaw alike could eat the grass and survive on that diet, where the fragile Sons of Freyr would perish.

Nevertheless, the components of the High Nyktryhk kept away from the grasslands leading to Sibornal unless some special objective lured them there. Sibornal was feared by the ancipitals. In their pale harneys remained a memory of a terrible fly.

That memory—more of a programme than a memory—told them that the chill regions of Sibornal were the resort of flies, and of one fly in particular. That fly made almost intolerable the existence of the countless head of flambreg which inhabited the plains below the Circumpolar Regions. The yellow-striped fly lived on the flambreg herds, the female sinking her ovipositor into the hide of the animals. There the larvae, when they hatched, entered into the bloodstream, eventually to form pockets of putrefaction under the skin until they were ready to burst forth into the world.

The grubs grew as big as the end of a man's thumb. They finally chewed their way through their host's hide, dropping to the ground to pupate.

It might seem that this yellow-striped terror fulfilled no role in life except to make miserable the lives of the flambreg. That was not so. No other animal would venture into the territory ruled by the yellow-striped fly; and so the domain of the flambreg did not become overgrazed in the normal course of events.

Yet the fly remained as a curse, a scourge to the flambreg—who frequently galloped along the most windswept ridges, careless of danger, in a vain attempt to escape their fate. The ancipitals, descended from the flambreg, retained in their eotemporal minds a record of that yellow-striped torment, and steered well clear of its empire.

But a broken human army wandering in the wilds of Chalce represented a special objective to the ancipitals. Travelling into the wind, like the wind, with a supply of spears and rifles in the quivers at their backs, they bore down on the Sons of Freyr.

All they encountered they killed. Even those phagors who served in Asperamanka's army were mowed down with no compunction, and their eddre strewn across the lands.

Some groups of men maintained a semblance of military order. They formed up behind their supply wagons and fired at the enemy in a disciplined way. Many phagors fell.

Then the marauders stood off awhile, watching the men deteriorate from thirst and cold, before attacking again. They spared no one.

It was useless for the soldiers to surrender. They fought to the last, or blew their own brains out. Perhaps in them too was some kind of a racial memory: that summer was the time of human supremacy, when Freyr was bright; that when the long winter came, the ancipitals in their turn prevailed upon the globe, as once they had before mankind arrived upon the scene. So they defended themselves without hope, to die without help. The women who were with the men died too.

But sometimes the ammunition ran out and then the phagors, instead of killing everyone, took the humans into slavery.

Although the Oligarch did not know it, ancipitals proved his best ally. They eliminated what was left of Asperamanka's once great army.

Such phagor components as there were in Sibornal manifested a less warlike spirit. They were largely composed of ancipital slaves who had escaped their masters, or lowland phagors accustomed to generations of hard work and servility. These creatures roamed the countryside in small bands, doing their best to avoid human settlements.

Of course anything vulnerable belonging to the Sons of Freyr became their target; their deep-seated antagonism never died. When one such group sighted the brig *New Season* close to the coast, it became the object of scrutiny. The group followed it as the ship drifted along the bleak Loraj coast to the west of Persecution Bay, where Uskuti territory ended.

Eight gillots, a fillock, three ageing stalluns, and a runt comprised the band. All but the runt were dehorned. They had with them as baggage animal a yelk which was loaded with their chief items of diet, pemmican and a thick porridge. They were armed.

Although a stiff offshore wind blew the brig from the land, the coastal current, running westwards, was slowly bringing it closer. The phagors paced it, mile by unweary mile, as the distance between them lessened. They knew in their eddre that the time would come when they could seize and destroy the vessel.

Visible activity on board was intermittent. Several shots were fired one night. At another time, a man was seen to run to the starboard rail, pursued by two screaming women. Knives flashed in the hands of the women. The man threw himself overboard, made some attempt to swim ashore, and drowned without a cry in the cold sea.

Small icebergs, sailing like swans, moved in a westward direction after spilling out of Persecution Bay. They occasionally banged against the sides of the *New Season*. Luterin Shokerandit heard them as he sat in the wretched closet where Toress Lahl lay.

He had locked the door, but sat clutching a small chopper. The bulimia engendered by the Fat Death made everyone on ship a potential enemy. He used the chopper occasionally to hack into the beams of the ship. The wood was needed to fuel the small fire on which he roasted joints cut from the last flehbiht. Shokerandit and Toress Lahl between them had all but devoured the four long-legged goats in what he estimated was eight or nine days at sea.

The Fat Death generally ran its course in about a week. By that time, the sufferer was dead or on his way to recovery, faculties unimpaired but physiologically altered. He watched as the woman struggled and thickened. In her fight to get free, Toress Lahl had torn the clothes from herself, often using her teeth. She had gnawed the upright to which she was secured. Her mouth was bruised and bleeding. He looked at her with love.

The time came when she was able to return his gaze. She smiled.

She slept for some hours and then was better, with that feeling of well-being which accompanies those who survive the Fat Death.

Shokerandit untied her limbs and bathed her with a cloth and salt water in a bowl. She kissed him as he tried to help her to her feet. She surveyed her naked form and wept.

"I'm like a barrel. I was so slim."

"It's natural. Look at me."

She stared at him through her tears and then laughed.

They laughed together. He took in the marvellous architecture of her new body, still gleaming from its wash, the beauty of her shoulders, breasts, stomach, thighs.

"These are the proportions of a new world, Luterin," Toress Lahl said; he heard her using his first name for the first time.

He threw up his arms, scraping his knuckles on the bulkhead. "I'm relieved that you survived."

"Because you looked after your captive."

It was natural to wrap his arms about her, natural to kiss her bruised mouth, and natural to sink with her to the deck on which they had recently wrestled with agony. There they wrestled with sexual rejoicing.

Later, he said to her, "You are no longer my captive, Toress Lahl. We are now captives of each other. You are the first woman I have loved. I will take you to Shivenink, and we will go into the mountains where my father lives. You shall see the wonders of the Great Wheel of Kharnabhar."

She was already beginning to forget what had happened, and answered indifferently.

"Even in Oldorando we have heard of the Great Wheel. I will come with you if you say so. The ship is very silent. Shall we see how the others fare? They may all be sick with the plague—Odim and his vast brood, and the crew."

"Wait here with me a little longer." Lying with his arms about her, looking down into her dark eyes, he was reluctant to break the spell. At that time he was incapable of distinguishing between love and restored health.

She said briskly, "Back in Oldorando I was a doctor. It's my duty to tend the sick." She turned her face from Luterin.

"Where does the plague come from? From phagors?"

"From phagors, we believe."

"So our brave captain spoke the truth. Our army was going to be prevented by force from returning to Sibornal, just in case we spread the plague; it was among us. So what the Oligarch decreed was wise rather than evil."

Toress Lahl shook her head. She began to comb her hair with slow strokes, luxuriously, looking into a small mirror rather than at him as she spoke. "That's too easy. What the Oligarch decreed is entirely wicked. To destroy life is always wicked. What he did may not only be evil; it may prove ineffective too. I do know something about the contagious nature of the Fat Death—although since the Fat Death is latent for most of the Great Year it is difficult to study. Knowledge hard-learnt one year is forgotten by the next."

He expected her to continue but she fell silent, continuing to regard her face even when she had set down her comb, licking a finger to smooth her eyebrows.

"Be careful what you say about the Oligarch. He knows more than we."

Then she turned to look at him. Their regards met as she said with some emphasis, "I don't have to respect your Oligarch. Unlike the Oligarchy, the Fat Death has elements of mercy in its functioning. It's mainly the old and very young who die of it: a majority of fit adults survive—over half. They successfully metamorphose, as we do." She prodded him with a still moist finger, not without humour. "We in our compact shapes represent the future, Luterin."

"Yet half the population will die . . . whole communities destroyed . . . The Oligarch wouldn't allow that to happen in Sibornal. He'd take strong measures—"

She gestured dismissively. "Such die-back has its merciful side at a time when crops are failing and famine threatens. The healthy survivors benefit. Life goes on."

He laughed. "In fits and starts . . ."

She shook her head as if suddenly impatient. "We must see who has survived on the ship. I don't like the silence."

"I hope to thank Eedap Mun Odim for his kindness."

"I trust you will be able to."

They stood close in the small stale room, gazing at each other through the stramineous light. Shokerandit kissed her, although at the last moment she moved her lips away. Then they ventured into the corridor.

The scene was to come back to him much later. He would see then, as not at the time, how much of herself Toress Lahl withheld from him. Physically, she was very desirable to him; but her attitude of independence was more attractive to him than he could then realise. Only when that independence was eroded by time could they come to any true understanding.

But Shokerandit's proper appreciation of that fact could scarcely be arrived at while his whole outlook was based upon certain misunderstandings which left him, whichever way he turned, insecure, unable to develop emotionally. His innocence stood between him and maturity.

Shokerandit went first. Beyond the companionway, the corridor led to the main hold, where the relations of Odim had been settled. He went to listen at the door and heard stealthy movement within. From the cabins on either side of the corridor came silence. He tried the door of one, and knocked; it was locked, and no answer came.

As he emerged on deck, with Toress Lahl behind him, three naked men ran swiftly into hiding. They left a female corpse spread-eagled beneath the mizzenmast. It had been partially dismembered. Toress Lahl went over and looked at it.

"We'll throw it overboard," Shokerandit said.

"No. This woman is already dead. Leave her. Let the living be fed."

They turned their attention to the situation of the *New Season* itself. The ship, as their senses had told them, was no longer in motion. The ocean currents had brought it slowly to fetch up against the shore. The *New Season* was trapped against a tongue of sand which curled out from the land.

Towards the stern, a small cluster of icebergs had accumulated. At the bows, it would be an easy matter to jump over the side and walk ashore without getting a foot wet. The guardians of this spit of sand were two large rocks, one taller than the masts of the ship, which stood on the shore, deflecting ocean tides. They had probably been thrown to their present position by some long-gone volcanic explosion, though nothing so dramatic as a volcano could be seen inland. The coast offered a vista only of low cliffs, so tumbled that they might have been an old wall part-demolished by cannon fire, and, beyond the cliffs, mustard-coloured moorland, off which a chill wind blew, bringing tears to the viewer's eyes.

Blinking the water away, Shokerandit looked again at the larger rock. He was sure he had seen movement there. In a moment, two phagors appeared, walking with their curious glide away from the shore. It became apparent that they were going to meet a group of four of their kind who materialised over a rise, dragging with them the carcass of an animal of some kind. More phagors appeared from behind the rock to greet the hunters.

The original party of thirteen ancipitals had that morning met up with a second and larger party, a party also comprising escaped slaves, as well as four phagors who had served as transport animals in the Oligarch's soldiery. There were now thirty-six phagors in all. They had a fire burning in a cavity in the landward side of the rock, on which they intended to roast whole flambreg their hunting party had speared.

Toress Lahl looked at Shokerandit in dismay.

"Will they attack us?"

"They have a marked aversion to water, but they could easily get along that spit of sand and board us. We'd better see if we can find any fit members of the crew—and quickly."

"We were the first to go down with the Fat Death, so we may be the first to recover."

"We must see if there are any weapons to defend the ship with."

Their search of the ship horrified them. It had become a slaughter-house. There had been no escape from the plague. Those who had locked themselves into cabins alone had succumbed and, in some cases, died alone. Where two or three had shut themselves away, the first to show symptoms had perhaps been killed. Any animals aboard had been killed and devoured, their remains fought over. Cannibalism had prevailed in the large hold, where the Odim family was. Of twenty-three members of the family, eighteen were already dead, killed mainly by their relations. Of the five remaining alive, three were still suffering from the madness of the disease and fled when shouted at. Two young women were able to speak; they had undergone the full metamorphosis. Toress Lahl took them to the safety of the closet where she and Shokerandit had sheltered.

The hatches to the crew's quarters were locked in place. From below came animal noises and a peculiar singsong, intoning endlessly

> *"He saw his fair maid's incision*
> *O, that terminal vision . . .*
> *O, that terminal vision . . ."*

In a forward storage cupboard, they discovered the bodies of Besi Besamitikahl and the old grannie. Besi lay staring upwards, a puzzled expression frozen on her face. Both were dead.

In the forward hold, they came on some sturdy square boxes which had remained untouched throughout the disaster which had overwhelmed the ship.

"Praise be, cases of rifles," Shokerandit exclaimed. He opened the nearest box and pulled away some sacking. There, each item wrapped in tissue paper, lay a complete dinner set in purest porcelain, decorated with pleasant domestic scenes. Other boxes contained more porcelain, the finest that Odim exported. These were Odim's presents for his brother in Shivenink.

"This will not keep the phagors off," Toress Lahl said, half laughing.

"Something has to."

Time seemed to be suspended as they wandered the bloodied ship. Because it was small summer, the hours of Batalix's daylight were long. Freyr was rarely far above the horizon, rarely far below. The cold wind blew continually. Once a sound like thunder came with its breath.

After the thunder, silence. Only the dull pound of the sea, the occasional knock of a small ice floe against the wooden hull. Then the thunder again, this time clear and continuous. Shokerandit and Toress Lahl looked at each other in puzzlement, unable to imagine what the noise was. The phagors understood it without thought. For them, the noise of a flambreg herd on the move was unmistakable.

The flambreg lived in their millions below the skirts of the polar ice cap. Their progeny filled the Circumpolar Regions. Loraj, of all the countries of Sibornal, offered a variety of territories most suited to flambreg, with extensive forests of the hardy eldawon tree, and a landscape of low rolling hills and lakes. The flambreg, unlike yelk, were mildly carnivorous, with a fondness for any rodents and birds they could catch. Their main diet was of lichen, fungi, and grass, supplemented with bark. The flambreg also ate the indigestible moss called flambreg moss by the primitive tribes of Loraj which hunted them. The moss contained a fatty acid which protected the animals' cell membranes from the effects of cold, enabling the cells to continue efficient functioning at low temperatures.

A herd of over two million individuals was nearing the coast. Many of the Loraj packs were several times larger. This herd had emerged from an eldawon forest and was running almost parallel with the sea. The ground shook under its multitudinous hoofs.

On the shore, the phagors showed signs of unease. Their crude cooking operations were suspended. They marched back and forth, scanning the horizon, manifesting a humanlike uncertainty.

Two escape routes lay open to them. They could climb to the top of the house-sized boulder, or they could attack and take possession of the ship. Either alternative would save them from the approaching stampede.

There was a living forerunner of the herd. Above the heaving shoulders of the animals flew a cloud of midges, intent on drawing blood from the furry noses of the flambreg. The midges were the enemies also of a fly the size of a queen wasp. This fly now darted ahead into freer air. It appeared from nowhere and landed smartly between the eyes of one of the phagors. It was a yellow-striped fly.

The ancipital group broke into an uncharacteristic panic, rushing back and forth. The individual whose face the fly had alighted on turned and ran straight into the rock. He squashed the fly and laid himself out senseless.

The rest of the group gathered together to confer on a plan of action. Some of the newly arrived group carried with them a small and wizened emblem, an ancestor in tether. This shrunken symbol of themselves, this illustrious and moth-eaten great-grandstallun, though almost entirely transformed into keratin, was still a degree or two from nonbeing. In it, some faint spark still served to focus their attempts at ratiocination. Comprehension left their harneys. They communed. The currents of their pale harneys entered into tether.

From an area of total whiteness, a spirit emerged. It was no bigger than a rabbit. The phagor whose ancestor it was said inwardly, "O sacred forebear, now integrating with earth, here you see us in grave danger by the edge of the drowning world. The Beasts-we-were run upon us and will trample us down. Strengthen our arms, direct us from danger."

Through their harneys the keratinous figure transmitted pictures the ancipitals knew well, pictures flowing fast, one to another. Pictures of the Circumpolar Regions with their ice, their bogs, their sombre enduring forests, and of the teeming life that ran there, even there, on the edge of the ice cap. The ice cap then much greater in extent, for Batalix ruled alone in the heavens. Pictures of hunted creatures hiding in caves, making an alliance with that mindless spirit called fire. Pictures of the humble Others taken as pets. Terrifying pictures of Freyr roaming, coming mottled black down the air-octaves, a giant spider-form, eddre-chilling. The retreat of beautiful T'Sehn-Hrr, once silver in the tranquil skies. The Others proving themselves Sons of Freyr, running off carrying the mindless spirit fire on their shoulders. Many, many ancipitals dying, in flood, in heat, in battle with the monkey-browed Sons of Freyr.

"Go fast, remember enmities. Retreat to safety of the wooden thing afloat on the drowning world, kill all Sons of Freyr. Stay safe there against the running of the Beasts-we-were. Be valiant. Be large. Hold horns high!"

The tiny voice fled to lands beyond knowing. They thanked the great-grandstallun with a deep churring in their throats.

They would obey its word. For the voice was his and the voice was theirs and there was no difference. Time and opinion had no place in their pale harneys.

They advanced slowly on the beached ship.

It was an alien thing to them. The sea was their dread. Water swallowed and extinguished them. The ship was outlined against the smouldering orange of Freyr, snoring just below the horizon, ready to leap from its hiding place in that same hungry sea.

They clutched their spears and moved with reluctant step towards the New Season.

The sand crunched beneath their tread. All the while, their twitching ears picked up the thunder of the approaching flambreg.

To one side lay the icebergs, no taller than the runt which walked close to its gillot. Some icebergs clung to the sides of the vessel; some, as if possessed by a mysterious will, described slow intricate figures over the still sea, ghostly in the dim light, their reflections caught as if in tether in the water.

As the sand spit narrowed, so the ancipital group had to narrow its front. Finally, two stalluns led the rest. The ship loomed above them without movement.

Things clattered and broke beneath the feet of the stalluns. They tried to halt, but those behind pushed them forward. More breaking, more clattering. Looking down, they saw the thin white shards beneath their feet, and the whiteness stretching cracked all the way to the ship's hull.

"There is ice and it breaks," they said to each other, using the continuous present tense of Native Ancipital. "Go back or we fall into the drowning world."

"We must kill all Sons of Freyr, as it is said. Go forward."

"That we cannot do with the drowning world protecting them."

"Go back. Hold horns high."

Crouching by the rail of the New Season, Luterin Shokerandit and

Toress Lahl watched their enemies shuffle back to the shore and seek for shelter by the rock.

"They may return. We have to get the ship afloat as soon as possible," Shokerandit said. "Let's see how many of the crew have survived."

Toress Lahl said, "Before we leave the coast, we should kill some flambreg if they get within range. Otherwise everyone is going to starve."

They looked uneasily at each other. The thought crossed their minds that they sailed with a cargo of the dead and the mad.

Standing with their backs to the mainmast, they set up a great shout, which rolled away across the wastes of water and land. After a pause, an answering cry came. They called again.

A man appeared from the forecastle, staggering. He had undergone the metamorphosis, and presented the typical barrel-figure of a survivor. His clothes were ill-fitting, his once boney face now broad and presenting a curiously stretched appearance. They hardly recognised him as Harbin Fashnalgid.

"I'm glad you're alive," Shokerandit said, going towards him.

The transformed Fashnalgid put out a warning hand and sat down heavily on the deck.

"Don't come near me," he said. He covered his face with his hands.

"If you are fit enough, we need help in getting the ship on course again," Shokerandit said.

The other gave a laugh without looking up. Shokerandit saw that there was blood caked on his hands and clothes.

"Leave him to recover," Toress Lahl said. At this Fashnalgid uttered a harsh cackle and started to shout at them, " 'Leave him to recover!' How can a man recover? Why should he recover . . . I've been through the last few days eating raw arang—yes, and killing a man for the privilege of doing so . . . Entrails—everything . . . And now I find Besi's dead. Besi, the dearest, truest girl there ever was . . . Why do I want to recover? I want to be dead."

"You'll feel better soon," said Toress Lahl. "You scarcely knew her."

"I'm sorry about Besi," Shokerandit said. "But we have to get the ship on course."

Fashnalgid glared up at him. "That's typical of you, you skerming conformist! No matter what happens, do what you're supposed to do. Let the ship rot, for all I care."

"You're drunk, Harbin!" He felt morally superior to this abject figure.

"Besi's dead. What else matters?" He sprawled on the deck.

Toress Lahl motioned to Shokerandit. They crept away.

They took fire hatchets to break into cabins and went below.

As Shokerandit reached the bottom of the companionway, a naked man threw himself on him. Shokerandit went down on one knee and was seized by the throat. His attacker—an Odim relation—snarled, more like a maddened animal than a human being. He clawed at Shokerandit without any coherent attempt to overcome him. Shokerandit stuck two knuckles in the man's eyes, straightened his arm, and pushed hard. As the man fell away, he kicked him in the stomach, jumped on him, and pinned him to the deck.

"Now what do we do? Throw him to the phagors?"

"We'll tie him up and leave him in a cabin."

"I'm not taking any chances." He picked up the hatchet he had dropped and clouted the prone man across the temple with the handle. The man went limp.

They tackled the captain's cabin in the stern. The lock broke under their assault, and they burst in. They found themselves in a comfortably appointed quarter galley with windows opening above the water.

They drew up short. A man with an old-fashioned bell-mouthed musket was sitting with his back to the windows, aiming the gun at them.

"Don't shoot," Shokerandit said. "We intend no harm."

The man rose to his feet. He lowered the weapon.

"I would have blasted you if you were loonies."

He was proportioned in the unaccustomed thickset way. He had passed through the Fat Death. They recognised him then as the captain. His officers lay about the cabin, their hands tied. Some were gagged.

"We've had a high old time here," said the captain. "Fortunately, I was the first to recover, and we have lost only the first mate—for eating purposes, that was, excuse the expression. A few more hours and these officers will be back in action."

"Then you can leave them and see to the rest of your ship," said Shokerandit sharply. "We're beached, and there's a threat from phagors ashore."

"How's Master Eedap Mun Odim?" asked the captain, as he accompanied them from the cabin, his gun under his arm.

"We haven't found Odim yet."

They found him later. Odim had locked himself in his cabin with a supply of water, dried fish, and ship's biscuits as he felt the first fever upon him. He had undergone the metamorphosis. He was now a few inches shorter, and of much more rounded bulk than before. His characteristic straight-backed stance had disappeared. He wore a floppy sailor's garb, his own clothes having become too tight for him. Blinking, he emerged on deck like a hibernatory bear from its cave.

He looked round quickly frowning, as they hailed him. Shokerandit approached slowly, well aware that it was he who had passed the Fat Death to all aboard. He humbly reminded Odim of his name.

Ignoring him, Odim went to the rail and gestured over the side of the ship. When he spoke, his voice choked with rage.

"Look at this barbarism! Some wretch has thrown my best plate overboard. It's an atrocity. Just because there's illness on the ship, it doesn't excuse . . . Who did it? I demand to know. The culprit is not going to sail with me."

"Well . . ." said Toress Lahl.

"Er . . ." said Shokerandit. He took a grip on himself and said, "Sir, I have to confess that I did it. We were being attacked by phagors at the time."

He pointed to where phagors could be seen by the rock.

"You shoot phagors, you do not throw precious plates at them, you imbecile," Odim said. He reined in his temper. "You were mad—is that your excuse?"

"The ship has no weapons with which to defend itself. We saw that the phagors were going to attack—they will try again if they get desperate. I threw the plate over the side deliberately, to cover the sand spit. As I expected, the fuggies believed they were treading on thin ice, and retreated. I'm sorry about your porcelain, but it saved the ship."

Odim said nothing. He stared down at the deck, up at the mast. Then he brought a little black notebook out of his pocket and perused it. "That service would have fetched a thousand sibs in Shivenink," he said in low tones, darting swift glances at them.

"It has saved all the rest of the porcelain on the ship," Toress Lahl said. "Your other crates are intact. How is the rest of your family?"

Muttering to himself, Odim made a pencilled note. "Perhaps more than a thousand . . . Thank you, thank you . . . I wonder when such fine ware will again be manufactured? Probably not until the spring of next Great Year, many centuries in the future. Why should any of us care about that?"

He turned bemusedly, to shake hands with Shokerandit while looking elsewhere. "My gratitude for saving the ship."

"Now we'll get it afloat again," said the captain.

The noise of the flambreg herd was louder now. They turned to see the animals pour by, not more than a mile inland. Odim disappeared unnoticed.

Only later did they discover the reason for his slightly eccentric behaviour. It was not his dear Besi's death alone which had unsettled Odim. Of his three children, only the eldest boy, Kenigg, had survived the ravages of the Fat Death. His wife was also dead. Little was found of her bar skull, torso, and a pile of bones.

The flotation was not to come about for several hours. With the captain and a few crew on their feet again, some attempt was made to

bring the ship back into order. Those still sick were settled as comfortably as possible in the surgeon's cabin. The injured were tended.
The convalescent were brought to fresh air. The dead were wrapped in
blankets and lined up in a row on the upper deck. The dead numbered
twenty-eight. The survivors were twenty-one in number, including the
captain and eleven of his crew.

When everyone had been accounted for and order prevailed, the fit
assembled for a service of thanksgiving for their survival to God the
Azoiaxic, who ordered all things.

In their innocent hymns, they did not see that the complexity of their
survival was beyond the capacity of any local deity.

Helliconia was at this period receding towards something like the
original conditions which had existed before its parent sun Batalix became locked into the gravitational field of the A-type supergiant. The
planet had then carried a remarkable number of phyla, ranging in size
from viruses to whales, while being denied the energy levels or the
complexity to support beings with that intensity of cellular organisation
required as building blocks for higher mental functions—the thinking,
deducing, perceiving functions associated with full consciousness. The
ancipitals were Helliconia's supreme effort in this respect.

The ancipitals were a part of the integrated living system of Helliconia's biosphere. One of the functions of that systemic gestalt—of
which, needless to say, its component parts were entirely unaware—
was to maintain optimum conditions for the survival of all. As the
yellow-striped fly could not live without the flambreg, so ultimately, the
flambreg could not live without the yellow-striped fly. All life was
interdependent.

The capture of Batalix by the supergiant was only an event of the
first magnitude and not a catastrophe for Helliconian life, although it
was catastrophic for many phyla and many individuals. The impact of
the capture was gradual enough for the biosphere to sustain it. The
planet looked after its own. Its moon was lost; its vital processes continued, although through a disruption which brought storms and
blizzards raging for hundreds of years.

The fierce output of high-energy radiation from the new sun caused
more damage. More phyla were eradicated, while others survived only
through genetic mutation. Among the new species were some which
were, in evolutionary terms, hastily developed; they survived in the
new environment only at some cost to themselves. The assatassi in the
sea, which were born as maggots from the decaying bodies of their
parents; the yelk and biyelk, necrogenes which resembled mammals but
were without wombs; and human stock; these were among the new
creatures which rose to abundance under the energy-rich conditions
which came about eight million years before the present.

The new creatures were products of the biospheric striving for unity, and cobbled into it at the time of maximum change. Before its capture by Freyr, Helliconia's atmosphere had contained a large amount of carbon dioxide, protecting its life with a greenhouse effect, and producing a mean temperature of $-7°$ C. After capture, the atmospheric carbon dioxide was much reduced, combining at periastron with water to form carbonate rocks. Oxygen levels increased to amounts suitable for the new creatures: humans could not live in the oxygen-scarce Nyktryhk, as phagors did. In the seas, greater concentrations of macromolecules led to stepped-up activity all along the food chain. All these new parameters for existence came within the regulatory functions of Helliconia's biosphere.

The humans, as the most complex life form, were the most vulnerable. However they might rebel against the idea, their corporate lives were never more than part of the equipoise of the planet to which they belonged. In that, they were no different from the fish, the fungi, or the phagors.

In order that they might function at optimum efficiency in Helliconia's extremes, evolutionary pressure had introduced a system for regulating the masses of the humans. The pleomorphic helico virus had as its vector a species of arthropoda, a tick, which transferred itself readily from phagor to human. The virus was endemic during two periods of the Helliconian year, in the Spring and in the late Autumn of the Great Year, with minor epicycles between these cycles. These two pandemics were known as bone fever and the Fat Death.

Sexual dimorphism between the sexes was negligible; but both sexes showed seasonal dimorphism. Male and female could be said to average approximately one hundred and twelve pounds over an entire Great Year. But spring and autumn brought dramatic variations in body weight.

Survivors of the spring scourge of bone fever weighed a lanky ninety-six pounds, and presented a skeletal appearance to those who were brought up to the old way of things. This decreased body weight was an inheritable factor. It persisted throughout the generations as a crucial survival trait during the increasing heat. But the effect slowly became less apparent, until populations achieved the median of one hundred and twelve pounds.

Towards winter, the virus returned, partly in obedience to glandular signals. Survivors of these attacks increased in bulk, rather than losing it, generally gaining an average of about fifty percent body weight. For a few generations, the population averaged one hundred and sixty-eight pounds. They had transformed from ectomorph at one extreme to endomorph at the other.

This pathological process performed a vital function in preserving the human stock, with a side effect which benefitted the entire biosphere. As the expanding energy quota of the spring planet demanded a much more variegated biomass for efficient systemic working, so the contracting energy quota of winter required a decrease in total biomass. The virus culled the human population to conform with the total food-chain organisation of the biosphere.

Human existence was not possible without the virus, just as the flambreg herds would have ceased ultimately to exist without the curse of the yellow-striped fly.

The virus destroyed. But it was a life-giving destruction.

VIII

THE RAPE
OF THE MOTHER

The stiff breeze blew off the coast. The clouds parted, revealing Batalix overhead. The sea sparkled, tossing up foam made of finest pearl. The *New Season* raced west by southwest, with music in her shrouds.

Along the Loraj coast on the north stood the Autumn Palaces, terrace after terrace of them. The dreams of forgotten tyrants were imprisoned in their stone, extending along the shore in distance and time. According to legend, King Denniss had once lived within their hallowed walls. Since the days of their fashioning, the Palaces, like some inconclusive human relationship, had never been entirely occupied or entirely deserted. They had proved too grandiose for those who created them and for those who followed after. Yet they were used still, long after whatever autumn had first seen the rise of their towers above the granite strand. Human beings—whole tribes of beings—lived in them like birds under neglected eaves.

The learned, who are always attracted to the past, lodged also in the Autumn Palaces. For them, the Palaces were the greatest archaeological site in the world, their ruinous cellars taproots to an earlier age of man. And what cellarage! Mazes of almost infinite depth stretched down into the rock, as if to syphon up warmth from the heart of Helliconia. Here were reckonings inscribed on stone and clay, pot shards, skeletons of leaves from vanished forests, skulls to be measured, teeth to be fitted to jawbones, middens, weapons dissolving in rust . . . the history of a planet patiently awaiting interpretation, yet as tantalisingly beyond complete comprehension as a vanished human life.

The Palaces lay pallid with distance, and the *New Season* passed them far to starboard.

The depleted crew occasionally saw other ships. As they sailed by the port of Ijivibir, they passed fleets of herring-coaches about their business. Farther out to sea, an occasional warship was sighted, reminding them that the quarrel between Uskutoshk and Bribahr was still active. Nobody molested them or even signalled to them. Ice dolphins sported alongside the vessel.

After Clusit, the captain decided to make a landing on the coast. He was familiar with these waters and determined to stock the ship with food before they made the last part of the run for the Shivenink port of Rivenjk. His passengers were doubtful about the wisdom of going ashore after their recent close encounter with the phagor band, but he reassured them.

This part of Loraj was within the northern tropics and still fertile. Behind the coast lay a glittering country of woods, lakes, rivers, and marshes, scarcely inhabited by mankind. Behind that country stood ancient eldawon and caspiarn forests, stretching all the way to the ice cap.

On the shore, helmeted seals basked, roaring as the passengers and crew of the *New Season* walked among them. They offered no resistance as they were clubbed to death. This clubbing was done with an oar. The oar had to hit the creature under the jaw in the vulnerable part of its throat. With its air passages blocked, the seal died of suffocation. This took some while. The passengers averted their gaze while the seals rolled in agony. Their mates often tried to help them, whimpering pitifully.

The heads of the seals were covered by something resembling a helmet. The helmet was an adaptation of horns, the seals having been land animals in the distant past, driven back into the oceans by the cold of Weyr-Winter. The adaptation protected the ears and eyes of the creatures, as well as the skull.

As the human party turned away from the seals they were killing, legged fish heaved themselves out of the waves and rushed up the steeply shelving shingle. They began attacking the dying seals, tearing chunks of their blubbery flesh.

"Hey!" shouted Shokerandit, and struck out at the fish.

Some scattered and ran under stones. One lay wounded by Shokerandit's blow. He picked it up and showed it to Odim and Fashnalgid.

The fish was the best part of a metre long. Its six "legs" were finlike. It had a lantern jaw, behind which trailed a number of fleshy whiskers. As its head flicked from side to side, jaw snapping, its filmy grey eyes stared at its captor.

"See this creature? It's a scupperfish," said Shokerandit. "Soon these creatures will be coming ashore in the thousands. Most of them get eaten by birds. The others survive and tunnel into the earth for safety. Later, they'll become longer than snakes, once the Weyr-Winter's here."

"They're Wutra's worms, that's what they're called," said the captain. "Best throw it away, sir. They're not fit even for the sailors to eat."

"The Lorajans eat them."

The captain said, deferentially but firmly, "Sir, the Lorajans do eat the worms as a delicacy, that's true. They are poison nonetheless. The Lorajans cook them with a poisonous lichen, and 'tis said that the two poisons cancel each other out. I've eaten the dish myself, sir, when wrecked on this coast some years past. But I still hate the sight and taste of the things, and certainly don't want my men filling their bellies with them."

"Very well." Shokerandit flung the still wriggling scupperfish out to sea.

Cowbirds and other sorts of birds were wheeling above them, screaming. The sailors cut up six of the helmeted seals as quickly as possible and carried the chunks of meat over to the jolly boat. The offal was left to the other predators.

Toress Lahl was weeping in silence.

"Get back in the boat," Fashnalgid said. "What are you weeping for?"

"What a horrible place this is," the woman said, turning her face away. "Where things with legs crawl from the sea and everything eats some other living thing."

"That's how the world is, lady. Jump in."

They rowed back towards the ship, and the birds followed, crying, crying.

The *New Season* hoisted sail and began to move over the still water, its bows swinging towards Shivenink. Toress Lahl tried to speak to Shokerandit, but he brushed her to one side; he and Fashnalgid had matters to attend to. She stood by the rail, hand to brow, watching the coastline dwindle.

Odim came up and stood beside her.

"You need not be sorrowful. We'll soon reach the safety of the harbour of Rivenjk. There my brother will take us in, and we can rest and recover from our various shocks."

Her tears burst forth again. "Do you believe in a god?" she asked, turning a tear-stained face towards him. "You've undergone such sorrow this voyage."

He was silent before answering. "Lady, all my life until now I have lived in Uskutoshk. I behaved like an Uskuti. I believed like an Uskuti. I conformed—which means that I regularly worshipped God the Azoiaxic, the God of Sibornal. Now that I have come away from that place, or have been driven away, as one might say, I can see that I am no Uskuti. What is more, I find I have absolutely no belief in God. At his passing, I felt a weight lifting." He patted his chest in illustration. "I can say this to you, since you are not an Uskuti."

She gestured towards the shore they were leaving. "This hateful place ... those dreadful creatures ... all I've been through ... my husband killed in battle ... the gruesomeness of this ship ... Everything just gets steadily worse, year by year ... Why wasn't I born in the spring? I'm sorry, Odim—this isn't like me. . . ."

After a pause, he said gently, "I understand. I've also undergone bereavement. My wife, my younger children, dear Besi ... But I speak to my wife's gossie in pauk, and she comforts me. Do you not seek out your husband in pauk, lady?"

She said to him in a low voice, "Yes, yes, I sink down to his gossie. He is not as I desire to see him. He comforts me and tells me I should find happiness with Luterin Shokerandit. Such forgiveness . . ."

"Well? Luterin is a pleasant young man, by all I see and hear."

"I can never accept him. I hate him. He killed Bandal Eith. How can I accept him?" She startled herself by her own antagonism.

Odim shrugged his broad shoulders. "If your husband's gossie so advises you . . ."

"I am a woman of principle. Maybe it is easier to forgive when you are dead. All gossies speak with the same voice, sweet like decay. I may cease the habit of pauk ... I cannot accept the man who has enslaved me—however tempting the terms he uses to bribe me. Never. It would be hateful."

He rested a hand on her arm. "All is hateful to you, eh? Yet perhaps you should try to think as I do that a new life is being presented to us—us exiles. I am twenty-five and five tenners—no chicken! You are much younger. The Oligarch is supposed to have observed that the world is a torture chamber. That is the case only for those who believe so.

"When we walked on the shore, killing off those seals—only six out of thousands, after all!—a feeling overcame me that I was being shaped for the winter season in some wonderful way. I had put on flesh but I had shed the Azoiaxic. . . ." He sighed. "I find difficulty talking profoundly. I'm better at figures. I'm only a merchant, as you know, lady. But this metamorphosis through which we have come—it is so wonderful that we must, *must*, try to live in accord with nature and her generous accountancy."

"And so I'm supposed to yield to Luterin, is that it?" she said, giving him a straight look.

A smile turned the corner of his mouth. "Harbin Fashnalgid has a soft spot for you also, lady."

As they laughed, Kenigg, Odim's one surviving son, ran up to him and hugged him. He stooped and kissed the boy on his cheek.

"You're a marvellous man, Odim, I really think it," Toress Lahl said, patting his hand.

"You are marvellous too—but try not to be too marvellous for happiness. That's an old Kuj-Juvec saying."

As she nodded her head in agreement, a tear shone in her eye.

Worse weather came in as the ship approached the coasts of Shivenink. Shivenink was a narrow country consisting almost entirely of an enormous mountain range—the Shivenink Chain, which had lent its name to the nation. The range divided the territories of Loraj and Bribahr.

The Shiveninki were peaceful, god-fearing people. Their rages had been drained by the original chthonic angers which had built their mountains. In the recesses of their natural fortress, they had built an artifact which embodied their particular brand of holiness and determination, the Great Wheel of Kharnabhar. This wheel had become a symbol, not merely to the rest of Sibornal but to the rest of the globe as well.

Great whales thrust their beaked heads up to observe the *New Season* as it entered Shiveninki waters. Sudden snow blizzards, battering the ship, almost immediately hid them from sight.

The ship was in difficulties. The wind howled through its rigging, spray dashed across the deck; the brig pitched from side to side as if in fury. In something like darkness—though the hour was Freyr-dawn—the sailors were sent up the ratlines. In their new metamorphosed shape, they were clumsy. To the yardarm they climbed, soaked, drenched, battered. The unwilling sails were furled. Then back down to a deck ceaselessly awash.

With the crew depleted, Shokerandit and Fashnalgid, together with some of Odim's more able relations, helped to man the pumps. The pumps were amidships, just abaft the mainmast. Eight men could work on each pump, four on either handle. There was scarcely room for the sixteen together in the pump well. Since this part of the main deck caught the worst of the seas breaking inboard, the pumpers were constantly inundated. The men cursed and fought, the pumps wheezed like old grandfathers, the waters smashed against them.

After twenty-five hours the wind abated, the barometer steadied, the sea became less mountainous. The snow fell silently, blowing off the land. Nothing could be seen of the shore, yet its presence could be felt, as if some great thing lay there, about to wake from its ancient sleep of rock. They all sensed it, and fell silent. They looked for it, peering into the muffling snow, and saw nothing.

Next day brought improvement, a calm passage in the orchestration of the elements.

The snow showers fell away across the green water. Batalix shone through overhead. The sleeping thing was slowly revealed. At first only its haunches were visible.

The ship was reduced to toy dimensions by a series of great blue-green bastions whose tops were lost in cloud. The bastions unfolded as the ship, again under full sail, sped westwards. They were immense headlands, each greater than the last. At sea level, pillars of gigantic proportions irresistibly suggested that they had been sculpted by a hand with intent behind it; they supported brows of rock which went almost vertically up. Here and there, trees could be observed, clinging to folds in the rock. White horizontal veins of snow defined the curves of each headland.

Cleft between the headlands were deep bays—pockets in which the mountains kept reserves of murk and storm. Lightning played in these recesses. White birds hovered where the current raced at their mouths. Strange sounds and resonances issued across the waters from the veiled cavities, touching the minds of the humans like the salt that lighted on their lips.

Fitful bursts of sun, penetrating such bays, revealed at their far end cataracts of blue ice, great waterfalls frozen as for eternity, which had tumbled down from the high homes of rock, ice, hail, and wind concealed almost perpetually by cloud.

Then a bay greater than the previous ones. A gulf, flanked by black walls. At its entrance, perched on a rock where the highest seas could not overwhelm it, a beacon. This token of human habitation reinforced the loneliness of the scene. The captain nodded and said, "There's the Gulf of Vajabhar. You can put in there at Vajabhar itself—it sticks out like a tooth in the lower jaw of the Gulf."

But they sailed on, and the great bulk of the planet to their starboard seemed to move with them.

Later, the coast became more massive still, as they reached the waters off the Shiven Peninsula. Round this they had to sail to reach the port of Rivenjk. The peninsula had no bays. It was almost featureless. Its chief characteristic was its size. Even the crew, when off duty, gathered silently on deck to stare.

The tall slopes of Shiven were shrouded in vegetation. Climbers hung down, falling free as if in imitation of the many small waterfalls which began their descent and never finished, whipped away by winds scouring the sheer faces. Occasionally the clouds would part to reveal the great head of snow-clad rock which climbed to the sky. This was the southern end of a mountain range which curved northwards to join the enormous lava plateau sequences under the polar ice cap.

Within a comparatively few miles of where the ship sailed, the ridge of the peninsula rose to heights of over six and a quarter miles above sea level. Far higher than any mountain peaks on Earth, the Shivenink Chain rivalled the High Nyktryhk of Campannlat in scale. It formed one of the grandest spectacles on the planet. Shrouded in its own storms, its own climatic conditions, the great chain revealed itself to few human eyes, except from the deck of a passing ship.

Lit by the almost horizontal rays of Freyr, the formation clad itself in breathtaking lights and shadows. To the perceptions of the passengers, all appeared brilliant, all new. They became uplifted just to regard such titanic scenery. Yet what they beheld was ancient—ancient even in terms of planetary formation.

The heights that dominated them had come into being four thousand and more million years earlier, when the unevolved Helliconian crust had been struck by large meteors. The Shivenink Chain, the Western Barriers in Campannlat, as well as distant mountains in Hespagorat, were remaining testaments to that event, forming between them segments of a great circle comprising the ejecta material of a single impact. The Climent Ocean, regarded by sailors as of almost infinite extent, lay within the original crater.

For day after day they sailed. As in a dream, the peninsula remained to starboard, unchanging, as if it would never go away.

Once they rounded a small island, a pimple in the ocean, which might have dropped from the overhanging landmass. Although it looked a terrifying place on which to live, the island was inhabited. A smell of wood smoke drifted out to the ship; that and the sight of huts nestling among trees made the passengers long for a spell ashore, but the captain would hear nothing of it.

"Those islanders are all pirates, many of them desperate characters lost off ships in storms. Were we to set foot there, they'd murder us and steal our ship. I'd sooner befriend vultures."

Three long skin canoes put out from the island. Shokerandit passed his spyglass round, and they looked at the men, bent of back, who rowed towards them as if their life depended on it. In the stern of one of the boats stood a naked woman with long black hair. She carried a baby which suckled at her breast.

A snowstorm blew off the mountains at that time, falling like a shawl to the sea. The flakes settled on the woman's bare breasts and melted.

The *New Season* was carrying too much sail for the canoes to catch up. They fell astern. Still the men rowed with undiminished zeal. Still they rowed when lost to sight, like madmen.

Once or twice, cloud and mist parted enough for the passengers to catch a glimpse of the Shiven heights. Then whoever saw the gap would give a cry, and other passengers would come running, and gasp to see how far above their heads stretched those dripping rocks, those vertical jungles, those snows.

Once a landslide started. A part of the cliff fell away. It dropped and dropped, carrying away more rock with it. Where it struck the sea, a great wave was raised. A wedge of ice fell, disappeared under the surface, bobbed up again. Larger wedges tumbled after it—having fallen from the edge of some glacier invisibly housed in the clouds. The falls caused terrifying reverberations of sound.

A colony of brown birds sped out from shore in their thousands, whistling their fright. So great was their wingspan that, when they passed over the ship, the noise of their movements was like low thunder. The colony took half an hour to pass overhead, and the captain shot several for the pot.

When at last the brig rounded the peninsula and began to sail north, within two days of Rivenjk, another storm struck. It was less severe than the previous one. They were whirled up in fog and snow, which arrived in great flurries. For a whole day the light of the suns glittered through thick mists and hail, the hailstones being as large as a man's fist.

As the storm abated and the men at the pumps were able to stagger away and sleep, the coastline slowly revealed itself again.

Here the cliffs were less vertical, though as awesome as ever, husbanding their own clouds and rainstorms. From out of one obscuring storm emerged the gigantic figure of a man, swathed in mist.

The man appeared to be intending to spring from the shore and land on the deck of the *New Season*.

Toress Lahl cried in alarm.

"That's the Hero, ma'am," said the second mate reassuringly. "He's a sign we're nearly at journey's end—and a good thing too."

Once the scale of the coast was grasped, it was plain that the statue was gigantic. The captain demonstrated with his sextant that it stood over a thousand metres high.

The Hero's arms were upraised and carried slightly forward over the head. The knees were slightly bent. The man's stance suggested that he was either about to jump into the ocean or take flight. The latter alternative was suggested by what might have been a pair of wings, or else a cloak, flowing back from the broad shoulders. For stability, the figure's lower legs had not been separated from the rock face from which it was sculpted.

The statue was stylised, cut with curious whorls as if to confer an aerodynamic shape. The face was sharp and eaglelike, yet not entirely inhuman.

Increasing the solemnity of the sight, a distant bell tolled. Its brazen voice rolled across the grey waters to the brig.

"He's a splendid figure, isn't he?" Luterin Shokerandit said with pride. The passengers in their metamorphosed state all gathered at the rail to stare uneasily across at the gigantic statue.

"What does he represent?" Fashnalgid asked, plunging his hands into his coat pockets.

"He represents nothing. He is himself. He's the Hero."

"He must represent something."

Annoyed, Shokerandit said, "He stands there, that's all. A man. To be seen and admired."

They fell uneasily silent, listening to the melancholy note of the bell.

"Shivenink is a land of bells," Shokerandit said.

"Has the Hero got a bell in his belly?" young Kenigg asked.

"Who would build such a thing in such a place?" Odim enquired, to cover his son's impertinent question.

"Let me tell you, my friends, that this mighty figure was created ages ago—some say many Great Years past," Shokerandit said. "It was built, legend has it, by a superior race of men, whom we call the Architects of Kharnabhar. The Architects constructed the Great Wheel. They are the finest builders the world has ever known. When they finished their labours on the Wheel, they sculpted this giant figure of the Hero. And the Hero has guarded Rivenjk and the way to Kharnabhar ever since."

"Beholder, what are we coming to?" Fashnalgid asked himself aloud. He went below to smoke a veronikane and read a book.

When the desolation of a post-apocalyptic Earth yielded to the ice age, signals had been received from Helliconia for the past three centuries. As the glaciers moved south, there were few who possessed the ability to watch that newly discovered planet's history, apart from the androids on Charon.

At least this could be said for the ice age. It wiped the Earth clear of the festering shells of defunct cities. It obliterated the cemeteries which all previous habitation had become. Voles, rats, wolves, ran where highways had once been. In the southern hemisphere, too, the ice was on the move. Solitary condors patrolled the empty Andes. Penguins moved, generation by generation, towards the desired ice shelves of Copacabana.

A drop of only a few degrees had been enough to throw the intricate mechanisms of climatic control out of gear. The nuclear blast had induced in the living biosphere—in Gaia, the Earth mother—a state of shock. For the first time in epochs, Gaia met a brute force she could not accommodate. She had been raped and all but murdered by her sons.

For hundreds of millions of years, Earth's surface had been steadily maintained within the narrow extremes of temperature most congenial to life—maintained by an unwitting conspiracy between all living things in conjunction with their parent world. This despite increases in the sun's energy, causing dramatic changes in the constitution of the atmosphere. The regulation of the amount of salt in the sea had been maintained at a constant percentage of 3.4. If that had ever risen to a mere 6 percent, all marine life would have ceased. At that percentage of salinity, cell walls disintegrate.

The amount of oxygen in the atmosphere had similarly been maintained at a steady 21 percent. The percentage of ammonia in the atmosphere had also been maintained. The ozone layer in the atmosphere had been maintained.

All these homeostatic equilibria had been maintained by Gaia, the Earth mother in whom all living things, from sequoias to algae, whales to viruses, had their being. Only mankind had grown up and forgotten Gaia. Mankind had invented its own gods, had possessed those gods, had been possessed by them, had used them as weapons against enemies, and against their own inner selves. Mankind had enslaved itself, in hate as much as love. In that madness of isolation, mankind invented formidable weapons of destruction. In committing genocide, it almost slew Gaia.

She was slow to recover. One striking symptom of her illness was the death of trees. Those abundant organisms, which had spread from the tropical rain forests to the northern tundras, were killed by the radioactivity and an inability to photosynthesise. With the disappearance of trees, a vital link in the homeostatic chain was broken; the homes they provided for a myriad of life forms were lost.

Conditions of cold prevailed for almost a thousand years. Earth lay in a chill catalepsy. But the seas lived.

The seas had absorbed much of the large clouds of carbon dioxide released by the nuclear holocaust. The carbon dioxide remained trapped in the water, retained in deep ocean circulation and not to be released for centuries. The ultimate release initiated a period of greenhouse warming.

As had happened before, life came forth from the seas. Many components of the biosphere—insects, microorganisms, plants, man himself—had survived, thanks to isolation, freak winds, or other providential conditions. They again became active, as white gave place to green. The ozone layer, shielding living cells from lethal ultraviolet, reestablished itself. Once more, as the firn melted, the pipe of separate instruments reached towards orchestral pitch.

By 5900, better conditions were evident. Antelope sprang among low thorn trees. Men and women muffled themselves in skins and trudged north after the glaciers.

At night, those humbled revenants huddled together for comfort and gazed upwards at the stars. The stars had scarcely changed since the time of paleolithic man. It was the human race which had changed.

Whole nations had gone forever. Those enterprising people who had developed mighty technologies and had struck out first for the planets and then for the stars, who had forged clever weapons and legends— those peoples had wiped themselves out. Their sole heirs were the sterile androids working on the outer planets.

Races came forth who, under an earlier dispensation, could be regarded as losers. They lived on islands or in wildernesses, at the tops of mountains or on untamed rivers, in jungles and swamps. They had once been the poor. Now they came forth to inherit the Earth.

They were peoples who took delight in life. In those first generations, as the ice retreated, they had no need to quarrel. The world awoke again. Gaia forgave them. They rediscovered ways of living with the natural world of which they were a part. And they rediscovered Helliconia.

From 6000 and for the next six centuries, Gaia could be said to convalesce. The tall glaciers were withdrawing fast to their polar fortresses.

Some of the old ways of life had survived. As the land returned, old bastions of the technophile culture were uncovered—generally hidden underground in elaborate military complexes. In the deepest bastions, there were descendants still living whose ancestors had been part of the ruling elite of the technophile culture; they had ensured their own survival while those who had been subject to them had perished. But these living fossils, on reaching the sunshine, died within a few hours— like fish brought up from the enormous pressures of the ocean deeps.

In their foul warrens, a hope was found—the link with another living planet. Summonses were sent through space to Charon, and a company of androids fetched back to Earth. These androids, with untiring skill, set about building auditoria in which the new population could observe all that happened on the far-distant planet.

The mentalities of the new populations were shaped to a large extent by the unfolding story they saw. Survivors on the other planets, cut off from Earth, also had their links with Helliconia.

In fresh green lands, auditoria stood like conch shells upended in sand. Each auditorium was capable of housing ten thousand people. In their sandalled feet, roughly clothed in skin, and later cloth, they came to look on with wonder. What they saw was a planet not greatly different from their own, emerging slowly from the grip of a long winter. It was their story.

Sometimes an auditorium might remain deserted for years. The new *populations* also had their crises, and the natural catastrophes which attended Gaia's recovery. They had inherited not only the Earth but its uncertainties.

When they could, the new generations returned to watch the story of lives running parallel to their own. They were generations without terrestrial gods; but the figures on the giant screens appeared like gods. Those gods endured mysterious dramas of possession and religion which gripped yet puzzled their terrestrial audiences.

By the year 6344, living forms were again in moderate abundance. The human population took a solemn vow that they would hold all possessions in common, declaring that not only life but its freedom was sacred. They were much influenced by the deeds of a Helliconian living in an obscure hamlet in the central continent, a leader called Aoz Roon. They saw how a good man was ruined by a determination to get his own way. To the new generations, there was no "own way"; there was only a common way, the journey of life, the uct of the communal spirit.

As they viewed the immense figure of Aoz Roon, saw water blow from his lips and beard as he drank from his hands, they watched drops which had fallen a thousand years earlier. The human understanding of past generations had made past and present merge. For many years, the picture of Aoz Roon drinking from his hands became a popular ikon.

To the new generations, with their empathic feel for all life, it was natural to wonder whether they could assist Aoz Roon and those who lived with him. They had no idea of setting out in starships, as preglacial peoples might have done. Instead, they decided to focus their empathic sense and broadcast it outwards through conch shells.

So it was that signals went from Earth to Helliconia, responding for the first time to the signals which had long flowed in the opposite direction.

The characteristics of the human race were now drawn from a slightly different genetic pool than formerly. Those who had inherited the Earth were strong on empathy. Empathy had not been dominant in the preglacial world. That gift of entering into the personality of another, of experiencing sympathetically his or her state of mind, had never been rare. But the elite had despised it—or exploited it. Empathy ran against their interest as exploiters. Power and empathy were not happy teammates.

Now empathy was widely dispersed among the race. It became a dominant feature, with survival characteristics. There was nothing inhuman about it.

There was an inhuman aspect to the Helliconians. The terrestrials puzzled greatly about it. The Helliconians knew the spirits of their dead and communed regularly with them.

The new race on Earth took no particular account of death. They understood that when they died they were taken back and absorbed into the great Earth mother, their elementary particles to be re-formed into future living things. They were buried shallowly with flowers in their mouths, symbolising the force that would spring up from their decay. But it was different on Helliconia. They were fascinated by the Helliconians' descent into pauk to commune with their gossies, those sparks of vital energy.

And it was observed that the ancipital race had a similar relationship with its dead. Dead phagors sank into a "tether" state and appeared to linger, dwindling, for several generations. The phagors had no burial customs.

These macabre extensions to existence were regarded on Earth as a compensation for the extremities of climate which living things endured in the course of a Helliconian Great Year. There was, though, a marked difference between the defunct of the ancipital kind and the defunct of the human kind.

Phagors in tether supported their living descendants, formed a reservoir of wisdom and encouragement, comforted them in adversity. The spirits of humans visited in pauk, on the other hand, were unmitigatedly spiteful. No gossie ever spoke except to utter reproaches and to complain about a spoilt life.

Why this difference? asked the new intellects.

They answered from their own experience. They said: Dreadful though the phagors are, they are not estranged from the Original Beholder, the Helliconian Gaia figure. So they are not tormented by the spirits about them. The humans are estranged; they worship many useless gods who make them ill. So their spirits can never be at peace.

How happy for the Helliconian peoples—said the empathic ones among themselves—if they could have comfort from their gossies in the midst of all their other troubles.

So a determination developed. Those fortunate enough to experience life, to rise up from the molecular and surface into the great light of consciousness, like a salmon leaping from a stream to take a winged life, should radiate their happiness towards Helliconia.

The living of Earth, in other words, should beam empathy like a signal to Helliconia. Not to the living of Helliconia. The living, estranged from their Original Beholder, busy with their affairs, their lusts and hatreds, could not be expected to receive such a signal. But the gossies—for ever hungry for contact—might respond! The gossies in their event-free existence, suspended in obsidian as they sank towards the Original Beholder, the gossies might be capable of receiving a beam of empathy.

A whole generation discussed the daringly visionary proposal.

Was the attempt worth making? went the question.

It would be a great unifying experience even if it failed, came the answer.

Could we possibly hope to affect alien beings—the very dead—so far away?

Through us, Gaia could address the Original Beholder. They are kin, not alien. Perhaps this amazing idea is not ours but hers. We must try.

But when we are so far distant in space and time . . . ?

Empathy is a matter of intensity. It defies space and time. Do we not still feel for the exile of Iphigenia in that ancient story? Let's try. Shall we?

On all counts, it is worth it. The spirit of Gaia commands.

And so they tried.

The attempt was long-sustained. Wherever they sat and watched, wherever they came or went in their rough sandals, the living generations put away worldly things and radiated empathy towards the dead of Helliconia. And even when they could not resist including the living, such as Shay Tal or Laintal Ay, or whomever they might personally favour, they were still empathising with those long dead.

And over the years the warmth of their empathy took effect. The fessups ceased to grieve, the gossies ceased to chide. Those of the living who communed through pauk were not reproved but comforted. An unpossessive love had triumphed.

IX

A QUIET DAY ASHORE

A biogas fire burned in the grate. Before it sat two brothers talking. Every now and again, the thin brother would reach out to pat the sturdy one, as the latter told his tale. Odirin Nan Odim, referred to by all his kin as Odo, was a year and six tenners older than Eedap Mun Odim. He much resembled his brother, except in the crucial matter of girth, for the Fat Death had yet to make its dread appearance in Rivenjk.

The two brothers had much to tell each other, and much planning to do. A ship bearing the Oligarch's soldiery had recently arrived in the port, and the set of regulations against which Odim had fought was beginning to trouble Odo too. However, the Shiveninki were less ready than the Uskuti to take orders. Rivenjk was still a comfortable place in which to live.

The remaining precious porcelain which Odim had brought to his elder brother had been well received.

"Soon such porcelain will become even more precious," said Odo. "Such fine quality may never be achieved again."

"Because the weather deteriorates towards winter."

"What follows from that, brother, is that fuel for firing the kilns will become short, and so increase in price. Also, as people's lives grow harsher, they will be content with tin plates."

"What do you plan to do then, brother?" asked Odim.

"My trade links with Bribahr, the neighbouring country, are excellent. I even despatch my goods to Kharnabhar, far north of here. Porcelain and china are not the only goods that need to travel such routes. We must adapt, deal in other goods. I have ideas for—"

But Odirin Nan Odim was never allowed peace for long. He, like his brother, housed a number of relations. Some of them, voluble and voluminous, rushed to the fireside now, heads full of a quarrel that only Odo could settle. Some of Eedap Mun's relations, surviving plague and voyage, had been billeted with their Rivenjk relations, and the old question had arisen of floor space being encroached upon.

"Perhaps you would not mind coming with me to see what is happening," said Odo.

"I would be pleased. From now on, I shall be your shadow, brother."

Homesteads in Rivenjk were arranged round a courtyard and protected from the elements by a high wall. The more prosperous the family, the higher the wall. Round this courtyard lived the various branches of the Odim family—very little more enterprising here than the relatives in Koriantura had been.

With the families lived their domestic animals, housed in stalls adjoining the human habitations. Some of the animals had been crowded together to permit the newly arrived relatives shelter. This arrangement was the cause of the present quarrel: the resident relations prized their animals above the newly arrived relations—and with some justice.

The sanitary arrangements of most Shiveninki courtyard homesteads depended on a commensalism between animals and humans. All excretions from both house and stall were washed down into a bottle-shaped pit carved in the rock under the courtyard. The pit could be maintained from an inspection flap in the courtyard, through which all vegetable refuse was also thrown. As the refuse rotted underground, it gave off biogas, chiefly methane.

The biogas rising from the pit was trapped and piped into the houses, to be used for cooking and lighting.

This civilised system had been developed throughout Shivenink to cope with the extremes of the Weyr-Winter.

As the Odim brothers inspected the complaints of their relatives, they discovered that two cousins had been housed in a stall where there was a small gas leak. The smell offended the cousins, who had insisted on bundling into the adjoining house, which was already packed with people.

The gas leak was plugged. The cousins, protesting for form's sake, went back to their appointed stall. Slaves were despatched to see that the biogas tank was not malfunctioning.

Odo took his brother's arm. "The church is nearby, as you will observe when we take you on a tour of the city. I have arranged this evening for a small service of thanksgiving to be held there. Praise will be offered to God the Azoiaxic for your preservation."

"You are most kind. But I warn you, brother, I am free of religious belief."

"This little service is necessary," said Odo, raising a dismissive finger. "There you will be able to meet all our relatives formally. There is something downcast in your spirit, brother, owing to your multiple bereavements. You must take a good woman, or at least a slave, to make you happy. What is the status of that foreign woman in your party, Toress Lahl?"

"She's a slave, belonging to Luterin Shokerandit. A doctor, very spirited. He is a fine young man, and from Kharnabhar. About Captain Fashnalgid, I am less certain. He's a deserter, not that I blame him for that. I started out the voyage, before the Fat Death overcame us, with a woman who meant much to my comfort. Alas, she died in the epidemic."

"Was she from Kuj-Juvec, brother?"

"No, but she became like a dove to the tree of my self. She was faithful and good. Her name, for I must speak it, was Besi Besamitikahl. She was more to me even than my—"

Odim broke off sharply, for up ran Kenigg, with a newfound friend. As Odim smiled and took his son's hand, his brother said, "Let me help you find another dove for that good tree of your self. You have only one brother, but the air is full of doves waiting for a suitable branch on which to alight."

⸙

Luterin Shokerandit and Harbin Fashnalgid had been given a small room under the roof, thanks to Odo's generosity. It was lit by one little garret window overlooking the courtyard, from which they could watch the comings and goings of the family and their slaves. In an alcove stood a stove on which their slave could cook their meals.

Both the men had beds of wood, raised above the floor and covered in rugs. Toress Lahl was supposed to lie on the floor beside Shokerandit's bed.

Shokerandit took her in with him while Fashnalgid still slept. He lay all night with his arms round her. Only as he was rising did Fashnalgid stir.

"Luterin, why so energetic?" he asked, yawning cavernously. "Didn't you drink enough of the Odim family's wine last night? Rest, man, and for the Azoiaxic's sake, let's recover from that terrible voyage."

Shokerandit came and looked down at him, smiling. "I had enough wine. Now I want to be off to Kharnabhar as soon as possible. My status is uncertain. I must see how my father is."

"Damn fathers. May their gossies eat shoe leather."

"I have another anxiety too—one you had better heed. Although the Oligarch is well occupied with the war against Bribahr, he has a ship here in port. More may arrive. They may be watching for us both. The sooner I start for Kharnabhar, the better. Why not come with me? There'd be safety and work with my father."

"It's always cold in Kharnabhar. Isn't that what they say? How far north is it from here?"

"The Kharnabhar road covers over twenty-two degrees of latitude."

Fashnalgid laughed. "You go. I'll stay here. I'll find a ship sailing for Campannlat or Hespagorat. Anything rather than your frozen refuge, thanks for all that."

"Please yourself. We don't exactly please each other, do we? Men have to get along well, to survive the drive to Kharnabhar."

Fashnalgid brought an arm up from his furs and held out a hand to Shokerandit. "Well, well, you're a man for the system, and I'm against it, but never mind that."

"You like to think I'm a man for the system, but since my metamorphosis I've broken from it."

"Yes? Yet you long to get back to Father in Kharnabhar." Fashnalgid laughed. "True conformists don't know they conform. I like you well enough, Luterin, though I know you think I wrecked your life by capturing you. On the contrary, I saved you from the claws of the Oligarch, so be grateful. Be grateful enough to heave your Toress over to my bed for the morning, will you?"

A flush spread over Shokerandit's face. "She'll get you water or food while I'm out. Otherwise, she is mine. Ask Odim's brother for what *you* want—he has plenty of slaves for whom he cares nothing."

They looked each other in the eye. Then Shokerandit turned to leave the room.

"Can I come with you?" Toress Lahl called.

"I shall be busy. You can stay here."

As soon as he was gone, Fashnalgid sat up in bed. The woman was hurriedly dressing. She cast the odd glance across at the captain, who smoothed his moustache and gave a smile.

"Don't be so hasty, woman. Come over to me. Sweet Besi's dead and I want comforting."

When she made no answer, he climbed naked out of bed.

Toress Lahl made a run for the door, but he caught her by the wrist and pulled her back.

"Don't be in such a hurry, I said, didn't I? Didn't you hear me?"
He gave her long brown hair a gentle tug. "Women are generally pleased
to be attended by Captain Fashnalgid."

"I belong to Luterin Shokerandit. You heard what he said."

He twisted her arm and grinned down at her. "You're a slave, so
you're anyone's. Beside, you hate his guts—I've seen the looks you
give him. I never forced a woman, Toress, that's the truth, and you'll
find me a good deal more expert than he, from what I overheard."

"Please let me go. Or I shall tell him and he'll kill you."

"Come on, you're too pretty to threaten me. Open up. I saved you
from death, didn't I? You and he were riding into a trap. He's a fatal
innocent, your Luterin."

He put a hand between her legs. She got her right hand free and
slapped him across the face.

With a burst of anger, Fashnalgid wrenched her off her feet and
threw her down on his bed. He fell on top of her.

"Now you listen to me before you provoke me beyond words, Toress
Lahl. You and I are on the same side. Shokerandit is all very well, but
he is going home to security and position—all the things you and I have
lost. What is more, he plans to drive you countless skerming miles
northwards. What's up there but snow and holiness and that gigantic
Wheel?"

"It's where he lives."

"Kharnabhar's fit only for rulers. The rest die in the cold. Haven't
you heard of the Wheel's reputation? It used to be a prison, the worst
on the planet. Do you want to finish up in the Wheel?

"Throw your lot in with me. I have seen the sort of woman you are.
You've seen the sort of man I am. I am an outcast, but I can fend for
myself. Before you get taken miles to some fortress in the northern ice
from which you will never escape, achieve wisdom, achieve wisdom,
woman, and throw in your lot with me. We'll sail from here to
Campannlat and better climes. Maybe we'll even get back to your
precious Borldoran."

She had gone very pale. His face, close above hers, was a blur, nothing
more than eyebrows, those piercing eyes, and that great dead moustache.
She was afraid that he would strike her or even kill her—and that
Shokerandit would not care. Her will was already ebbing under the
burden of captivity.

"He owns me, Captain. Why discuss it? But you may have your
way with me if you must. Why not? He has."

"That's better," he said. "I'll not hurt you. Throw your clothes off."

Luterin Shokerandit knew the port of Rivenjk well. It had always
been the great city, spoken of in Kharnabhar with longing, visited—

when visited—with excitement. Now that he had seen more of the world, he recognised that it was rather small.

At least there was pleasure in being ashore again. He could swear he still felt a slight rolling movement underfoot. Walking down to the harbour, he went into one of the inns and drank a measure of yadahl while listening to the talk of the sailors.

"They're nothing but a nuisance here, these soldiers," a man nearby was saying to a companion. "You heard, I suppose, that one was knifed last night down Perspicacity Alley, and I don't wonder at it."

"They'll set sail tomorrow," his friend said. "They'll be confined aboard ship tonight, you'll see, and good riddance." He lowered his voice. "They're off under Oligarch's orders to fight against the good people of Bribahr. What harm Bribahr have done the rest of us, I don't know."

"They may have captured Braijth, but Rattagon is impregnable. The Oligarch is wasting his time."

"Set in the middle of a lake, I hear."

"That's Rattagon."

"Well, I'm glad I'm not a soldier."

"You're too much of a fool to be anything but a sailor."

As the two men laughed together, Shokerandit fixed his gaze on a poster on a wall by the door. It announced that henceforth Anyone Entering the State of Pauk committed an Offence. To Enter into Pauk, whether alone or in company, was to Encourage the Spreading of the Plague known as the Fat Death. The Penalty for defying this law was One Hundred Sibs and, for a Second Offence, Life Imprisonment. By Order of the Oligarch.

Although Shokerandit never practised pauk, he disliked the stream of new orders the State was issuing.

Shokerandit thought to himself as he drained his glass that he probably hated the Oligarch. When the Archpriest-Militant Asperamanka had sent him to report to the Oligarchy, he had felt honoured. Then Fashnalgid had stopped him almost at the Sibornalese frontier; and it had taken him some while to believe what the man claimed, that he would have been cold-bloodedly killed with the rest of the returning army. It was even more difficult to realise that all of Asperamanka's force had been wiped out on the Oligarch's orders.

It made sense to take rational measures to keep the plague from spreading. But to suppress pauk was a sign that authoritarianism was spreading. He wiped his mouth with his hand.

As a result of circumstance, Shokerandit was no hero but a fugitive. He could not imagine what his fate would be if he was arrested for desertion.

"What did Harbin mean, I'm a man of the system?" he muttered. "I'm a rebel, an outcast—like him."

It behoved him to get home to Kharnabhar and remain under his father's powerful protection. At least in distant Kharnabhar the forces of the Oligarch would not reach him. Thought of Insil could be left for later.

With this reflection came another. He owed Fashnalgid something. He must take him on the arduous journey north if Fashnalgid could be persuaded to come. Fashnalgid would be useful in Kharnabhar: there he could help bear witness to the massacre of thousands of young Shiveninki by their own side.

He said to himself, I had courage in battle. I must have courage to fight against the Oligarchy if necessary. There will be others at home who feel as I do when they hear the truth.

He paid his coin and left the inn.

Along the waterfront stood a grand avenue of rajabarals. As temperatures dropped, the trees prepared for the long winter. Instead of shedding their leaves, they drew in their branches, pulling them into the tops of their vast trunks. Shokerandit had seen pictures in natural history books of how branches and leaves would dissolve to form a solid resin plug, protecting the featureless and undecaying tree until it released its seed in the following Great Spring.

Under the rajabarals, soldiers from a ship which flew the flags of Sibornal and the Oligarchy were parading. Shokerandit had a momentary fear that someone might recognize him; but his metamorphosed shape was protection. He turned inland, towards the marketplace, where there were agents who handled the affairs of travellers intending to visit Kharnabhar.

The cold winds from the mountains made him turn up his collar and lower his head. But at the agent's door, pilgrims eager to visit the shrines of the Great Wheel were gathered, many poor and scantily clad.

It took him a while to arrange matters to his liking. He could travel to Kharnabhar with the pilgrims. Or he could travel independently, hiring a sledge, a team, a driver, and a jack-of-all-trades. The former way was safer, slower, and less expensive. Shokerandit decided on the latter as more befitting the son of the Keeper of the Wheel.

All he needed was cash or a letter of credit.

There were friends of his father's at hand, some men of influence in the town's affairs. He hesitated, and eventually chose a simple man called Hernisarath, who ran a farm and a hostel for pilgrims on the edge of town. Hernisarath welcomed Shokerandit in, immediately supplied a letter of credit for the agent, and insisted that Shokerandit join him and his wife for a midday meal.

He embraced Shokerandit on the doorstep when it was time to take leave.

"You're a good and innocent young man, Luterin, and I'm happy to help. Every day as Weyr-Winter approaches, farming becomes more difficult. But let's hope we shall meet again."

His wife said, "It's so nice to meet a young man with good manners. Our respects to your father."

Shokerandit glowed as he left them, pleased to have made a good impression; whereas Harbin was probably drunk by now. But why did Hernisarath call him "innocent"?

Snow began to fall from the heights, whirling as it came, like fine white sugar dissolving in a stirred glass of water. It thickened, muffling the sound of his boots on the cobbles. The streets cleared of people. Long grey shadows sprouted penumbras, dark for Freyr, lighter for Batalix, until the cloud extended over the bay and enveloped all Rivenjk in murk.

Shokerandit halted suddenly behind a rajabaral.

Another man came on from behind, clutching his collar to his throat. He walked past the tree, glanced back, shuffled his feet, and hurried into a side street. Shokerandit saw with some amusement that it was called Perspicacity Alley.

With uncharacteristic forethought, he had not told his fellow travellers that on the head of the Hero guarding entry to Rivenjk harbour was a heliograph signalling station. Warning of the deserters aboard the *New Season* could have reached the port long before the brig docked. . . .

He returned to Odo's house by as devious a route as he could contrive. By then, the worst of the snow shower was over.

"How fortunate that you arrive in time," Odo said, as Shokerandit entered the door. "My brother and I and the rest of the family are about to go to church to give thanks for the *New Season*'s survival. You will come along, please?"

"Oh . . . yes, of course. A private ceremony?"

"Absolutely private. Only the priest and the family."

Shokerandit looked at Odim, who nodded encouragingly. "You are about to embark on another journey, Luterin. We who have known each other such a short while must part. The ceremony seems appropriate, even if you don't believe in prayer."

"I will see if Fashnalgid will come too."

He hastened up the winding wooden stair to the room Odo had lent them. Toress Lahl was there, lying under her skins on his bed.

"You're meant to be working, not lying about," he said. "You're not still mourning your husband? Where's the captain?"

"I don't know."

"Find him, will you? He'll be drinking somewhere."

He ran back downstairs. As soon as he was gone, Fashnalgid climbed out from under his bed and laughed. Toress Lahl refused to smile.

"I want food, not prayer," he said, peering cautiously out of the window. "And that drink your friend mentioned would be welcome. . . ."

The Odim clan was gathering in the courtyard, where slaves were still meddling inefficiently with long rods, climbing in and out of the biogas inspection pit, despite the sleet in the air. The place was filled with excited talk.

Shokerandit appeared. Some of the ladies who had been on the *New Season* ran up and embraced him, in a manner more reminiscent of Kuj-Juvec than of the rest of Sibornal. Shokerandit no longer contrasted such free behaviour with his own formal upbringing.

"Oh, this is such a good place, this Rivenjk," said one well-wrapped grand-aunt, taking his arm. "There are many fine buildings, and much statuary. I shall be happy here, and mean to set up a press to print poetry. Do you think your countrymen like poetry?"

But before Shokerandit could reply, the lady had turned in the other direction to grasp Eedap Mun Odim by the sleeve. "You are our little hero, cousin, bringing us safe from oppression. Let me be in the church next to you. Walk there with me and make me proud."

"I shall be proud to walk with *you*, auntie," said Odim, smiling kindly at her. And the whole jostling crowd began to move out of the courtyard gate and along the street to the church.

"And we are proud to have you with us, too, Luterin," said Odim, anxious that Shokerandit should not feel left out of the party. He looked round with pleasure at so many Odims gathered together. Although their ranks had been culled by the Fat Death, the bulk of the survivors was a compensation of sorts.

When they filed into the high-roofed church, Odim ranged himself against his brother, elbows touching. He wondered if Odo, like him, had no belief in God the Azoiaxic. He was far too polite to put such a personal question; secrecy was for men, as the saying went. If his brother wished to confess one evening, over a little wine, that was another matter. For now, it was enough that they were together and that the service allowed them to mourn for those who had died, including his wife and children and the beloved Besi Besamitikahl, and to rejoice in the fact that their own lives were spared.

A treble voice, disembodied, sexless, free of lust, traced a thread of theatrical penitence which rose from the well of the church to its inter-laced roof beams.

Odim smiled as he sang and felt his soul lifted towards the rafters. Belief would have been good. But even the wish to believe was consolatory.

As the voices of the congregation were raised in song inside, ten beefy soldiers marched down the street outside accompanied by an officer, and halted outside Odirin Nan Odim's gate. The watchman opened up to them, bowing. The soldiers brushed him aside and marched into the centre of the courtyard, trampling the already trodden carpet of snow.

The officer barked orders to his men. Four men to search the houses set at each point of the compass, remainder to stand where they were and be alert for escapees.

"Abro Hakmo Astab!" Fashnalgid shouted, jumping up from his bed. He had been sitting half-dressed, watching both the window and Toress Lahl, to whom he occasionally read lines of poetry from a small book. She was obeying his orders to prepare a meal, and was carrying a flaming brand obtained from a slave downstairs to light their stove.

She flinched at the obscenity of his oath, although she was used to the swearing of soldiers.

"How I love the sound of a military voice! 'No song like yours under spring skies . . .'" Fashnalgid said. "And the clump of army boots. Yes, there they are. Look at that young fool of a lieutenant, uniform gleaming. All I once was . . .''

He glared down at the scene in the courtyard, where, in front of the soldiers, slaves still worked, rodding out the biogas drains, glancing mistrustfully at the invaders.

A pair of boots started to clump up the stairs to the attic room.

Fashnalgid snarled, showing white teeth under the wave of his moustache. He rushed for his sword and glared round the room like a cornered beast. Toress Lahl stood petrified, one hand to her mouth, the other holding the flaming brand at arm's length.

"Haaa . . ." He dashed forward and snatched the brand from her, trailing the smoke across the room as he ran for the window. Pushing it open, he forced his head and shoulders out and hurled the brand with all his strength.

He had not lost his military skills. No grenade could have flown truer. The flame drew a parabola down the darkened air and disappeared into the open trap of the biogas chamber. For a second, silence. Then the whole place exploded. Slabs of the courtyard went flying. A great flame rose in the midst of everything, burning blue at its core.

With a roar of satisfaction, Fashnalgid crossed to the door and flung it wide. A young soldier stood there, hesitating, looking back the way he had come. Without thought, Fashnalgid ran him through. As the man doubled, Fashnalgid kicked out, sending him head first down the stairs.

"Now we've got to run for our lives, woman," he said, taking hold of Toress Lahl's hand.

"Luterin—" she said, but she was too frightened to do anything but follow him. They ran downstairs. The courtyard was a scene of panic. The gas still burned. Odims too old, too young, or too voluminous to attend the church service, together with their animals, were running about among the soldiers. The smart lieutenant aimed a bullet or two at the clouds. Slaves were screaming. One of the houses had caught fire. It was an easy matter to skirt the melee and leave by the gate.

Once they were in the street, Fashnalgid dropped to an easier pace and sheathed his sword, so as to be less conspicuous.

They hurried into the churchyard. He pulled the woman against a buttress, panting. Inside, hymns rose to God the Azoiaxic. In his excitement, he gripped her painfully by the upper arm.

"Those sherbs, they're after us. Even in this piddling dump . . ."

"Oh, do let me go. You're hurting me."

"I'll let you go. You're going to go inside this church and get Shokerandit. Tell him that the military have caught up with us. There'll be no escaping by boat now. If he has arranged a sledge, then we all start for Kharnabhar as soon as we can. Go in and tell him." He gave her a push to encourage her. "Tell him they want to hang him."

By the time Toress Lahl reappeared with Shokerandit, many people were about in the street—and not only innocent bystanders. As the Odims ran shouting with distress, Fashnalgid said, "Luterin, have you got a sledge? Can we get out of here right away?"

"Need you have wrecked the Odim home after all they have done for us?" Shokerandit said, regarding the other's disarray.

"Don't trust Odim. He's a tradesman. We have to leave. The army's woken up. Don't forget your lovely Toress Lahl is officially a runaway slave. You know the penalty for that. Where's the sledge?"

"We can get it when the stables open at Batalix-dawn. You have changed your mind suddenly, haven't you?"

"Where do we hide till dawn?"

Shokerandit thought. "There's a family friend, by name Hernisarath. He and his wife will give us shelter until the morning. . . . But I must go and say good-bye to Odim."

Fashnalgid pointed a thick finger at him. "You'll do no such thing. He'll hand you over. Soldiers are swarming everywhere. You *are* an innocent, aren't you?"

"All right, and you're an eccentric. Insults apart, why the change of plan? Only this morning you were going to sail for Campannlat."

Fashnalgid smiled. "Suppose it occurred to me that I ought to be nearer to God? I've decided to come with you and your lady slave to Holy Kharnabhar."

X

"THE DEAD NEVER
TALK POLITICS"

On the sixth day of the sixth tenner of every sixth small year, the Synod of the Church of the Formidable Peace met in Askitosh. The lesser fry met in conventials behind the Palace of the Supreme Priest. The fifteen dignitaries who formed the standing synod lived and met in the Palace itself. They represented both the ecclesiastical and the secular or military arms of the organisation of the Church. The burdens of office were heavy upon them. They were not men given to drollery.

Being human, the fifteen had their faults. One was regularly overcome by alcohol by sixteen twenty every day. Others kept young female or male slaves in their chambers. Some enjoyed peculiar defilements. Nevertheless, at least a part of each of them was dedicated to the good continuance of the Church. Since good men were hard to find, the fifteen could be accounted good men.

And the most dedicated man of all was Chubsalid, a man of Bribahr birth, brought up by holy fathers within the cloisters of their church, now Priest-Supreme of the Church of the Formidable Peace, the appointed representative on Helliconia of God the Azoiaxic, who existed before life and round whom all life revolves.

Even the most watchful ecclesiastical eye had never seen Chubsalid raise a bottle to his lips. If he had any sexual proclivities whatsoever, they were a secret kept between him and his maker. If he ever experienced anger, fear, or sorrow, no shadows of those emotions ever reached his rosy face. And he was no fool.

Unlike the Oligarchy, whose meeting place on Icen Hill was not a mile away, the Synod had wide popular support. The Church genuinely ministered to the needs of its people; uplifted their hearts and supported them in adversity. And preserved tactful silence about pauk.

Unlike the Oligarch, who was never seen and whose image in the fearful popular imagination most resembled a huge crustacean with hyperactive nippers, Priest-Supreme Chubsalid travelled among the poor and was a popular visitor with his congregations. He looked every inch a Priest-Supreme, with his large stature, craggy but kindly countenance, and mane of white hair. When he spoke, people wished to listen. His addresses were spun from piety and often fringed by wit: he could make his congregations laugh as well as pray.

The discussion at the synodical meetings was conducted in the highest Sibish, with multiple clauses, elaborate parentheses, and spectacular verb formations. But the matter on this occasion was strictly practical. It concerned the strained relationship between the two great estates of Sibornal, the State and the Church.

The Church watched with alarm as the edicts of the Oligarchy increased in severity. One of the synodic priesthood was speaking to the assembly on this subject.

"The new Restrictions of Persons in Abodes Act and similar regulations are/continue represented by the State as a move to curtail the plague. Already they are causing as much disruption as the plague does/will/can. The poor are evicted and arrested for vagrancy, or else perish from the increasing cold."

He was a silvery man and spoke in a silvery voice, but its conviction carried to the end of the room. "We can see the political thinking behind this iniquitous Act. As more northerly farms fail/failing, the peasants and small farmers who worked those farms drift into town, where they must find shelter where they can, generally in overcrowded conditions. The Act seeks to confine them to their failed farms. There they will starve. I hope I am not unduly uncharitable when I say that their deaths would suit the State well. The dead never talk politics."

"You foresee a revolt starting in the towns if the Act were repealed?" asked a voice from the other end of the table.

"In my youth, it was said that a Sibornalese worked for life, married for life, and longed for life," replied the silvery voice. "But we never rebel. We leave that to the people of the Savage Continent. The Church has so far said nothing about these restrictive Acts. Now I suggest that we have reached a sticking point with the Act against pauk."

"We have no policy on pauk."

"Neither had the State till now. Again, the dead have no politics, and that the State has/continuous recognises. Nevertheless, the Oligarchy have now legislated against pauk. This causes/has/will further misery to our congregations for whom—if you will forgive my saying so—pauk is as much a part of life as parturition.

"The poor are being unfairly punished to fit them for the coming winter. I move that the Church speaks out publicly against the recent actions of the State."

An aged and bald man, completely lacking hair or colour, rose with the aid of two sticks and spoke.

"It may be as you say, brother. The Oligarchy may be tightening its grip. I suggest to you that it has to do so. Think of the future. All too soon, our descendants will be faced/facing three and a half centuries of the bitter Weyr-Winter. The Oligarchy reasons that the harshness of nature must be matched by the harshness of mankind.

"Let me remind you of that terrible Sibish oath which must not be spoken. It is regarded as a supreme blasphemy, and rightly. Yet it is admirable. Yes, admirable. I would not/admonitorily have it spoken in my diocese, yet I admire the defiance of it."

He steadied himself. There were those who thought the venerable man was about to defile his lips with the oath. Instead, he took a different tack.

"In the Savage Continent of Campannlat, chaos descends with the cold. They have no overriding order as we have. They crawl back to their caves. Sibornal survives intact. We will/shall/have perpetual survive by organisation. That organisation has to tighten like an iron fist. Many have to die that the state will survive.

"Some of you have complained because all phagors are to be shot regardless. I say they are not human. Get rid of them. They have no souls. Shoot them. And shoot all that defend them. Shoot the farmers whose farms fail. This is no time for individual gestures. Individuality itself must soon/will be punished by death."

In the silence, his sticks rattled like bones as he seated himself again.

A murmur of shock went round the room, but Priest-Supreme Chub-salid from his ermine-lined seat said mildly, "No doubt they make such speeches all the while on Icen Hill, but we must keep to our chosen profession, which involves/continuous tempering our dealings even with failed farmers with mercy. Our Church stands for the individual, for individual conscience, individual salvation, and our duty is to remind our friends in the Oligarchy of this from time to time, so that the people are also clear in their minds on that point.

"The seasons may grow harsh. We do not have to imitate them, so that even in harshest times the essential teaching of the Church may/will/must live. Otherwise there is no life in God. The State sees this time of crisis as one in which it must show its strength. The Church must do at least as much. Who here of the fifteen agrees that the Church should stand against the State?"

All of the fourteen he had addressed turned to mutter with their neighbours down the long table. They could guess the retribution which would follow the move advocated by their leader.

One of the number raised a gold-ringed hand and said, in a quavering voice, "Sire, the time may/potential come when we do indeed have to take the kind of stance you suggest. But for pauk? When we have carefully avoided for eons—when perhaps some doubt as to the legitimacy of challenging—when the myth of the Original Beholder opposes our . . ."

He left that theatrical thought unstated.

The youngest member of the Synod was a Priest-Chaplain named Parlingelteg, a delicate man, though it was whispered that some of his activities were indelicate. He was never afraid to speak up, and he addressed his words directly to Chubsalid.

"That last miserable speech convinces me at least—and I imagine all of you—that we must stand against the State. Perhaps specifically on the issue of pauk. Let's not pretend pauk isn't real, or that the gossies don't exist, just because they don't fit with the Teaching.

"Why do you think the State has tried to forbid pauk? For one reason only. The State is guilty of genocide. It killed off thousands of men in Asperamanka's army. The mothers of those sons thus slain have communed with them after death. The gossies have spoken. Who here said the dead have no politics? That's nonsense. Thousands of dead mouths cry out against the State and the murderous Oligarch. I support the Priest-Supreme. We must speak against Torkerkanzlag and have him thrown out of office."

He blushed red to the roots of his fair hair, as several of his seniors applauded. The meeting broke up. Still they drew back from taking a decision. Had not Church and State always been inseparable? And to speak aloud of that massacre . . . They loved peace—some of them at all costs.

An hour's break followed. It was too chilly to go outdoors. They loitered in the heated withdrawing rooms while scouts served water or wine in porcelain cups. They talked among themselves. Perhaps there was a way of avoiding actual consultation; apart from what the gossies said, there was no real evidence, was there?

A bell rang. They reconvened. Chubsalid spoke privily to Parlingelteg and both looked solemn.

The debate was continuing when a liveried slave knocked and

entered. He bowed low before the Priest-Supreme and handed him a note on a tray.

Chubsalid read the note, then sat for a moment with his elbow on the table before him and his hand touching his tall forehead. The talk died. All waited for him to speak.

"Brothers," he said, looking round at them. "We have a visitor, an important witness. I propose to summon him before us. His words, I fancy, will carry more weight than would further discussion." He gestured to the slave, who bowed and hurried from the room.

Another man entered the chamber. With deliberation, he turned and closed the doors behind him, only then advancing towards the table where the fifteen leaders of the Church sat. He was dressed in deep blue from head to foot; boots, breeches, shirt, jacket, cloak, all were blue; so was the hat he carried in his hand. Only his hair was white, although black remained over each temple. When the Synod had last seen him, his hair had been entirely black.

The white hair emphasised the size of his head. His straight brows, eyes, mouth, emphasised the anger that lurked like thunder there.

He bowed deeply to the Priest-Supreme and kissed his hand. He turned to salute the Synod.

"I thank you for giving me audience," he said.

"Archpriest-Militant Asperamanka, we had been informed of your death in battle," said Chubsalid. "We rejoice in the inaccuracy of our information."

Asperamanka formed his lips into a chilling smile. "I all but died— but not in battle. The story of how I managed to reach Askitosh, almost alone of all my army, is an extraordinary one. I was shot in Chalce, on the very frontiers of our continent, I was captured by phagors, I escaped, I was lost in marshland—well, in brief, it is God's miracle that I stand before you now. God protected me, and sharpened me as an instrument of justice. For I come as proof of a crime of perfidy unequalled in the illustrious history of Sibornal."

"Pray take a seat," said the Priest-Supreme, motioning to a lackey. "We wait to hear what you have to tell us. You will prove a better informant than any gossie."

As Asperamanka told his story of the ambush, of the withering fire directed by the Oligarch's guard against his returning forces, as the full extent of what had happened was borne home to everyone, it became clear that Parlingelteg had spoken truly. The Church would have to confront the State. Otherwise, the Church became party to the massacre.

It took Asperamanka over an hour to unfold the whole story of the campaign and its betrayal. Finally he was silent. Silent only for a minute. Then he unexpectedly hid his face in his hands and burst into tears.

"The crime is mine too," he cried. "I worked for the Oligarch. I fear the Oligarch. To me, Church and State were one and synonymous."

"But no more," said Chubsalid. He rose and rested his hand on Asperamanka's shoulder. "Thank you for being God's instrument and making our duty plain to us.

"The Oligarchy has had jurisdiction over humanity's bodies, the Church over its souls. Now we must gird ourselves to assert the supremacy of the soul above the body. We must oppose the Oligarchy. Is it here so resolved?"

The fourteen members gave cries of assent. Sticks rattled under the table.

"Then it is unanimous."

After more discussion, agreement was reached that the first move should be to send out a firmly worded Bill to all churches the length and breadth of the land. The Bill would declare that the Church defended the ancient practice of pauk, which it regarded as an essential freedom of every man and woman in the realm. There was no evidence that the so-called gossies spoke other than Truth. The Church in no way accepted that the practice of pauk spread the Fat Death. Chubsalid set his name to the Bill.

"This is probably the most revolutionary Bill the Church has ever put out," said the silvery voice. "I just want to state that fact. And by acknowledging pauk, are we not acknowledging also the Original Beholder? And are we not thus allowing heathen superstition into the Church?"

"The Bill makes no mention of the Original Beholder, brother," said Parlingelteg softly.

The Bill was approved and sent to the ecclesiastical printer. From the printer it went out to all the churches in the land.

Four days passed. In the Palace of the Priest-Supreme, churchmen waited for the storm to break.

A messenger, clad in oilskins against the weather, came down from Icen Hill and delivered a sealed document at the Palace.

The Priest-Supreme broke the seal and read the message.

The message said that subversive pamphlets put out by the Synod preached treason, in that they set out deliberately to flout recent Acts promulgated by the State. Treason was punishable by death.

If there was an explanation for these vile offences, then the Priest-Supreme of the Church of the Formidable Peace should present himself before the Oligarch forthwith, and deliver it in person.

The letter was signed with the signature of Torkerkanzleg II.

"I do not believe that man exists," Chubsalid said. "He has reigned for over thirty years. Nobody has ever seen him. No portrait exists of his face. He could be a phagor for all we know to the contrary . . ."

He continued for a while in this vein, tut-tutting absently, and visiting the Synod library to compare signatures, toying with magnifying glasses and shaking his head.

This activity made the Priest-Supreme's advisors nervous; they felt he should be concentrating on the gravity of a summons which, on the face of it at least, appeared to be his death warrant. Senior advisors, speaking among themselves, suggested that the entire centre of the Church should move immediately from Askitosh to a safer place—possibly to Rattagon, although it was under siege, since its position in the middle of a lake rendered it secure; or even to Kharnabhar, despite its extreme climate, since it was a religious refuge.

But Chubsalid had his own ideas. Retreat never entered his mind. After an hour of pottering about comparing signatures, he announced that he would meet the Oligarch. An acceptance note was written by his scribe to that effect. It suggested that the meeting should be in the great entrance hall of Icen Castle, and that anyone who wished might come there and hear the debate between the two men.

As Chubsalid appended his name to the document, Priest-Chaplain Parlingelteg, who was standing nearby, came forward and knelt by the Priest-Supreme's chair.

"Sire, when you go to that place, permit me to accompany you. Whatever there befalls you, let it also befall me."

Chubsalid set his hand on the young man's shoulder.

"It shall be as you suggest. I shall be grateful for your presence."

He turned then to Asperamanka, who was also in the company.

"And you, our Priest-Militant, will you also come to Icen Castle, to bear witness to the Oligarch's crime?"

Asperamanka looked here and there, as if seeking out an invisible door. "You speak better than I, Priest-Supreme. I think it unwise to bring up the subject of the plague. We have no cure for the Fat Death, any more than the State. The Oligarch may have reasons we know nothing of for wishing to suppress pauk."

"Then we will hear them. You will come with Parlingelteg and me?"

"Perhaps we should take doctors with us."

Chubsalid smiled. "We shall be able to stand against him, I trust, without the aid of doctors."

"Surely we ought to try and compromise," said Asperamanka, looking wretched.

"We shall see if that is possible," said Chubsalid. "And thank you for saying you will accompany us."

The day dawned. Priest-Supreme Chubsalid put on his ecclesiastical robes and bade good-bye to his colleagues. One or two he embraced.

The silvery man shed a tear.

Chubsalid smiled at him. "Whatever happens this day, I will require your courage as well as mine." His voice was firm and serene.

He climbed into his carriage, where Asperamanka and Parlingelteg waited. The carriage moved off.

It made its way through silent streets. The police, at the Oligarch's command, had cleared onlookers away, so that there was none of the cheering which usually greeted the appearance of the Priest-Supreme. Only silence.

As the carriage ground its way up the treacherous paving stones of Icen Hill, the presence of soldiery was all too noticeable. At the gates of the castle, armed men stepped forward and fended off those priests who had followed behind their leader's carriage. The carriage passed under the ponderous stone arch. The great iron gates closed behind it.

Many windows looked down on the front courtyard, enforcing silence with their oppressive dead shine. They were mean windows, less like eyes than blunt teeth.

The party of three was led unceremoniously from the carriage into the chill of the building. Their footsteps echoed as they traversed the great entrance hall. Soldiers in elaborate national uniform stood on guard. None moved.

The party was shown to the rear, to a dingy passage where the skirting was scuffed by innumerable boots, as if a tormented animal had tried to fight its way to freedom. After a wait, a signal was given their guide and they ascended by a narrow wooden stair which wound up two flights without a window by way of punctuation. They emerged into another passage, no more congenial to tormented animals than the first, and halted at a door. The guide knocked.

A voice bade them enter.

They came into a room which displayed all the festive cheer for which the Oligarchy was noted. It was a reception room of a kind, lined with chairs on which only the most emaciated anatomies could have found rest. The one window in the room was draped in heavy leather curtains, evidently designed to be capable of repelling the onslaughts of daylight.

The niggardly proportions of the room, in which the height of the ceiling was matched only by the depth of gloom it engendered, was reinforced by its lighting. One fat viridian candle burned in a tall stand in the middle of the otherwise empty floor. A chilling draught caused its shadows to stir wakefully on the creaking parquet.

"How long do we wait here?" Chubsalid enquired of the guide.

"A short while, sire."

Short whiles were of long duration in such a room, but eventually inner doors opened. Two uniformed men with swords dragged the doors apart, allowing the party to view a further room.

This further room was lit by gas flares, which imparted a sickly light over everything but the face of a man sitting berobed in a large chair at the far end of the room. Since the gas lights were behind his throne, his face was cast into shadow. The man made no movement.

Chubsalid said in a clear voice, "I am Priest-Supreme Chubsalid of the Church of the Formidable Peace. Who are you?"

And an equally clear voice came back. "You address me as the Oligarch."

The visiting party, although they had prepared themselves for the encounter, were silenced by a momentary awe. They shuffled forward to the door of the inner chamber, where soldiers barred their way with naked swords.

"Are you Torkerkanzlag II?" asked Chubsalid.

Again the clear voice. "Address me as the Oligarch."

Chubsalid and Asperamanka looked at each other. Then the former spoke out.

"We have come here, Dread Oligarch, to discuss the curtailment of traditional liberties in our state, and to speak with you regarding a recent crime committed—"

The clear voice cut in. "You have come here to discuss nothing, priest. You have come here to speak of nothing. You have come here because you preached treason, in deliberate defiance of recent edicts issued by the State. You have come here because the punishment for treason is death."

"On the contrary," said Parlingelteg. "We came here anticipating reason, justice, and an open debate. Not some sort of tawdry melo-dramatics."

Asperamanka set his chest against one of the drawn swords and said, "Dread Oligarch, I have served you faithfully. I am Priest-Militant Asperamanka, who, as no doubt you know, led your armies to victory in the field against the thousand heathen cults of Pannoval. Did you not— were not those armies destroyed on their return to your domains?"

The unmoved voice of the Oligarch said, "In the presence of your ruler, you do not ask questions."

"Tell us who you are," said Parlingelteg. "If you are human you give no evidence of it."

Ignoring the interruption, Torkerkanzlag II gave the guard an order: "Draw back the window curtain."

The guide who had led the three into the stifling chamber creaked his way across the floor and grasped the leather curtain with both hands. Slowly, he pulled the curtain back from the long window.

Grey light filtered into the room. While the other two turned to see out, Chubsalid looked back towards the Oligarch. Some of the light filtered even to where he sat motionless on his shadowed throne; some-thing of his features was revealed.

"I recognise you! Why, you're—" But the Priest-Supreme got no further, for one of the soldiers grasped him unceremoniously by the shoulder and swung him to the long window, where the guide stood pointing downwards.

A courtyard lay beneath the window, surrounded entirely by tall grey walls. Anyone walking down there would have been crushed by the weight of disapproving windows ranged above him.

In the middle of the courtyard, a wooden cage had been built. Inside the cage was a tall, sturdy pole. What made this arrangement remarkable was the fact that cage and pole stood on a slatted wooden platform, which was built over piles of logs. Tucked in among the logs were bundles of brushwood. Bunches of twigs and kindling skirted the brushwood.

The Oligarch said, "The punishment for treason is death. That you knew before you entered here. Death by burning. You have preached against the State. You will be burnt."

Parlingelteg spoke up boldly as the curtain was pulled back over the window. "If you dare burn us, you will turn the religion of Sibornal against the State. Every man's hand will be against you. You will not survive. Sibornal itself may not survive."

Asperamanka made a run for the door, shouting, "I'll see to it that the world hears of this villainy."

But there were soldiers outside the door who turned him back.

Chubsalid stood in the middle of the room and said soothingly to him, "Be firm, my good priest. If this crime is committed here in the centre of Askitosh, there will be those who will never rest until the Azoiaxic triumphs. This is the monster who believes that treachery costs less than armies. He will find that this treachery costs him everything."

The unmoving man in the chair said, "The greatest good is the survival of civilisation over the next centuries. To that end all else must be sacrificed. Fine principles have to go. When plague's rampant, law and order break down. So it has always been at the onset of previous Great Winters—in Campannlat, in Hespagorat, even in Sibornal. Armies run mad, records burn, the finest emblems of the state are destroyed. Barbarism reigns.

"This time, this winter, we shall/will survive that crisis. Sibornal is to become a fortress. Already none may enter. Soon, none shall leave. For four centuries, we shall remain a haven of law and order, whilst the cold tears out the gizzards of wolves. We will live from the sea.

"Values will be maintained, but those values must be the values of survival. I will not have Church and State at loggerheads. That is what the Oligarchy has decided. Ours is the only plan which can/determined save the maximum number of people.

"Next spring, we shall rise up strong while Campannlat is still given over to primitivism and its women lug carts like beasts of burden—if they haven't forgotten how to make wheels by then. At that time, we shall resolve the endless hostility with those savage lands for good and all.

"Do you call that wicked? Do you call that wicked, Priest-Supreme? To see our beloved continent triumph?"

Garbed in his canonicals, Chubsalid made a fine figure. He drew himself up. He let silence cover the Oligarch's rhetoric before he replied.

"Whatever you may arrogantly believe to the contrary, yours is the argument of a weak man. We have in Sibornal a harsh religion, forged, like the Great Wheel itself, out of an adverse climate. But what we preach is stoicism, not cruelty. Yours is the ancient argument of ends justifying means. You will find that if you pursue your proposed course the cruel means will subvert the end, and your plan will fail utterly."

The man in the chair moved his hand scarcely an inch as a substitute for a gesture. "We may make mistakes, Priest-Supreme, that I grant. Then we shall simply bury our dead and remain on course."

Parlingelteg's clear young voice rang out: "And all the dead will bear witness against you. Word will go from gossie to gossie. All will hear of your crimes."

The Oligarch's darker tone replied. "The dead may bear witness. Happily, they cannot bear arms."

"When this deed is known, many will bear arms against you!"

"If you have nothing to say beyond the airing of threats, then the time has come for you to meet those unarmed millions below ground yourselves. Or do any of you care to reconsider your loyalty to the State in view of what I have said?"

He motioned to the guards. Parlingelteg shouted the forbidden curse. "Abro Hakmo Astab, damned Oligarch!"

Armed guards marched across the room with heavy tread, to take up positions behind the ecclesiastics.

Asperamanka could say nothing for the trembling of his jaw. He rolled his eyes at Chubsalid, who patted him on the shoulder. The youngest priest took Chubsalid by the arm and called out again, "Burn us and you set all Askitosh afire!"

Chubsalid said, "I warn you, Oligarch, if you cause a schism between Church and State, your plans will never succeed. You will divide the people. If you burn us, your plan will already have failed."

In a composed voice, the Oligarch said, "I shall find others who will cooperate, Priest-Supreme. Dozens of the obedient will rush to fill your place—and think it honourable. I know men well."

As the guards took hold of the captives, Asperamanka broke free. He ran towards the Oligarch's throne and went down on one knee, bowing his head.

"Dread Oligarch, spare me. You know that I, Asperamanka, was your faithful servant in war. You surely never intended that such a valuable

instrument should be killed. Do with these other two as you will, but
let me be saved, let me serve again! I believe that Sibornal must
survive as you say. Harsh times call for harsh measures. Spiritual power
must make way for temporal power to secure the way. Just let me live,
and I will serve . . . for the glory of God."

"You may do it for your own base sake, but never for God's," said
Chubsalid. "Get up! Die with us, Asperamanka—'twill be less pain."

"Living or dying, we accept the role of pain in our existence," said
the Oligarch. "Asperamanka, this comes unexpectedly from you, the
victor of Isturiacha. You entered here with your brothers; why not
burn with your brothers?"

Asperamanka was silent. Then, without rising from his knees, he
burst out in a flood of eloquence.

"What has been said here belongs not so much to politics or morals
as to history. You wish to change history, Oligarch—perhaps the
obsession of all great men. Indeed our cyclic history stands in need of
reform—reform which must be brutal to be effective.

"Yet I speak for our beloved Church, which I have also served—
served with devotion. Let *these* burn for it. I'd rather live for it. History
shows us that religions can perish just like nations. I have not forgotten
my history lessons as a child in the monastery of Old Askitosh, where I
was taught of the defeat of the religion of Pannoval at the hand of a
wicked King of Borlien and his ministers. If Church and State here
fall apart, then our Supreme God is similarly threatened. Let me, as a
Man of God, serve your ends."

As the other priests were marched out, Parlingelteg took a flying kick
at Asperamanka, sending him sprawling on the floor. "Hypocrite!" he
called as he was dragged out of range.

"Take those two down to the courtyard," said the Oligarch. "If a
little fear is struck into the heart of the Church, the Church may not
be so vocal in future."

He sat motionless as Priest-Supreme Chubsalid and Priest-Chaplain
Parlingelteg were marched away.

The chamber emptied. Only one guard remained, silent in the
shadows, and Asperamanka, still crouching on the floor, face pale.

The Oligarch's cold stare turned in Asperamanka's direction.

"I can always find work for your kind," he said. "Get up on your
feet."

XI

STERN DISCIPLINE
FOR TRAVELLERS

Most of Sibornal's rivers ran south. Most of them, for most of the year, were fast and ill-natured, as befitted waters born of glaciers.

The Venj was no exception. It was wide, full of dangerous currents, and could be said to hurtle rather than flow on its way to its outlet at Rivenjk.

In the course of centuries, however, the Venj had scoured itself a valley through which it might flow or flood as the mood took it, and it was along this valley that the road led which would eventually bear a north-bound traveller to Kharnabhar.

The road wound upward through pleasant country, protected from prevailing winds by the mass of the Shivenink Chain. Large bushes, indifferent to frost, grew here, putting out immense blossoms. Small flowers grew by the wayside, picked by pilgrims because they were never seen elsewhere.

The pilgrims were carefree on this, the first stage of their land journey to Kharnabhar. They travelled alone or in groups, dressed in all manner of garb. Some went barefoot, claiming that they controlled their bodies so as not to experience cold. There was singing and music among the groups. This was a serious exercise in piety—one that would stand them in good stead at home for the rest of their lives—but nevertheless it was a holiday, and they rejoiced accordingly. For some miles out of Rivenjk, stalls stood by the side of the way, where fruit or emblems of the Wheel could be bought. Or peasants from Bribahr—for the frontier was close here—climbed up from the valley to sell produce to the travellers. This stage of the way was easy.

The way became steeper. The air grew a little thinner. The blossoms on the leathery-leaved bushes were brighter but smaller. Fewer peasants climbed up from the valley. Not so many of the pilgrims had the lung power to blow their musical instruments. There was nervous talk of robbers.

But still—well, this special trip must be an adventure, perhaps the great adventure. They would all return home as heroes. A little difficulty was welcome.

The hostels where the pilgrims slept for the night, if they could afford it, became rougher, the dreams of the pilgrims more troubled. The nights were filled with the sound of water forever falling—a reminder of the heights lost in the clouds above them. Next morning, the travellers would get silently on their way. Mountains are enemies of talk. Conversation was born a lowland art.

Still the road wound upward, still it followed the ill-tempered Venj. Still the travellers followed the road. And at last they were rewarded by fine views.

They were approaching Sharagatt, five thousand metres above sea level. When the clouds dispersed, views were to be had northwestward, down the tangled mountainsides, into terrifying gorges where vultures soared. Even farther, if the pilgrim was lucky and eagle-eyed, he might see the plains of Bribahr, blue with distance or possibly frost.

Before Sharagatt, a few pokey wayside shops began again. Some had nuts and mountain fruits to sell, some offered paintings of the landscape, as badly drawn as they were highly idealised. Signs appeared. A bend in the road—and yet another bend—and how tired the calf muscles suddenly seemed—and a stall selling waffles—and a glimpse of a wooden spire—and then another bend—and people—crowds—and Sharagatt, yes, that haven!—Sharagatt and the prospect of a bath and a clean bed.

Sharagatt was full of churches, some modelled on the ones in Kharnabhar. Paintings and engravings of Kharnabhar were on sale. Some claimed that, if you knew where to go, you could purchase genuine certificates to say that you had visited the Great Wheel.

For Sharagatt—considerable though the achievement was to reach it—was nothing. It was but a halt, a beginning. Sharagatt was where the real journey to Kharnabhar began. Sharagatt was as far as many travellers ever got. Promising everything, it was a milestone of lost hopes. Many people found themselves too old, too tired, too ill, or simply too poor to get further. They stayed for a day or two. Then they turned round and made their way back down to Rivenjk, at the mouth of the unforgiving river.

For Sharagatt was little past the tropical zone. To the north, further up the mountain, the climate rapidly grew more severe. Many hundreds of miles lay between Sharagatt and Kharnabhar. More than determination was needed to make that journey.

Luterin Shokerandit, Toress Lahl, and Harbin Fashnalgid slept in the Sharagatt Star Hotel. More precisely, they slept on a verandah under the broad eaves of the Sharagatt Star Hotel. For even Shokerandit's careful booking of all details in Rivenjk had not prevented a muddle at the hotel, which was fully occupied. A creaky three-decker bunk bed had been carried onto the verandah for their comfort.

Fashnalgid lay in the top bunk, with Shokerandit next and the woman at the bottom. Fashnalgid had not been pleased with the arrangement, but Shokerandit had bought them each a pipe full of occhara, the weed grown from a mountain plant, and they were full of peace. A light wagon had brought them and other privileged passengers this far. Tomorrow they would take to a sledge. Tonight was for rest. When the mists cleared over the mountain, the night sky blazed with familiar constellations, the Queen's Scar, the Fountain, the Old Pursuer.

"Toress Lahl, you see the stars? Can you name them?" Shokerandit asked in a dreamy voice.

"I name them all—stars. . . ." She gave a faint laugh.

"Then I shall climb down into your bunk and teach you."

"There are so many."

"It will take me a long time. . . ."

But he fell asleep before he could move, and even animal cries from further down the mountainside did not awaken him.

Shokerandit was up early next morning, feeling stale and tired. He pulled his chilly top clothes on before rousing Toress Lahl.

"We sleep in all our clothes from now until the end of the journey," he said. Without waiting for her to follow he was off to the stores to see to the equipment that would be needed for the month ahead. NORTH TRAVEL STORES it announced over the door, with a painting of the Great Wheel.

He was anxious. Fashnalgid, a true Uskuti, thought of Shivenink as a mountainous backwater. Luterin Shokerandit knew better. Remote though it was from the capital, Shivenink was well provided with police and informers. After Fashnalgid's killing of a soldier, both police and military would be on their track. He grieved to think of the trouble he had left with Eedap Mun Odim and Hernisarath.

Using an assumed name, he bought various necessary items at the store, and then went to inspect the team, already booked, which would transport them to Kharnabhar and the safety of his father's estates.

Fashnalgid took the processes of the morning more slowly. Directly Shokerandit was gone from the verandah, he ceased to feign sleep and climbed down into the lower bunk with Toress Lahl. Now that he had broken her spirit, she offered no resistance. The occhara had left her listless.

"Luterin will kill you when he discovers what you are doing," she said.

"Shut up and enjoy it, you hussy. I'll take care of him when the time comes." He seized her in a bear's embrace, and with his ankles wrapped about hers, parted her thighs, and thrust into her. His thrusting set the rickety bunk banging against the rail of the verandah.

Sharagatt was divided into two parts. There was Sharagatt and North Sharagatt. The two parts were close. Little more than a hundred yards and a clifflike corner of rock separated them. Sharagatt was protected by wedges of mountainside above it. On North Sharagatt cold katabatic winds poured, lowering the temperature by several degrees. The teams that made the northward journey were stabled only in North Sharagatt. Sharagatt itself would have made them soft.

It took Shokerandit two hours to see that all was arranged for the journey. He knew the folk he had to deal with. They were mountain people who called themselves Ondod, which meant—according to who was translating from their complex language—either "Spirit People" or "Spirited People."

One Ondod would be driver. With him would be his phagor slave. He had a good sledge and an eight-dog asokin team.

While he was inspecting the harness inch by inch, Toress Lahl appeared, her face pale and sullen.

"It's freezing here," she said listlessly.

He went over to the supplies he had acquired and brought back a woollen one-piece undergarment. Smiling, he handed it to her. "This is for you. Put it on now."

"Where?"

"Here." He caught her meaning, glanced at the Ondod and phagors standing there. "Oh, these people have no shame. Put your new garment on."

"I'm the one with shame," she said. But she did as she was told, while the others watched smiling.

He went back to checking everything and interrogating their Ondod driver, by name Uuundaamp, a small person with brilliant black eyes, pockmarked cheeks, and a narrow moustache that faded out into lashes across his cheekbones. He was fourteen, and had made the difficult journey many times.

As Uuundaamp took Shokerandit out to see the team, Toress Lahl joined them in her new gear, glancing at the Ondod questioningly.

"All drivers are young," Shokerandit told her. "They live on meat, and generally die young."

At the back of the store, a door opened into a yard. Here were the pens, separated by high wire. Dirty snow lay on the ground. The noise of the dogs was deafening.

Uuundaamp walked the narrow path between the pens. On either side, asokins hurled themselves at the wire, teeth snapping, saliva running from their jaws. The horned dogs stood as high as a man's hip, and were covered in thick fur, brown, white, grey, black, or mixed.

"This our team—gumtaa team—very good asokin," Uuundaamp said, pointing out the contents of one pen and glancing slyly up at Shokerandit. "Before we go here, you two give one meat chunk for lead dog, make friend together him. Then you alway friend together him. Ishto?"

"Which is the lead dog, the black one?" Shokerandit asked.

Uuundaamp nodded. "Same black one, he lead dog. He name Uuundaamp, all same me. People say, he same size me, only not so fierce."

The black asokin had finely marked and curled horns, pointing outwards at the ends. Uuundaamp's body was covered with bristling black fur. Only his chest was white, and the underside of his tail. The Ondod Uuundaamp pointed out this latter feature; it was distinctive, making Uuundaamp easy for the rest of the pack to follow.

Uuundaamp turned to Toress Lahl. "Lady, to you warning. You give one meat this Uuundaamp, like I say. Then never no more. You never give no meat other asokin, understand? These asokin, they keep rules. We obey. Ishto?"

"Ishto," she said. That mountain word of acceptance she had picked up on the way from Rivenjk.

He stared up at her, black eyes merry. "You big woman. I no feed you one piece meat. Beside, my woman, she come Kharnabhar together us. One thing more. Most important. Never you try pat these asokin, see? He take him hand like one piece meat."

Toress Lahl shivered and laughed. "I wouldn't dare try to pat them."

"We'll collect Fashnalgid and then we'll be away," Shokerandit said when he had checked everything thoroughly. The stores and provisions were adequate; the sledge would not be overloaded. He linked his arm in hers. "You are well, aren't you? It's completely useless to be ill on the trail."

"Can't we leave Fashnalgid behind?"

"No. He's okay. He'd be a good man if anything happened. Let me tell you that I am anxious in case the Oligarch's agents are on our track. Perhaps they think that if we reach my father and tell him our history, he will turn the army against the Oligarchy. Many of my father's associates are military. I checked here, and one of the sledges is booked to leave at fifteen—just an hour after us. They said that four men hired it. If we can leave earlier, all the better for us. I have a gun."

"I'm frightened. Can you trust these Ondod?"

"They're not human. They're related to the Nondads of Campannlat. He's got eight fingers on each hand—you'll see when he takes his gloves off. They tolerate the phagors but they never really ally themselves with humans. They're tricky. You must pay them and please them, or they can be difficult."

While they were talking, they were walking back from North Sharagatt to Sharagatt. The change in temperature was marked.

She clung to his arm and said resentfully, "Why did you make me strip off in front of them? You don't have to humiliate me just because I'm a slave."

He laughed. "Oh, that was part of pleasing them. They wanted to see. They'll think the better of me for it."

"I don't think the better of you for it."

"Ah, but I am lead dog."

She said viciously, "Why didn't you come into my sleeping bag? Are you weird or something? Aren't I supposed to be yours to biwack whenever you feel the urge?"

"Oh, you want me now? That's a change of tune." He gave a short angry laugh. "Then you'll be pleased about tonight's arrangements."

They collected Fashnalgid, who was drinking spirits at a wayside stall. Shokerandit then spent a while in a small shop, haggling over the price of a bright yellow-and-red striped blanket. The inevitable pattern of the Great Wheel was woven among its stripes.

"Beholder, how you waste your money!" Fashnalgid said. "I thought you'd been so careful to get all the necessary supplies already."

"I like the look of this blanket. Pretty, isn't it?"

He paid up and draped the colourful blanket over his shoulder before starting back for North Sharagatt. Other travellers took no apparent notice of him; all were dressed unpredictably against the cold mountain air. Fashnalgid looked on in amazement as, at another stall, Shokerandit paid dear for a skinned smoked kid.

A man at the North Travel Stores said that Uuundaamp was asleep. Shokerandit went alone to the makeshift dwelling carved from the rock at the back of the store, behind the asokin pens. Some Ondod were sitting on the floor eating strips of raw meat. Others slept with their women on shelves built against the cliff.

Uuundaamp was wakened, and came forward scratching his armpits and yawning, showing teeth almost as sharp as those of his animals.

"You make hard chief, start three hour too much. I no your man till fifteen."

"Sorry. Look, I want to start soonest. I bring you present, ishto?"

He threw the smoked baby goat on the floor. Uuundaamp immediately sat down on the floor and called to his friends. He pulled out a knife and beckoned to Shokerandit with it. "All come eat, friend. Gumtaa. Then make quick start."

As everyone gathered round, Uuundaamp called to his wife as an afterthought. She rolled off the shelf she had shared and came forward, bundled in bedding. All that was visible of her was a round face with black eyes much like Uuundaamp's. She made no attempt to join the greedy circle of men. Instead, she stood meekly behind Uuundaamp, deftly catching a scraggy slice of meat when he tossed it to her over his shoulder.

While Shokerandit chewed his meat, he observed the hands of the men. They were narrow and sinewy, and bore eight fingers. The blunt clawlike nails were uniformly black, gleaming with filth and fat lodged under them.

"Gumtaa," said Uuundaamp, with his cheeks bulging.

"Gumtaa," agreed Shokerandit.

"Gumtaa," agreed the other Ondod. The woman, being a woman, was not called upon to say whether she thought the food was good or not.

Soon, nothing but bones and horns were left of the kid. Uuundaamp rose immediately, wiping his hands on his suit of fur. "By way, chief," he said, still chewing, "this horrid bag behind me with belly full of gas and babies is my woman. Name Moub. You can forget. She come together us. You no mind."

"She is as welcome as she is beautiful, Uuundaamp. I am carrying this blanket for myself, which I did not intend to give away, but in view of Moub's loveliness, I wish you to give it to her as a present."

"Loobiss. You give, chief. Then she not lose it. She kiss you."

So Shokerandit presented the yellow-and-red striped blanket to Moub.

"Loobiss," she said. "Far too good for any bag belong this vile Uuundaamp." She hopped nimbly forward and kissed Shokerandit with her full and greasy lips.

"Gumtaa. Any time you want biwack, chief, you use Moub. She look horrid but she got all that stuff there, ishto?"

"Loobiss!" Their friendship had been properly cemented. Happiness swept through Shokerandit, as he recalled sleigh rides with his mother when he was a child, and playing with Ondod children on their estates. His mother had always found the Ondod coarse and beastly, perhaps because of the peculiar conventions between the sexes, which relied on insult. Later, he and his friends had visited a shack on the edge of the caspiarn forests. His first sexual experiences had been with Ondod females. He remembered a rotund girl called Ipaak. To Ipaak he had always been "the pink stinker."

Stern discipline for asokins, stern discipline for travellers. That was the rule for journeys between Kharnabhar and the outside world.

Uuundaamp sat at the front of the sledge with the whip, Moub

lumpish just behind him. The phagor, Bhryeer, rode at the back, standing upright to steer the long vehicle, often jumping off to left or right,
sometimes pushing when the incline was steep enough for the asokins
to require help. The three humans sat astride the tarpaulin-covered
supplies, on one side or the other according to the direction of the wind.

It was easy to fall off the sledge. An eye had to be kept on the driver,
for a hint of which way they might be turning. Sometimes Uuundaamp
could hardly be seen for the snow that fell in flurries from the heights
of the chain above them. They had crossed the treacherous Venj by
wooden bridge, and were now proceeding on a roughly north-north-
easterly course under the high spine of Shivenink, where ice prevailed
above the ten-thousand-metre line for all of the Great Year.

Even when the air was clear of snow, the breath of the dogs rose like
steam and concealed them from the passengers. The team included one
bitch, to keep the other seven doing their utmost. The dogs frequently
broke wind at the start of a new lap of the journey. Their panting
could be heard above the shrill of the metal runners. Otherwise, sounds
were muffled. There was no visibility, except for white walls on either
side. The smell of the dogs and of stale clothes became part of the
scene. Monotony dulled the sense of danger. Weariness, the reflections
of the snow, reveries that ran half-formed through the mind, these
filled the days.

The asokins were attached to the sledge by twenty feet of leather
harness. They were allowed to rest for ten minutes every three hours.
Then all eight would lie down except for Uuundaamp the leader. The
man Uuundaamp was at least as close to his asokins as he was to Moub.
They were his life.

During the break, Uuundaamp did not rest. He and Moub would
walk restlessly about, studying natural phenomena—the shape of clouds,
the flight of birds, any nuance of change in weather, tracks of animals,
sounds and signs of landslides.

Sometimes they met pilgrims coming or going, making the great
journey on foot. There were other sledges on the route, bells ringing.
Once they were caught behind a slow herring-train and forced to tag
along slowly before the vehicle moved into a passing place. The
herring-train was a land version of the herring-coach. It bore barrels of
pickled fish up to the distant rendezvous.

The asokins barked furiously whenever they met with another
vehicle, but the rival drivers never moved a muscle in greeting.

The night's break also had its set pattern. Uuundaamp pulled the
team off the track in selected places he knew about. He then immediately went about settling the dogs, which had to be staked
separately and away from the sledge, so that they did not eat its skins.
Each asokin was fed two pounds of raw meat every third day; they
worked best when starved. But each night they got a herring apiece,

which Uuundaamp threw to each asokin in turn, starting with Uuun-daamp. They caught the fish in midair, swallowing it at a gulp. The bitch was last to be fed. The lead dog slept some way from the rest of the team. If snow fell during the night, the dogs remained under it, in small caverns carved by their own heat. Bhryeer the phagor slept with them.

At a night's stop, everything had to be made ready for the evening meal inside fifteen minutes.

"It's not possible. What's the point?" Fashnalgid complained.

"The point is that it's possible and must be done," Shokerandit said. "Stretch the tent, hold tight."

They were stiff with cold. Their noses were peeling, their cheeks blackened by frost.

The sledge had to be unloaded. The tent was pitched over it and secured, which often entailed a battle against wind. Skins were stretched across the sledge. On this, the five of them slept, to be off the ground. Belongings required overnight were arranged nearby: food, stove, knives, oil lamp. Although the temperature in the tent generally remained below zero, they found themselves sweating in the confined space, after the cold of the journey.

When Uuundaamp entered on the first night, he found the three humans quarrelling.

"No more speak. Be good. Anger bring smrtaa."

"I can't stand four weeks of this," Fashnalgid said.

"If you disobey him, he will simply leave," Shokerandit said. "All he asks is that you put your personality away to sleep for the journey. The cold will not allow quarrels, or death will strike."

"Let the sherb leave."

"We'd die here without him—can't you understand that?"

"Occhara soon, soon," said Uuundaamp, nudging Fashnalgid. He handed Moub a pair of silver foxes to cook. They came from traps he had set on his previous journey.

A pleasant fug arose in the tent. The meat smelt good. They ate with filthy hands, afterwards drinking melted snow water from a communal mug.

"Food ishto?" asked Moub.

"Gumtaa," they said.

"She bad cook," Uuundaamp said, as he lit up pipes of occhara and handed them round. The lamp was providently extinguished and they smoked in peace. The howl of the wind seemed to die away. Good feelings overcame them. The smoke filtering through their nostrils was the breath of a mysterious better life. They were the children of the mountain and it had them in its care. No harm comes to those who have eaten silver fox. For all the differences between men and women, and between men and men, all have this good thing in common—that the divine smoke pours from their noses, and perhaps from eyes and ears and other orifices. Sleep itself is but another orifice in the mountain god. Sometimes in sleep men become the dream of the silver fox.

In the morning, when they struggled in the dull, bitter air to fold the tent, Toress Lahl said secretly to Shokerandit, "How degraded you are and how I hate you! Last night, you biwacked with that bag of lard, Moub. I heard you. I felt the sledge tremble."

"I was being courteous to Uuundaamp. Pure courtesy. Not pleasure."

He had discovered that the Ondod female was far gone with child.

"No doubt your courtesy will be rewarded with a disease."

Uuundaamp came up smiling with the two silver fox tails. "Carry these at teeth. Gumtaa. Keep off cold from face."

"Loobiss. Have you one for Fashnalgid?"

"That man, he got tail grow along face," said Uuundaamp, indicating the captain's moustache, and laughing merrily.

"At least he means to be kind," Toress Lahl said, hesitatingly placing the tail between her teeth to protect her chapped nose and cheeks.

"Uuundaamp is kind. And when we stop tonight you must be kind to him. Return his favour."

"Oh, no . . . Luterin . . . not that, please. I thought you had some feeling for me."

He turned savagely on her. "I have some feeling for getting us safe to Kharnabhar. I know the conventions of these people and these journeys and you don't. It's a code, a matter of survival. Stop thinking you are so special."

Bitterly hurt, she said, "So you don't care, I suppose, that Fashnalgid rapes me whenever your back is turned."

He dropped the tent and grasped her jacket.

"Are you lying to me? When did he do it? Tell me when. Then and when else. How many times?"

He listened bleakly as she told him.

"Very well, Toress Lahl." He spoke in no more than a whisper, his face hard. "He has broken the honour that existed between us as officers. We need him on this journey. But when we get to my father's home, I shall kill him. You understand? For now, you say nothing."

Without further words, they loaded up the sledge. Smrtaa—retribution. A prominent feature of life in these parts. Uuundaamp was harnessing up the dogs, and in a few minutes they were once more on their way through the mist, Shokerandit and Toress Lahl biting on their fox tails.

The unsleeping machines of the Avernus still recorded events below, and transmitted them automatically back to Earth. But the few humans surviving on the Observation Station took little interest in that primary function; their own primary function was to survive. Their numbers were so far down—lowered by disease as well as fighting—that defence became a less pressing need.

Much time was spent establishing tribes and tribal territory, to obviate pitched battles. In neutral territory between tribes, the obscene pudendolls survived, to become something sacroscanct, something between gods and demons.

Though a measure of "peace" descended, the earlier destruction of food synthesising plants meant that cannibalism was still prevalent. There was almost no meat but human meat. The heavy tabus against this practice fell with great force upon the delicately trained sensibilities of the Avernians. To descend to barbarism and worse within a generation was more than their psyches could easily endure.

The tribes became matriarchies, while many of the younger men, mainly adolescent, developed multiple personalities. As many as ten different personalities could house themselves in one body, differing in inclination, age, and sex, as well as habits. Ascetic vegetarians were common, living an eye's blink away from stone age savages, tempestuous dancers from lawgivers.

The complex separation from nature undergone by the Avernian colonisers had now reached its limits. Not only did individuals not know each other: they were now strangers to themselves.

This adaptation to stress situations was not for everyone. When severe fighting first broke out, a number of technicians left the Avernus. They stole a craft from one of the Observation Station's maintenance bays and fled. They landed on Aganip.

Tempting though the green, white, and blue planet of Helliconia looked, its danger was known to all. Aganip occupied a special place in the mythology of Avernus, for it was here, many centuries ago, that Earth's colonising starship had established a base while the Avernus was being constructed.

Aganip was a lifeless planet, with an atmosphere consisting almost entirely of carbon dioxide, together with a little nitrogen. But the old base still stood, and offered something of a welcome.

The escapers built a small dome. There they lived in restricted circumstances. At first they sent out signals to Earth and then—being naturally unwilling to wait two thousand years for an answer—to the Avernus. But the Avernus had its own problems and did not reply.

The escapers had failed to understand the nature of mankind: that it, like the elephant and the common daisy, is no more and no less than a part and function of a living entity. Separated from that entity, humans, being more complex than elephants and daisies, have little chance of flourishing. The signals continued automatically for a long while.

No one heard.

XII

KAKOOL ON THE TRAIL

And when that massed human spirit we have called empathy reached out across space and communicated with the gossies of Helliconia, what then? Did nothing important happen—or did something unprecedentedly magnificent, something quantally different, happen?

The answer to that question will perhaps remain forever clouded in conjecture; mankind has its umwelt, however bravely it strives to enlarge that confining universe of its perceptions. To become part of a greater umwelt may prove biologically impossible. Or perhaps not. It must be sufficient to admit that if something unprecedentedly magnificent, something quantally different, happened, it happened in a greater umwelt than mankind's.

If it happened, then it was a cooperation, and perhaps a cooperation of various factors not unlike the cooperation forced on differing individuals on the trail to Kharnabhar.

If it happened, then it left an effect. That effect can be traced by looking at the contrasting fates of Earth, where Gaia resided, and New Earth, which was without a tutelary biospheric spirit. . . .

To start with the case of Earth, after which New Earth was named:

The intermission between the two postnuclear ice ages has been understood as the swing of a pendulum. Gaia was trying to regulate her clock. But it was less simple than that, just as the biosphere was less simple than the mechanism of a clock. The truth may be put more accurately. Gaia had been almost terminally ill. She was now convalescent, and subject to relapses.

Or, abandoning the dangers of personifying a complex process, it may be said that the carbon dioxide released by the deep oceans initiated a period during which the ice retreated. At the end of the period of greenhouse heating, there was an overshoot of the return to normal, as the whole biosphere and its ruined biosystems strove for adjustment. The ice returned.

This time, the cold was less severe, the spread of the ice caps less extensive, and the duration of the cold briefer. The period was marked by a series of oscillations, in the way that a clock's pendulum gradually slows to a stationary median position. It was a time of discomfort for many generations of the thin-spread human race. In the remission in the 6900s, for instance, there was a small war in what had once been India, followed by famine and pestilence.

Could that trivial war be likened to a convalescent's tantrum?

The restlessness of the period awoke a corresponding restlessness in the human spirit. Fences were no longer going to be possible. The old world of fences had died, and was never going to be rebuilt.

"We belong to Gaia." And with the declaration went the understanding that human beings were not exactly Gaia's best allies. To see those best allies, a microscope was needed.

Throughout the ages—and long before the invention and development of nuclear weapons—there had been those who prophesied that the world would end because of man's wickedness. Such prophecies were always believed, no matter how many times they had been proved wrong in the past. There was a wish for, as well as a fear of, punishment.

Once nuclear weapons were invented, the prophecies gained plausibility, although now they were couched in lay terms rather than religious ones.

Evidence, the more convincing because governments tried to suppress it, proved that the world could be ended at the touch of a button.

Eventually, the button was touched. The bombs came.

But human wickedness proved too feeble to end the world. Set against that wickedness were industrious microbes of which wickedness took little cognisance.

Large trees and plants disappeared. The carnivores, including man, disappeared from the scene for a while. They were superfluous to requirements. These large beings were merely the superstars in Earth's drama. The dramatists themselves still lived. Under the soil, on the *seabeds of the continental shelves, thick microbial life continued Gaia's story, undisturbed by radioactivity or increased ultraviolet. The ecosystems of unicellular life were rebuilding nature. They were Gaia's pulse.*

Gaia regenerated herself. Mankind was a function in that regeneration. The human spirit was triggered into a quantum leap in consciousness.

As nature had formed a diverse unity, so now did consciousness. It was no longer possible for a man or woman merely to feel or merely to think; there was only empathic thinkfeel. Head and heart were one.

One immediate effect was a mistrust of power.

There were people who understood what the greed for power in all its forms had done to the world. That chill faded from the mind. Humanity began truly to be adult and to live and enjoy with adult comprehension. Men and women looked about at the territory they happened to occupy and no longer asked, "What can we get out of this land?" Instead, they asked, "What best experience can we have on this land?"

With this new consciousness came less exploitive ties and more ties everywhere, an abundance of new relationships. The ancient structure of family faded into new superfamilies. All mankind became a looseknit superorganism. It did not happen at once, nor did it happen to everyone. There were those who could not undergo the metamorphosis. But their genes were recessive and their strain would die away. They were the insensible in a new world of new empathies. They were the only ones not smiling.

When more generations passed, the new race could feel itself to be the consciousness of Gaia. The ecosystems of unicellular life had been given a voice—had, in a sense, invented a voice for themselves.

Even as this was happening, the convalescence of the biosphere continued. While humanity evolved, an entirely new type of being was born to the Earth.

Many phyla had vanished for ever. The cummerbund of tropical forest with its various myriad lives had withered from the equator under the nuclear onslaught. Its fragile soils had been lost into the oceans and could not be recovered. Now a replacement of a startlingly different kind came forth.

The new thing was not born of the oceans. It came from the snows and frosts of the arctic. It fed on ultraviolet radiation and it began moving southward as the glaciers began a fresh retreat northwards.

The first men to meet the new thing fell back in astonishment.

White polyhedrons were slowly advancing. Some of the shapes were no larger than giant tortoises. Others reached as high as a man's head.

Beyond their various planes, they had no features. No visible means of movement. No arms or tentacles. No mouths of any kind. No orifices. No eyes or ears. No appendages whatsoever. Just white polyhedrons. Some sides were perhaps less white than others.

The polyhedrons left no track. They sailed where they would. They moved slowly, but nothing could stop them, although brave men tried to. They were christened geonauts.

The geonauts multiplied and sailed the Earth.

The geonauts provided a new wonder. The old wonder remained. The great conchlike auditoria were still scattered across Earth, maintained by androids who had found no other function, having been programmed to none.

On the holoscreens, the spring of the Great Year turned to summer just as the snows of Earth were dying. The history of the beautiful MyrdemInggala, known as the Queen of Queens, was familiar to all. The new race found much to learn from that thousand-year-old story.

They attended. They gloried in the benevolent effect their empathy had on the gossies. But their own new world was calling urgently, with a fresh beauty that could not be resisted. A thousand years of spring was theirs.

But what of that unprecedentedly magnificent, quantally different something—that empathic linking of two worlds? Were its traces visible to those capable of looking for signs?

So to the case of New Earth:

On the other planets also, some slight recovery had been made. There were no Mother Natures on the dead worlds of Mars and Venus. Their surface temperatures were generally intolerable, their atmospheres coffins full of carbon dioxide. Yet the unfortunate colonists who had settled there managed to survive, by wits and by technology.

These Outlanders had succumbed to a psychosis regarding Earth. Their generations were smothered by cosmic anomie. To Earth they would never return. They felt themselves dispossessed.

When advanced technology was again within their power—and they were quicker to solve technical problems than social ones—they built a starship and set off for the nearest planet which mankind had colonised earlier, so-called New Earth.

This was an all-male expedition. The men left their women at home, preferring to take with them on their journey svelte robotic partners, styled as abstract ideals of womanhood. They enjoyed coupling with these perfect metal images.

New Earth retained breatheable air. Its one small ocean remained surrounded by desert—desert and inhospitable mountain ranges. There was a spaceport on the equator, with a city nearby. The spaceport had not been in use for ages. Nor had the city grown; the roads from it led nowhere. People lived in the city knowing nothing of that great ocean of space above their roofs.

The New Earthers were like neutered animals. Something vital and rebellious had gone from their spirits. They had no aspirations, no feeling for the immensities of space, no love for the world that was their home, no tremulous intimations at dawn and sunset. The degenerate language they spoke had no conditional tense. Music had been entirely lost as an art.

Hardly surprising. Their world was without spirit.

These New Earthers occasionally visited the shores of their salt sea. The visits were not to refresh themselves but to collect cartloads of the kelp which grew in the sea. The kelp was one of the few living things on the planet. The people of New Earth spread it on their fields, growing cereals brought from Earth ages previously.

They did not dream because they existed on a world which had never nurtured a Gaia figure. But they had a myth. They believed that they lived in a giant egg, of which the desert was the yolk and the cloudless sky was the shell. One day, said the myth, the sky would crack and fall. Then they would be born. They would acquire yellow wings and white tails, and they would fly to a better place, where trees like giant seaweeds grew everywhere in pleasant vales and it always rained.

When the Outlanders arrived, they did not like New Earth much.

They flew to examine the neighbouring planet, like New Earth the size of a terrestrial planet.

Whereas New Earth was a world of sand, its sister was a world of ice.

An observation drone was sent out to take computer-corrected photographs of the surface and of what lay below the ice.

It was a forbidding world. Glaciers engulfed mountain ranges. Trackless snowfields filled the lowlands. Helliconia in the grip of apastron winter was never as dead as this rigid globe.

The reconnaissance photographs showed frozen oceans beneath the ice. More. They showed the ruins of great cities and the routes of astonishly wide roads.

The Outlanders descended to the surface. Below an icefield remains of a vast building could be glimpsed. Fragments of it lay about the surface; some fragments had been carried far from source by the glacier. By blasting, the men got down to a sector of the ruins.

One of the first artefacts they brought up was a head, carved in a durable artificial material. The head was of an inhuman creature. In a slender tapering skull four eyes were set, lidless. Small feathers lay under the eyes. A short beak counterbalanced the backward thrust of the skull.

One side of the head was blackened.

"It's beautiful," a robot partner said.

"Ugly, you mean."

"It was once beautiful to someone."

Dating was not difficult. The city had been destroyed 3.2 thousand years earlier, at a time when New Earth was being strenuously colonised.

The whole planet had been destroyed by nuclear bombardment, and the avian race had perished with it.

The Outlanders called this planet Armageddon. They remained on the frigid surface for some while, discussing what should be done, spellbound by melancholy.

One of the powerful leaders spoke. "I think we might agree that we have found here on Armageddon an answer to one of the questions which has plagued mankind for many generations.

"How was it that when man went into space, he found no other intelligent species? It was always assumed that the galaxy would be full of life. Not so. How was it that there were scarcely any other planets like Earth?

"Well, we do realise that Earth is a pretty unusual place, where a number of fine specifications are met. Take just one example—the amount of oxygen in Earth's atmosphere is close to twenty-one percent. If it was twenty-five percent or over, forest fires would be started by lightning—even damp vegetation would burn. On New Earth, the oxygen percentage is eighteen; there are no plants to lock away the carbon dioxide and release oxygen molecules. No wonder the poor boobies there live in a dream.

"Nevertheless, statistics suggest that there must be other planets like Earth. Maybe Armageddon was one. Suppose a race with a wide-ranging diet reaches supremacy and dominates the planet, as happened on Earth before the nuclear war. That race must use technology to do so—from the club and bow-and-arrow onwards. It masters the laws of nature.

"The time comes when technology is advanced enough for the race to choose alternatives. It can put out into space, or it can destroy its enemies with nuclear weapons."

"Suppose there are no enemies on the planet?" someone called.

"Then the race invents them. The pressure of competition which technologies generate makes enemies necessary, as we know. And there's my point. At that stage, poised for a whole new way of life, no longer to be confined to the planet of its birth, on the brink of major discoveries —right then that race is set the big examination question: Can I develop the international social skills required to bring my aggression under control? Can I excel myself and make a lasting truce with my enemies, so that we throw away these vile weapons for good and all?

"You see what I mean? If the race fails the exam, it destroys its planet and itself, and shows that it was unfit to cross that vital quarantine area space provides.

"*Armageddon was unfit. Its people failed the exam. They destroyed themselves.*"

"*But you're saying everyone everywhere was unfit. We never have found another space-going race.*"

The leader laughed. "*We're still only on Earth's doorstep, don't forget. Nobody is going to come looking for us until they know we're trustworthy.*"

"*And are we trustworthy?*"

Amid general laughter, the leader said, "*Let's tackle Armageddon first. Maybe we can get the old place going again, if we press the right button.*"

Further surveys showed what the world had once been. One notable feature was a considerable high-latitude sea which—before the nuclear disaster—had been only partially ice-covered. After the disaster, atmospheric contamination had cooled the umbrella of air, leaving the water of the high-latitude sea warmer than its overlying air. The air was in consequence heated from below, and moisture drawn upwards. Violent high-latitude storms had resulted, probably enough in themselves to finish off any survivors of the nuclear strike. Plentiful snow fell on middle-altitude ground, a plateau once covered by urbanisation. The major glaciation which set in became self-sustaining.

The Outlanders decided to drop what the leader had called vile weapons on the frozen high-altitude sea, in order to "*get things started*" again. But the ice wilderness remained an ice wilderness. Here, the local tutelary spirit, the biospheric gestalt, was dead.

They were now almost out of fuel. They decided to return to New Earth and conquer it. Their discoveries on Armageddon had provided them with a strategy. Their idea was that one—just one—thermonuclear device dropped over New Earth's north pole would cause heavy rainfall, transforming the planet. The sea could be enlarged; the local zombies could make themselves useful by cutting canals. More kelp could be encouraged to grow, and eventually more oxygen released into the air. The calculations looked good. To the Outlanders, the decision to try just one more nuclear bomb was a sane one.

So they climbed into their ship, leaving Armageddon to its eons of frost.

For the people who lived on New Earth, one part at least of their only myth came true. The sky cracked and fell.

What were the vital differences here? Why could New Earth never recover, while Earth flourished and put forth new forms like the geonauts?

When the terrestrials developed their empathic link with the gossies of Helliconia, a new factor entered the universe. The terrestrials,

*whether or not they knew it, were acting as a focus of consciousness for
the whole biosphere. The empathic link was not a weak thing. It was a
psychic equivalent of magnetism or gravity; it bound the two planets.*

*A more startling way of putting it would be to say that Gaia com-
municated directly with her lusty sister, the Original Beholder.*

*Of course it is speculation. Mankind cannot see into the greater
umwelts about him. But he can train his ample senses to look for evidence. All the evidence suggests that Gaia and the Original Beholder
made contact through their progeny's projecting the link. One can only
guess at the ripples of shock that contact caused—unless the second ice
age and its ripples of remission provide evidence of that contact.*

*It is speculation that Gaia's recovery was prompted by the refresh-
ment of encountering a sister spirit in the void nearby.*

*There were the geonauts: serene, calm, apparently amiable, a new
thing. They can be understood not as an evolutionary freak but as an
inspiration born of a fresh and powerful friendship . . .*

*While on Helliconia, the august processes of the seasons were in
undeniable stride.*

In the northern hemisphere, small summer was nearly over. Frosty
nights foretold colder nights ahead. In the winding passes of the Shivenink Chain, frost already ruled, and the living creatures who ventured
there were subject to that rule.

It was morning. A screaming windstorm, the frigid breath from the
pole. The supplies were being stacked away. The phagor and Uuundaamp were harnessing up their asokins. Seventeen days had elapsed
since leaving Sharagatt. They had seen no sign that they were being
pursued.

Of the three passengers Shokerandit had fared best. Toress Lahl had
lapsed into speechlessness. She lay in the tent at night as if dead.
Fashnalgid seldom spoke, except to curse. Their eyebrows and lashes
were frosty white within a minute of leaving shelter, their cheekbones
black with frostbite.

The last section of the trail ran above six thousand metres. To their
right, in fuming cloud, was a solid mountain of ice. Visibility was down
to a few feet.

Uuundaamp came to Shokerandit, eyes merry in his frosted face.
"Today soft going," he shouted. "Downhill through tunnel. You
'member tunnel, chief?"

"Noonat Tunnel?" It was an effort to talk in the wind.

"Yaya, Noonat. Tonight we be there. Takit drink, bit meal, occhara,
gumtaa."

"Gumtaa. Toress tired."

The Ondod shook his head. "She soon make meat together asokin.

No much biwack gumtaa no more, eh?" He laughed with closed mouth.

Shokerandit sensed the man had something more to say. Simultaneously they turned their backs on the others working at lashing up the sledge. Uuundaamp folded his arms.

"Your friend got tail grow along face." One quick sly look from his profile.

"Fashnalgid?"

"Your friend got tail along face. Team no like him. Team give plenty kakool. Make bad time. We lose that sherb in Noonat Tunnel, ishto?"

"Has he been molesting Moub?"

"Mole sting? No, he stick him prodo up Moub las' night again. Biwack the bag, ishto? She no like. She full baby Uuundaamps." He laughed. "So we lose in Tunnel, you see."

"I'm sorry, Uuundaamp. Loobiss for telling me—but no smrtaa in Tunnel, please. I speak him friend in Noonat. No more biwack your Moub."

"Chief, you better lose that friend. Else big kakool, I see." He laughed and scowled, tapping his forehead, then turned abruptly on his heel.

The Ondod rarely showed anger. But they were treacherous—that Shokerandit knew. Uuundaamp remained friendly; without at least an appearance of friendship, the journey could never be made; but he had lost face by telling a human of his wife's disgrace.

Shokerandit had been invited to copulate with Moub. Such was Ondod courtesy, and Shokerandit would have offended by declining the invitation. But Fashnalgid had done it uninvited, and had broken Ondod law. Ondod laws were simple and stark; transgression meant death, smrtaa. Fashnalgid would be killed without compunction. If Uuundaamp had decided to lose Fashnalgid in Noonat Tunnel, Shokerandit's plea would count for nothing.

Both Toress Lahl and Fashnalgid shot him curious looks from their red-rimmed eyes. He gave them no word, though deeply troubled. Uuundaamp was always watching, and would see if Shokerandit passed Fashnalgid a warning. That would count as kakool.

The shaggy bulk of Bhryeer emerged from the murk, trudging down the length of the sledge. His eyes gleamed cerise as he swung his head momentarily to contemplate them. His morose gaze settled on Shokerandit. There was no interpreting the phagor's expression.

He clicked his milt up one ice-encrusted nostril and then shouted above the wind, "Team ready go. Climb your plaze. Hol' tight."

Harbin Fashnalgid pulled a flask from inside his skins, thrust the neck between his flaking lips, and swallowed. As he stowed the flask away, Shokerandit said, "Be advised, don't drink. Hold tight, as he said."

"Abro Hakmo Astab!" Fashnalgid growled. He belched and turned away.

Toress Lahl looked appealingly at Shokerandit. He shook his head severely, mutely saying, Don't give up, bite tightly on the silver fox tail.

As they took their places on the sledge, they could just see the bundles that were Uuundaamp and Moub, the latter wrapped in her bright blanket. The dogs were invisible. Uuundaamp brought the long whip forward over his head. *Ipsssssisiii*. Then the first squeal of the steel runners as they chastised the snow. The place where they had spent the night, marked by yellow stains of human and asokin urine, was immediately lost.

Within an hour, they were moving downhill towards Noonat Tunnel. Shokerandit felt the sickness of fear in his throat. He would lose face himself by allowing an Ondod to kill a fellow human, whatever the justification. His anger turned against both Uuundaamp and Harbin Fashnalgid. The man was next to him, back hunched in misery. No communication passed between them.

Their speed increased. They were moving at perhaps five miles an hour. Shokerandit kept staring ahead, squeezing his eyes between cheeks and brow. Only the eternal grey to be seen, although somewhere above was a suspicion of light. Spectral white trees flitted by.

Beyond the customary noises, the sledge creaks, the whistle of whip, the dog farts, the crack of ice, the wind song, another noise grew, hollow, threatening. It was the sound of the wind keening in Noonat Tunnel. Moub answered it with blasts on a curled goat horn.

The Ondod were giving warning of their presence to other teams which might be coming in the other direction.

The suspicion of light overhead was abruptly cut off. They were in the tunnel. The phagor gave a hoarse cry and applied the rear cross-beam brake to slow their progress. Uuundaamp's whip made a different note as he flicked it just before the nose of his lead dog who bore his name, to slow their pace.

A freezing wind struck them like a solid object. This tunnel through the mountainside was a shortcut to the Noonat station. The road, by which heavier traffic or marching men went, was some miles longer but less dangerous. In the tunnel, there was always the chance of two sledges meeting head on, the traces of the teams entangling hopelessly as the rival asokins fought to the death, a fatal knife fight taking place. Since the tunnel had been cut to show an almost circular cross-section, it was theoretically possible for teams to pass by driving partway up opposite walls, but this chance was so remote that most drivers spurred onwards in terror, screaming warning as they went.

There were nine miles of tunnel. What with rockfalls and the force of the wind, the sledge swayed from one side to the other like a rudderless ship.

The attempt by Uuundaamp to slow down caused greater vibrations. Fashnalgid cursed. The driver and his woman slid to either side of the sledge's front and stuck heels into the snow to increase the braking effect.

Bhryeer leaned forward and shouted to Fashnalgid, "You bottle juzz now drop out."

"My bottle? Where?"

As Fashnalgid leant forward over the side of the sledge, looking where the phagor indicated, the phagor struck him a blow across the small of his back. Fashnalgid fell with a cry, landing on hands and knees and rolling over in the snow.

Immediately, there was a shrill cry from Uuundaamp and he lashed on the asokins. The phagor pulled off the rear brake. They sizzled forward, aided by the slope.

Fashnalgid was already on his feet. Already he was fading into the dimness. He began to run. Shokerandit yelled to him to come on. The wind roared, the Ondod shrieked, the runners screamed. Fashnalgid was catching up. As he came level with the rear of the sledge, his face contorted with effort, the phagor lifted an arm to strike another blow.

To be alone in the long tunnel was to face certain death. Other sledges, thrusting through the gloom, would simply run a man over. This was Ondod smrtaa.

Shouting at the top of his voice, Shokerandit drew his revolver and ran back on his knees over the loaded sledge. He clamped the muzzle against the phagor's long skull.

"I'll blast your sherbing harneys out." The silver fox tail fell from his mouth and was gone.

The phagor cowered back.

"Throw the brake on."

Bhryeer did so, but the downhill impetus was such that it made little difference, beyond sending a spume of fine snow over the running man.

Still the whip whistled and the driver shrieked at his team. Fashnalgid was falling back, mouth open, blackened face distorted. His never-too-certain will was failing him.

"Don't give up," yelled Shokerandit, stretching out a hand to the captain.

Making a new effort, Fashnalgid increased speed. His boots drummed on the snow as he slowly drew level with the rear of the sledge. Bhryeer cowered out of harm's way. The wind shrilled.

Clutching a cord securing the tent with one gloved hand, Shokerandit leant forward and extended his other hand. He shouted encouragement. Fashnalgid was tiring. The sledge was still gaining speed. The two men stared into each other's wide eyes. Their gloved hands touched.

"Yes," yelled Shokerandit. "Yes, leap aboard, man, fast!"

Their grips locked. Just as Shokerandit tugged, Uuundaamp gave a swerve to the left, flicking the runners of the sledge up the sloping side of the tunnel, and almost overturning his vehicle. Shokerandit was flung free. He clutched at and missed a runner as it sizzled past his face. Fashnalgid stumbled over him and they sprawled flat.

When they picked themselves up, the sledge was disappearing in the dimness.

"Lousy biwacking drivers," Fashnalgid said, bending forward and trying to get his breath back. "Animals."

"That was deliberate. That's Ondod smrtaa—vengeance. Because of your ape tricks with the woman." He had to turn his back to the wind flow to speak.

"That stinking tub of lard? He said himself that she was not good enough even for an asokin to enjoy." He bent double, panting.

"That's how they talk, you fool. Now listen, and take in what I say. This tunnel is death. Another sledge may come through at any moment, from one end or the other. There's no way we could stop it, except with our bodies. We have about seven miles to go, I'd guess, and we'd better do it fast."

"How about going back and taking the road?"

"That way's about thirty miles. We've no provisions and we'd still be walking when dark fell. We would be dead. Now, are you going to run? Because I am."

Fashnalgid straightened up, groaning. He said, "Thanks for trying to save me."

"Astab you, you arrogant fool. Why couldn't you have tried to obey the system?"

Luterin Shokerandit started to run. At least it was downhill. His knee hurt from his fall. He listened for the sound of another sledge but heard only the wind roaring in his ears.

The footsteps of Fashnalgid echoed behind him. He never looked back. All his faculties were concentrated on getting through the tunnel to Noonat.

When he thought he could run no further, he made himself keep on. Once there was a gleam of light to one side. In relief, he halted and went to look. Part of the rock of the outer wall had fallen away, revealing daylight. Nothing could be seen but cloud and, just beyond arm's reach, a stalactite of ice. He threw a piece of rock into the void, listened, but never heard it fall.

Fashnalgid caught up with him, blowing hard.

"Let's get out through this hole."

"It's a sheer mountainside."

"Never mind. Bribahr somewhere down there. Civilisation. Not like this place."

"You'll kill yourself."

As Fashnalgid was trying to lever his body through the hole in the rock, a distant horn announced an oncoming sledge—this one also arriving from the south. Shokerandit saw a light looming. He pressed into the natural alcove, forcing himself back against the jagged rock close to Fashnalgid.

Next moment, a long black sledge shot by, teamed by ten dogs. A bell dangling over the driver jangled madly. Several men sat aboard, twelve possibly, all crouching masked against the cold. It was by in a flash.

"Military," Fashnalgid said. "Could they be after us?"

"After you, you mean. What does it matter? With them travelling ahead, clearing the way, this is our best chance to get out of the tunnel safely. Unless you like thousand-foot jumps, you'll come too."

He started off again. After a while, the running became automatic. He could feel the knock of his lungs against his ribs. Ice formed on his chin. The lids of his slitted eyes froze. He lost count of time.

When the brightness came, it assailed him. He could not prise open his eyes. He jogged on before realising that he had at last left the tunnel. Sobbing, he staggered to one side and clung to a boulder. There he lay, panting as if he would never stop. Two sledges passed nearby, horns blowing, but he did not look up.

A lump of falling snow forced him into action. He scrubbed his face with the snow and peered ahead. The light still seemed brilliant. The wind had dropped. There was a break in the cloud. Only a short distance away, people were strolling, smoking veronikanes, wearing blankets. A woman was buying something at a stall. An ancient bowed man was driving horned sheep down the street. A welcoming sign said PILGRIM LODGE: *No Ondods*. He had reached Noonat.

Noonat was the last stop before Kharnabhar. It was nothing more than a halt in the wilds, a place where teams could be changed. But it had something else to offer. The trail between Kharnabhar, Northern Sharagatt, and Rivenjk followed the contours of the chain, taking every advantage of the protection against the polar winds which the mountains provided. But at Noonat there was a junction, and a road led westward, over the great falls and valleys and plateaux of the western chain, to enter at last into the plains of Bribahr. Kharnabhar was now nearer than those plains. But the plains were nearer than Rivenjk, by a long measure.

The state of hostility which existed between Uskutosh and Bribahr might account for an increased number of military uniforms visible in

Noonat, and for the fact that an imposing new wooden building, which
would face westwards, was being built.

Shokerandit was almost too exhausted to take much care for himself.
But he had the presence of mind to stagger behind the boulder that
had sheltered him and follow a footpath uphill until he came to a
stone-built goat shed. He climbed in with the goats and fell asleep.

When he woke, he felt refreshed, and was angry with himself for
wasting time. He could not greatly care what had happened to Fashnalgid, so great was his need to find Toress Lahl and to get the sledge
on to Kharnabhar. Once there, his problems would be over.

The straggle of Noonat lay below him. Its poor houses clung to the
mountainside like burrs to an animal's flank. Most of the houses took
advantage of eldawon trees, a species with thin multiple trunks, and
cowered against them or were actually built into them. Since most of
the houses were constructed from the timber of the eldawon, it was
difficult to distinguish habitation from vegetation.

Cottages crouched here and there, linked by trails followed by humans, animals, and fowls. They stood higgledy-piggledy, so that one
man's doorstep came level with the next man's chimney. Fields were
coterminous with roofs. Every homestead boasted a pile of chopped logs.
Some piles leant against the houses, some houses against the piles.
Woodmen could be heard, busy with axes, adding to either the number
of piles or the number of homesteads.

For a short while, the air was free of cloud and possessed a brilliance
unique to high mountain places. Batalix shone over a distant crag. Boys
in the stoney fields, supposedly herding sheep and goats, flew kites
instead.

A crowd of pilgrims had just arrived on foot from Kharnabhar. Their
voices carried in the clear air. Most had shaven heads, some went barefoot, despite the hard snow on the ground. All ages were represented
among them; there was even an old yellowed woman being carried in
a wicker chair to which shafts had been attached. A few local traders
were watching them attentively, but without great interest. This lot
had already been fleeced on their way northwards.

Having travelled the trail before, Shokerandit knew that Uuundaamp
would have to stop here. He and Moub would rest. All the asokins
would be staked separately and fed, with extra meat for Uuundaamp,
the leader. Sledge and harness would be thoroughly overhauled for the
last lap of the journey if the Ondods intended to go on to Kharnabhar.
And what would they do with Toress Lahl?

Not murder her. She was too valuable. As a slave, she could be sold;
but few humans would buy a human slave from an Ondod. Ancipitals
on the other hand . . . He was frightened for her, and forgot Fashnalgid.

Although the ancipital kind were rare in Sibornal as a whole, those who escaped slavery often made their way to Shivenink, finding in the wilderness of the chain congenial habitation. Having experienced slavery themselves, they were the more inclined to use human slaves. Once she vanished into the hills with them, Toress Lahl would be lost to human knowledge.

Negotiating the paths at the rear of the houses, he covered the whole village. On its outskirts, he came to a palisade. Furious barking sounded on the other side as he approached. He peered over and saw trail asokins, staked out separately, or in cages. They launched themselves as far as chain and mesh would allow as he appeared.

This was unmistakably the staging post. He remembered it now. It had been snowing the last time he was through, when almost nothing could be seen in the blizzard. Something like fifty half-starved asokins were waiting in the pound.

Without provoking them further, he moved cautiously round by the side.

The staging post was the last building to the north of Noonat. A shout indicated that he had been sighted, although he saw no one. The Ondod were too cautious to be caught unawares.

Three of them appeared immediately, carrying whips. He knew how deadly they were with whips, halted, made the sign of peace on his forehead.

"I want my friend Uuundaamp, give him loobiss. Speak him loobiss, ishto?"

They were surly. They made no move.

"No see Uuundaamp. Uuundaamp no want loobiss together you. Uuundaamp fat lady plenty kakool."

He said. "I know. I bring help. Moub give birth, yaya?"

Sullenly they let him through. He told himself it was a trap, and that he should be ready for anything.

At the entrance to a barnlike building, the Ondods clustered, pausing, giving each other sullen eye glances. Then they motioned him to go in. The interior was dark and unwelcoming. He smelt occhara.

They thrust him in from behind and slammed the door.

He ran forward and threw himself flat. The sharp tongue of a whip passed lightly across his shoulder. He rolled over and dived to a side wall.

With one swift glance he observed Moub naked except for the blanket he had given her, which was now wrapped round her breasts. She lay on a plank, legs spread wide. Toress Lahl crouched over her. Toress Lahl was tied by the upper arm, in such a way that she could use her hands. The other end of the rope was held by one of three dehorned phagors who stood motionless against the wall opposite the one against which Shokerandit crouched. Uuundaamp's lead dog,

Uuundaamp, was staked in the middle of the barn, snapping savagely at the end of his leash in a futile attempt to eat the nearest portion of Shokerandit.

And Uuundaamp. He had heard or seen—for the barn had slit windows—Shokerandit's approach. With the ability of his kind, he had jumped above the lintel of the door, and stood poised there, about to lash out with his whip again. He smiled as he did so, without mirth.

Shokerandit had his gun in his hand. He knew better than to point it at the Ondod—the gesture would have provoked both Uuundaamp and phagors. Nor would any threat to Moub halt Uuundaamp in his present state of mind.

Shokerandit pointed the gun at the dog.

"I kill you dog dead, finish, gumtaa, ishto? You fall down here smart, drop whip. You come here, boy, you Uuundaamp. Else your dog plenty kakool one second quick!"

As he spoke, Shokerandit rose up, pointing the gun with both hands down the throat of the raging dog.

The whip fell to the floor. Uuundaamp jumped down. He smiled. He bowed, touched his forehead.

"My friend, you tumble off sledge in tunnel. No gumtaa. I very worry."

"You'll have a dead lead dog if you give me that sherb. Untie Toress Lahl. Are you all right, Toress?"

In a shaky voice, she said, "I have delivered babies before, and here comes another. But I am greatly relieved to see you, Luterin."

"What was the plan here?"

"The phagors were going to do something for Uuundaamp. I was the exchange gift. I've been terrified but I'm unharmed. And you?" Her voice trembled.

The phagors never moved. As he worked at the knots in the cord, Uuundaamp said, "This very nice lady, yaya. Shaggie he much enjoy . . . give him chance, yaya. No harm." He laughed.

Shokerandit bit his lip; the creature had to be allowed to save face. Almost penniless, they were forced to rely on him to get them to Kharnabhar.

When she was free, Toress Lahl said to Uuundaamp, "You very kind. When your baby is born, I buy you and Moub pipes of occhara, ishto?"

Shokerandit marvelled at her coolness.

Uuundaamp smiled and whistled through his teeth. "You buy extra pipe for baby too? I smoke three pipe together."

"Yaya, if you will kick out these shaggy brutes while I perform the delivery." Her face was white as she confronted him, but her voice no longer shook.

Still Uuundaamp felt that honours had not yet been made equal. "You give money now. Moub go buy three pipe occhara now. Better leave Noonat before is darkness."

"Moub's water broken, give birth directly."

"Baby no come maybe twenty minutes. She go buy fast. Smoke, give birth." He clapped his eight-fingered hands and laughed again.

"The baby is almost hanging out of her."

"That woman lazy bag." He grasped Moub by the arm. She sat up without protest. Toress Lahl and Shokerandit exchanged glances. When he nodded, she produced some sibs and gave them to the woman. Moub wrapped her entire body in the red and yellow blanket and waddled out of the barn without protest.

"Stay there," Shokerandit said. Toress Lahl sat on the water-stained bench. The lead dog settled down on its haunches, its red tongue lolling. At a gesture from Uuundaamp, the phagors filed out of the far end of the barn, pushing through a broken door. Outside, by the dog cage, stood Uuundaamp's sledge, unharmed.

"Where your friend grow tail on face?" Uuundaamp asked innocently.

"I lost him. Your plan did not work well."

"Ha ha. *My* plan work fine. You still want go Kharber?"

"Are you going that way? You've been paid, Uuundaamp."

Uuundaamp held his hand wide in a gesture of frankness, exposing his sixteen black-gleaming nails.

"If your friend tell police, no gumtaa. Hard for me. That bad man no understand Ondod like you. He want smrtaa. Better we go fast, ishto, once that bag throw her baby from her bottom-part."

"Agreed." No point in quarrelling now. He tucked his gun into his pocket. The apparent friendship of the trail could be resumed.

They remained watching each other, and the asokin waited at the end of its leash. Moub padded back, still swathed in the blanket. She gave two pipes to Uuundaamp and resumed her place on the plank by Toress Lahl, the third pipe in her mouth.

"Baby now come. Gumtaa," she said. And a small Ondod male was born into the world without further ado. As Toress Lahl lifted it, Uuundaamp nodded and then turned away. He spat into a corner of the barn.

"Boy. Is good. Not like girl. Boy do much work, soon have biwack, maybe one year."

Moub sat up and laughed. "You no make good biwack, you fool sherb. This boy belong Fashnalgid."

They both burst into laughter. He went across and hugged her. They kissed each other over and over.

This scene so much took everyone's attention that they did not heed whistles of warning from outside. Three police carrying rifles at the ready entered the barn from the road end.

The leader said coolly, "We have offence orders against you all. Uuundaamp, you and that woman have a number of murders to your name. Luterin Shokerandit, we have followed you from Rivenjk. You are an accomplice in blowing up an army lieutenant, and killing a soldier in the course of his duties. Also guilty of deserting from the army. In consequence of which, you, Toress Lahl, slave, are also guilty of escaping. We have a dispensation to execute you at once here in Noonat."

"Who these humans people?" asked Uuundaamp, pointing indignantly at Shokerandit and Toress Lahl. "I no see them. They just come here one minute, cause plenty kakool."

Ignoring him, the police leader said to Shokerandit, "I have orders to shoot you if you try to escape. Throw down any arms you have. Where is your recent companion? We want him too."

"Who do you mean?"

"You know who. Harbin Fashnalgid, another deserter."

"I'm here," said an unexpected voice. "Drop your rifles. I can shoot you and you can't hit me, so don't try. I'll count three and then I shall shoot one of you in the stomach. One. Two."

The rifles dropped. By then they had seen the revolver poking through one of the slit windows.

"Grab the guns, then, Luterin, look alive."

Shokerandit unfroze and did as he was told. Fashnalgid entered by the rear door, setting all the asokins barking.

"How did you come so providentially?" Toress Lahl asked.

He scowled. "I imagine the same way these dummies did. By following that unmistakable red-and-yellow striped blanket. Otherwise I had no idea where you were. As you see, I'm going in for disguise."

They had noticed. Fashnalgid had had his immense moustache shaved off and his hair cut short. He kept his revolver levelled at the police in a professional manner as he spoke.

"Rifle get much money," Uuundaamp suggested. "Cut these man throat first, ishto?"

"Never mind that, you little scab-devourer. If your shaggie was here, I'd drop him. Luckily he is not, because this place is swarming with police and soldiers."

"We'd better leave fast," Shokerandit said. "Excellent timing, Harbin. You'll make an officer yet. Uuundaamp, if we keep these three police quiet, can you and Moub get the dogs harnessed up really quickly?"

The Ondod became very active. He got the two women to drag the sledge into the barn and grease the runners, which he insisted was necessary. The police were made to stand with their trousers round their ankles and their hands up the wall. Everyone stood back as lead dog Uuundaamp was unleashed and he and the other seven asokins were secured to the traces, each in its appropriate place. As he worked, Uuundaamp cursed each of them in different tones of affection.

"Please hurry," said Toress Lahl once, betraying her nervousness.

The Ondod went and sat down on the plank where his wife had recently given birth.

"Jus' take small rest, ishto?"

They waited it out, no one moving, until his honour was satisfied. Snow came in through the rear door as he methodically checked over the harness.

From the direction of the street they could hear shouts and whistles. The three police had already been missed.

Uuundaamp picked up his whip.

"Gumtaa. Get on."

The rifles were tucked hastily under the sledge straps as they jumped aboard. Uuundaamp called encouragingly to Uuundaamp, and the sledge started to move. The police at once began to shout at the top of their voices. Answering shouts came. The sledge bumped out of the rear door.

Outside, ravening asokins leaped furiously against the mesh of their cage. Uuundaamp raised himself, twirled his whip, sent its tip flying towards the cage door. The hasp of the cage was secured in position by a thick wooden wedge. The whip end flicked the wedge free as the sledge went by.

Under the weight of the dogs, the cage door crashed open, and the brutes hurled themselves to freedom in a torrent of fur and fangs. Into and through the barn they rushed. Ghastly cries came up from the police.

The sledge gathered speed, bumping across rough ground, swinging round. Uuundaamp shouted commands, plying his whip expertly, licking each dog with it in turn, arms tireless. The passengers hung on. The barking and sounds of pain from behind died as they went over the hillside and jarred down onto the northward road.

Shokerandit looked back. No one was following. Faintly through the snow, sounds of growling still reached his ears. Then the road turned. Toress Lahl clutched him. Under one arm, wrapped in a bundle of dirty rag, she sheltered the newborn babe. It looked up at her and grinned, showing sharp baby teeth.

A mile along the trail, Uuundaamp slowed and turned.

He pointed the handle of the whip at Fashnalgid.

"You, kakool man. You jump off. No want."

Fashnalgid said nothing. He looked at Shokerandit, grimaced. Then he jumped.

Within a few yards, his figure was concealed in a whirl of snow. His last words reached them faintly—the terrible oath: "Abro Hakmo Astab!"

Uuundaamp turned to scan the trail ahead.

"Kharber!" he cried.

Avoiding Noonat, Fashnalgid met up with a group of Bribahrese pilgrims, returning from Kharnabhar and Noonat and making their way home, down the winding trails to the western valleys. He had shaved off his moustache in order to avoid identification and had every intention of disappearing from human ken.

Hardly had he been with the pilgrims for twenty-five hours when the group met another party climbing up from Bribahr. The latter had such a tale of disaster to tell that Fashnalgid became convinced that he was heading in the wrong direction. Perhaps right directions did not exist anymore.

According to the refugees, the Oligarch's Tenth Guard had descended on the Great Rift Valley of Bribahr, with orders to take possession of or destroy the two great cities of Braijth and Rattagon.

Most of the rift valley was filled by the cobalt blue waters of Lake Braijth. In the lake was an island on which stood an immense old fortress. This was the city of Rattagon. There was no way of attacking the fortress except by boat. Whenever an enemy attempted to cross, it was sunk by the batteries of the frowning castle walls.

Bribahr was the great grain-producing land of Sibornal. Its fertile plains reached down into the tropical zones. In the north, before the ice sheets began, there stretched the tundra barrier, skirted by mile upon mile of caspiarn trees, which could withstand even the onslaught of Weyr-Winter.

The inhabitants of Bribahr were mainly peasant farmers. But a warrior elite, based in the two cities of Braijth and Rattagon, had recklessly threatened Kharnabhar, the Holy City. Braijth would have liked a greater share of Sibornal's prosperity. Bribahr farmers sent grain to Uskutoshk for little return; to put pressure on the Oligarchy, they had made a tentative move against Holy Kharnabhar, capable of being approached from their plains.

In return for their threats, Askitosh had sent an army. Braijth had already fallen.

Now the Tenth sat on the shores of Lake Braijth, looked towards Rattagon, and waited. And starved. And shivered.

The frosts of the brief autumn had come. The lake also began to freeze.

There would be a time, and the Rattagonese knew it, when the ice would be firm enough to permit an enemy force to cross, walking. But that time was not yet. So far, nothing heavier than a wolf could get across. It might take a tenner before the ice would bear a platoon of soldiers. By then, the enemy on the banks would have starved and crawled away home. The Rattagonese knew the habits of their lake.

They did not entirely starve behind their battlements. The ancient rift valley had numerous faults. There was a tunnel below the lake to the northwestern shore. It was a wet way to travel, the water in it always knee-deep. But food could pass by that route; the defenders of Rattagon could afford to wait, as they had done before in times of crisis.

One night, when Freyr was lost behind dense gales of snow blowing from the north, the Tenth put a desperate plan into action.

The ice was strong enough to bear wolves. It would also bear men with kites flying above them, supporting much of their weight, making them no heavier than wolves, and as ferocious.

The officers encouraged their men by telling them tales of the voluptuous women of Rattagon who stayed by their men in the fortress, keeping their beds warm.

The wind blew, strong and steady. The kites tugged and lifted the shoulders of the men. Bravely they ran onto the thin ice. Bravely they permitted themselves to be carried across the ice, right up to the grey walls of the fortress.

Inside the fortress walls, even the sentries slept, huddled in any warm nook to shelter from the storm. They died with hardly a cry.

The volunteers of the Tenth cut away their kite cords and ran to the central keep. They slew the commander of the garrison in mid-snore.

Next day, the flag of the Oligarchy flew over fallen Rattagon.

This dreadful story, related with great drama over camp fires, persuaded Harbin Fashnalgid that there was wisdom in returning to Noonat and seeking a way southwards.

It's always painful to become involved in history, he told himself, and accepted a bottle that was making the rounds of the pilgrims.

XIII

"AN OLD ANTAGONISM"

The night was alive. So thickly was the snow falling that, brushing against a human face in its descent, it resembled the fur of a great beast. The fur was less cold than suffocating: it occupied space normally taken up by air and sound. But when the sledge stopped, the staid brazen tongue of a bell could be distantly heard.

Luterin Shokerandit helped Toress Lahl down from the sledge. The churn of snowflakes had confused her. She stood with bowed shoulder, sheltering her eyes.

"Where are we?"

"Home."

She saw nothing, only the animal dark, rolling, rolling towards her. Dimly, she made out Shokerandit, a bear walking, as he staggered towards the front of the sledge. There he embraced both Uuundaamp and the Ondod mother, clutching her infant into the coloured blanket.

Uuundaamp lifed his whip in farewell and flashed his unreliable smile. Came the jar-jar of his warning bell, the slice of his whip over the team, and the outfit was swallowed immediately by the whirling murk.

Bent almost double, Shokerandit and Toress Lahl made their way to a gate beyond which a dim light burned. He pulled a metal bell handle. They leaned exhaustedly against the stone pillar of the gate until a muffled military figure appeared from a shelter somewhere beyond the bars. The gate swung open.

They sheltered, panting, saying nothing to each other, until the guard returned after securing the gate and scrutinised them under his lantern.

The guard's lineaments were those of an old soldier. His mouth was tight, his gaze evaded other eyes, his expression gave nothing away. He stood his ground and asked, "What do you want?"

"You're speaking to a Shokerandit, man. Where are your wits?"

The challenging tone made the guard look more closely. With no change of expression, he said finally, "You wouldn't be Luterin Shokerandit?"

"Have I been away that long, you fool? Will you stand there and have me freeze?"

The man allowed his glance to take in Luterin's metamorphosed bulk in one mute, insulting glare. "A cab to take you up the drive, sir."

As he turned away, Luterin, still nettled at not being recognised, said, "Is my father in residence?"

"At present not, sir."

The guard put his free hand to the side of his mouth and bawled to a slave lurking at the rear of the guardhouse. In a short while, the cabriolet appeared through the blizzard, drawn by two yelk already encrusted in snow.

It was a mile from the gate to the ancient house, through land still known as the Vineyard. Now it was rough pasturage, where a local strain of yelk was bred.

Shokerandit alighted. The snow whirled round the corner of the house as if personally interested in turning them to ice. The woman closed her eyes and clutched Shokerandit's skins. Following ghostly materialisations of the structure, they climbed steps to the iron-banded front door. Above them sounded the dismal tolling bell, long drawn out, like a sound heard underwater. Other bells, drowning farther off, added their tongues.

The door opened. Dim guardian figures showed, helping the two new arrivals inside. The snow ceased, the roaring and clanging ceased, as bolts were shot home behind them.

In an echoing darkened hall, Shokerandit exchanged words with a servant unseen. A lamp glittered high on a marble wall, not yielding its illumination beyond the frosty surface which reflected it. They padded upstairs, each step with its own protesting noise. A heavy curtain was drawn back as if to abet the powers of darkness and stealth. They entered. While the woman stood, the servant lit a light and quit the room, bowing.

The room smelt dead. Shokerandit turned up the wick of his lamp.

An impression of space, a low ceiling, shutters ineffectively barring out the night, a bed . . . They struggled out of their filthy garments.

They had been travelling for thirty-one days and, since Sharagatt, had been allowed only six and a half hours of sleep a day, rarely more, sometimes less, according to whether Uuundaamp considered the police were closing on them. Their faces were blackened by frost and lined by exhaustion.

Toress Lahl took a blanket from a couch and prepared to lie beside the bed. He climbed into the bed and beckoned her to join him.

"You sleep with me now," he said.

She stood before him, her expression still dazed from the journey. "Tell me what place we are in now."

He smiled. "You know where we are. This is my father's house in Kharnabhar. Our troubles are over. We are safe here. Get in."

She attempted a smile in return. "I am your slave and so I obey, master."

She got in beside him. Her answer did not satisfy him, but he put his arms about her and made love to her. After which, he fell asleep immediately.

When she awoke, Shokerandit had gone. She lay gazing at the ceiling, wondering what he was trying to demonstrate by leaving her on her own. She felt herself unable to move from the comfortable bed, to face the challenges that would have to be met. Luterin was well disposed to her, and more than that; she had no doubts on that score. For him, she could feel only hatred. His casual handing over of her to the animal who drove the sledge, a humiliation still fresh in her mind, was merely the latest of his coarse treatments. Of course, she reflected, he did not do these things to *her* personally; he was merely conforming to fashion and treating her as slaves were treated.

She had good reason to hope that he might restore her social status. She would be a slave no more. But if that entailed marrying him, her husband's murderer, she did not think she could go through with it, even to ensure her own safety.

To make matters worse, she felt a dread of this place to which she had been brought. A spirit seemed to brood over it, chill, hostile.

She rolled over unhappily in the great bed, to discover that a female slave was waiting silently, kneeling by the door. Toress Lahl sat up, pulling the sheet over her naked breasts.

"What are you doing there?"

"Master Luterin sent me in to attend you and bathe you when you woke, lady." The girl bowed her head as she spoke.

"Don't call me lady. I am a slave just as you are."

But the response merely embarrassed the girl. Resigning herself to the situation and half-amused, Toress Lahl climbed naked from the bed. She raised an imperious hand.

XIII · "AN OLD ANTAGONISM" 199

"Attend me!" she said.

Nodding compliantly, the girl came forward and escorted Toress Lahl to a bathroom, where warm water ran from a brass tap. The whole mansion was heated by biogas, the slave explained, and the water too.

As Toress Lahl reclined in the luxurious water, she surveyed her body. It had grown less bulky with the rigours of the journey. Down both sides of her thighs, the scratches inflicted by Uuundaamp's claws were slowly healing. Rather worse, she suspected that she might be pregnant. By whom she could not say, but she thanked the Beholder that matings between Ondods and humans were never fertile.

Borldoran and her home town of Oldorando were thousands of miles away. If she ever saw the pleasant land of her birth again, she would be more than lucky. A female slave's life was generally wretched and short. She thought to ask the girl attending her about that, then considered it wiser to hold her tongue. If Luterin married her, she would be a thousand times better off.

What would he say? Would he ask her? Tell her? She would have to go through with it, whatever he did.

After the maid had dried her, she put on a satara gown provided for her. She sank back on the bed and delivered herself into a state of pauk. It was the first time that she had descended into the world of the gossies since leaving Rivenjk. There below her, in obsidian where all decisions had finally been made, waited the spark of her dead husband, calling her to him.

The estate looked as beautiful as ever. The continuing wind from the north had blown most of the night's snow into drifts. Exposed areas were clear. To the south of every tree lay a line of snow, fine honed as a bird's bone. The Chief Steward, an agreeable man Luterin had known since his childhood accompanied him on his survey. Ordinary life was beginning again.

Great caspiarns and brassimips stood in wind-deflecting parade. On all sides, distant or near, rose snowy peaks, the daughters of the chain, generally sulking in cloud. To the north, the cloud allowed glimpses of the Holy Mountain, in which was the Great Wheel. Luterin broke off the conversation to raise his gloved hand in salute.

He wore a warm greatcoat over his clothes, and had attached his hip-bell to his belt. In the stable yard, slaves naked to the waist had brought a young gunnadu for him to ride. These two-legged, large-eared creatures balanced themselves by means of long tails, and ran on clawed birdlike feet. Like the yelk and biyelk with which they associated in the wild, the gunnadu were necrogenes. Thus they belonged to a category of animal which could give birth only through its own death. Luterin's mother had said bitterly to him once, "Not unlike humanity."

Gunnadu were without wombs; the sperm developed into grubs inside the stomach, where they fed, working outwards until reaching an artery. From there they exploded throughout the maternal body, causing rapid death. The grubs pupated through several stages, feeding on the carion, until of a size to survive in the outside world as small gunnadu.

Fully grown gunnadu made docile mounts, but tired easily. They were ideal for short journeys, such as an inspection of the Shokerandit estate.

He felt himself safe here. The police would never enter one of the great estates. While his father was away enjoying the hunt, Luterin was in charge. Despite his long absence, despite his metamorphosis, he fell into the role with ease. From the Chief Steward down to the lowest slave, everyone knew him. It was absurd to think of any other life. And he was the perfect only son.

He had duties. Those he would attend to. He must introduce Toress Lahl to his mother. And he would have to speak to Insil Esikananzi; that might be a little awkward. . . . Meanwhile, there were more important duties.

He had matured. He caught himself reflecting that it was no bad thing that his father was absent. Always before this, he had missed him. Lobanster Shokerandit's word hereabouts was law, as it was with his one remaining son. But the formidable Keeper of the Wheel was frequently absent. He liked to live rough, he said, and his hunting trips took up two or three tenners at a time. Off he would go, taking his dogs and his yelk with him. Sometimes he went accompanied only by his mute hunt captain, Liparotin. A farewell wave and he would be away, into the trackless wilds.

From his childhood, Luterin remembered that casual gesture of the hand upraised. Less a sign of love for him and his mother as they watched him depart, more a sign of acknowledgement to the spirit which presided over the lonely mountains.

Luterin had grown up missing his father. His withdrawn mother was hardly compensating company. Once he had insisted on accompanying his father and his brother, Favin. He had been proud then, among the proud caspiarns; but Lobanster had appeared vexed with his sons, and they had returned home after no more than a week away.

He sniffed. He told himself that he too was a solitary, like his father. And then his thoughts swung back to Harbin Fashnalgid, last seen when Uuundaamp had turned him off the sledge. Only now did he realise he liked Fashnalgid, and should try to do something for him. His jealous anger at the man for possessing Toress Lahl was over.

Now he could recall Harbin uttering his unseemly oath, and smile. What an outcast the man was! Perhaps that was why it rankled when he called Luterin a victim of the system, or whatever the phrase was. The captain also had had a good side to his nature.

He and the Chief Steward visited the stungebag enclosure. The slow creatures were much as he remembered them. It was said that the Shokerandits had bred stungebags through four Great Years. The stungebags looked like badly thatched caterpillars or, when stretched to their full length, like fallen trees. They were combined animal and plant, a sport born at the melting time when the planet was showered by high-energy radiation.

Slaves were working in the hoxney paddock. Droves of hoxneys had once roved the uplands. Now they were starting to go into hibernation. In one of the corners of the estate, slaves were collecting the animals and storing them away in dry barns, prising them out of the nooks and crannies in which they had hidden. The animals relapsed swiftly into a shrunken, glassy state, their energies draining. They would come to resemble small translucent figures. Already, some were losing their dull brown colour and exhibiting colourful horizontal stripes, as they had done in the Great Spring.

In the hibernatory state, the hoxneys were known as glossies, perhaps not only for their shine, but because, like gossies, they were not entirely dead.

The estate manager, a freeman, came up and touched his hat.

"Glad to see you back, master. We're packing the glossies with hay between, as you may observe, to protect the creatures. They should be all right when spring arrives, if so happen it ever does."

"It'll come. It's only a matter of centuries."

"So you scholars say," said the man, with a conspiratorial grin at the steward.

"The principle is to organise for spring now. By storing these hoxneys safely, instead of leaving them to the vagaries of nature, we guarantee a good riding herd when the time comes."

" 'Twill be long past our lifetimes."

"Someone will be here, I don't doubt, to be grateful for our providence."

But he spoke absentmindedly, with Fashnalgid still on his mind.

When he got back to the mansion, he summoned his father's secretary, a learned withdrawn man called Evanporil. He gave Evanporil instructions that four armed liegemen were to be sent on two giant biyelk as far down the road as Noonat, to seek out Fashnalgid if he was to be found. Fashnalgid was to be brought back to the safety of the Shokerandit estate. The secretary left about his task.

Luterin ate some lunch, and only then thought that he should visit his mother.

The hall of the great house was gloomy. There were no windows on the lower floor, so as to render the structure more impervious to ice, snow, and flood. A great heavy chair stood empty on the marble tiling; as far as Luterin knew, no one had ever sat in it.

Between the dim wall lamps, fed from the biogas chambers, skulls of
phagors projected from the walls. These were specimens that Lobanster
and other Shokerandits before him had killed. They remained now with
their horns held high, their shadowed eye sockets observing with
melancholy the far recesses of the hall.

He paused on the way to his mother's quarters, aware of an uproar
outside. Someone was shouting in a thick drunken voice. Shokerandit
ran for a side door, hip-bell clattering. A slave hastily flung back the
bolts to allow him passage.

In a court overlooked by the upper windows of the mansion, a liegeman and two freemen were brandishing swords. They had cornered six
dehorned phagors. One of the phagors, a gillot with thin withered
dugs which spoke of years in captivity, was calling out in a hoarse
voice, in Sibish, "You not to kill, you vile Sons of Freyr! This Hrl-Ichor
Yhar come back belong to us, the ancipitals! Stop! Stop!"

"Stop!" Shokerandit said.

The men had already killed one of the ahumans. A swordsman had
disembowelled a stallun with a downward slash of his sword. Ancipital
eddre lodged in their carcasses above their lungs. As Shokerandit bent
over the corpse, which was still in spasm, the intestines slithered forth
on a tide of yellow blood.

The mass loosened itself and began slowly to evacuate the cavern of
the ribs like a concoction of soft-boiled eggs in jelly. Beige shadows ran
between little glistening mounds which came creeping out of the wound
like a living mass, flowing thickly over the flags and into the cracks
between the flags, flowing until all poured forth, separate organs no
longer distinguishable in the general exodus, leaving a hollow behind
them.

Shokerandit tugged back the dead creature's ear to expose its blaze
mark.

He glared at the men.

"These are our slave ancipitals. What are you doing?"

The liegeman was scowling. "Best mind out the way, master. Orders
are to kill off all phagors, whether ours or otherwise."

The five phagors began shouting hoarsely and scrambling to get past
the men, who immediately brought their swords to the ready.

"Stop. Drikstalgil, who gave you these orders?" He remembered the
liegeman's name.

Keeping one eye on the ancipitals and his sword ready, the liegeman
dipped into his left pocket and brought out a folded paper.

"Secretary Evanporil issued me this this morning. Now, stand back,
if you would not mind, master, or you'll get crushed."

He handed Shokerandit a poster, which Shokerandit flapped open
with an angry gesture. It was printed in heavy black letters.

The poster announced that a New Act had been passed, in a further attempt to keep down the Plague known as the Fat Death. The Ancipital Race had been identified as the main Carrier of the Plague. All Phagors must therefore be killed. Phagor slaves must be put down. Wild Phagors should be shot on sight. A bounty would be paid of One Sib per ancipital head by the appropriate authority in each District. Henceforth, the possession of Phagors was illegal, under Penalty of Death. By Order of the Oligarch.

"Put up your swords until I give you further orders," Shokerandit said. "No more killing till I say so. And get this corpse away from here."

When the men reluctantly did as he instructed, Shokerandit went back into the house, marching angrily upstairs to see the secretary.

The mansion was full of ancient prints, many of them engraved by a steel process in Rivenjk, when that city had boasted an artistic colony. Most of the prints depicted scenes suitable to wild mountainous areas: hunters coming unexpectedly upon bears in clearings, bears coming unexpectedly upon hunters, stags at bay, men mounted on yelk leaping into chasms, women being stabbed in gloomy forests, lost children dying in pairs upon exposed crags.

Beside the secretary's door was a print of a soldier-priest on guard before the very portals of the Great Wheel. He stood stiffly upright while spearing to death an immense phagor which had leaped from a hole to attack him. The engraving was entitled—the Sibish lettering executed with many a curlicue—"An Old Antagonism."

"Very appropriate," Shokerandit said aloud, thumped on Evanporil's door, and entered.

The secretary was standing by his window, looking out, and enjoying a cup of pellamountain tea. He inclined his head and looked slyly at Shokerandit without speaking.

Shokerandit spread the poster out on his desk.

"You did not tell me about this when I was here earlier. How's that?"

"You did not ask me, Master Luterin."

"How many ancipitals do we employ on the estate?"

The secretary answered without hesitation. "Six hundred and fifteen."

"It would be a tremendous loss to slaughter them. The new Act is not to be complied with. First, I am going into town to see what the other landlords make of it."

Secretary Evanporil coughed behind his fingers. "I wouldn't advise a visit to town just now. We have reports of some disturbance there."

"What kind of disturbance?"

"The clergy, Master Luterin. The live cremation of Priest-Supreme Chubsalid has caused a great deal of disaffection. A tenner has passed since his death, and I'm given to understand that the occasion was marked this morning by the burning of an effigy of the Oligarch. Member Ebstok Esikananzi led some men to quell the display, but there has been trouble since."

Shokerandit sat himself on the edge of the desk.

"Evanporil, tell me, do you consider that we can afford to kill over six hundred phagors out of hand?"

"That's not for me to say, Master Luterin. I am only an administrator."

"But the Act—it's so arbitrary. Don't you think so?"

"I would say, since you ask me, Master Luterin, that, if scrupulously carried out, the Act will rid Sibornal of the ancipital kind for ever. An advantage, wouldn't you say?"

"But the immediate loss of cheap labour to us . . . I don't imagine my father will be best pleased."

"That may be, sir, but for the general good . . ." The secretary let the sentence hang.

"Then we will not implement the Act until my father returns. I shall write to Esikananzi and the other landlords to that effect. See that the managers are clear on that score immediately."

Shokerandit spent the afternoon happily riding about the estate, ensuring that no more phagors were harmed. He rode out some miles to call on his father's cousins, who had another estate in a mountainous region. With his mind full of plans, he forgot entirely about his mother.

That night he made love to Toress Lahl as usual. Something in the words he uttered, or in the way he touched her, woke a response in her. She became a different person, yielding, imaginative, fully alive. An exhilaration beyond mere happiness filled Luterin. He thought he had won a great gift. All the pains of life were worth such delight.

They spent the whole night in the closest embraces, moving slowly, moving wildly, moving scarcely at all. Their spirits and bodies were one.

Towards morning, Luterin fell asleep. He was immediately in the dreamworld.

He was walking through a sparse landscape almost bereft of trees. It was marshy underfoot. Ahead lay a frozen lake whose immensity could not be judged. It was the future: all-powerful night prevailed in a small winter during the Weyr-Winter. Neither sun was in the sky. A lumbering animal with rasping breath followed him.

It was also the past. On the shores of the lake were camped all the men who had died violently in the Battle of Isturiacha. Their wounds still remained, disfiguring them. Luterin saw Bandal Eith Lahl there, standing apart with his hands in his pockets, gazing down at the ground.

Under the ice of the lake, something gigantic was penned. He recognised that this was where the breathing came from.

The being surged forth from the ice. The ice did not break. The being was a huge woman with a lustrous black skin. She rose and rose into the sky. No one saw her but Luterin.

She cast a benevolent gaze on Luterin and said, "You will never have a woman to make you entirely happy. But there will be much happiness in the pursuit."

Much more she said, but this was all Luterin could remember when he woke up.

Toress Lahl lay beside him. Not only were her eyes shut: her whole countenance presented a closed appearance. A lock of hair lay across her face; she bit it, as recently she had bitten the fox tail to preserve her from the cold of the trail. She scarcely breathed. He recognised that she was in pauk.

Finally she returned. She stared and looked at him almost without recognition.

"You never visit those below?" she said in a small voice.

"Never. We Shokerandits regard it as gross superstition."

"Do you not wish to speak with your dead brother?"

"No."

After a silence, he clutched her hand and asked, "You have been communing with your husband again?"

She nodded without speaking, knowing it was bitter to him. After a moment, she said, "Isn't this world we live in like an evil dream?"

"Not if we live by our beliefs."

She clung to him then and said, "But isn't it true that one day we shall grow old, and our bodies decay, and our wits fail? Isn't that true? What could be worse than that?"

They made love again, this time more from fear than affection.

After he had done the rounds of the estate the next day, and found everything quiet, he went to visit his mother.

His mother's rooms were at the rear of the mansion. A young servant girl opened the door to him, and showed him into his mother's anteroom. There stood his mother, in characteristic pose, hands clasped tightly before her, head slightly on one side as she smiled quizzingly at him.

He kissed her. As he did so, the familiar atmosphere that she carried round with her enveloped him. Something in her attitude and her gestures suggested an inward sorrow, even—he had often thought it—an illness of some kind: and yet an illness, a sorrow, so familiar that Lourna Shokerandit drew on them almost as a substitute for other marked characteristics.

As she spoke gently to her son, not reproaching him for failing to come earlier, compassion rose in his heart. He saw how age had increased its

tyranny upon her since their last meeting. Her cheeks and temples were
more hollow, her skin more papery. He asked her what she had been
doing with herself.

She put out a hand and touched him with a small pressure, as if
uncertain whether to draw him nearer or push him away.

"We won't talk here. Your aunt would like to see you too."

Lourna Shokerandit turned and led him into the small wood-panelled
room within which much of her life was spent. Luterin remembered
it from childhood. Lacking windows, its walls were covered with paintings of sunlit glades in sombre caspiarn forests. Here and there, lost
among representations of foliage, women's faces gazed into the room
from oval frames. Aunt Yaringa, the plump and emotional Yaringa,
was sitting in a corner, embroidering, in a chair upholstered somewhat
along her own lines.

Yaringa jumped up and uttered loud soblike noises of welcome.

"Home at last, you poor poor thing! What you must have been
through . . ."

Lourna Shokerandit lowered herself stiffly into a velvet-covered chair.
She took her son's hand as he sat beside her. Yaringa perforce retreated
to her padded corner.

"It's happiness to see you back, Luterin. We had such fears for you,
particularly when we heard what happened to Asperamanka's army."

"My life was spared through a piece of good fortune. All our fellow
countrymen were slain as they returned to Sibornal. It was an act of
deep treachery."

She looked down at her thin lap, where silences had a habit of
nestling. Finally she said, without glancing up, "It is a shock to see you
as you are. You have become so . . . fat." She hesitated on the last word,
in view of her sister's presence.

"I survived the Fat Death and am in my winter suit, Mother. I like
it and feel perfectly well."

"It makes you look funny," said Yaringa, and was ignored.

He told the ladies something of his adventures, concluding by saying,
"And I owe my survival in great part to a woman called Toress Lahl,
widow of a Borldoranian I killed in battle. She nursed me devotedly
through the Fat Death."

"From slaves, devotion is to be expected," said Lourna Shokerandit.
"Have you been to see the Esikananzis yet? Insil will be eager to see
you again, as you know."

"I have not yet spoken to her. No."

"I shall arrange a feast for tomorrow night, and Insil and her family
shall come. We will all celebrate your return." She clapped her hands
once, without sound.

"I shall sing for you, Luterin," said Yaringa. It was her speciality.

Lourna's expression changed. She sat more upright in her chair.

"And Evanporil tells me that you are countermanding the new Act to destroy all phagors."

"We could cull them gradually, Mother. But to lose all six hundred at once would be to disrupt the working of the estate. We are hardly likely to get six hundred human slaves to replace them—apart from the greater expense of human slaves."

"We must obey the State."

"I thought we would wait for Father's return."

"Very well. Otherwise, you will comply with the law? It is important for us Shokerandits to set an example."

"Of course."

"I should tell you that a foreign female slave was arrested in your rooms this morning. We have her in a cell, and she will go before the local Board when they meet next."

Shokerandit stood up. "Why was this done? Who dared intrude into my rooms?"

With composure, his mother answered, "The servant you had ordered to attend the slave woman reported that she went into a state of pauk. Pauk is proscribed by law. No less a personage than Priest-Supreme Chubsalid has gone to the stake for refusing to comply with the law. Exception can hardly be made for a foreign slave woman."

"In this case, an exception will be made," Shokerandit said, pale of face. "Excuse me." He bowed to his mother and aunt and left their rooms.

In a fury, he stamped through the passages to the Estates Office. He relieved his anger by bellowing at the staff.

As he summoned the estate guard captain, Shokerandit said to himself, Very well, I shall marry Toress Lahl. I must protect her from injustice. She'll be safe, married to a future Keeper of the Wheel . . . and perhaps this scare will persuade her not to visit the gossie of her husband so often.

Toress Lahl was released from the cell without trouble and restored to Shokerandit's rooms. They embraced.

"I bitterly regret this indignity imposed on you."

"I have become used to indignity."

"Then you shall become used to something better. When the right opportunity arises, I will take you to meet my mother. She will see the kind of person you are."

Toress Lahl laughed. "I am sure that I shall not greatly impress the Shokerandits of Kharnabhar."

The feast to mark Luterin's return was well attended. His mother had shaken off her lethargy to invite all local dignitaries as well as such Shokerandit relations as were in favour.

The Esikananzi family arrived in force. With Member Ebstok Esikananzi came his sickly-looking wife, two sons, his daughter Insil Esikananzi, and a train of subsidiary relations.

Since Luterin and Insil had last met, she had developed into an attractive woman, though a heaviness in her brow prevented true beauty—as well as suggesting that tendency to meet fate head-on which had long been a quality of the Esikananzis. She was elegantly dressed in a grey velvet gown reaching to the floor, adorned by the sort of wide lace collar she favoured. Luterin noted how the formal politeness with which she covered her disgust at his metamorphosis studiedly emphasised that disgust.

All the Esikananzis tinkled to a great extent; their hip-bells were very similar in tone. Ebstok's was the loudest. In a loud whisper, he spoke of his bottomless sorrow at the death of his son Umat at Isturiacha. Luterin's protest that Umat was killed in the great massacre outside Koriantura was swept aside as lies and Campannlatian propaganda.

Member Ebstok Esikananzi was a thickset man of dark and intricate countenance. The cold endured on his frequent hunts had brought a maze of red veins creeping like a species of plant life over his cheeks. He watched the mouths, not the eyes, of those who addressed him.

Member Ebstok Esikananzi was a man who believed in being unafraid to speak his mind, despite the fact that this organ, when spoken, had only one theme to sound: the importance of his opinion.

As they demolished the maggoty fists of venison on their plates, Esikananzi said, addressing both Luterin and the rest of the table, "You'll have heard the news about our friend Priest-Supreme Chubsalid. Some of his followers are kicking up a bit of trouble here. Wretched man preached treason against the State. Your father and I used to go hunting with Chubsalid in better days. Did you know that, Luterin? Well, we did on one occasion.

"The traitor was born in Bribahr, so you don't wonder. . . . He paid a visit to the monasteries of the Wheel. Now he takes it into his head to speak against the State, the friend and protector of the Church."

"They have burnt him for it, Father, if that's any consolation," said one of the Esikananzi sons, with a laugh.

"Of course. And his estates in Bribahr will be confiscated. I wonder who will get them? The Oligarchy will decide on what is best. The great thing is, as winter descends, to guard against anarchy. For Sibornal, the four main tasks are clear. To unify the continent, to strike rapidly against all subversive activity, whether in economic, religious, or academic life . . ."

As the voice droned on, Luterin Shokerandit stared down at his plate. He was without appetite. His eventful time away from Shivenink had so widened his outlook on life that he was oppressed by the sight and sound of the Esikananzis, of whom he had once been in awe. The pattern of the plate before him penetrated his consciousness; with a wave of nostalgia, he realised that it was an Odim export, despatched from the warehouse in Koriantura in better times. He thought with affection of Eedap Mun Odim and his pleasant brother—and then, with guilt, of Toress Lahl, at present locked in his suite for safety. Looking up he caught Insil's cool gaze.

"The Oligarchy will have to pay for the death of the Priest-Supreme," he said, "no less than for the slaughter of Asperamanka's army. Why should winter be an excuse for overturning all our human values? Excuse me."

He rose and left the room.

After the meal, his mother employed many reproaches in order to induce him to return to the company. Sheepishly, he went and sat with Insil and her family. They made stiff conversation until slaves brought in a phagor who had been taught to juggle. Under guidance from her master's whip, the gillot jiggled a little from one foot to another while balancing a plate on her horns.

An ensemble of slaves appeared next, dancing while Yaringa Shokerandit did her party piece and sang love songs from the Autumn Palaces.

If my heart were free, if my heart were free,
And wild as the dashing Venj is . . .

"Are you being uncivil or merely soldierly?" Insil asked, under cover of the music. "Do you anticipate our marrying in a kind of dumb show?"

He gazed at her familiar face, smiled at her familiar teasing tone. He admired the froth of lace and linen at shoulders and breasts, and observed how those breasts had developed since their last meeting.

"What are your expectations, Insil?"

"I expect we shall do what is expected of us, like creatures in a play. Isn't that necessary in times like these—when, as you tactfully reminded Pa, ordinary values are cast off like garments, in order to meet winter naked."

"It's more a question of what we expect from ourselves. Barbarism may come, certainly, but we can defy it."

"Word has it that in Campannlat, following the defeat you administered to their various savage nations, civil wars have broken out and civilisation is already crumbling. Such disturbances must be avoided here at all costs . . . Notice that I have taken to talking politics since we parted! Isn't that barbarism?"

"No doubt you have had to listen to your father preaching about the perils of anarchy many times. It's only your neckline I find barbaric."

When Insil laughed, her hair fell over her brow. "Luterin, I am not

sorry to see you again, even in your present odd shape, disguised as a
barrel. Let's talk somewhere privately while your relation sings her heart
out about that horrible river."

They excused themselves and went together to a chill rear chamber,
where biogas flames hissed a continual cautionary note.

"Now we can trade words, and let them be warmer than this room,"
she said. "Ugh, how I hate Kharnabhar. Why were you fool enough
to come back here? Not for my sake, was it?" She gave him a look
askance.

He walked up and down in front of her. "You still have your old
ways, Sil. You were my first torturer. Now I've found others. I am
tormented—tormented by the evil of the Oligarchy. Tormented by the
thought that the Weyr-Winter might be survived by a compassionate
society, if men thought that way, not by a cruel and oppressive one
like ours. Real evil—the Oligarch ordered the destruction of his own
army. Yet I can also see that Sibornal must become a fortress, submitting
to harsh rules, if it is not to be destroyed as Campannlat will be by the
oncoming cold. Believe me, I am not my old childish self."

Insil appeared to receive the speech without enthusiasm. She perched
herself on a chair.

"Well, you certainly don't look yourself, Luterin. I was disgusted at
the sight of you. Only when you condescend to smile, when you are not
sulking over your plate, does your old self reappear. But the size of
you . . . I hope my deformities remain inside me. Any measures, however harsh, against the plague, are justified if they spare us that." Her
personal bell tinkled in emphasis, its sound calling up a fragment of
the past for him.

"The metamorphosis is not a deformity, Insil; it's a biological fact.
Natural."

"You know how I hate nature."

"You're so squeamish."

"Why are you so squeamish about the Oligarch's actions? They're
all part of the same thing. Your morality is as boring as Pa's politics.
Who cares if a few people and phagors are shot. Isn't life one big
hunt anyway?"

He stared at her, at her figure, slender and tense, as she clutched
her arms against the chill of the room. Some of the affection he had
once felt broke through. "Beholder, you still argue and riddle as before.
I admire it, but could I bear it over a lifetime?"

She laughed back. "Who knows what we shall be called upon to
endure? A woman needs fatalism more than a man. A woman's role in
life is to listen, and when I listen I never hear anything but the howl
of the wind. I prefer the sound of my own voice."

He touched her for the first time as he asked, "Then what do you
want from life, if you can't even bear the sight of me?"

She stood up, looking away from him. "I wish I were beautiful. I know I haven't got a face—just two profiles tacked together. Then I might escape fate, or at least find an interesting one."

"You're interesting enough."

Insil shook her head. "Sometimes I think I am dead." Her tone was unemphatic; she might have been describing a landscape. "I want nothing that I know of and many things I know nothing of. I hate my family, my house, this place. I'm cold, I'm hard, and I have no soul.

"My soul flew out of the window one day, maybe when you were spending your year pretending to be dead . . . I'm boring and I'm bored. I believe in nothing. No one gives me anything because I can give nothing, receive nothing."

Luterin was pained by her pain, but only that. As of old, he found himself at a loss with her. "You have given me much, Sil, ever since childhood."

"I am frigid, too, I suspect. I cannot bear even to be kissed. Your pity I find contemptible." She turned away to say, as if the admission cost her dear, "As for the thought of making love with you as you are now . . . well, it repels me . . . at least, it does not attract me at all."

Although he had no great depth of human understanding, Luterin saw how her coldness to others was part of her habit of maligning herself. The habit was more ingrained than formerly. Perhaps she spoke truth: Insil was always one for truth.

"I'm not requiring you to make love with me, dear Insil. There is someone else whom I love, and whom I intend to marry."

She remained half turned from him, her narrow left cheek against the lace of her collar. She seemed to shrink. The wan gaslight made the skin at the nape of her neck glisten. A low groan came from her. When she could not suppress it by putting hands to mouth, she began to beat her fists against her thighs.

"Insil!" He clutched her, alarmed.

When she turned back to him, the protective mask of laughter was back on her face. "So, a surprise! I find that there was after all something I wanted, which I never expected to want. . . . But I'm too much of a handful for you, isn't that true?"

"No, not that, not a negative."

"Oh, yes . . . I've heard. The slave woman in your quarters . . . You want to marry a slave rather than a free woman, because you've grown like all the men here, you want someone you can possess without contradiction."

"No, Insil, you're wrong. You're no free woman. You are the slave. I feel tenderly for you and always will, but you are imprisoned in your self."

She laughed almost without scorn. "You now know what I am, do you? Always before you were so puzzled by me, so you said. Well, you

are callous. You have to tell me this news without warning? Why did
you not tell my father, as convention demands? You're a great respecter
of convention."

"I had to speak to you first."

"Yes? And have you broken this exciting news to your mother? What
of the liaison between the Shokerandits and the Esikananzis now?
Have you forgotten that we shall probably be *forced* to marry when
your father returns? You have your duty as I have mine, from which
neither of us has so far flinched. But perhaps you have less courage than
I. If that day comes when we are forced into the same bed, I will repay
you for the injury you do me today."

"What have I done, for the Beholder's sake? Are you mad because
I share with you your lack of enthusiasm for our marriage? Speak
sense, Insil!"

But she gave him a cold look, her eyes dark under her disordered
hair. Collecting up her heavy skirt with one hand, she set the other
hand pale against her cheek and hastened from the chamber.

Next morning, after Toress Lahl had bathed and a slave woman had
dressed her, Luterin took her before his mother and announced formally
that he intended to marry her and not Insil Esikananzi. His mother
wept and threatened—and in particular threatened the wrath of Luterin's
father—and finally retreated to her inner room.

"We shall go for a ride," Luterin said coolly, strapping on his
revolver and clipping a sling onto a short rifle. "I'll show you the Great
Wheel."

"Am I to ride behind you?"

He regarded her judiciously. "You heard what I said to my mother."

"I heard what you said to your mother. Nevertheless, at present I am
not a free woman, and this is not Chalce."

"When we return, I will have the secretary issue you a declaration
of your freedom. There are such things. Just now, I wish to be outside."
He moved impatiently to the door, where two stablemen stood holding
the reins of two yelk.

"I'll teach you the points of a yelk one day," he said, as they moved
into the grounds. "These are a domestic breed—bred by my father,
and his father before him."

Once outside the grounds of the estate, they moved into the teeth
of the wind. There was no more than a foot of snow underfoot. On
either side of the track, striped markers stood, awaiting the time when
the snow was deep.

To get to Kharnabhar, the peak, they had to pass the Esikananzi
estates. The track then wound through a tall stand of caspiarns, the
branches of which were fuzzy with frost. As they advanced, bells of

differing voice told of Kharnabhar, as it emerged gradually from the cloud.

Everything here was bells, indoors and out. What had once had a function—to guard against the possibility of being lost in snow or fog—was now a fashion.

Toress Lahl reined her yelk and stared ahead, holding a cloaked arm up to her face to protect her mouth. Ahead lay the village of Kharnabhar, the lodgings for pilgrims and the stalls on one side of the main track, the housing for those who worked with the Great Wheel on the other side. Most of the buildings had bells on their roofs, housed in cupolas, each with its distinctive tongue; they could be heard when the weather was too bad for them to be seen.

The track itself led uphill to the entrance to the Great Wheel. That entrance, almost legendary, had been adorned by the Architects with gigantic bird-faced oarsmen. It led into the depths of Mount Kharnabhar. The mount dominated the village.

Up the face of the mountain the buildings climbed, many of them chapels or mausoleums erected by pilgrims on this holiest of sites. Some of them stood boldly above the snow, perched on rock outcrops. Some were in ruins.

Shokerandit gestured largely ahead. "Of all this my father is in charge."

He turned back to her. "Do you want to look more closely at the Wheel? They don't take you in there by force. These days, you have to volunteer to get a place in the Wheel."

As they moved forward, Toress Lahl said, "I somehow imagined that we should see a part of the Wheel from outside."

"It's all inside the mountain. That's the main idea. Darkness. Darkness bringing wisdom."

"I thought it was light brought wisdom."

Jostling locals stared at their metamorphosed shapes. Some locals bore prominent goitres, a common malady in such mountainous inland regions. They superstitiously made the symbol of the circle as they moved towards the entrance of the Wheel with Shokerandit and Toress Lahl.

Nearer, they could see a little more: the great ramplike walls leading in from either side, as if to pour humanity down the gullet of the mountain. Above the entrance, protected from landslides by an apron, was a starkly carved scene embodying the symbolism of the Wheel. Oarsmen clad in ample garments rowed the Wheel across the sky, where could be recognised some of the zodiacal signs: the Boulder, the Old Pursuer, the Golden Ship. The stars sprang from the breast of an amazing maternal figure who stood to one side of the archway, beckoning the faithful to her.

Pilgrims, dwarfed by the statuary, knelt at the gateway, calling aloud the name of the Azoiaxic One.

She sighed. "It's splendid, certainly."

"To you, it may be no more than splendid. To those of us who have grown up in the religion, it is our life, the mainspring that gives us confidence to face the vicissitudes of this life."

Jumping lightly from his yelk's back, he took hold of her saddle and said, looking up at her, "One day, if my father finds me fit enough, I may in my turn become Keeper of the Wheel. My brother was to have been heir to the role, but he died. I hope my chance will come."

She looked down at him and smiled in a friendly way, without understanding. "The wind's dropped."

"It's generally calm here. Mount Kharnabhar is high, the fourth highest mountain in the world, so they say. But behind it—you can't see it for cloud—is the even grander Mount Shivenink, which shelters Kharnabhar from the winds of the pole. Shivenink is over seven miles high, and the third highest peak. You'll catch a glimpse of it some other time."

He fell silent, sensing that he had been too enthusiastic. He wished to be happy, to be confident, as he had been. But the encounter with Insil the previous evening had upset him. Abruptly he jumped back on his yelk and led away from the entrance to the Wheel.

Without speaking, he wended a way through the village street, where pilgrims were crowding among the clothing shops and bell stalls. Some munched waffles stamped with the sign of the Great Wheel.

Beyond the village was a steep ravine, with a path winding down into a distant valley. The trees grew close, with massive boulders between them. Drifts of snow lay here and there, making the route treacherous. The yelk picked their way with care, the bells on their harness jingling. Birds called in the branches high above them and they heard the sound of water falling onto rock. Shokerandit sang to himself. Batalix weakly lit their way. In the chasmlike valley below them, shadow ruled.

He halted where the track divided. One fork ran upwards along the slopes, one down. When she caught up with him, he said, "They say this valley will fill with snow when the Weyr-Winter really comes— say in my grandchildren's time, if I have any. We should take the upper track. It's the easiest way home."

"Where does the lower track lead?"

"There's an old church down there, founded by a king from your part of the world, so you might be interested. And next to it is a shrine my father built in memory to my brother."

"I'd like to see."

The way became steeper. Fallen trees obstructed their way. Shokerandit pursed his lips to see how the estate was being neglected. They passed under a waterfall, and picked their way through a bed of snow.

Cloud clung to the hillside. Every leaf about them shone. The light was bad.

They circled past the cupola of the chapel. Its bell hung silent. When they reached level ground, they saw that a great drift of snow had sealed the door of the building.

As a native of Borldoran, Toress Lahl recognised immediately that the church was built in what was known as the Embruddockan style. Most of it lay below ground level. The steps which wound down its curving outer dome were intended to give worshippers a chance to clear their minds of worldly things before entering.

She scooped away snow so that she could peer through a narrow rectangular window set in the door. Darkness had been created inside, such light as there was penetrating from above. An old god's portrait gazed down from behind a circular altar. She felt her breath come faster.

The name of the deity eluded her memory, but she knew well the name of the king whose bust and titles stood, sheltered from the elements, under the porch above the outer door. He was JandolAnganol, King of Borlien and Oldorando, the countries which later became Borldoran.

Her voice shook when she spoke. "Is this why I am brought here? This king is a distant ancestor of mine. His name is proverbial where I come from, though he died almost five centuries ago."

Luterin's only response was to say, "I know the building is old. My brother lies nearby. Come and see."

In a moment, she collected herself and followed him, saying, "JandolAnganol . . ."

He stood contemplating a cairn. Stone was piled on stone, and capped with a circular block of granite. His brother's name—FAVIN—was engraved on the granite, together with the sacred symbol of circle within circle.

To show reverence, Toress Lahl dismounted and stood with Luterin. The cairn was a brutal object in comparison with the delicately worked chapel.

Finally, Luterin turned away and pointed to the rocks above them. "You see where the waterfall begins?"

High overhead, a spur of rock protruded. Water spouted over its lip, falling clear for seventy feet before striking stone. They could hear the sound of its descent into the valley.

"He rode out here one day on a hoxney, when the weather was better. Jumped—man and mount. The Azoiaxic knows what made him do it. My father was at home. He it was who found my brother, dead on this spot. He erected this cairn to his memory. Since then, we have not been allowed to speak his name. I believe that Father was as heartbroken as I."

"And your mother?" she asked, after a pause.

"Oh, she was upset too, of course." He looked up again at the waterfall, biting his lip.

"You think greatly of your father, don't you?"

"Everyone does." He cleared his throat and added, "His influence on me is immense. Perhaps if he were away less, he would not be so close to me. Everyone knows him hereabouts for a holy man—much like your ancestor, the king."

Toress Lahl laughed. "JandolAnganol is no holy man. He is known as one of the blackest villains in history, who destroyed the old religion and burnt the leader of it, with all his followers."

"Well, we know him here as a holy man. His name is revered locally."

"Why did he come here?"

He shook his head impatiently. "Because this is Kharnabhar. Everyone wants to be here. Perhaps he was doing penance for his sins . . ."

To that she would say nothing.

He stood staring down into the valley, into the confused hillsides.

"There is no finer love than that between son and father, don't you agree? Now I have grown up, I know other kinds of love—all with their lure. None has the purity—the clarity—of the love I bear for my father. All others are full of questions, of conflicts. The love for a father is unquestioning. I wish I were one of his hounds, that I could show him unquestioning obedience. He's away in the caspiarn forests for months at a time. If I were a hound, I could be forever at his heel, following wherever he led."

"Eating the scraps he threw you."

"Whatever he wished."

"It's not healthy to feel like that."

He turned towards her, looking haughty. "I am not a lad anymore. I can please myself or I can subdue my will. So it must be with everyone. Compassion and firmness are needed. We must fight unjust laws. As long as anarchy does not take over, Weyr-Winter will be endurable. When spring comes, Sibornal will emerge stronger than ever. We are committed to four tasks. To unify our continent. To rectify work, and consolidate it organisationally with regard to depleted resources . . . Well, all that's no concern of yours. . . ."

She stood apart from him. The clouds of their breath formed and dispersed without meeting. "What role do I play in your plans?"

He was uneasy with the question, but liked its bluntness. Being in Toress Lahl's company was like occupying a different world from Insil's. With a sudden impulse, he turned and grasped her, staring into her eyes before kissing her briefly. He stepped back, drawing deep breath, drinking in her expression. Then he moved forward again and this time kissed her with greater concentration.

Even when she made some response, he could not banish the thought

XIII · "An Old Antagonism"   217

of Insil Esikananzi. For her part, Toress Lahl too struggled against her late husband's phantom lips.

They broke apart.

"Be patient," he said, as if to himself. She gave no answer.

Luterin climbed back on his mount, and led the way up the track which wound through the dark trees. The bells on the animals' harness jingled. The little snowbound chapel sank behind them, soon becoming lost in the obscurity.

When he returned, a sealed note from Insil awaited him. He opened it with reluctance, but it contained only an oblique reference to their quarrel of the previous evening. It read:

Luterin:

You will think me hard, but there are those who are harder. They offer you greater danger than ever I could.

Do you recall a conversation we once had about the possible cause of your brother's death? It took place, unless I dreamed it, after you had recovered from that strange horizontal interlude which followed the death. Your innocence is heroic. Let me say more soon.

I beg you use guile now. Hold "our" new secret for a while, for your own sake.

Insil

"Too late," he said impatiently, screwing the note up into a ball.

XIV

THE GREATEST CRIME

But how could anyone be sure that those tutelary biospheric spirits, the Original Beholder and Gaia, had a real existence?

There was no objective proof, just as empathy cannot be measured. Microbacterial life has no knowledge of mankind: their umwelts are too disparate. Only intuition can permit mankind to see and hear the footsteps of those geochemical spirits who have managed the life of a functioning whole world as a single organism.

It is intuition, again, which tells humanity that to live according to the spirit it must not possess, must refrain from dominating. It was precisely those men who met so secretively on Icen Hill, shut away from human contact, secure from contact with the outside world, who most feverishly tried to possess the world.

And if they succeeded?

The biospheric spirits are forgiving and adaptable. Intuition tells us that there are always alternatives. Homeostasis is not fossilisation but the balance of vitality.

The early tribal hunters who burned the forests to secure their prey gave birth to the ecosystems of the great savannahs. Mutability informs Gaia's cybernetic controls.

*The Original Beholder's grey cloak was sweeping across Helliconia.
Human beings defied it or accepted it, according to their individual
natures.*

Beyond the pale of human possession, the creatures of the wild made
their own dispositions. The brassimip trees greedily stored food resources
far below ground, in order that they might continue to grow. The little
land crustaceans, the rickybacks, congregated in their thousands on the
underside of stones of alabaster, working lodgements for themselves in
the stone with secretions of acid; they would derive such light as they
needed to sustain them through the stone itself. The horned sheep of
the mountains, the wild asokin, the badgered timoroon, the flambreg on
their scoured plains, indulged in fierce courtship battles. There was
time for one more mating and perhaps one more: the number of living
offspring born would be decided by temperature, by the food supply, by
courage, by skill.

All those beings which could not be described as part of the human
race, but remained suspended by a quirk of evolution just outside the
hearths of humanity—wistfully looking towards the camp fires—those
beings too made their dispositions.

The Driat tribes, given the gift of language and well able to curse in
it, cursed and moved down from the hills to rocky shores of their continent, where they would find food in abundance. The migratory Madis
were driven from their dying ucts to seek shelter in the West and to
haunt the ruined cities mankind had deserted. The Nondads burrowed
down between the roots of great trees, living their elusive lives little
differently from in the scorching days of summer.

As for the ancipital race, each generation saw global conditions re-
verting to what they had been before the invasion of Freyr into their
skies. To their eotemporal minds, the stereotype of the future was coming more nearly to resemble the stereotype of the past. On the broad
plains of Campannlat, phagors became increasingly dominant, relying
for meat on the herds of yelk and biyelk, which appeared in growing
numbers, and becoming bolder in their attacks on the Sons of Freyr.
Only in Sibornal, where their presence had never been strong, were they
subject to organised counterattacks from humanity.

All these creatures could be seen as vying with one another. In a sense
it was true. But in a wider sense, all were a unity. The steady disappearance of green things destroyed their numbers, but they remained
intact. For all of them depended on the anaerobic muds on the Helliconian seabeds, working to bury carbon and maintain the oxygen of the
atmosphere, so that the great processes of respiration and photosynthesis
were maintained over land and ocean.

All these creatures, again, could be seen as the vital life of the planet.
In a sense it was true. But fully half of the mass of Helliconian life lived
in the three-dimensional pasturages of the seas. That mass was com-

posed for the most part of single-celled microflora. They were the true monitors of life, and for them little changed, whether Freyr was close or distant.

The Original Beholder held all living forces in balance. How was life possible on the planet? Because there was life on the planet. What would happen without life? There could be no life. The Original Beholder was a spirit who dwelt over the waters: not a separate spirit endowed with mind, but a vast cooperative entity, creating well-being from the centre of a furious chemical storm. And the Original Beholder was forced to be even more ingenious than her sister goddess, Gaia, on nearby Earth.

Somewhat apart from all other living things, from algae and rutting sheep and rickybacks, were the humans of Helliconia. These creatures, although fully as dependent on the homeostatic biosphere as other units of life, had nevertheless elevated themselves to a special category. They had developed language. Within the wordless universe, they had assembled their own umwelt of words.

They had songs and poems, dramas and histories, debate, lament and proclamation, with which to give tongue to the planet. With words came the power to invent. As soon as words came, there was story. Story was to words as Gaia was to Earth and the Original Beholder to Helliconia. Neither planet had a story until mankind came chattering onto the scene and invented it—to fit what each generation saw as the facts.

There were visionaries on Helliconia who, at this time of crisis in human affairs, divined the existence of the Original Beholder. But visionaries had always been there, often inarticulate because they worked close to the thresholds of inarticulacy. They perceived something azoiaxic in the universe, something beyond life round which all life revolves, which was itself at once unliving and the Life.

The vision did not fit easily into words. But because there were words, their listeners could not tell whether the vision was true or false. Words have no atomic weight. The universe of words has no ultimate criteria corresponding to life and death in the tongueless universe. This is why it can invent imaginary worlds which have neither life nor death.

One such imaginary world was the perfectly functioning Sibornalese state as visualised by the Oligarchy. Another was the perfectly functioning universe of God the Azoiaxic as visualised by the elders of the Church of the Formidable Peace. With the defiance of the Oligarch's edicts and the subsequent burning of Priest-Supreme Chubsalid and his fellow ecclesiastics, the two imaginary perfections ceased to coincide. After long periods of near identity, Church and State discovered to their mutual horror that they were in opposition.

Many of the leading clergy, like Asperamanka, were too much in the pocket of the State to protest. It was the rank and file of the Church, the lowly friars, the unlovely monks, those closest to the people, who raised the alarm.

One Member of the Oligarchy cried out against "those preachers in their cowls running to and fro, spreading false rumours among the common folk"—thus unconsciously echoing Erasmus on Earth many centuries earlier. But the Oligarchy was no defender of humanism. It could respond to the oppressed only with more oppression.

Enantiodromia once more. Just when the ranks were closing, a gulf opened; when unity was within reach, the divisions became widest.

The Oligarchy turned everything to its advantage. It could use the new unrest in its countries as an excuse for yet firmer measures. The army returning from its success in Bribahr was redeployed in the towns and villages of Uskutoshk. A sullen and cowed population stood by while its village priests were shot.

The dissention reached even Kharnabhar.

Ebstok Esikananzi called upon Luterin to discuss the trouble, and watched his mouth rather than his eyes when Luterin counselled caution. Other worthy officials representing one side or other also called. Luterin found himself closeted with Secretary Evanporil and staff for many hours. With his own fate hanging over him, he was unable to decide the fate of his province.

The Great Wheel was involved in the dispute. While it was itself run by the Church, its territory was under the control of a lay governor appointed by the Keeper. The gulf between lay and ecclesiastic widened. Chubsalid was not forgotten.

After two days of argumentation, Luterin did what he had done before when feeling oppressed. He escaped.

Taking with him a good hound and a huntsman, he rode off into the wilds, the almost limitless wilderness of mountain round Kharnabhar. A blizzard was blowing, but he disregarded it. Lost here and there among the valleys, or punctuating breaks in the caspiarn forests, were hunting lodges and shrines where a man could stable his mount, shelter, and sleep. Like his father, he simply disappeared from human ken.

Often he hoped that he might encounter his father. He saw the meeting in his mind's eye. Saw his father the centre of a group of heavily garbed hunters, the snow swirling about them. Masked hawks sat on leather shoulders. A biyelk dragged a sled carrying dead game. The breath of the hounds rose up. His father descended stiffly from his saddle and came towards him, arms outstretched.

Always his father had learnt of his heroism at Isturiacha, and congratulated him on his escape from death at Koriantura. They embraced . . .

He and his companion met no one, heard nothing but the clash of glaciers. They slept in remote lodges, where the aurora flickered high above the forests.

However tired he was, however many animals they had slain, the nights brought bad dreams to Luterin. The obsession overwhelmed him that he was climbing, not amid forests, but through rooms stuffed with meaningless furniture and ancient possessions. In those rooms, a sense of horror gathered. He could neither find nor evade the thing that hunted him.

Often he awoke and imagined that he was again laid flat by paralysis. Knowledge of his real surroundings returned only slowly. Then he would try to calm his mind with thoughts of Toress Lahl; but ever and again Insil stood beside her.

At least his mother had taken to her bed after the feast she had given in his honour, so news that he would not marry Insil had not spread.

He saw in how many ways Insil was fitted to be his wife in the years to come; in her was the true unyielding Kharnabhar spirit.

Toress Lahl, by contrast, was an exile, a foreigner. Had he said he would marry her merely to prove his independence?

He hated the fact that he was still undecided. Yet he could not decide finally until his own uncertain situation was made clear. That entailed a confrontation with his father.

Night after night, lying with beating heart inside his sleeping bag, he came to see that confrontation there must be. He could marry Insil only if his father did not force him to it. His father must accept his viewpoint.

He must be hero or outcast. There were no other alternatives. He had to face rejection. Sex, when all was said, was a question of power.

Sometimes, as the aurora cast its glow inside the dark lodges, he saw his brother Favin's face. Had he also challenged his father in some way—and lost?

Luterin and the huntsman rose early every dawn, when night birds were still in flight. They shared their food together as equals, but never a private thought did they let pass from one to the other.

However badly the nights passed, the days were all happiness. Every hour brought a changing light and changing conditions. The habits of the animals they stalked differed from hour to hour. With the decline of the small year, the days grew shorter, and Freyr remained always close to the horizon. But sometimes they would climb a ridge and see through foliage the old ruler himself, still blazing, throwing his light into another valley brimming in its depths with shadow like a sea, as a king might carelessly fill a glass with wine.

The stoic silence of nature was all about them, increasing their sense of infinity. Infinity came through all their senses. The rocks down which they scrambled to drink at some snow-bearded mountain stream seemed

new, untouched by time. Through the silence ran a great music, trans-
lated in Luterin's blood as freedom.

On their sixth day in the wilderness, they spied a party of six horned
phagors crossing a glacier on kaidaw-back. The cowbirds sailing above
their shoulders gave them away. They stalked the phagors for a day and
a half, until they could get ahead of them and ambush them in a ravine.

They killed all six ancipitals. The cowbirds fled, screeching. The
kaidaw were good specimens. Luterin and the huntsman managed to
round up five of them and decided to drive them back to the family
estate. It was possible that the Shokerandit stables could breed a
domesticated strain of kaidaw.

The expedition had ended in modest triumph.

The tongues of the sullen bells of the mansion could be heard to toll
long before the building loomed out of the blue mists.

So Luterin returned home, to find uproar, and his father's yelk being
combed down in the stables, dead game lying everywhere, and his
father's bodyguard throwing back fresh-brewed yadahl in the gunroom.

Unlike Luterin's imagined meeting with Lobanster Shokerandit, the
real reunion between father and son contained no embraces.

Luterin hurried into the reception hall, throwing off only his outer
garments, retaining his boots, his revolver, his bell. His hair was long
and unkempt. It fluttered about his ears as he ran towards his father.

Skewbald hounds skulked about the chamber and pissed against the
wall hangings. A group of armed men stood by the door, backs to the
main party, looking round suspiciously as if plotting.

About Lobanster Shokerandit were gathered his wife, Lourna, and
her sister, and friends such as the Esikananzis—Ebstok, his wife, Insil,
and her two brothers. They were talking together. Lobanster's back was
turned to Luterin, and his mother saw him first. She called his name.

The talk ceased. They all turned to look at him.

Something in their faces—an unpleasant complicity—told him they
had been discussing him. He faltered in mid-stride. They continued to
regard him and yet, curiously, their true attention still remained with
the black-clad man in their midst.

Lobanster Shokerandit could command the attention of any group.
This was less by his stature, which was no more than average, than by
a sort of stillness which emanated from him. It was a quality all noticed,
yet no one had word for it. Those who hated him, his slaves and servants, said that he froze you with a glance; his friends and allies said
that he had an amazing power of command or that he was a man apart.
His hounds said nothing, but slunk about his legs with their tails tucked
down.

His hands were neat and precise, his nails pointed. Lobanster Shokerandit's hands were noticeable. They were active while the rest of him remained rigid. They frequently travelled up to visit his throat, which was always swathed in black silk, moving with a startled action not unlike that of crabs or hawks searching for concealed prey. Lobanster had a goitre, which his cravat concealed and his hands betrayed. The goitre lent a pillarlike solidity to the neck, sufficient to support a large head.

The white hair of this remarkable head was brushed straight back as if raked, receding from a broad forehead. There were no eyebrows, but the pallid eyes were surrounded by thick dark lashes—so thick that some people suspected Madi blood somewhere. The eyes were further bolstered by grey pillows or bags below them; these pillows, having a certain goitrous quality, acted as embankments behind which the eyes watched the world. The lips, though ample, were almost as pale as the eyes, and the flesh of the face almost as pale as the lips. A sebacious sheen covered forehead and cheeks—sometimes the busy hands went up to wipe at the film—so that the face gleamed as if it had recently been recovered from the sea.

"Come near, Luterin," said the face now. The voice was deep and somewhat slow, as if the chin was reluctant to disturb the mound of goitre lying below it.

"I am glad you are back, Father," said Luterin, advancing. "Had you good hunting?"

"Well enough. You are so metamorphosed that I scarcely recognised you."

"Those fortunate enough to survive the plague take on compact shape for the Weyr-Winter, Father. I assure you I feel excellently fit."

He took his father's neat hand.

Ebstok Esikananzi said, "We may assume that phagors feel themselves to be fit, yet they are proven carriers of the plague."

"I have recovered from the plague. I cannot carry it."

"We certainly hope you can't, dear," said his mother.

As he turned to her, his father said sternly, "Luterin, I wish you to retire to the hall and await me. I shall be there presently. We have some legal matters to discuss."

"Is there something the matter?"

Luterin took the full force of his father's stare. He bowed his head and retired.

Once in the hall, he paced about, heedless of the tongue of his bell. What had made his father so cold he could not guess. True, that august figure had always been distant even when present, but that had been merely one of his qualities, as much taken for granted as the hidden goitre.

He summoned a slave and sent him to fetch Toress Lahl from her quarters.

She came questioningly. As she approached, he thought how appeal-

ing her metamorphosed shape was. And the frost prints on her face had
healed.

"Why have you been so long away? Where have you been?"

There was a hint of reproach, although she smiled and took his hand.

As he kissed her, he said, "I'm entitled to vanish on the hunt. It's in
the family blood. Now listen, I am anxious for you. My father's back
and evidently displeased. This may be something that concerns you,
since my mother and Insil have been talking to him."

"What a pity you were not here to welcome him, Luterin."

"That can't be helped," he said dismissively. "Listen, I want to give
you something."

He led into an alcove off the hall, where a wooden cupboard stood.
With a key taken from his pocket, he unlocked the cupboard. Within
hung dozens of heavy iron keys, each labelled. He ran a finger along the
rows, frowning.

"Your father has a mania for locking things," she said, half laughing.

"Don't be silly. He is the Keeper. This place has to be fortress as well
as home."

He found what he wanted and picked out a rusted key almost a
hand's span long.

"Nobody will miss this," he said, locking up the cupboard. "Take it.
Hide it. It is the key to that chapel built by your countryman, the king-
saint. You remember, in the woods? There may be a little trouble—I
can't tell what. Perhaps about pauk. I don't want you harmed. If anything happens to me, you will be in danger of arrest at the least. Go and
hide in the chapel. Take a slave with you—they're all longing to escape.
Choose a woman who knows Kharnabhar, preferably a peasant."

She slipped the key into the pocket of her new clothes.

"What can happen to you?" She clutched his hand.

"Nothing, probably, but—I just feel an apprehension. . . ."

He heard a door opening. Hounds came scurrying, nails clicking on
the tiles. He pushed Toress Lahl into the shadows behind the cupboard,
and stepped forth into the hall. His father was emerging. Behind him
came half a dozen of the conspiratorial men, bells clanking.

"We'll speak together," said Lobanster, lifting one finger. He led
into a small wooden room on the ground floor. Luterin followed, and
the conspiratorial men moved in behind them. The last one in locked
the door on the inside. The biogas hissed when turned up.

This room had a wooden bench and table and little else in the way
of furniture. People had been interrogated here. There was also a wooden
door fortified with iron straps, which was kept locked. It was a private
way down into the vaults, where the well was whose waters never froze.
Legend had it that precious brood animals had been preserved down
there in the coldest centuries.

"Whatever we discuss should be said privately, Father," Luterin said.

"I don't even know who these other gentlemen are, though they make free in our house. They are not your huntsmen."

"They are returned from Bribahr," said Lobanster, speaking the words as if they gave him a cold pleasure. "Eminent men need bodyguards in these times. You are too young to understand how plague can cause the dissolution of the state. It breaks up first small communities and then large. The fear of it disintegrates nations."

The conspiratorial men all looked very serious. In the limited space, it was impossible to stand away from them. Only Lobanster was separate, poised without movement behind the table, on the surface of which he played his fingers.

"Father, it is an insult that we should have to converse before strangers. I resent it. But I say to you—and to them, if they are capable of hearing—that although there may be truth in what you say, there is a greater truth you neglect. There are other ways of disintegrating nations than by plague. The harsh measures being brought against pauk—the common people, the Church—the cruelty behind those measures—will eventually bring greater destruction than the Fat Death—"

"Cease, boy!" His father's hands went to the region of his throat. "Cruelty is also part of nature. Where is mercy, except with men? Men invented mercy, but cruelty was here before them, in nature. Nature is a press. Year by year, it squeezes us tighter. We cannot fight it but by bringing to bear cruelty of our own. The plague is nature's latest cruelty, and must be fought with its own weapons."

Luterin could not speak. He could not find, under that chill, pale gaze, words to explain that while there might be a casual cruelty in circumstances, to formulate cruelty into a moral principle was a perversion of nature. To hear such pronouncements from his father turned him sick. He could only say, "You have swallowed utterly the words of the Oligarch."

One of the conspiratorial men spoke in a loud, rough voice. "That is everyone's duty."

The sound of this stranger's voice, the claustrophobia of the room, the tension, his father's coldness, all mounted to Luterin's brain. As if from afar, he heard himself shouting, "I hate the Oligarch! The Oligarch is a monster. He murdered Asperamanka's army. I'm here as a fugitive instead of a hero. Now he will murder the Church. Father, fight this evil before you are yourself devoured by it."

This he said and more, in a kind of seizure. He was scarcely aware of their bringing him from the room and helping him outside. He felt the bite of the chill wind. There was snow in his face. He was pushed through a courtyard where the biogas inspection pit was, and into a harness room.

The stablemen were sent away, the conspiratorial men were sent away. Luterin was alone with his father. Still he could not bear to look at him, but sat clutching his head, groaning. After a while he listened to what his father was saying.

". . . only son left to me. You I must groom to take over the role of Keeper. For you there are particular challenges, and you must meet them. You must be strong—"

"I am strong! I defy the system."

"If the order is to wipe out pauk, then we must wipe it out. If to destroy all phagors, then we must destroy all phagors. Not to do so is weakness. We cannot live without a system—all else is anarchy.

"I hear from your mother that you have a female slave who has influence over you. Luterin, you are a Shokerandit and you must be strong. That slave must be destroyed, and you will marry Insil Esikananzi, as we have planned since your childhood. There is no question but that you must obey. You obey not for my sake, but for the sake of freedom and Sibornal."

Luterin gave a laugh. "What freedom would there be in such circumstances? Insil hates me, I believe, but for you that's neither here nor there. There's no freedom under the laws now being imposed."

Lobanster moved as if for the first time. It was a simple gesture, a mere removal of one hand from the throat, to extend it in appeal towards Luterin.

"The laws are harsh. That's understood. But there is no freedom, nor any life, without them. Without laws firmly applied, we shall die. Just as Campannlat dies without law, though the climate favours it above Sibornal. Campannlat already disintegrates under the coming of the Great Winter. Sibornal can survive.

"Let me remind you, my son, that there are one thousand eight hundred and twenty-five small years in a Great Year. This Great Year has but five hundred and sixteen more years to run before its death, before the time of greatest cold, the winter solstice, when Freyr is farthest from us.

"We have to live like iron men until that time. Then the plague will be gone, and conditions will improve once more. We have known these facts since birth, for we hold Kharnabhar. The life of the Great Wheel is dedicated to getting us through that black time, to bringing us again to the light and warmth—"

Now Luterin confronted his father and spoke composedly.

"Agreed, the Wheel does as you say, Father. Why, then, do you approve—as I gather you must—these wicked deeds whereby Chubsalid, Priest-Supreme of our Church, is burnt and the Church in general attacked?"

"Because the Wheel is an anachronism." Lobanster made a throaty noise resembling a laugh, so that his goitre trembled under its black covering. "It is an anachronism, without meaning. It cannot save Helliconia. It cannot save Sibornal. It is a sentimental concept. It functioned

properly only when it imprisoned murders and debtors. It conflicts with
the scientific laws of the Oligarchy. Those laws, and those alone, can
bring us through the Weyr-Winter which will be upon our children.
We cannot have two sets of laws in conflict. Therefore the Church must
be demolished. It was as a first step towards that demolition that the
Act against pauk was passed."

Again Luterin found no words.

"Is that what you brought me here to tell me?" he asked at last.

"I was not going to have others hear our discussion. I'm chiefly concerned with your contempt for the laws concerning pauk and the ex-
termination of phagors, as reported by Evanporil. If you weren't my son,
I would have killed you. Do you understand?"

Luterin shook his head once. He cast his gaze to the floor of the
tack room. As in childhood, he was unable to face his father's eyes.

"Do you understand?"

Still Luterin could not speak. He was utterly dismayed by his father's
imperviousness to his feelings.

Lobanster wiped his shining brow and crossed to the table, on which
lay a saddle bag among other pieces of harness. He flicked open the
buckle on the saddle bag so that a wad of posters came spilling out. He
handed one to his son.

"Since you are so fond of Acts, have a look at the latest one."

Sighing, Luterin took it. He barely glanced at it before letting it drop.
The sheet sailed into a corner of the room. It stated in black letters that,
as a further measure to prevent plague, persons found in a metamorphosed state would be put to death. By Order of the Oligarch. Luterin
said nothing.

His father spoke. "You see that if you do not obey my wishes I cannot protect you. Can I?"

At last Luterin stared at his father in misery. "I have served you,
Father. I have done as you wished all my life. I went into the army
without protest—and acquitted myself well. I have been—and desired
nothing better than to be—your *possession*. No doubt something of the
same was in Favin's mind when he leaped to his death. But now I have
to oppose you. Not for my sake. Not even for religion's sake, or for the
State. After all, what are they but abstractions? I must oppose you for
your own sake. Either the season or the Oligarch himself has driven you
mad."

A terrible fire shone on his father's face, while the eyes remained as
stoney as ever.

He snatched a long black shoeing knife from the table and held it out
to his son. "Take this, you fool, and come outside with me. You must be
made to see who is mad."

The snow was coming down fast, whirling round a grey angle of the mansion as if bent on filling up the courtyard to the very top of its walls as soon as possible. The conspiratorial men stood in a group, hands tucked under their belts, waiting under a porch, heels knocking together for warmth. To one side stood yelk, still saddled, with an anxious stableman still standing among them. Near at hand was a pile of phagor corpses; they had been dead for some while: the snow settled on them without steaming.

To one side, close to an outer gate, a row of rusty iron hooks stuck out from the wall above head level. The naked bodies of four men and a woman dangled by ropes from the hooks.

Lobanster pushed his son in the back, urging him forward. The touch was like fire.

"Cut these dead things down and look at them. Have a good look at their monstrousness and then ask if the Oligarch is not just. Go on."

Luterin drew near. The killing appeared recent. Moisture stood on the distorted faces of the dead. All five corpses were of people who had survived the Fat Death and metamorphosed.

"Laws have to be obeyed, Luterin, obeyed. Laws are what make society, and without society men are only animals. We caught these people on the way to Kharnabhar today, and we hanged them here because of the law. They died so that society can survive. Do you now think the Oligarch mad?"

As Luterin hesitated, his father said harshly, "Go on, cut them down, look at the agony in their faces, and then ask yourself if you prefer that state to life. When you reach an answer, you can get down on your knees to me."

The lad looked in appeal at his father. "I loved you as a dog its master. Why do you make me do this?"

"Cut them down!" One hand flew convulsively to the throat.

Choking, Luterin came level with the first corpse. He raised the knife and looked up into its distorted face.

It was someone he knew.

For a moment, he hesitated. But there was no mistaking that face, even without its moustache. Luterin recalled vividly seeing it in the Noonat Tunnel, livid with exertion. Swinging the knife, he cut down the remains of Captain Harbin Fashnalgid. At the same time, his mind opened. Just for a second, he was the boy about to prefer a year's paralysis to the truth.

He turned to his father.

"Good. That's one. Now the next. To rule you must obey. Your brother was weak. You can be strong. I heard of your victory at Isturiacha when I was in Askitosh. You can be Keeper, Luterin, and your children. You can be more than Keeper."

Flecks of spittle flew from his mouth, to be carried along in a vortex of snow. The expression on his son's face made him pause. In an instant, his demeanour altered. His bell rattled at his hip almost for the first time as he turned to look for his conspiratorial men.

The words burst from Luterin. "Father, you are the Oligarch! You! That's what Favin discovered, wasn't it?"

"No!" Lobanster suddenly changed. All command was gone. As he raised his crablike hands, every line of his body expressed fear. He clutched his son's forearm as Luterin drove the knife up under his rib cage, straight into his heart. Blood burst from the torn clothing and covered both their hands.

The courtyard became a scene of confusion. First to move was the saddler, who cried in terror and rushed out of the gate. He knew what befell menials who witnessed murder. The conspiratorial men were less quick to respond. Their leader was falling to his knees in the snow and then collapsing slowly, one reddened hand tugging weakly at his goitre, over the body of Fashnalgid. They stared at the sight as if paralysed.

Luterin did not wait. Horrified though he was, he ran over to the yelk and flung himself on one of them. As he galloped from the yard, a shot came, and he heard the men behind him rushing to follow.

Slitting his eyes against the snow, he spurred on the yelk. Across the rear square. Men shouted. His father's recently returned cavalcade was still being unloaded. A woman ran, shrieking, slipped, fell. The yelk leaped over her. At the gate there was a move to stop him. It was ill-coordinated. He struck out with his revolver, trying to smash the face of a guard who made to grab his rein. Then he was in the grounds.

As he rode, heading for a belt of trees and the side road, he was saying something over and over again. His mind had lost its rationality. Only a while later could he grasp and understand what he said.

What he constantly repeated to himself was, "Patricide is the greatest crime."

The words formed a rhythm to his escape.

Nor did he make any conscious decision as to where he was going. There was but one place in Kharnabhar where he might be safe from pursuit. The trees flashed by on either side, smeared across his slitting vision. He rode with his head low on the yelk's neck, breathing its misty breath, shouting at the creature to tell it what the greatest crime was.

The gates of the Esikananzi estate loomed out of the flying twilight. There was a flicker of lamplight at the lodge, and a man ran out. Then he was torn from view. Beyond the drum of the yelk's hoofs, above the whistle of the wind, came sounds of pursuit.

He was into the village before he knew it. Bells clashed about his ears as he passed the first monastery. There were people about, muffled to the eyes. Pilgrims screamed and scattered. He glimpsed a waffle stall overturned. Then it too was gone and there were only guardhouses before him until—out of the murk—loomed the ramparts of Mount Kharnabhar. The tunnel with its mighty figures was before him.

Without waiting to do more than check the yelk's pace, Luterin flung himself off the animal and ran forward. Above, a great bell tolled. It spoke in solemn tones of his guilt. But the instinct for self-preservation drove him onwards. He ran down the ramp. Priestly figures came forward.

"The soldiers!" he gasped.

They understood. The soldiers were no longer their allies. They hurried him into the gloom, while the great metal doors clanged fast together behind him.

The Great Wheel had claimed him.

XV
INSIDE THE WHEEL

The geonauts were the first life systems on Earth not to consist of living cells, and therefore not to depend on bacteria. They formed a complete break from all life that had gone before, including those amazing gene cities, humanity.

Perhaps Gaia had turned her metaphorical thumbs down on humanity. They had proved themselves more of a curse than an adjunct to the biosphere. Possibly they were now being phased out, or merged with a greater thing.

At all events, the white polyhedrons were now everywhere, covering every continent. They appeared to do no harm. Their ways were as inscrutable as the ways of kings to cats, or of cats to kings. But they emitted energy.

The energy was not the old energy which mankind had used for centuries and termed electricity. The humans called the new energy egonicity, perhaps in memory of the old.

Egonicity could not be generated. It was a force which flowed only from large white polyhedrons when they were about to replicate, or were meditating on the subject. It could, however, be felt. It was felt as a mild singing noise in the lower stomach or hora region. It did not register on any instrument the post-ice age humans could devise.

The post-ice age humans were itinerant. They no longer wished to possess land but rather to be possessed by it. The old world of fences was dead for ever.

Wherever they went, they walked. And it so turned out that it was the easiest thing to follow a suitable geonaut. Humanity had not lost its old ingenuity, or its skill with its hands. As generations passed, a group of men on one of the new continents discovered a way of harnessing enough egonicity to move a small carriage. Soon, small carriages were to be seen everywhere, moving at a slow rate over the land, trundling in front of a geonaut.

When the geonaut replicated, letting slip a stream of tiny polyhedrons like sheets of paper in the wind, the egonicity ceased, and those who sat in the carriage had to push it to another source.

However, that was just a beginning. Later developments would bring different arrangements.

The human race, greatly reduced from its former numbers, roamed the new Earth, and developed a dependence on the geonauts which increased generation by generation.

Nobody worked as once people had worked, bent double planting rice or sowing potatoes in the dirt. They did plant vegetables occasionally, but that was for pleasure; and others inherited the fruits of their labours, since they had by that time moved on—though rarely by more than a mile a day. Egonicity was not a violent power source.

Nobody worked at desks. Desks were extinct.

It might have been supposed that these people were always on holiday, or perhaps that they inhabited some rather spartan version of the Garden of Eden. Such was not the case. They were intensely involved with work of their own specific kind. They were doing what they termed rethinking.

The storms of radioactivity which had followed the nuclear war had left their brand upon the genetic pool. The survival of mankind increasingly favoured those with new connections among the neural pathways of their brains. The neocortex had been, in geological terms, a hasty development. It had functioned well on ordinary occasions but, in times of stress, it had been bypassed by emotion. In prenuclear times, this deficiency had been regarded as a norm, sometimes as a desirable norm. Violence was regarded as an acceptable solution to many problems which would never have originated had violence not been in the air in the first place.

In these more pacific times, violence was unwelcome. It was seen as a failing, never as a solution. Generation by generation, the neocortex developed better connections with other parts of the brain. Mankind began to know itself for the first time.

234

HELLICONIA WINTER

These itinerant people did see themselves as on holiday. Such are the ways that Gaia works through evolution. They found pleasure in doing exactly those things which improved their stock, and those couples excelled whose children in the next generation would do best at the new sport of rethinking.

Mainly they searched for deep structures in the human consciousness. While seeking out those guiding determinants which had shaped the history of the human race so far, they were guided by what happened on Helliconia. The records of terrestrial history before the nuclear destruction were almost entirely destroyed; only one or two caches of knowledge had been disinterred from the ruins. But Helliconia was reckoned to present in its people a fair parallel of the deep structures which had once prevailed on Earth.

Those terrestrials who had so feared their own violent nature, who had walled themselves about with fences, armaments, and harsh laws— so it was reckoned—were not greatly different from the troubled young man who killed his father. Aggression and killing had been an escape from pain: in the end, the planet itself had been murdered by its own sons.

Although there was scarcely a person on the whole planet who had not heard of the Great Wheel of Kharnabhar, few had visited it. None had seen it in its entirety.

The Great Wheel lay underground, buried in the heart of Mount Kharnabhar. The Architects had built it, and none had come after them who could even emulate their work.

Nothing was known of the Architects of Kharnabhar, but one thing was certain. They were devout men. They had believed that faith could move worlds. They had set about building a machine of stone which could haul Helliconia across the darkness and cold until it docked again to bask in the warmth of God the Azoiaxic's favour. So far, the machine had always worked.

The machine was powered by faith, and the faith was in the hearts of men.

The way by which men entered the Wheel had been unchanged throughout the ages. After a preliminary ceremony at the gates of the tunnel, the newcomer was led down a wide flight of stairs which curved into the mountain. Biogas jets lit the way. At the bottom of the steps was a funnel-shaped chamber, the far wall of which was a section of the Wheel itself. The newcomer was then helped or propelled, depending on his state of mind, into the cell of the Wheel there visible. After a while, after a jerk, the Wheel began to rotate. Slowly, the view of the outer world was cut off from the cell's new occupant by the rock face. The outer world disappeared from view. Now the newcomer was alone

—except for all the occupants of all the other cells nearby, who would remain unseen throughout his tenure of the Wheel.

Luterin Shokerandit was not untypical of those who entered the Wheel. Others had sought refuge there. Some had been saints, some sinners.

Originally, the plan of the Architects had been followed by the Church. There had been no shortage of volunteers to take their places in the Great Wheel and row it across the firmament to its rightful port beside Freyr. But when the long centuries of light returned at last, when Sibornal was again bathed in daylight, then the faith declined. It became more difficult to attract the faithful, to persuade them into the darkness.

The Wheel would have come to a standstill had not the State stepped in to aid the Church. It had sent its criminals to Kharnabhar, in order that they might serve their sentences in the Wheel and, crouched deep in rock, haul their world and themselves to remission. Thus had come about the close collaboration of Church and State which had sustained the strength of Sibornal for more Great Years than could be remembered.

Throughout the summer and the long lazy autumn, the Wheel was hauled as often by malefactors as by priests. Only when life became more difficult, when snows began to fall and crops to fail, did the old faith grow strong again. Then the religious returned, begging for a guaranteed place among the righteous. The criminals were sent off to become sailors or soldiers, or were dumped unceremoniously in Persecution Bay.

> *Father father what headwaters are these*
> *The rock so red hot like a forehead*
> *And me so fevered in the rude red darkness*
> *Are you there above below me*
> *Waiting not to die   O death*
> *Its energies   You scream in the walls*
> *Of my existence by my side   The lights go by*
> *Go by and are gone and I in the snoring*
> *Rock   I revile myself   That thing*
> *I never did in mind but of a sudden*
> *With your knife cutting our mutual*
> *It was I swear our mutual artery*
> *This place of terror screaming*
> *Where I'll forever bleed like lava*
> *Clogging the rude red rock darkness*

His thoughts ran in curious patterns, seemed to him to flow through him forever. Time was marked in the entombed soul by protracted squeals of rock against rock and by hideous groans. Gradually, the groans caught his attention. His mind became quieter listening to them.

He was uncertain of his whereabouts. He imagined himself lying in the subterranean stall of some great wounded beast. Though close to death, the beast was still searching for him, looking here, looking there. When it found him, it would fall upon him and crush him to death in its own final agonies.

At last he roused himself. It was the wind he heard. The wind blew down the orifices of the Wheel, creating a harmony of groans. The squealing was the movement of the Wheel.

Luterin sat up. The priests of the Wheel had not only let him in, thus saving him from his father's avengers, they had absolved him from all his sins before guiding him into his cell. Such was their standard practice. Men who were imprisoned with their sins upon them were more likely to go mad.

He stood up. The terrible thing he had done filled all his mind. He looked with horror at his right hand, and at the bloodstain on his right sleeve.

Food arrived. It could be heard rumbling down a chute in the rock overhead. It consisted of a round loaf of bread, a cheese, and a chunk of something which was probably roast stungebag, tied up in a cloth. So it was Batalix-dawn overhead. Soon the small winter would prevail, and then Batalix would not be seen again for several tenners. But little difference that made in the entrails of Mount Kharnabhar. As he munched on a piece of bread, he walked about his cell, examining it with the attention a man gives his surroundings when he knows that a narrow box is to become his life.

The Architects of Kharnabhar had arranged every measurement to correspond in some way with the astronomical facts which governed life on Helliconia. The height of the cell was 240 centimetres, corresponding to the six weeks of a tenner times the forty minutes of the hour, or to five times the six weeks times the eight days in a week.

The width of the cell at its outer end was 2.5 metres—250 centimetres, corresponding to the ten tenners of a small year times the number of hours in a day.

The depth of the cell was 480 centimetres, corresponding to the number of days in a small year.

Against one wall was a bunk, the cell's sole furniture. Above the bunk was the chute down which provisions came. On the far side of the cell was the opening which served as a latrine. The wastes fell down a pipe to biogas chambers below the Wheel, which, supplemented by vegetable and animal wastes from the monastery overhead, supplied the Wheel with its methane lighting.

Luterin's cell was separated from those on either side by walls .64159 metres in thickness—a figure which, added to the cell width, gave the value of pi. As he sat on his bunk with his back against this partition, he regarded the wall on his left. It was solid unmoving rock, and formed the fourth wall of the cell with scarcely a crack between it and its neighbours in the Wheel. Carved in this rock were two sets of alcoves: a high series containing the biogas burners, which provided the cells with what light and warmth they enjoyed, and, set twice as frequent, a lower series containing lengths of chain, firmly stapled into place.

Still munching his bread, Luterin crossed to the outer wall and lifted the heavy links of chain. They seemed to sweat in his hands. He dropped them. The chain fell back into its narrow alcove. It consisted of ten links, each link representing a small year.

He stood there without movement, his gaze locked on the length of chain. Beside the horror of his deed, another horror was growing, the horror of imprisonment. By these ten-link chains, the Great Wheel was to be moved through space.

He had not yet taken his turn with the chains. He had no notion how long he had lain in a delirium, while words winged like birds through his head. He recalled only the shrill noise of trumpets from the monks somewhere above the Wheel, and then the lurching horizontal movements of the Wheel itself, which continued for half a day.

Contemplating the outer wall frightened Luterin. The time would come when he would feel differently. That wall was the only changing element of his environment. Its markings formed a map of the journey; by those excoriations, a practised prisoner could chart his way through time and granite.

The inner walls, the permanent walls of the cell, had been elaborately incised by previous occupants. Portraits of saints and drawings of genital organs testified to the mixed occupancy of the cell. Poems were engraved here, calendars, confessions, calculations, diagrams. Not an inch had been spared. The walls preserved fossils of spirits long dead. They were palimpsests of suffering and hope.

Revolutionary slogans could be read. One was cut on top of an earnest prayer to a god called Akha. Many of the earliest markings were obliterated by later ones, as one generation obliterates another. Some of the early inscriptions, though faint, were legible and delicately formed. Some were in ornate scripts which had disappeared from the world.

In one of the faintest, most elaborate scripts, Luterin read the basic details of the Wheel itself. These were figures which had a power over all who were incarcerated here.

The Wheel might more properly be described as a ring, revolving about a great central finger of granite.

The height of the Wheel was a uniform 6.6 metres, or twelve times 55, the northern latitude of the Wheel itself. Counting its base, its thickness was 13.19 metres, 1319 being the year of Freyr-set, or Myrkwyr, at latitude 55°N, dating the years from the nadir year of apastron. The diameter of the Wheel was 1825 metres, the number of small years in one Great Year. And 1825 was the number of cells set in the outer circumference of the Wheel.

Close to this numeration, and allowed to remain intact, was an intricately engraved figure. It represented the Wheel in its correct dimensions, set in the rock. Above it was the cavern, large enough to permit the monks from the monastery to walk on top of the Wheel and drop supplies to the prisoners below. Entry to the cavern could be gained only through Bambekk Monastery, which perched on the hillsides of Mount Kharnabhar, above the buried Wheel.

Whoever had incised the figure on the granite had evidently been well informed. The river that ran below the Wheel, assisting its revolutions, was also depicted. Other schematic lines carried a connection from the heart of the Wheel out to Freyr and Batalix and to the constellations of the ten houses of the zodiac—the Bat, Wutra's Ox, the Boulder, the Night Wound, the Golden Ship, and the others.

"Abro Hakmo Astab!" Luterin exclaimed, uttering the forbidden oath for the first time. He hated these supposed connections. They lied. There were no connections. There was only himself, embedded in rock, no better than a gossie. He flung himself down on the bunk.

He used the oath again. As one of the damned, he was permitted it.

The dimmer the vision, the louder the noises. Luterin presumed that the other occupants of the Wheel slept when it was not moving. He lay awake, gazing vacantly about the dull box he inhabited.

His water supply ran down into a trough near the foot of his bunk. Its drips and splashes were close, and as regular as the tick of clocks.

Deeper in tone were the flows of water beneath the mobile floor. These were lazy noises, like a continuous drunken monologue. Luterin found them soothing.

Other watery noises, drips and plops, coming more distantly, reminded him of the outside world of nature, of freedom, of the hunt. He could imagine himself wandering free in the caspiarn forests. But that illusion could not be sustained. Ever and again he saw his father's face in its final agony. The brooks, waterfalls, torrents, disappeared from his mind's eye, to be replaced by blood.

His lethargy was pierced only when he opened his daily woven bundle of food, and found a message in it.

He carried the scrap of paper over to the blue flame in the outer wall and peered at it. Someone had written in small script, "All is well here. Love."

There was no signature, not even an initial. His mother? Toress Lahl? Insil? One of his friends?

The very anonymity of the message was an encouragement. There

was someone outside who thought well of him and who could—at least
on one occasion—communicate with him.

That day, when the priests' trumpets sounded, he leaped up and
seized hold of the chain hanging in its alcove in the outer wall. Bracing
his feet against the partition wall, he heaved on the chain. His cell
moved—the Wheel moved.

Another heave, and the movement was less reluctant this time. A
few centimetres were gained.

"Pull, you biwackers!" he shouted.

The encouraging bugles sounded at intervals for twelve and a half
hours, then fell silent as long. By the end of a day's work, Luterin had
advanced himself by some 119 centimetres, almost half the width of his
cell. The flame which lit his cell was close to the dividing wall. By the
end of another day's work, it would be eclipsed—would be in the following cell—and a new one would be revealed.

A mass of 1284551.137 tons had to be shifted: that was the burden
which holiness had placed on the incumbents of the Wheel. It appeared
to be merely a physical labour. But, as the days were to pass, Luterin
would find himself regarding it more and more as a spiritual task; while
more and more it became apparent to him that there were indeed connections out from his heart, and from the Wheel, to Freyr and Batalix
and to the far constellations. The perception would come that the
Wheel contained not merely hardship but—as legend claimed—the
beginnings of wisdom.

"Pull!" he shouted again. "Pull, you saints and sinners."

From then on, he became fanatical, leaping up eagerly from his bunk
as soon as the awaited bugle blew. He cursed those who, in his imagination, did not rise as swiftly to the task as he did. He cursed those who
would not labour at their chains at all, as he had once done. It was
beyond his understanding why the work periods were not longer.

At night—but here only night existed—Luterin lay down to sleep
with a head full of the image of that great slow-grinding Wheel, crush-
ing men's lives away like a grindstone. The Wheel moved every day,
as it had done since the great Architects had established it.

It revolved about a harsh irony. The captives, nested like maggots
each in separate cells on the perimeter of the Wheel, were forced to
propel themselves into the heart of the granite mountain. Only by submitting to that cruel journey, by actively collaborating in it, was it
possible to emerge. Only by that collaboration was it possible to effect
the revolution of the Wheel which meant freedom. Only by plunging
deep into the entrails of the mountain was it possible to issue forth a
free man.

"Pull, pull!" shouted Luterin, straining every muscle. He thought of
the 1824 others, captive each in his separate cell, each bound to pull if
ever they were to escape.

He knew not what crises prevailed in the outside world. He knew not what sequence of events he had precipitated. He knew not who lived or died. Increasingly, as the tenners went by, his mind was filled with loathing for those other prisoners—some perhaps sick or even dead— who did not pull with a whole heart. He felt that he alone was bearing the weight of rock on his sinews, he alone heaving the Wheel through its firmament of granite towards the light.

The tenners passed, and the small years. Only the scratchings on the outer rock wall changed. Otherwise, all remained always the same.

The sameness overpowered his youthful mind. He became dull, re- signed. He did not always move now when the priests' trumpets blew overhead, their noise made reedy by the thickness of roof.

His thoughts of his father receded. He had come to terms with his guilt by believing that his father had himself been overwhelmed by guilt, and had handed his son the knife before taunting him in order that he might meet death. That face, always shining with sebum, had been a face of misery.

It took him a long while to contemplate the possibility of visiting his father in pauk. But the idea preyed on his mind. In the second year of his incarceration, Luterin climbed onto his bunk and lay flat. He scarcely knew what to do. Gradually, the pauk state overcame him, and he drifted down into a darkness greater than any in the heart of the mountain.

Never before had he entered into that melancholy world of the gossies, where all who had once lived and lived no more sank slowly through the terrible silences into nonbeing. Disorientation overwhelmed him. At first he could not sink; then he could not stop himself sinking. He drifted down towards the sparks dim below him like guttering stars, all arranged in a static uniformity possible only within the regions of death.

The barque of Luterin's soul moved steadily, peering without sight into the fessup ranks which filtered down all the way to the heart of the Original Beholder. Viewed closely, every gossie resembled something like singed poultry, hanging to dry. Through their rib cages, their trans- parent stomachs, particles could be seen, circulating slowly like flies in a bottle. In their sketchy heads, little lights flickered through hollow eye sockets. Obeying a direction no compass could detect, the soul of Luterin fluttered before the gossie of Lobanster Shokerandit.

"My father, you need say one word only and I shall be gone, I who loved you best and harmed you most."

"Luterin, Luterin, I wait here, sinking towards extinction, only in the hope of seeing you. What sight could be more welcome to my eyes than you? How fare you, child, in the ranks of those who must still undergo the hour of their mortality?" On the last word, puffs of sparks were transpired.

"Father, ask not of me. Speak of yourself. My thoughts are never free of that crime I committed. Those terrible moments in that fatal courtyard always haunt me."

"You must forgive yourself, as I forgave you when I reached this place. We were of different generations, your mind had not yet composed itself, you were unable to take the long view of human affairs that I could. You obeyed a principle, just as I did. There's honour in that."

"I did not intend to kill you, my beloved father—only the Oligarch."

"The Oligarch never dies. There is always another." As the gossie spoke, a cloud of dull particles issued from the cavity where once a mouth had been. They hung and dispersed but slowly, like snow sinking into coal dust.

The cinder of Lobanster described how he had taken on the duties of the Oligarch because he believed that there were values in Sibornal worth preserving. He spoke long about these virtues, and many times his discourse wandered.

He spoke of the way he had hidden the truth of his august position from his family. His long hunting trips were no such thing. Somewhere in the wilderness of the mountains, he had a secret retreat. There his hunting dogs were kept, while he went on with a small guard to Askitosh. He collected the hounds on the way home. Once his older son had discovered the hounds and pieced the truth together. Rather than speak of what he found, Favin had leaped to his death.

"You may easily imagine the grief that overwhelmed me, son. Better to be here, to be safe in obsidian, knowing that no more bitter shocks can assail flesh and spirit."

The soul of the son was overcome but not convinced by this eloquence.

"Why could you not confide in me, Father?"

"I let you guess when I believed the time to be right. The plague must be stopped, the people must learn obedience. Otherwise, civilisation will sink and die under the impact of centuries of cold. Only with that thought in mind could I persevere as I did."

"Respected Father, you could not represent civilisation when the blood of thousands was on your hands."

"They are here with me now, son, those men of Asperamanka's army. Do you imagine they have a single complaint against me? Or your brother, also here?"

The soul uttered the equivalent of a cry. "Matters are different after death. There is no real feeling, only benevolence. What about that unnecessary war you caused to be waged against our neighbors in Bribahr, when the ancient city of Rattagon was destroyed? Was that not sheer cruelty?"

"Only if necessity is cruelty. My speediest way from Kharnabhar to distant Askitosh was to turn westwards from Noonat and speed down the Bribahrese river, the Jerddal—a much more easily navigable river than our ill-tempered Venj. So I came to the coast where ships awaited me, and was not recognised, as in Rivenjk I would have been recognised. Do you comprehend me, my son? I speak only to set your mind at rest.

"It is important that the Oligarch remain anonymous. It lessens danger of assassination and jealousy between nations. But a party of nobles from Rattagon sailing on the Jerddal did recognise me. In view of the hostility between our countries, they planned to dispose of me. I disposed of them instead, in self-defence. You must do likewise, my dear son, when your turn comes. Protect and cherish yourself."

"Never, Father."

"Well, you have plenty of time to mature," said the glimmering shade indulgently.

"Father, you have also struck out against the Church." The soul paused. It was unable to master its feelings, at once of respect and hatred, towards this smokey fragment. "I must ask you—do you think that God ever listens or speaks?"

The hollow which had once been mouth made no movement when it replied. "It is given to us gossies here below to perceive wherefrom our visitors come. I know well, my son, that you come from the heart of our nation's holiness. Therefore I ask you: in this purgatory, do you hear God speak? Do you feel him listen?"

In the questions moved a kind of leaden evil, as if misery could be happy only in propagating itself.

"If it were not for my sins, he might listen, he might speak. That I believe."

"If there were a God, boy, do you not reckon that we here below in all our legions would know of him? Look around you. There's nothing here but obsidian. God is mankind's greatest lie—a buffer against the bleak truths of the world."

For the soul, it was as if a strong current was drawing it towards an unknown place, and it felt close to suffocation.

"Father, I must leave."

"Come nearer to me that I may embrace you."

Accustomed to obey, Luterin drifted nearer to the battered cage. He was about to hold out a hand in a gesture of affection when a strong rain of particles shot up from the gossie, enveloping it as if with fire. He scudded away. The glow died. Just in time, he recalled the stories which claimed that the gossies, for all their resignation to death, would seize a living soul and change places with it if they could.

Once more, he uttered his protestations of affection and rose up slowly through the obsidian, until the whole congregation of gossies and fessups was not more than a dwindling star field. He returned to his own prostrate form in its cell. Sluggishly, he became aware of the warmth of the living body.

There were still eight years to go before his cell was hauled round to the exit, still three before his cell had reached even halfway, in the heart of the dolorous mountain.

The environment never changed. But Luterin's revulsion for himself began to stale, and change came to colour his thought. He began to brood on the division which had been growing between the Church and the State. Supposing that division became still wider and, for whatever reason, recruitment to the Wheel ceased. Supposing that ten-yearers continued to be released and were not replaced. Gradually the Wheel would slow. There would be too few men to budge its mass. Then, despite all the world's bugles, the Wheel would stop. He would be entombed deep within the mountain. There would be no escape.

The thought pursued him like a yellow-striped fly, even in his slumbers. He did not doubt that it pursued many another prisoner. Certainly the Wheel had never failed since the Architects finished their work long ago; but the past was no guarantee for the future. He lived in a suspense that was scarcely life, thinking with resignation of the old saying, "A Sibornalese works for life, marries for life, and longs for life." Apart from the clause regarding marriage, he would have sworn that the proverb originated in the Wheel.

He was tormented by the thought of women, and by the lack of male companionship. He tried to signal through the rock to his nearest fellow sufferers, but no response came. Nor did he receive any more messages from outside. Hope of them died. He had been forgotten.

Through the spells of work and silence, a riddle rose to haunt him. Of the 1825 cells of the Wheel, only two had access to the outer world at one time, the cell by which one entered and the adjacent cell by which one left. How, then, had the Wheel been loaded with its pilgrims in the first instance? How had the giants who had erected this machine started it into motion?

He burdened his mind with visions of ropes and hawsers and pulleys, and of gushing underground rivers which turned the Wheel into a waterwheel. But he could never resolve the riddle to his satisfaction.

Even the processes of his mind remained incarcerated within the holy mountain.

Occasionally a rickyback would make a journey across his cell floor. With joy, he seized it up, holding it gently, watching its fragile legs wave as it struggled to be free. The rickyback understood freedom and was undividedly interested in the subject. Infinitely more complex humans were more divided.

What transcendental pain caused men to imprison themselves for a large portion of their lives within the Great Wheel? Was this indeed the path towards self-understanding?

He wondered if the rickyback understood itself. His efforts to identify with the tiny creatures, so as to enjoy a fraction of their freedom, left him feeling ill. He lay for hours at a time on the floor of the cell, staring at minute moving things, small white ants, microscopic worms. Sometimes he caught pink-eyed rats and mice observing him. If I died, he thought, these would be my only witnesses. The unconsidered.

Many men must have died during their confinement in the intestines of the Wheel. Some had confined themselves from choice, as some were celibate from choice. Perhaps they had been goaded by a wish to escape into changelessness, away from the bustle of the world—that bustle framed, if he understood the astronomers, within the greater commotion of the universe.

But for him, the changelessness of the cell was a kind of death. There had been no yesterday. There would be no tomorrow. His spirit fought against a withering process.

Then the day's trumpets echoed, and he scrambled up, ran to the outer wall of his cell, and grasped the nearest chain. Heaving the Wheel through the rock had become the only meaningful activity left. By 119 centimetres a day, the machine progressed each of its occupants through the darkness.

He never sank into pauk again. But the visit to his father's ember had removed the burden of his guilt. He found after a while that he had ceased to think of his father; or, if he thought at all, he thought only of the spark spluttering in the world beyond mortality.

The father who had been real to him, the brave hunter, forever stalking with his gallant friends through the wilds of the caspiarn forest, was lost, had never existed. Instead there was a man who—in place of that free life—had chosen to incarcerate himself in Icen Hill, in the slatey castle in Askitosh.

There were curious parallels between the dead man's life and Luterin's own. Luterin was also self-imprisoned.

For the third time, his life had come to a standstill. After the year's paralysis, on the threshold of adulthood, the hiatus of the Fat Death, with its subsequent metamorphosis; now this. Was he at last to cease to be what Harbin Fashnalgid had called a creature of the system? Was there a last metamorphosis awaiting him?

It remained to be seen if he could throw off his father's influence. His father, though head of the system, had also been its victim, as had his family through him. Luterin thought of his mother, for ever incarcerated in the family mansion: she might as well be where he was.

As the years passed, he saw Toress Lahl more dimly. The glow of her presence went out. By becoming a slave, she had become no more than a slave; as his mother had pointed out, her devotion was merely the devotion of a slave, self-seeking, self-preserving, not from the heart. Without social status—dead to society, as people said of slaves—the heart did not move. There could be only tactical moves. He thought he understood that a slave must always hate its captor.

Insil Esikananzi glowed more brightly as the tenners and centimetres passed. Incarcerated in her own home, entombed within her own family, she carried the spark of rebellion; her heart beat strongly under her velvets. He spoke to her in the dark. She answered always mockingly, teasing him for his conformity; yet he was comforted by her concern, and by her perception of the world.

And he hauled on his chain whenever the trumpets blew.

High above the Great Wheel rode a structure to some extent resembling it. The Earth Observation Station Avernus also relied on faith for its working.

That faith had failed. Matriarchal societies ruled over small groups of people now entirely devoted to the spiritual playacting of multiple personalities. The giant aberrant sexual organs, the pudendolls, had all been ceremonially put to death—often by aberrant means. But a revulsion from all things mechanical or technological had left the tribes prey to a spiritless eudaemonism in which the sexual motif predominated.

The genders became hopelessly confused. From childhood, individuals adopted female and male personalities, sometimes as many as five of each. These multiple personalities might remain forever strangers to each other, speaking different dialects, pursuing different ways of life. Or they might fall into violent quarrels with each other, or become hopelessly enamoured of another.

Some of these personalities died, while their originator lived on.

Gradually, a general disintegration took place, as if the genetic coding on which inheritance depended had itself become confused.

A diminishing population continued to play its intricate games. But the sense of an ending was in the air. The automatic systems were also breaking down. The drones programmed to service faulty circuits were becoming themselves fit only for regeneration. Regeneration required human supervision, which was not forthcoming.

The signals passing back to Earth became more partial, less coordinated. Soon they would cease entirely. It needed only a few more generations.

XVI
A FATAL INNOCENCE

I t was summer in the northern hemisphere of Earth in a year that
would once have been called 7583.

A group of lovers was travelling in a slowly moving room. Other
rooms were moving nearby, also at a leisurely pace. They perambulated
before a mountainous geonaut. The geonaut perambulated in the
tropics.

Sometimes, one of the lovers would climb down from the room and
cross to another room. Seventy rooms clustered round the geonaut.
Soon it would replicate.

A man called Trockern was talking, as he liked to do in the after-
noons, when the morning's rethinking session was over. Like the others
present, male and female, Trockern wore nothing but a light gauze
veil over his head.

He was a lightly built olive-skinned man, with good features and an
irrepressible smile which broke forth even when he was speaking
seriously.

"If I've got the fruits of this morning's rethink right, then the bizarre
peoples who lived in the ages before the nuclear war failed to realise one
fact which now seems obvious to us. They had not developed suffi-

*ciently to escape from the same sort of territorial possessiveness which
still governs birds and animals."*

He was addressing two sisters, Shoyshal and Ermine, who were currently sharing his room with him. The sisters looked much alike; but
there was a greater clarity about Shoyshal, and she was the leader of
the pair.

"At least part of the old race denounced the evils of landownership,"
Ermine said.

"They were regarded as cranks," Trockern said. "Listen, my theory,
which I hope we can explore, is that possession was everything for the
old race. Love—for them, even love was a political act."

"That's far too sweeping," Shoyshal said. "Admittedly, over most of
the globe in those times one sex dominated the other—"

"Possessed them as slaves."

"Well, dominated them, you argumentative hunk. But there were
also societies where sex became just good clean fun, without any spiritual or possessive connotations, where 'liberation' was the watchword,
and—"

Trockern shook his head. "Darling, you prove my point. That mi-
nority was rebelling against the predominant ethos, so they too treated
—were forced to treat—love as a political act. 'Liberation' or 'free love'
was a statement, therefore political."

"I don't suppose they thought like that."

"They didn't see clearly enough to think like that. Hence their perpetual unease. My belief is that even their wars were welcome as an
escape from their personal predicaments. . . ." Seeing that Shoyshal was
about to argue, he went on hastily, "Yes, I know war was also linked to
territory. That sense of territoriality extended from the land to the
individual. You were supposed to be proud of your native land and to
fight for it, and equally you were supposed to be proud of and fight for
your lover. Or wife, as they then called it. Do you imagine I am proud
of you or would fight for you?"

"Is that a rhetorical question?" Ermine asked, smiling.

"Look, take an example. This obsession the old race had with owner-
ship. Slavery was a common condition on Earth up to and including
the Industrial Revolution. Long after that, in many places. It was just
as bad as we witness it on Helliconia. It gave you power to possess
another person—an idea now almost past belief to us. It would bring us
only misery. But we can see how the slave owner also becomes enslaved."

As Trockern raised both his left hand and his voice for emphasis, the
old man sleeping away the afternoon on a nearby bunk muttered irri-
tably, snorted, and rolled over onto his other side.

"Again, darling, there were plenty of societies without slaves," Shoyshal said. "And plenty of societies which abhorred the idea."

"They said they abhorred it, but they kept servants when they could

—possessed them as far as possible. Later they employed androids. Officially nonslave societies went in for multiple possessions instead. Possessions, possessions . . . It was a form of madness."

"They were not mad," Shoyshal said. "Just different from us. They'd probably find us pretty strange. Besides, it was the adolescence of mankind. I've listened to your preaching often enough, Trockern, and can't deny I've enjoyed it—more or less. Now listen to what I am going to say.

"We're here because of astonishing luck. Forget about the Hand of God, about which the Helliconians are always agonising. There's just luck. I don't mean only luck that a few humans survived the nuclear winter—though that's a part of it. I mean by luck the series of Earth's cosmic accidents. Think of the way plantlike bacteria released oxygen into an otherwise unbreathable atmosphere. Think of the accident of fish developing backbones. Think of the accident of mammals developing placenta—so much cleverer than eggs—though eggs, too, were winners in their day. Think of the accident of the bombardment which altered conditions so sharply that the dinosaurs failed, to give mammals their chance. I could go on."

"You always could," said her sister half-admiringly.

"Our old adolescent ancestors feared accident. They feared luck. Hence gods and fences and marriage and nuclear arms and all the rest. Not your possessiveness, but the fear of accident. Which eventually befell them. Perhaps such prophecies are self-fulfilling."

"Plausible. Yes. I'll agree, if you will allow that possessiveness itself might have been a symptom of that fear of accidents."

"Oh, well, Trockern, if you're going to agree, let's get back to the subject of sex." They all laughed. Outside their windows, the mobile city could be seen trundling on its inelegant way, drinking egonicity from the white polyhedrons.

Ermine put an arm about her sister's shoulder and stroked her hair.

"You talk about one person possessing another; I suppose you would say that the old institution of marriage was like that. Yet marriage still sounds rather romantic to me."

"Most squalid things are romantic if you get far enough away from them," Shoyshal said. "Anything seen through a haze . . . But marriage is the supreme example of love as a political act. The love was just a pretence, or at best an illusion."

"I don't see what you mean. Men and women did not have to marry, did they?"

"It was voluntary in a way, yes, but there was the pressure of society to marry. Sometimes moral pressure, sometimes economic pressure. The man got someone to work for him and have sex with. The woman got someone to earn money for her. They pooled their cupidities."

"How awful!"

"All those romantic postures," continued Shoyshal, enjoying herself. "Those raptures, those love songs, that sticky music, that literature they so prized, the suicide pacts, the tears, the vows—all just social mating displays, the baiting of the trap they couldn't see they were setting or falling into."

"You make it sound awful."

"Oh, it was worse than that, Ermine, I assure you. No wonder so many women chose prostitution. I mean, marriage was another version of the power struggle, with both husband and wife battling for supremacy over the other. The man had the bludgeon of the purse strings, the woman the secret weapon between her legs."

They all burst out in laughter. The old man on the other bunk, SartoriIrvrash by name, began to snore in self-defence.

"It's a long while since yours was secret," Trockern said.

When a city became too crowded for someone's liking, it was not difficult to change to another geonaut and head off in a new direction. There were many other cities, other alternatives. Some people liked to follow the long light days; others travelled to enjoy spectacular scenery; others developed longings to view the sea or the desert. Every environment offered a different kind of experience.

And those kinds of experience were of a different order from the kinds that once had been. No longer did the people cry out. Their agile brains had at last led their emotions to accept a role of modesty, subordinate but never acquiescent to Gaia, spirit of Earth. Gaia did not seek to possess them, as their imagined gods had once done. They were themselves part of that spirit. They had a vision.

In consequence, death ceased to play the leading role of Inquisitor in human affairs, as once it had done. Now it was no more than an item in the homely accounting which included mankind: Gaia was a common grave from which fresh increment continually blossomed.

There was also the dimension of a real involvement with Helliconia. From watchers, men and women had graduated to participators. As the images failed to arrive from the Avernus, as the mere pictures died in the shell-like auditoria, so the empathic link was forged ever more strongly. In a sense, humankind—humanmind—leaped across space to become the eye of the Original Beholder, to lend strength to their distant fellows on the other planet.

What the future might bring to that spiritual extension of being was a matter for expectation.

By accepting a role proper and comfortable to them, the terrestrials had again entered the magic circle of being. They had forsworn their old greeds. Theirs was the world, as they were the world's.

When it was growing dark, Ermine said, "Talking about love as a political act. It takes a little getting used to. But what was that legalistic arrangement the old race suffered when a marriage broke up? Jandol-

Anganol had one? Oh, a divorce. That was a quarrel over possessions, wasn't it?"

"And over who possessed the children," Shoyshal said.

"That's an example of love all entangled in economics and politics. They didn't understand that the random cannot be escaped. It's one of the caprices by which Gaia keeps herself up to date."

Trockern glanced out the window and gestured at the geonaut. "I wouldn't be surprised if Gaia hasn't sent that object to supersede us," he said, with an air of mock gloom. "After all, geonauts are more beautiful and more functional than we are—present company excepted."

As the stars came out, the three climbed down onto the earth and walked by the side of their slow-trundling room. Ermine linked arms with the other two.

"We can judge from the example of Helliconia how many lives of the old race were ruined by territoriality and the lust to possess those who were loved. No matter that it killed love. At least the nuclear winter freed our race from that sort of territoriality. We have risen to a better kind of life."

"I wonder what else is wrong with us that we don't know about?" Trockern said, and laughed.

"In your case we know," said Ermine, teasingly. He bit her ear. Inside the room, SartoriIrvrash stirred on his bunk and grunted, as if in approval, as if he would have relished biting that pink lobe himself. It was about the hour when he generally decided to wake and enjoy the hours of tropical darkness.

"That reminds me," Shoyshal said, looking up at the stars. "If my randomness theory is in any way correct, it might account for why the old race never found any other life forms out there, except on Helliconia. Helliconia and Earth were lucky. We were accident-prone. On the other planets, everything went according to some geophysical plan. As a result, nothing ever happened. There was no story to tell."

They stood looking up into the infinite distances of the sky.

A sigh escaped Trockern. "I always experience intense happiness when I look up at the galaxy. Always. On the one hand, the stars remind me that the whole marvellous complexity of the organic and inorganic universe resolves itself down to a few physical laws awesome in their simplicity—"

"And of course you are happy that the stars provide a text for a speech. . . ." She imitated his posturing.

"And on the other hand, darling, and on the other hand . . . Oh, you know, I'm happy that I'm more complex than a worm or bluebottle, and thus able to read beauty into those few awesome physical laws."

"All those age-old rumours about God," Shoyshal said. "You can't help wondering if there isn't something in them. Perhaps the truth is that God's a real old bore you wouldn't want to be seen dead with. . . ."

". . . Sitting brooding for ever over planets piled with nothing but sand . . ."

". . . And counting every grain," finished Ermine.

Laughing, they had to run to catch up with their room.

The years went by. It was simple. All one had to do was haul on the chains, and the years passed. And the Wheel moved through the starry firmament.

Despair gave way to resignation. Long after resignation came hope, flooding in without fanfares, like dawn.

The nature of the graffiti on the encompassing outer wall changed. There were representations of nude women, hopes and boasts about grandchildren, fears about wives. There were calendars counting down the final years, the figures growing larger as the tenners shrank.

Yet still there were religious sayings, sometimes repeated obsessively on every few metres of wall until, after many tenners, the writer grew tired. One such which Luterin read musingly was ALL THE WORLD'S WISDOM HAS ALWAYS EXISTED: DRINK DEEP OF IT THAT IT MAY INCREASE.

Once, as he hauled on his chains with the rest of the unseen host, as trumpets blew and the whole structure shrieked on its pinions, Luterin Shokerandit was aware of a faint luminosity in his cell. He worked. Every hour hauled the mass of the Wheel under 10 centimetres forward, but every hour increased the luminosity. An halosis of yellow twilight crept in.

He thought himself in paradise. Throwing off his furs, he tugged at the ten-link chain with extra vigour, shouting for his unhearing fellows to do the same. Near the end of the twelve-and-a-half-hour work period, the cell's leading wall slipped forward to reveal the merest slit of light. The cell became filled with a holy substance which flickered and flowed into the least corner of the cell. Luterin fell down on his knees and covered his eyes, crying and laughing.

Before the work period ceased, all of the slit was contained within his outer wall space. It was 240 millimetres wide—and there was now half a small year to go before Luterin had hauled his cell once more to the exit under Bambekk Monastery. Concisely engraved lettering in the granite read: YE HAVE BUT HALF A YEAR LEFT AWAY FROM THE WORLD: SEE YE BENEFIT FROM IT.

The window was cut deep into the rock. It was difficult to see how far it extended before it became a window to the outside. Bars were secured over it at the far end. Through the bars a distant tree could be seen, a caspiarn blowing before a storm wind.

Luterin stared out for a long while before going to sit on his bunk to contemplate the beauty about him. The cleft by which the daylight entered was silted with rubble. Through it filtered a precious quality which brimmed the entire volume of the cell with transforming fluids of beauty. All the light in the world seemed to him to be pouring blessing on his head. Before him lay both the brightest of illuminations, as well as exquisite shadows which painted the corners of the modest room with such gradations of tone as he had never observed in the world of freedom. He drank the ecstasy of being a living biological creature again.

"Insil!" he cried into the twilight. "I shall be back!"

He did not work the next day, but watched the life-giving window being moved by others across the outer wall. On the following day, when again he refused to work, the window moved again and all but disappeared. Even the crack remaining was sufficient to spill an exquisite pearly luminosity into his confinement. When, on the fourth workday, even that vanished—presumably to charm the inmate of the following cell—he was disconsolate.

Now began a period of self-doubt. His longing to be free changed to a fear of what he would find. What would Insil have done with herself? Would she have left the place she hated?

And his mother. Perhaps she was dead by now. He resisted the impulse to sink into pauk and find out.

And Toress Lahl. Well, he had set her free. Perhaps she had made her way back to Borldoran.

And what of the political situation? Was the new Oligarch carrying out the old Oligarch's edicts? Were phagors still being slain? What of the quarrel between Church and State?

He wondered how he would himself be treated when he emerged into the world. Perhaps a party of execution would await him. It was the old question, still unanswered over almost ten small years: was he saint or sinner? A hero or a criminal? Certainly he had forfeited any claim to the position of Keeper of the Wheel.

He began talking to an imagined woman, achieving an eloquence that was never his when he was face to face with anyone else.

"What a maze life is to humans! It must be so much simpler to be a phagor. They aren't tormented by doubt or hope. When you are young, you enjoy a sustained illusion that sooner or later something marvellous is going to happen, that you are going to transcend your parents' limitations, meet a wonderful woman, and be capable of being wonderful to her.

"At the same time, you feel sure that in all the wilderness of possibility, in all the forests of conflicting opinion, there is a vital something that can be known—known and grasped. That we will eventually know it, and convert the whole mystery into a coherent narrative. So that then one's true life—the point of everything—will emerge from the mist into a pure light, into total comprehension.

"But it isn't like that at all. But if it isn't, where did the idea come from, to torture and unsettle us? All the years I've spent here—all the thought that's gone by . . ."

He tugged mightily at each heavy chain that presented itself in that endless succession of chains. The days on the stone calendar dwindled. That impossible day would be upon him when he would be free again to move among other human beings. Whatever happened, he prayed to the Azoiaxic that he might make love to a woman again. In his imagination, Insil was no longer remote.

The wind blew from the north, carrying with it the taint of the permanent ice cap. Very few things could live within its breath. Even the tough leaves of the caspiarns furled themselves like sails against the trunks of the trees when the wind blew.

The valleys were filling with snow. The snow was packing down. Year by small year, the light grew less.

There was now a covered way to the small chapel of King Jandol-Anganol. It was roughly built of fallen branches, but it served to keep a path clear to the sunken door.

For the first time in many centuries, someone lived in the chapel. A woman and a small boy crouched over a stove in one corner. The woman kept the door locked, and screened the stove so that its light could not be seen from outside. She had no right to be here.

All round the chapel she had set traps which she found rusting in the vestry of the chapel. Small animals were caught in her traps, providing food enough. Only rarely did she dare show herself in the village of Kharnabhar, although she had a kind friend there who had established a store to sell fish brought up from the coast—for the old route she had once travelled was kept open, whatever the weather.

She taught her son to read. She drew the letters of the alphabet in the dust, or carried him to see the letters painted on the walls in various texts. She told him that the letters and words were pictures of ideal things, some of which existed or could exist, some of which should not exist. She tried to instil morality with his reading, but she also invented silly stories for him which made them both laugh.

When the child was asleep, she read to herself.

It was a perpetual source of wonder to her that the presiding presence in this building was a man from her own city of Oldorando. Their lives were united in a curious way, across miles and centuries. He had retreated to this place to be in seclusion and to do penance for his sins. Late in life, he had been joined by a strange woman from Dimariam, a distant country of Hespagorat. Both had left documents, through which she wandered by the hour. Sometimes she felt the king's restless spirit by her side.

As the years passed, she told the story to her growing son.

"This naughty King JandolAnganol did a great wrong in the country where your mother was born. He was a religious man, yet he killed his religion. It was a terrible paradox under which he found it hard to live. So he came to Kharnabhar and served in the Wheel for the full ten small years, as now does the one who is your father.

"JandolAnganol left two queens behind him to come here. He must have been very wicked, though the Sibornalese think him holy.

"After he emerged from the Wheel, he was joined by the Dimariam woman I told you about. Like me, she was a doctor. Well, she seems to have been other things besides, including a trader of some sort. Her name was Immya Muntras, and she, feeling the call of religion, sought out the king. Perhaps she comforted his old age. She stood by him. That's no ill thing.

"Muntras possessed learning which she thought precious. See, here is where she wrote it all down, long ago, during the Great Summer, when people thought the world was going to end, just as they do now.

"This lady Muntras had some information from a man who arrived in Oldorando from another world. It sounds strange, but I have seen so many amazing things in my life that I believe anything. Lady Muntras's bones now lie in the antechapel, beside those of the king. Here are her papers.

"What she learned from the man from another world concerned the nature of the plague. She was told by the strange man that the Fat Death was necessary, that it brought to those who survived a metamorphosis, a change in bodily metabolism which would enable them best to survive the winter. Without that metamorphosis, humans cannot hope to live through the heart of the Weyr-Winter.

"The plague is carried by ticks which live on phagors and transfer to men and women. The bite of the tick gives you plague. The plague brings metamorphosis. So you see that man cannot survive the Weyr-Winter without phagors.

"This knowledge the lady Muntras tried to teach in Kharnabhar, centuries past. Yet still they are killing phagors, and the State does everything in its power to keep the plague at bay. It would be better to improve medicine, so that more people who caught the plague could survive."

So she used to talk, scanning her boy's face in the semidarkness.

The boy listened. Then he went to play among the treasures left in the chests which had once belonged to the wicked king.

One evening, as he was playing and his mother reading by the firelight, there came a knocking at the door of the chapel.

Like the slow seasons, the Great Wheel of Kharnabhar always completed its revolutions.

For Luterin Shokerandit, the Wheel at last came full circle. The cell that had been his habitation returned to the opening. Only a wall 0.64 metres thick separated it from the cell ahead, into which a volunteer was even then stepping, to commence ten years in the darkness, rowing Helliconia towards the light.

There were guards waiting in the gloom. They helped him from his place of confinement. Instead of releasing him, they took him slowly up a winding side stair. The light grew steadily brighter; he closed his eyes and gasped.

They took him into a small room in the monastery of Bambekk. For a while he was left alone.

Two female slaves came, regarding him out of the corner of their eyes. They were followed by male slaves, bearing a bath and hot water, a silver looking glass, towels and shaving equipment, fresh clothes.

"These are by courtesy of the Keeper of the Wheel," said one of the women. " 'Tisn't every wheeler gets this treatment, be sure of that."

As the scent of hot water and herbs reached him, Luterin realised how he stank, how the methaney odours of the Wheel clung to him. He allowed the women to strip off his ragged furs. They led him to the bath. He lay glorying in the sensation as they washed his limbs. Every smallest event threatened to overwhelm him. He had been as if dead.

He was powdered and dried and dressed in the thick new clothes.

They led him to the window to peer out, although the light at first almost blinded him.

He was looking down on the village of Kharnabhar from a great height. He could see houses buried up to their roofs in snow. The only things that moved were a sledge pulled by three yelk and two birds circling in the sky overhead, creating that eternal spectre of the wheel.

Visibility was good. A snowstorm was dying, and clouds blew away to the south, leaving pockets of undiluted blue sky. It was all too brilliant. He had to turn away, covering his eyes.

"What's the date?" he asked one of the women.

"Why, 'tis 1319, and tomorrow's Myrkwyr. Now, how about having that beard cut off and looking a few thousand years younger?"

His beard had grown like a fungus in the dark. It was streaked with grey and hung to his navel.

"Cut it off," he said. "I'm not yet twenty-four. I'm still young, aren't I?"

"I've certainly heard of people being older," said the woman, advancing with the scissors.

He was then to be taken before the Keeper of the Wheel.

"This will be merely a formal audience," said the usher who escorted him through the labyrinth of the monastery. Luterin had little to say. The new impressions crowding in were almost more than he could receive; he could not help thinking how he had once regarded himself as destined to be Keeper.

He made no response when eventually he was left at one end of what seemed to him an immense chamber. The Keeper sat at the far end on a wooden throne, flanked by two boys in ecclesiastical garb. The dignitary beckoned Luterin to approach.

He stepped gingerly through the lighted space, awed by the number of paces it required to reach the dais.

The Keeper was an enormous man who had draped himself in a purple gown. His face seemed about to burst. Like his gown, it was purple, and mottled with veins climbing the cheeks and nose like vines. His eyes were watery, his mouth moist. Luterin had forgotten there were such faces, and studied it as an object of curiosity while it studied him.

"Bow," hissed one of the attendant children, so he bowed.

The Keeper spoke in a throttled kind of voice. "You are back among us, Luterin Shokerandit. Throughout the last ten years, you have been under the Church's care—otherwise you would probably have been poisoned by your enemies, in revenge for your act of patricide."

"Who are my enemies?"

The watery eyes were squeezed between folds of lid. "Oh, the slayer of the Oligarch has enemies everywhere, official and unofficial. But they were mainly the Church's enemies too. We shall continue to do what we can for you. There is a private feeling that . . . we owe you something." He laughed. "We could help you to leave Kharnabhar."

"I have no wish to leave Kharnabhar. It's my home." The watery eyes watched his mouth rather than his eyes when he spoke.

"You may change your mind. Now, you must report to the Master of Kharnabhar. Once, if you remember, the offices of Master and Keeper of the Wheel were combined. With the schism between Church and State, the two offices are separate."

"Sir, may I ask a question?"

"Ask it."

"There's much to understand . . . Does the Church hold me to be saint or sinner?"

The Keeper endeavoured to clear his throat. "The Church cannot condone patricide, so I suppose that officially you are a sinner. How could it be otherwise? You might have worked that out, I would have thought, during your ten years below. . . . However, personally, speaking ex officio . . . I'd say you rid the world of a villain, and I regard you as a saint." He laughed.

So this must be an unofficial enemy, thought Luterin. He bowed and turned to walk away when the Keeper called him back.

The Keeper heaved himself to his feet. "You don't recognise me? I'm Wheel-Keeper Ebstok Esikananzi. Ebstok—an old friend. You once

had hopes of marrying my daughter, Insil. As you see, I have risen to
a post of distinction."

"If my father had lived, you would never have become Keeper."

"Who's to blame for that? You be grateful that I'm grateful."

"Thank you, sir," said Luterin, and left the august presence, preoccupied by the remark regarding Insil.

He had no idea where he was supposed to go to report to the Master
of Kharnabhar. But Keeper Esikananzi had arranged everything. A
liveried slave awaited Luterin with a sledge, with furs to protect him
from the cold.

The speed of the sledge overwhelmed him, and the jingle of the
animals' harness bells. As soon as the vehicle started to move, he closed
his eyes and held tight. There were voices like birds crying, and the
song of the runners on the ice, reminding him of something—he knew
not what.

The air smelt brittle. From what little he glimpsed of Kharnabhar
the pilgrims had all gone. The houses were shuttered. Everything looked
drabber and smaller than he remembered it. Lights gleamed here and
there in upper windows or in trading stores which remained open. The
light was still painful to his eyes. He slumped back, marshalling his
memories of Ebstok Esikananzi. He had known this crony of his
father's since childhood, and had never taken to the man; it was Ebstok
who should be called to account for his daughter Insil's bitterness.

The sledge rattled and jolted, its bells merrily jingling. Above their
tinny sound came the tongue of a heavier bell.

He forced himself to look about.

They were sweeping through massive gates. He recognised the gates
and the gatehouse beside them. He had been born here. Cliffs of snow
three metres high towered on either side of the drive. They were driving
through—yes—the Vineyard. Ahead, roofs of a familiar house showed.
The bell of unforgettable voice sounded even louder.

Shokerandit was visited by a warming memory of himself as a small
boy, pulling a little toboggan, running towards the front steps. His
father was standing there, at home for once, smiling, arms extended to
him.

There was an armed sentry on the door now. The door was three parts
enclosed in a small hut for the sentry's protection. The sentry kicked
on the panels of the front door until a slave opened up and took charge
of Luterin.

In the windowless hall, gas jets burned against the wall, their nim-
buses reflected in the polished marble. He saw immediately that the
great vacant chair had gone.

"Is my mother here?" he asked the slave. The man merely gaped at
him and led him up the stairs. Without emotional tone, he told himself that he should be the Master of Kharnabhar, as well as Keeper.

At the slave's knock, a voice bade him enter. He stepped into his father's old study, the room that had so often been locked against him during earlier years.

An old grey hound lay sprawled by the fire, woofing pettishly at Luterin's arrival. Green logs hissed and smouldered in the grate. The room smelt of smoke, dog's piss, and something resembling face powder. Beyond the thick-paned window lay snow and the infinite wordless universe.

A white-haired secretary, the hinges of whose lumbar region had rusted to force on him a resemblance to a crooked walking stick, approached. He munched his lips by way of greeting and offered Luterin a chair without any needless display of cordiality.

Luterin sat down. His gaze travelled round the room, which was still crammed with his father's belongings. He took in the flintlocks and matchlocks of earlier days, the pictures and plate, the mullions and soffits, the orreries and oudenardes. Silverfish and woodworm went about their tasks in the room. The sliver of crumbling cake on the secretary's desk was presumably of recent date.

The secretary had seated himself with an elbow by the cake. "The master is busy at present, with the Myrkwyr ceremony to come. He should not be long," said the secretary. After a pause, he added, regarding Luterin slyly, "I suppose you don't recognise me?"

"It's rather bright in here."

"But I'm your father's old secretary, Secretary Evanporil. I serve the new Master now."

"Do you miss my father?"

"That's hardly for me to say. I simply carry out the administration." He became busy with the papers on his desk.

"Is my mother still here?"

The secretary looked up quickly. "She's still here, yes."

"And Toress Lahl?"

"I don't know that name, sir."

The silence of the rooms was filled with the dry rustle of paper. Luterin contained himself, rousing when the door opened. A tall thin man with a narrow face and peppery whiskers came in, bell clanking at waist. He stood there, wrapped in a black-and-brown heedrant, looking dcwn at Luterin. Luterin stared back, trying to assess whether this was an official or an unofficial enemy.

"Well . . . you are back at last in the world in which you have caused a great deal of havoc. Welcome. The Oligarchy has appointed me Master here—as distinct from any ecclesiastical duties. I'm the voice of the State in Kharnabhar. With the worsening weather, communications with Askitosh are more difficult than they were. We see to it that we get good food supplies from Rivenjk, otherwise military links are . . . rather weaker. . . ."

This was drawn out sentence by sentence, as Luterin made no response.

"Well, we will try to look after you, though I hardly think you can live in this house."

"This is my house."

"No. You have no house. This is the house of the Master and always has been."

"Then you have greatly profited by my act."

"There is profit in the world, yes. That's true."

Silence fell. The secretary came and proffered two glasses of yadahl. Luterin accepted one, blinded by the beauty of its ruby gleam, but could not drink it.

The Master remained standing rather stiffly, betraying some nervousness as he gulped his yadahl. He said, "Of course, you have been away from the world for a long time. Do I take it that you don't recognise me?"

Luterin said nothing.

With a small burst of irritation, the Master said, "Beholder, you are silent, aren't you? I was once your army commander, Archpriest-Militant Asperamanka. I thought soldiers never forgot their commanders in battle!"

Then Luterin spoke. "Ah, Asperamanka . . . 'Let them bleed a little' . . . Yes, now I remember you."

"It's hard to forget how the Oligarchy, when your father controlled it, destroyed my army in order to keep the plague from Sibornal. You and I were among the few to escape death."

He took a considered sip at his yadahl and paced about the room. Now Luterin recognised him by the anger lines incised into his brow.

Luterin rose. "I'd like to ask you a question. How does the State regard me—as a saint or a sinner?"

The Master's fingernails tapped against his glass. "After your father . . . *died*, there followed a period of unrest in the various nations of Sibornal. They're used to harsh laws by now—the laws that will see us safe through the Weyr-Winter—but then it was otherwise. There was, frankly, some bad feeling about Oligarch Torkerkanzlag II. His edicts weren't popular. . . ."

"So the Oligarchy circulated the rumor—and this was my idea—that they had trained you to assassinate your father, whom they could no longer control. They put out the idea that you had been spared at the massacre at Koriantura only because you were the Oligarchy's man. The rumour increased our popularity and brought us through a difficult time."

"You wrapped up my crime in a lie."

"We just made use of your useless act. One outcome of it was that the State recognised you officially as a—why do you say 'saint'?—as a hero. You've become part of legend. Though I have to say that personally I regard you as a sinner of the first water. I still keep my religious convictions in such matters."

"And is it religious conviction that has installed you in Kharnabhar?"

Asperamanka smiled and tugged at his beard. "I greatly miss Askitosh. But there was an opportunity open to govern this province, so I took it. . . . As a legend, a figure in the history books, you must accept my hospitality for the night. A guest, not a captive."

"My mother?"

"We have her here. She's ill. She's no more likely to recognise you than you were to recognise me. Since you are something of a hero in Kharnabhar, I want you to accompany me to the public Myrkwyr ceremony tomorrow, with the Keeper. Then people can see we haven't harmed you. It will be the day of your rehabilitation. There'll be a feast."

"You'll let me *feed* a little . . ."

"I don't understand you. After the ceremony, we will make what arrangements you wish. You might consider it best to leave Kharnabhar and live somewhere less remote."

"That's what the Keeper also hoped I might consider."

He went to see his mother. Lourna Shokerandit lay in bed, frail and unmoving. As Asperamanka had anticipated, she did not recognise him. That night, he dreamed he was back in the Wheel.

The following day began with a great bustle and ringing of bells. Strange smells of food drifted up to where Luterin lay. He recognised the savoury odours as rising from dishes he would once have desired. Now he longed for the simple fare he had reviled, the rations that came rolling down the chutes of the Wheel.

Slaves came to wash and dress him. He did as was required of him, passively.

Many people he did not know assembled in the great hall. He looked down over the bannisters and could not bring himself to join them. The excitement was overpowering. Master Asperamanka came up the stairs to him and said, taking his arm, "You are unhappy. What can I do for you? It is important that I am seen to please you today."

The personages in the hall were flocking outside, where sleighbells rattled. Luterin did not speak. He could hear the wind roar as it had done in the Wheel.

"Very well, then at least we will ride together and people will see us and think us friends. We are going to the monastery, where we shall meet the Keeper, and my wife, and many of Kharnabhar's dignitaries."

He talked animatedly and Luterin did not listen, concentrating on the exacting performance of descending a flight of stairs. Only as they went through the front door and a sleigh drew up for them, did the Master say sharply, "You've no weapon on you?"

When Luterin shook his head, they climbed into the sleigh, and slaves bundled furs round them. They set off into the gale among cliffs of snow.

When they turned north, the wind bit into their faces. To the twenty degrees of frost, a considerable chill factor had to be added.

But the sky was clear and, as they drove through the shuttered village, a great irregular mass appeared through its veils to loom over Mount Kharnabhar.

"Shivenink, the third highest peak on the planet," said Asperamanka, pointing it out. "What a place!" He made a moue of distaste.

Just for a minute the mountain's naked ribbed walls were visible; then it was gone again, the ghost that dominated the village.

The passengers were driven up a winding track to the gates of Bambekk Monastery. They entered and dismounted. Slaves assisted them into the vaulted halls, where a number of official-looking people had already gathered.

At a sign, they proceeded up several staircases. Luterin took no interest in their progress. He was listening to a rumble far below, which carried through the monastery. Obsessively, he tried to imagine every corner of his cell, every scratch on its enclosing walls.

The party came at last to a hall high in the monastery. It was circular in shape. Two carpets covered the floor, one white, one black. They were separated by an iron band which ran across the floor, dividing the chamber in half. Biogas shed a dim light. There was one window, facing south, but it was covered by a heavy curtain.

Embroidered on the curtain was a representation of the Great Wheel being rowed across the heavens, each oarsman sitting in a small cell in its perimeter, wearing cerulean garments, each smiling blissfully.

Now at last I understand those blissful smiles, thought Luterin.

A group of musicians was playing solemn and harmonious music at the far side of the room. Lackeys with trays were dispensing drinks to all and sundry.

Keeper of the Wheel Esikananzi appeared, raising his hand graciously in greeting. Smiling, half-bowing to all, he made his portly way towards where the Master of Kharnabhar and Luterin stood.

When they had greeted each other, Esikananzi asked Asperamanka, "Is our friend any more sociable this morning?" On receiving a negative, he said to Luterin, with an attempt at geniality, "Well, the sight you are about to witness may loosen your tongue."

The two men became surrounded by hangers-on, and Luterin gradually edged his way out of the centre of the group. A hand touched his sleeve. He turned to meet the scrutiny of a pair of wide eyes. A thin woman of guarded mien had approached, to observe him with a look of real or feigned astonishment. She was dressed in a sober russet gown, the hem of which touched the floor, the collar of which rioted in lace. Although she was near middle age and her face was gaunter than in bygone times, Luterin recognised her immediately.

He uttered her name.

Insil nodded as if her suspicions were confirmed and said, "They claimed that you were being difficult and refusing to recognise people. What a habit this lying is! And you, Luterin, how unpleasant to be recalled from the dead to mingle with the same mendacious crowd— older, greedier . . . more frightened. How do I appear to you, Luterin?"

In truth, he found her voice harsh and her mouth grim. He was surprised by the amount of jewellery she wore, in her ears, on her arms, on her fingers.

What most impressed him were her eyes. They had changed. The pupils seemed enormous—a sign of her attention, he believed. He could not see the whites in her eyes and thought, admiringly, Those irises show the depth of Insil's soul.

But he said tenderly, "Two profiles in search of a face?"

"I'd forgotten that. Existence in Kharnabhar has grown narrower over the years—dirtier, grimmer, more artificial. As might be expected. Everything narrows. Souls included." She rubbed her hands together in a gesture he did not recall.

"You still survive, Insil. You are more beautiful than I remembered." He forced the insincerity from him, conscious of pressures on him to be a social being again. While it remained difficult to enter into a conversation, he was aware of old reflexes awakening—including his habit of being polite to women.

"Don't lie to me, Luterin. The Wheel is supposed to turn men into saints, isn't it? Notice I refrain from asking you about *that* experience."

"And you never married, Sil?"

Her glare intensified. She lowered her voice to say with venom, "Of course I am married, you fool! The Esikananzis treat their slaves better than their spinsters. What woman could survive in this heap without selling herself off to the highest bidder?"

She stamped her foot. "We had our discussion of that glorious topic when you were one of the candidates."

The dialogue was running too fast for him. "Selling yourself off, Sil! What do you intend to mean?"

"You put yourself completely out of the running when you stuck your knife into that pa you so revered. . . . Not that I blame you, seeing that he killed the man who took away my cherished virginity—your brother Favin."

Her words, delivered with a false brightness as she smiled at those around them, opened up an ancient wound in Luterin. As so often during his incarceration in the Wheel, he thought of the waterfall and his brother's death. Always there remained the question of why Favin, a promising young army officer, should have made the fatal jump; the words of his father's gossie on that subject had never satisfied him. Always he had shied away from a possible answer.

Not caring who was looking on among the pale-lipped crowd, he grasped Insil's arm. "What are you saying about Favin? It's known that he committed suicide."

She pulled away angrily, saying, "For Azoiaxic's sake, do not touch me. My husband is here, and watching. There can be nothing between us now, Luterin. Go away! It hurts to look at you."

He stared about, his gaze darting over the crowd. Halfway across the chamber, a pair of eyes set in a long face regarded him in open hostility.

He dropped his glass. "Oh, Beholder . . . not Asperamanka, that opportunist!" The red liquid soaked into the white carpet.

As she waved to Asperamanka, she said, "We're a good match, the Master and I. He wanted to marry into a proud family. I wanted to survive. We make each other equally happy." When Asperamanka turned with a sign back to his colleagues, she said in venomous tones, "All these leather-clad men going off with their animals into the forests . . . why do they so love each other's stink? Close under the trees, doing secret things, blood brothers. Your father, my father, Asperamanka . . . Favin was not like that."

"I'm glad if you loved him. Can't we escape from these others and talk?"

She deflected his offer of consolation. "What misery that brief happiness inherited . . . Favin was not one to ride into the caspiarns with his heavy males. He rode there with me."

"You say my father killed him. Are you drunk?" There was something like madness in her manner. To be with her, to enter into these ancient agonies—it was as if time stopped. It was as if a fusty old drawer was being unlocked; its banal contents had become hallowed by their secret nature.

Insil scarcely bothered to shake her head. "Favin had everything to live for . . . me, for instance."

"Not so loud!"

"Favin!" she shouted, so that heads turned in her direction. She began to pace through the crowd, and Luterin followed. "Favin discovered that your father's 'hunts' were really journeys to Askitosh and that he was the Oligarch. Favin was all integrity. He challenged your father. Your father shot him down and threw him over the cliff by the waterfall."

They were interrupted by officious women acting hostess, and separated. Luterin accepted another glass of yadahl, but had to set it down, so violently was his hand shaking. In a moment, he found his chance to speak to Insil again, breaking in on an ecclesiastic who was addressing her.

"Insil—this terrible knowledge! How did you discover about my father and Favin? Were you there? Are you lying?"

"Of course not. I found out later—when you were in your fit of prostration—by my customary method, eavesdropping. My father knew everything. He was *glad*—because Favin's death punished me. . . . I could not believe I had heard aright. When he was telling my mother she was *laughing*. I doubted my senses. Unlike you, however, I did not fall into a year-long swoon."

"And I suspected nothing . . . I was fatally innocent."

She gave him one of her supercilious looks. Her irises appeared larger than ever.

"And you still are fatally innocent. Oh, I can tell . . ."

"Insil, resist the temptation to make everyone your enemy!"

But her look hardened and she burst out again. "You were never any help to me. My belief is that children always know intuitively the real natures of their parents, rather than the dissembled ones which they show the world. You knew your father's nature intuitively, and feigned dead to avoid his vengeance. But I am the truly dead."

Asperamanka was approaching. "Meet me in the corridor in five minutes," she said hastily, as she turned, smiling and gaily raising a hand.

Luterin moved away. He leaned against a wall, struggling with his feelings. "Oh, Beholder . . ." he groaned.

"I expect you find the crowds overpowering after your solitude," someone who passed by said pleasantly.

His whole inner life was undergoing revolution. Things had not been, he had not been, as he had pretended to himself. Even his gallantry on the field of battle—had that not been powered by ancient angers released, rather than by courage? Were all battles releases from frustration, rather than deeds of deliberate violence? He saw he knew nothing. Nothing. He had clung to innocence, fearing knowledge.

Now he remembered that he had experienced the actual moment when his brother died. He and Favin had been close. He had felt the psychic shock of Favin's death one evening: yet his father had announced the death as occurring on the following day. That tiny discrepancy had lodged in his young consciousness, poisoning it. Eventually—he could foresee—joy could come that he was delivered from that poison. But delivery was not yet.

His limbs trembled.

In the turmoil of his thoughts, he had almost forgotten Insil. He feared for her in her strange mood. Now he hurried towards the corridor she had indicated—reluctant though he was to hear more from her.

His way was barred by bedizened dignitaries, who spoke to him and to each other roundly of the solemnity of this occasion, and of how much more appalling conditions would be henceforth. As they talked, they devoured little meat-filled pastries in the shape of birds. It occurred to Luterin that he neither knew nor cared about the ceremony in which he had become involved.

Their conversation paused as all eyes focussed on the other side of the chamber.

Ebstok Esikananzi and Asperamanka were leaving by a spiral stair which wound to an upper gallery.

Luterin took the opportunity to slip into the corridor. Insil joined him in a minute, her narrow body leaning forward in the haste of her walk. She held her skirt up from the floor in one pale hand, her jewellery glittering like frost.

"I must be brief," she said, without introduction. "They watch me continually, except when they are in drink, or holding their ridiculous ceremonies—as now. Who cares if the world is plunged into darkness? Listen, when we are free to leave here, you must proceed to the fish seller in the village. It stands at the far end of Sanctity Street. Understand? Tell no one. 'Chastity's for women, secrecy's for men,' as they say. Be secret."

"What then, Insil?" Again he was asking her questions.

"My dear father and my dear husband plan to kick you out. They will not kill you, as I understand—that might look bad for them, and that much they owe you for your timely disposal of the Oligarch. Simply evade them after the ceremony and go down Sanctity Street."

He stared impatiently into her hypnotic eyes.

"And this secret meeting—what is it about?"

"I am playing the role of messenger, Luterin. You still remember the name of Toress Lahl, I suppose?"

XVII

SUNSET

Trockern and Ermine were asleep. Shoyshal had gone somewhere. The geonaut they preceded had come to a halt, and stood gently breathing out its little white hexagonal offspring.

SartoriIrvrash woke and stretched, yawning as he did so. He sat up on his bunk and scratched his white head. It was his habit to sleep for the second half of the day, waking at midnight, thinking through the dark hours, when his spirit could commune with the travelling Earth, and teaching from dawn onwards. He was Trockern's teacher. He had named himself after a dangerous old sage who once lived on Helliconia, whose gossie he had met empathically.

After a while, he heaved himself up and went outside. He stood for a long while looking at the stars, enjoying the feel of the night. Then he padded back into the room and roused Trockern.

"I'm asleep," Trockern said.

"I could hardly waken you if you weren't."

"Zzzz."

"You stole something of mine, Trockern. You stole my explanation of why things went awry on Earth, in order to impress your ladies."

"As you see, I impressed fifty percent of them." Trockern indicated

the peacefully sleeping Ermine, whose lips were pursed as if she was
awaiting the chance to kiss someone in her midsummer dream.

"Unfortunately you got my argument wrong. That possessiveness
which was once such a feature of mankind was not a product of fear,
as you claimed—although I believe you called it 'perpetual unease.' It
was a product of innate aggressiveness. The old races did not fear
enough: otherwise they would never have built the weapons they knew
would destroy them. Aggression was at the root of it all."

"Isn't aggression born of fear?"

"Don't get sophisticated before you can walk. If you take Helliconia
as an example, you can see how every generation ritualises its aggression
and its killing. The earlier terrestrial generations you were talking about
did not seek to possess only territory and one another, as you were
claiming."

"In truth, SartoriIrvrash, you cannot have slept well this afternoon."

"In truth I sleep, as I wake in truth." He put an arm about the
younger man's shoulders. "The argument can be taken to greater heights.
Those ancient people sought to possess the Earth also, to enslave it
under concrete. Nor did their ambitions die there. Their politicians
strove to make space their dominion; while the ordinary people created
fantasies wherein they invaded the galaxy and ruled the universe. That
was aggression, not fear."

"You could be right."

"Don't abandon your point of view so easily. If I could be right I
could be wrong. We ought to know the truth about our forebears who,
wicked though they were, have given us our chance on the scene."

Trockern climbed from his bunk. Ermine sighed and turned over,
still sleeping.

"It's warm—let's take a stroll outside," said SartoriIrvrash.

As they went out into the night, with the star field above them,
Trockern said, "Do you think we improve ourselves, master, by re-
thinking?"

"We shall always be as we are, biologically speaking, but we can
improve our social infrastructures, with any luck. I mean by that the
sort of work our extitutions are working on now—a revolutionary new
integration of the major theorems of physical science with the sciences
of mankind, society, and existence. Of course, our main function as
biological beings is as part of the biosphere, and we are most useful in
that role if we remain unaltered; only if the biosphere in some way
altered again could our role change."

"But the biosphere is altering all the time. Summer is different from
winter, even here so close to the tropics."

SartoriIrvrash was looking towards the horizon, and said, rather ab-
sently, "Summer and winter are functions of a stable biosphere, of Gaia
breathing in and out in her stride. Humanity has to operate within the

limits of her function. To the aggressive, that always seemed a pessimistic point of view; yet it is not even visionary, merely commonsensical. It fails to be common sense only if you have been indoctrinated all your life to believe, first, that mankind is the centre of things, the Lords of Creation, and, second, that we can improve our lot at the expense of something else.

"Such an outlook brings misery, as we see on our poor sister planet out there. We have only to step down from the arrogance of believing that the world or the future is somehow 'ours' and immediately life for everyone is enhanced."

Trockern said, "I suppose each of us has to find that out for ourself." He found it delightful to be humble after sunset.

With sudden exasperation, SartoriIrvrash said, "Yes, unfortunately that's so. We have to learn by bitter experience, not blithe example. And that's ridiculous. Don't imagine that I think the state of affairs is perfect. Gaia is an absolute ninny to let us loose in the first place. At least on Helliconia the Original Beholder planted phagors to keep mankind in check!" He laughed and Tockern joined in.

"I know you think me wanton," the latter said, "but isn't Gaia herself a wanton, spawning so riotously in all directions?"

His senior shot him a foxy look. "Everything else must bring forth in abundance, so that everything else can eat it. It's not the best of arrangements, perhaps—cooked up and cobbled together on the spur of the moment from a chemical broth. That doesn't mean to say we can't imitate Gaia and adopt, like her, our own homeostasis."

The moon in its last quarter shone overhead. SartoriIrvrash pointed to the red star burning low by the horizon.

"See Antares? Just north of it is the constellation Ophiuchus, the Serpent Bearer. In Ophiuchus is a large dark dust cloud about seven hundred light-years away, concealing a cluster of young stars. Among them lies Freyr. It would be one of the twelve brightest stars in the sky, were it not for the dust cloud. And that's where the phagors are."

The two men contemplated the distance without speaking. Then Trockern said, "Have you ever thought, master, how phagors vaguely resemble the demons and devils which used to haunt the imagination of Christians?"

"That had not occurred to me. I have always thought of an even older allusion, the minotaur of ancient Greek myth, a creature stuck between human and animal, lost in the labyrinths of its own lusts."

"Presumably you think that the Helliconian humans should allow the phagors to coexist, to maintain the biospheric balance?"

" 'Presumably . . .' We presume so much." A long silence followed. Then SartoriIrvrash said, reluctantly, "With the deepest respect to Gaia and her Serpent-Bearing sister out there, they are old biddies at

*times. Mankind learnt aggression in their wombs. I mean, to use an-
other ancient analogy, humans and phagors are rather Cain and Abel,
aren't they? One or other of them has to go . . ."*

Trumpets sounded above the heads of the gathering. Their voices
were muted and sweet, and in no way reminiscent of those work trumpets buried far below their feet—except to Luterin Shokerandit.

The dignitaries in the great chamber swallowed their last bird-shaped
pastries and put on reverential faces. Luterin moved among them feeling cumbersome among so many ectomorphic shapes. He lost sight of
Insil.

The Keeper and the Master, Insil's father and husband, were returning down the spiral stair. They had assumed silken robes of car-
mine and blue over their ordinary clothes, and put on odd-shaped hats.
Their faces were as if cast from an alloy of lead and flesh.

Side by side, they paraded to the curtained windows. There they
turned and bowed to the assembly. The assembly fell silent, the
musicians tiptoed away over creaking boards.

Keeper Esikananzi spoke first.

"You all know of the reasons why Bambekk Monastery was built,
many centuries ago. It was built to service the Wheel—and of course
you know why the Architects built the Wheel. We stand on the site of
the greatest act of faith ever achieved/to be by mankind. But perhaps
you will/permissive allow me to remind you why this particular position
was chosen by our illustrious ancestors, in what some people regard as
a remote part of the Sibornalese continent.

"Let me draw your attention to the iron band running under your
feet which divides this dome in half. That band marks the line of
latitude on which this edifice is built. We are here fifty-five degrees
north of the equator, and standing upon that actual line. As you scarcely
need reminding, fifty-five degrees north is the line of the Polar Circle."

At this point, he gestured to a servant. The curtains concealing the
windows were drawn apart.

A view over the town was revealed, looking south. The visibility was
good enough for everything to be seen clearly, including the far horizon,
bare except for a thin line of denniss trees.

"We are fortunate on this occasion. The cloud has cleared. We are
privileged to witness a solemn event which the rest of Sibornal will be
commemorating."

At this point, Master Asperamanka stood forward and spoke, stiffen-
ing his speech with High Dialect. "Let me echo my good friend and
colleague's word, 'fortunate.' Fortunate we are/tend indeed. Church
and State have kept/keeping/will the people of Sibornal united. The

plague has been/aspirational eradicated, and we have slain most of the phagors on our continent.

"You know that our ships have mastery of the seas. In addition, we are now/will building a Great Wall to serve as an act of faith comparable with our formidable Great Wheel.

"This is/proclamatory a New Great Age. The Great Wall will run right across the north of Chalce. There will be watchtowers on it every two kilometres, and the walls will be seven metres high. That Wall, together with our ships, will keep/keeping out all enemies from our territory. The Day of Myrkwyr is the harbinger of Weyr-Winter ahead, but we shall live through it, our grandchildren will live through it, and their grandchildren. And we shall emerge in the spring, the next Great Spring, ready to conquer all of Helliconia."

Cheers and handclaps had sounded throughout this speech. Now the applause was clamorous. Asperamanka stared down to hide the gleam of satisfaction on his face.

Ebstok Esikananzi raised a hand.

"Friends, it is five to noon on this solemn day. Watch the southern horizon. Since it is small winter, Batalix is below that horizon. She will rise again with her puny light in another four tenners, but—"

His words were lost, as everyone pressed to the windows.

Down in the village below, a bonfire had just been lit. The villagers were seen as ants, running about it, arms upraised, swaddled in woollens or furs.

Fresh drink was brought to the watchers in the dome. Mostly, it was drunk as soon as received, and the empty glasses thrust out for more. An unease had settled on the privileged crowd, whose faces made a gloomy contrast to the merry gestures of the ants far below.

A bell began to sound noon. As if in response to its brazen tongue, a change took place on the southern horizon.

On that horizon, the road could be seen as it wound from the village. Elsewhere was unbroken white, trees and buildings standing in frosty outline. Wisps of snow perpetually blew from lodgements, streaming out on the wind like smoke from candles newly extinguished. The horizon itself was clear, and bright with dawn—with sunrise.

Above its crusty line rose a rim of red, a red of heaviness, of congealing blood, the upper part of Freyr's orb.

"Freyr!" came the exclamation from the throats of all who watched, as if by naming the star they could have power over it.

A shaft of light spread upon the world, casting shadows, flooding a range of far hills with pink light till they gleamed against the slatey sky behind them. The faces of the privileged in the dome were made red. Only the village below, where the ants were circling, remained in shadow.

The privileged glared upon that sliver of disc. It remained as it was, growing no greater. The most intense scrutiny could not determine the instant at which, instead of increasing, it began to shrink. Sunrise was enantiodromic sunset.

Light was withdrawn from the world. The range of far hills faded, was absorbed into the increasing murk.

The precious slice of Freyr shrivelled still further. By now, the giant sun had in actuality set: what remained behind was an image of it, a refraction through the thickness of atmosphere of the real thing below the horizon. None could tell the image from the real. Myrkwyr had already begun, without their knowing it.

The red image shrivelled.

It divided itself into bars of light. Shattered.

Then it was gone.

In the centuries ahead, Freyr would hide like a mole beneath the mountain, never to be seen again. In the small summers, Batalix would shine as previously; the small winters would remain unlit, under the shadow of the greater winter. Auroras would unfold their mysterious banners in the skies above the mountain. Meteorites would briefly glitter. Comets would occasionally be sighted. The stars would still shine. Throughout the next ninety revolutions of the Great Wheel, the major luminary, that massive furnace which had given life to the Sons of Freyr, would be little more than a rumour.

For all who experienced it, Myrkwyr was a day of doom. The faceless deity who presided over the biosphere was powerless to intervene, relying perhaps on the shortsightedness of the humans, on their involvement in their own affairs, to damp down its psychic shock. She was carried along with her world. Seen in wider perspective, Freyr continued to shine, and ever would do until its comparatively brief lifespan was finished: its darkness was merely a local condition, of small duration.

For most of nature, there could be only submission to fate. On land, the sap, the seed, the semen, would wait, dormant for the most part. In the sea, the complex mechanisms of the food chain would continue unabated. Only mankind could lift itself above direct necessity. In mankind lay reserves of strength unknowable to those who held them, reserves which could be drawn upon in situations where survival demanded.

Such reflections were far from the minds of those in the assembly who watched Freyr shatter into fragments of light. They were touched by fear. They wondered for their family's survival and their own. The most basic question of existence faced them: How am I to keep fed and warm?

Fear is a powerful emotion. Yet it is easily overcome by anger, hope, desperation, and defiance. Fear would not last. The great processes of the Helliconian year would grind on towards apastron and the winter solstice. That turning point of the year was many generations away. By

then, the twilights of Weyr-Winter would have long since become all
that northern Sibornal knew. The rise of Freyr once more, majestic in
the Great Spring, would be greeted with the same awe as its departure.
But fear would have died long before hope.

How mankind would survive the centuries of Weyr-Winter would
depend upon its mental and emotional resources. The cycle of human
history was not immutable. Given determination, better could succeed
worse; it was possible to row into the light, to navigate in the tide of
Myrkwyr.

Keeper Esikananzi said solemnly, "The long night holds no fear for
those who trust in the Lord God the Azoiaxic, who existed before life,
and round whom all life revolves. With his aid, we shall bring this
precious world of ours through the long night, to bask again in his
glory." And Master Asperamanka shouted spiritedly, "To Sibornal—
united throughout the long Weyr-Winter to come!"

Their audience responded bravely. But in every heart lay the knowledge that they would never see Freyr again; nor would their children,
nor their children's children. On the latitude of Kharnabhar the brighter
sun of Freyr would never shine in the sky until another forty-two
generations had been born and died. Nobody present could ever hope
to see that brilliant luminary again.

A choir sang distantly the anthem, "Oh, May We All Find Light at
Last." Gloom settled in every heart. The loss was as sharp as the loss of
a child.

The lackey solemnly drew the curtains again, hiding the landscape
from view.

Many in the assembly stayed to drink more yadahl. They had little
to say to each other. The musicians played, but a mood of sullen
resignation had settled which would not be dispelled. Singly or in
groups, the guests were leaving. They evaded each other's gaze.

Stone steps wound down through the monastery to the entrance. A
carpet had been laid on the stairs in honour of the occasion. Cold drafts,
blowing upwards, lifted the edges of the carpet. As Luterin was descending, two men emerged from an archway on a landing and seized him.

He fought and shouted, but they locked his arms behind him and
carried him into a stone washroom. Asperamanka was waiting there.
He had divested himself of his ceremonial robes, and was putting on a
coat and leather gauntlets. His two men wore leather and carried guns
at their belts. Luterin thought of what Insil had said: "All those leather-
clad men . . . doing secret things."

Asperamanka put on a genial tone. "It isn't going to work, is it,
Luterin? We can't have you going free in a tight-knit community like
Kharnabhar. You'll be too disruptive an influence."

"What are you trying to preserve here—apart from yourself?"

"I wish to preserve my wife's honour for one thing. You seem to think there is evil here. The fact is, we have to fight to survive. The good—and the bad—will naturally survive in us. Most people understand that. You don't.

"You are inclined to play the part of a holy innocent, and they always make trouble. So we are going to give you a chance to help the whole community. Helliconia needs to be hauled back into the light. You are going to go into the Wheel for another ten-year spell."

He fought free and ran for the door. One of the huntsmen reached it in time to slam it in his face. He struck the man on the jaw, but was made captive again.

"Tie him," Asperamanka ordered. "Don't let him go again."

The men had no cord. One reluctantly yielded up the broad belt of his jacket, and with that they lashed Luterin's hands behind his back.

When Asperamanka opened the door, they marched down the rest of the stairs, the men flanking Luterin closely. Asperamanka seemed greatly pleased with himself.

"We said farewell to Freyr with courage and ceremony. Admire power, Luterin. I admired your father for his ruthlessness as Oligarch. What a fateful generation ours is. Either we'll be wiped out or we'll decide the course of the world. . . ."

"Or you'll choke on a fish bone," Luterin said.

They descended to the entrance hall. Through the broad archway, the outer world could be seen. The chill came in, and also the noise of the crowd and the bonfire. The simple people were dancing round the fires they had lit, faces gleaming in the light of the flames. Traders scurried about, selling waffles and spitted fish.

"For all their religion, they believe that lighting fires may bring Freyr back," Asperamanka said. He lingered at the entrance. "What they are really doing is ensuring that wood becomes short before it need be. . . . Well, let them get on with it. Let them go into pauk or do whatever they please. The elite is going to have to survive on the backs of just such peasants as these for the next few centuries or more."

There was shouting and a stir from the back of the crowd. Soldiers came into view as the crowd parted to make way for them. They carried something struggling between them.

"Ah, they've caught another phagor. Good. We'll see this," Asperamanka said, with a hint of ancient angers under his brows.

The phagor was lashed upside down to a pole. It struggled violently as its captors brought it to one of the fires.

Behind came a figure of a man, lifting his arms and shouting. Luterin could not hear what he said for the general hubbub, but he recognised him by his long beard. The man was his old schoolmaster, who had taught him—long ago in another existence—when he was lying paralysed in bed. The old man had kept a phagor as servant, being too poor to afford a slave. It was clearly his phagor which the soldiers had captured.

The soldiers dragged the creature nearer to the fire. The crowd ceased its dancing and shouted with excitement, the women egging the soldiers on along with the men.

"Burn it!" shouted Asperamanka, but he merely echoed the voice of the mob.

"It's just a domestic," Luterin said. "Harmless as a dog."

"It's still capable of spreading the Fat Death."

Fight though it would, the ancipital was pulled and pushed to the largest of the fires. Its coat began to burn. Another inch—a yell from the crowd—a heave—and then a mournful call sounded from beyond the gathering. Distant human screams. Into the marketplace poured armed ancipitals on kaidaws.

Each ancipital wore body armour. Some wore primitive skull shields. They rode their red kaidaws from a position behind the animals' low humps, at the crouch. In this position they could strike out with spears as they went.

"Freyr die! Sons of Freyr die!" they cried from their harsh throats.

The crowd began to move, less as separate individuals than as a wave. Only the soldiers made a stand. The captive phagor was left with its pale harneys boiling in its skull, but it rose up and made off, coat still smouldering.

Asperamanka ran forward, shouting to the soldiers to fire. Luterin, as an observer, could see that there were no more than eight of the invaders. Some of them sprouted black hairs, a mark of ancipital old age. All but one had been dehorned—a sure sign that these were no kind of threat from the mountains, such as tremulous imaginations in Kharnabhar fed on, but a few refugee phagors who had banded together on this special day, when conditions in Sibornal reverted to virtually what they had been before Freyr entered Helliconia's sky, many epochs ago.

He saw how members of the crowd who were impeded in some way fell first to the stabbing spears: pedlars with trays, women with babies or small children, the lame, the sick. Some were trampled underfoot. A baby was scooped up and flung into the heart of a fire.

As Asperamanka and his two bullies drew guns and started firing, the horned ancipital wheeled its russet-haired mount and charged at the Master. It came straight, its skull low over the massive skull of the kaidaw. In its eye was no light of battle, simply a dull cerise stare: it was doing what it did according to some ancient template set in its eotemporal brain.

Asperamanka fired. The bullets lost themselves in the thick pelage of animal. It faltered in mid-stride. The two bullies turned and ran. Asperamanka stood his ground, firing, shouting. The kaidaw fell suddenly on one knee. Up came the spear. It caught Asperamanka as he turned. The tip entered his skull through the eye socket and he fell back into the monastery entrance.

Luterin ran for his life. He had wrenched his arms free of the belt. He jumped down into the street, into the trampled snow, and ran. There were other running figures nearby, too concerned with saving their own lives to bother with his. He hid behind a house, panting, and surveyed the scene.

Blue shadows and bodies lay on the marketplace. The sky overhead was a deep blue, in which a bright star gleamed—Aganip. Hues of sunset lay to the south. It was bitterly cold.

The mob had surrounded one kaidaw and was pulling its rider to the ground. The others were galloping off to safety—another sign that this was not an arm of a regular ancipital component, which would not have abandoned a fight so easily.

He made his way without trouble towards Sanctity Street and his appointment with Toress Lahl.

Sanctity Street was narrow. Its buildings were tall. Most had been constructed in a better age to house the pilgrims who came to visit the Wheel. Now the shutters were up; many doors were barricaded. Slogans had been painted on the walls: God Keep the Keeper, We Follow the Oligarch—presumably as a form of life insurance. At the rear of the houses and hostels, the snow was piled up to the eaves.

Luterin started cautiously down the street. His mood was one of elation at his escape. He could see beyond the end of the street, where it seemed eternity began. There was an unlimited expanse of snow, its dimensions emphasised by occasional trees. In the distance stretched a band of pink of the most delicate kind, where the sun Freyr still lit on a far cliff, the southern face of the northern ice cap. This vista lifted his spirits further, suggesting as it did the endless possibilities of the planet, beyond the reach of human pettiness. Despite all oppression, the great world remained, inexhaustible in its forms and lights. He might be gazing upon the face of the Beholder herself.

He passed an entranceway where a figure lurked. It called his name. He turned. Through the dusk, he saw a woman wrapped in furs.

"You are almost there. Aren't you excited?" she said.

He went to her, clutched her, felt her narrow body under the furs. "Insil! You waited."

"Only partly for you. The fish seller has something I need. I am sick after that performance in there, with the silly drama and speeches. They think they have conquered nature when they wrap a few words round it. And of course my sherb of a husband mouthing the word Sibornal as if it were a mouthwash . . . I'm sick, I need to drug myself against them. What is that filthy curse which the commoners use, meaning to commit irrumation on both suns? The forbidden oath? Tell me."

"You mean, 'Abro Hakmo Astab'?"

She repeated it with relish. Then she screamed it.

Hearing her say it excited him. He held her tight and forced his mouth against hers. They struggled. He heard his own voice saying, "Let me biwack you here, Insil, as I've always longed to do. You're not really frigid. I know it. You're really a whore, just a whore, and I want you."

"You're drunk, get away, get away. Toress Lahl is awaiting you."

"I care nothing for her. You and I are meant for each other. That's been the case ever since we were children. Let's fulfill ourselves. You once promised me. Now's the time, Insil, now!"

Her great eyes were close to his.

"You frighten me. What's come over you? Let me be."

"No, no, I don't have to let you be now. Insil—Asperamanka is dead. The phagors killed him. We can be married now, anything, only let me have you, please, please!"

She wrenched herself away from him.

"He's dead? Dead? No. It can't be. Oh, the cur!" She started screaming and ran down the street, holding up her trailing skirt above the trodden snow.

Luterin followed in horror at her distress.

He tried to detain her but she said something which he at first could not understand. She was crying for a pipe of occhara.

The fish seller was, as she had said, at the end of the street. A short passage had been constructed beyond the original shop front, allowing passengers to enter without bringing the cold in with them. Above the door was a sign saying ODIM'S FINEST FISH.

They entered a dim parlour where several men stood, warmly wrapped, all of them metamorphosed winter shapes. Seals and large fish hung on hooks. Smaller fish, crabs, and eels were bedded in ice on a counter. Luterin took little notice of his surroundings, so concerned was he for Insil, who was now almost hysterical.

But the men recognized her. "We know what she wants," one said, grinning. He led her into a rear room.

One of the other men came forward and said, "I remember you, sir." He was youthful and had a vaguely foreign look about him.

"My name is Kenigg Odim," he said. "I sailed with you on that journey from Koriantura to Rivenjk. I was just a lad then, but you may recollect my father, Eedap Odim."

"Of course, of course," said Luterin distractedly. "A dealer in something. Ivory, was it?"

"Porcelain, sir. My father still lives in Rivenjk, and organises supplies of good fish to come up here every week. It's a paying business, and there's no demand for porcelain these days. Life's better down in Rivenjk, sir, I must say. Fine feelings is about as much good as fine porcelain up here."

"Yes, yes, I'm sure that's so."

"We also do a trade in occhara, sir, if you would care for a free pipe. Your lady friend is a regular customer."

"Yes, bring me a pipe, man, thank you, and what of a lady called Toress Lahl? Is she here?"

"She's expected."

"All right." He went through into the rear room. Insil Esikananzi was resting on a couch, smoking a long-stemmed pipe. She looked perfectly calm, and regarded Luterin without speaking.

He sat by her without a word, and presently the young Odim brought him a lighted pipe. He inhaled with pleasure and immediately felt a mood strangely compounded of resignation and determination steal over him. He felt he was equal to anything. He understood now Insil's expanded irises, and held her hand.

"My husband is dead," she announced. "Did you know that? Did I tell you what he did to me on our wedding night?"

"Insil, I've had enough confidences from you for one day. That episode in your life is over. We are still young. We can marry, can make one another happy or miserable, as the case may be."

Wreathing herself in smoke, she said from the centre of it, "You are a fugitive. I need a home. I need care. I no longer need love. What I need is occhara. I want someone who can protect me. I want you to get Asperamanka back."

"That's impossible. He's dead."

"If you find it impossible, Luterin, then please be quiet and leave me to my thoughts. I am a widow. Widows never last long in winter. . . ."

He sat by her, sucking on the occhara, letting his thoughts die.

"If you could also kill my father, the Keeper, this remote community could revert to nature. The Wheel would stop. The plague could come and go. The survivors would see the Weyr-Winter through."

"There will always be survivors. It's a law of nature."

"My husband showed me the laws of nature, thank you. I do not wish for another husband."

They fell silent. Young Odim entered and announced to Luterin that Toress Lahl awaited him in an upper room. He cursed and stumbled after the man up a rickety stair without a backward look at Insil, certain that she would remain where she was for some while.

Luterin was shown into a small cabin, before which a curtain did duty for a door. Inside, a bed served as the only furniture. Beside the bed stood Toress Lahl. He was astonished at her girth until he remembered that he was much the same size.

She had certainly grown older. There was grey in her hair, although she still dressed it as she had done ten years ago. Her cheeks were rough and florid with the abrasion of frost. Her eyes were heavier, although they lit as she smiled with recognition. In every way, she seemed unlike Insil, not least in the kind of calm stoicism with which she presented herself for his inspection.

She wore boots. Her dress was poor and patched. Unexpectedly, she removed her fur hat—whether in welcome or respect he could not tell.

He took a step towards her. She immediately came forward and embraced him, kissing him on both cheeks.

"Are you well?" he asked.

"I saw you yesterday. I was waiting outside the Wheel when they let you free. I called to you but you did not look my way."

"It was so bright." Still confused by the occhara, he could think of nothing to say. He wanted her to make jokes like Insil. When she did not, he asked, "Do you know Insil Esikananzi?"

"She has become a good friend of mine. We've supported each other in many ways. The years have been long, Luterin . . . What plans do you have?"

"Plans? The sun's gone down."

"For the future."

"This innocent is again a fugitive. . . . They may even try to blame me for Asperamanka's death." He sat down heavily on the bed.

"That man is dead? It's a mercy. . . ." She thought and then said, "If you can trust me, Luterin, I could take you to my little hideout."

"I would only be a source of danger."

"That's not what our relationship is based on. I'm still yours, Luterin, if you will have me." When he hesitated, she said pleadingly, "I need you, Luterin. You loved me once, I believe. What choices do you have here, surrounded by enemies?"

"There's always defiance," he said. He laughed.

They went down the narrow stairs together, taking care in the dark. At the bottom, Luterin looked into the rear room. To his surprise, the couch was empty and Insil had gone.

They bid good-bye to young Odim and made their way into the night.

In the gathering darkness, the Avernus passed overhead, making its swift transit of the sky. It was now a dead eye.

At last the splendid machine had run down. Its surveillance system was only partly functional. Many other systems—but not the vital ones—were still operational. Air still circulated. Cleaning machines still crawled through walkways. Here and there, computers still exchanged information. Coffee machines still regularly brought coffee to the boil.

Stabilisers kept the Earth Observation Station automatically on course. In the port departure lounge, a toilet regularly flushed itself, like a creature unable to suppress weeping fits.

But no signals were returning to Earth.

And Earth no longer had need of them, although there were many who regretted the termination of that unfolding story from another world. For Earth was moving beyond its compulsive stage, where civilisation was measured by the quantity of possessions, into a new phase of being where the magic of individual experience was to be shared, not stored; awarded, not hoarded. The human character became involuntarily more like that of Gaia herself: diffuse, ever changing, ever open to the adventures of the day.

As they went through the dusk, leaving the village behind them, Toress Lahl tried to talk of superficial things. Snow fell, blowing in from the north.

Luterin did not reply. After a silence, she told him how she had borne him a son, now almost ten years old, and offered Luterin anecdotes about him.

"I wonder if he will grow up to kill his father," was all Luterin said.

"He is metamorphosed, as we are. A true son, Luterin. So he will survive and breed survivors, we hope."

He trudged behind her, still with nothing to say. They passed a deserted hut and were heading for a belt of trees. He glanced back now and again.

She was following her own train of thought. "Still your hated Oligarchy is killing off all the phagors. If only they understood the real workings of the Fat Death, they would know that they are killing off their own kind too."

"They know well enough what they're doing."

"No, Luterin. You generously gave me the key to JandolAnganol's chapel, and I've lived there ever since. One evening, a knock came at the door and there was Insil Esikananzi."

He looked interested. "How did Insil know you were there?"

"It was an accident. She had run away from Asperamanka. They were then newly married. He had brutally sodomised her, and she was in pain and despair. She remembered the chapel as a refuge—your brother Favin had taken her there once, in happier days. I looked after her and we became close friends."

"Well . . . I'm glad she had a friend."

"I showed her the records left by JandolAnganol and the woman Muntras, with the explanations of how there was a tick which travelled from phagors to mankind carrying the plagues necessary to mankind's survival in the extreme seasons. That knowledge Insil took back with her, to explain to the Keeper and the Master, but they would take no notice."

He gave a curt laugh. "They took no notice because they already knew. They would not want Insil's interference. They run the system, don't they? They *knew*. My father knew. Do you imagine those old church papers were secret? Their knowledge became common knowledge."

The ground sloped. They picked their way more carefully toward where the caspiarn forest began.

Toress Lahl said, "The Oligarch *knew* that killing off all phagors meant ultimately killing the humans—yet still he passed his orders? That's incredible."

"I can't defend what my father did—or Asperamanka. But the knowledge did not suit them. Simply that. They felt they had to act, despite their knowledge."

He caught the scent of the caspiarns, inhaled the slight vinegary tang of their foliage. It came like the memory of another world. He drew it gratefully into his lungs. Toress Lahl had two yelk tethered in the shelter of the trees. She went forward and fondled their muzzles as he spoke.

"My father did not know what would happen if Sibornal was rid of phagors for ever. He just believed that it was something necessary to do, whatever the consequences. We don't know what will happen either, despite what it may say in some fusty old documents. . . ." More to himself, he said, "I think he felt some drastic break with the past was needed, no matter what the cost. An act of defiance, if you like. Perhaps he will one day be proved right. Nature will take care of us. Then they'll make a saint of him, like your wicked saint JandolAnganol.

"An act of defiance . . . that's mankind's nature. It's no good just sitting back and smoking occhara. Otherwise we should never progress. The key to the future must lie with the future, not the past."

The wind was getting up again; the snow came faster.

"Beholder!" she said. She put a hand up to her rough face. "You've grown hard. Are you going to come with me?" she asked.

"I need you," she said, when he did not answer.

He swung himself up into the saddle, relishing the familiarity of the act, and the response of the animal beneath him. He patted the yelk's warm flank.

He was an exile in his own land. That would have to change. Asperamanka was done for. The obscene Ebstok Esikananzi would have to be brought to an accounting. He did not wish for what Esikananzi had; he wanted justice. His face was grim as he gazed down at the yelk's mane.

"Luterin, are you ready? Our son is waiting for us in the chapel."

He stared across at the blur of her face and nodded. Snowflakes settled on his eyelids. As they nudged their mounts down among the trees, a wind cut through the forest, slicing down from the slopes of Mount Shivenink. Snow cascaded across their shoulders from branches overhead. The ground sloped towards the hidden chapel. They wound by what had once been a waterfall and was now a pillar of ice.

At the last moment, Luterin turned in the saddle to catch a last glimpse of the village. The light of its fires was reflected on the low cloud cover blowing in.

Holding the reins more firmly, he urged the yelk faster down the slope and into the thickening murk. The woman called to him with anxiety in her voice, but Luterin felt exhilaration rising in his arteries.

He raised a fist above his head.

"Abro Hakmo Astab!" he shouted, hurling his voice into the distances of the forest.

The wind took the sound and smothered it in the weight of falling snow.

THE END

For the nature of the world as a whole is altered by age. Everything must pass through successive phases. Nothing remains for ever what it was. Everything is on the move. Everything is transformed by nature and forced into new paths. One thing, withered by time, decays and dwindles. Another emerges from ignominy, and waxes strong. So the nature of the world as a whole is altered by age. The Earth passes through successive phases, so that it can no longer bear what it could, and it can now what it could not before.

Lucretius: *De Rerum Natura*

55 BC

My dear Clive,

There you have it. Seven years have passed since I began to consider these matters. This volume will achieve first publication in a year when we both reach a new decade, and when my age will be exactly double yours.

As I walk in Hilary's garden wondering what form of words to use, it occurs to me that the question to ask is, Why do individuals of the human race long for close community with each other, and yet remain so often apart? Could it be that the isolating factor is similar to that which makes us feel, as a species, apart from the rest of nature? Perhaps the Earth mother you meet in these pages has proved less than perfect. Like a real mother, she has had her troubles—on a cosmic scale.

So the fault is not all ours, or hers. We must accept a lack of perfection in the scheme of things, accept the yellow-striped fly. Time, in which the whole drama is staged, is, as J. T. Fraser puts it, "a hierarchy of unresolved conflicts." We must accept that limitation with the equanimity of Lucretius, and be angry only at those things against which one can be effectively angry, like the madness of making and deploying nuclear weapons.

Such matters are not generally the subject of literature. But I felt the necessity, as you see, to have a shot at incorporating them.

Now at last I have done. The rambling edifice of Helliconia is before you, with my hopes that you will enjoy the results.

Your affectionate
Father

Boars Hill
Oxford

ACKNOWLEDGEMENTS

Thanks for invaluable preliminary discussions go to Dr. J. M. Roberts (history) and Mr. Desmond Morris (anthropology). I also wish to thank Dr. B. E. Juel-Jensen (pathology) and Dr. Jack Cohen (biology) for factual suggestions. Anything sound philologically is owed to Professor Thomas Shippey; his lively enthusiasm has been of great help all along.

The globe of Helliconia itself was designed and built by Dr. Peter Cattermole, from its geology to its weather. For the cosmology and astronomy, I am indebted to Dr. Iain Nicolson, whose patience over the years is a cause for particular gratitude.

Dr. Mick Kelly and Dr. Norman Myers both gave up-to-date advice on winters other than natural ones. The structure of the Great Wheel owes much to Dr. Joern Bambeck. James Lovelock kindly allowed me to employ his concept of Gaia in this fictional form. Herr Wolfgang Jeschke's interest in this project from its early days has been vital.

My debt to the writings and friendship of Dr. J. T. Fraser is apparent.

To my wife, Margaret, loving thanks for letting Helliconia take over for so long, and for working on it with me.

Brian W. Aldiss has been a major science fiction author for more than thirty years. His work has won many honors, including the Hugo Award in 1962 for the novel *The Long Afternoon of Earth*, the Nebula Award for his novella "The Saliva Tree" in 1965, and the Prix Jules Verne in 1977 for the novel *Starship*. The *Helliconia* Trilogy is considered by many to be his most important fiction to date. In addition to novels and short stories, Aldiss has written two works of criticism, *The Billion-Year Spree* and *The Trillion-Year Spree*, which examine the history and development of science fiction.

Aldiss is noted for his precision of language, the complexity of his characters, and his ability to weave a multi-layered narrative that is both entertaining and intellectually challenging. He has experimented with a variety of narrative techniques over the course of his career, while maintaining a high literary standard. He lives with his family in Oxford, England.

Collier Nucleus Presents
the *Helliconia* Trilogy
by Brian W. Aldiss

Helliconia Spring (Volume I)

The great glaciers are melting, and life is awakening from a centuries-old sleep under a mantle of frost. The two great races, the dominant phagors and their physically puny but nettlesome enemies, mankind, inexorably head toward a terrible confrontation.

Change is sweeping the vast world on Helliconia as humanity, led by one far-thinking renegade, abandons the safety of Helliconia's underworld to bring a new order to the surface of the changing world.

One of the greatest epic science fiction novels ever written, *Helliconia Spring* is a robust adventure set against a vast and colorful world, vividly imagined by one of the finest SF authors of all time.

"This is *War and Peace* as distilled through the mind of a troubled futurologist, *Shōgun* as penned by a professional visionary."

—*The Washington Post Book World*

"A meaty, completely engrossing novel." —*Publishers Weekly*

Helliconia Summer (Volume II)

It is the middle of a centuries-long summer in the world of Helliconia as a magnificent drama unfolds. JandolAnganol, the beleaguered king of Borlien, struggling to keep the ship of state afloat, divorces his beautiful, popular queen to marry a young princess of the Oldorando empire. Beset by enemies from all sides, the king is the center of a storm of political trials, while the world goes mad around him.

Set amidst a colorful swirl of unforgettable characters, from Muntras the Ice Captain and CaraBansity the anatomist to Billy Xiao Pin, a visitor from a world beyond the sky, Helliconia's shifting fortunes race toward a climax that will sweep readers along by the power of Aldiss's compelling narrative.

But these turbulent events are only part of the story, for the forests of the planet are burning with a raging fire that threatens to engulf all the players before the unfolding drama ends.

"This is imaginative science fiction on a major scale, to be compared with the best of the masters in the field." —*St. Louis Post-Dispatch*

Also available in a Collier Nucleus edition is *Man in His Time: The Best Science Fiction Stories* of Brian W. Aldiss. This brilliant volume includes all of his finest SF, including the Nebula Award–winning novella, "The Saliva Tree."

Ask your bookseller for these and other Collier Nucleus Books, or use the order form on the last page of this book to order copies direct.

Great Science Fiction
by Award-Winning Authors
in Collier Nucleus Editions

Eye in the Sky **by Philip K. Dick**

In this science fiction classic, Dick poses a metaphysical puzzle that challenges readers to experiment with space and time.

"Philip K. Dick rivals Kurt Vonnegut." — *The New York Times Book Review*

Solar Lottery **by Philip K. Dick**

The psychologically gripping story of an ordinary man caught in a psychic power struggle set in the twenty-third century.

" . . . reality and madness, time and death, sin and salvation . . . [Philip K. Dick] is our own homegrown Borges . . ." — Ursula K. Le Guin

Gather, Darkness! **by Fritz Leiber**

Grand Master Fritz Leiber's futuristic tale of high-tech witchcraft involves an idealistic priest who finds himself caught between two warring factions—an all-powerful religious hierarchy and the cult of witches that rises up in opposition.

"A Fritz Leiber book is a real delight." — Marion Zimmer Bradley, author of *The Mists of Avalon*

A Specter Is Haunting Texas **by Fritz Leiber**

A politically barbed, post-atomic holocaust novel with the good sense to laugh at itself. Written as a satiric response to the political chaos that swirled around the Vietnam War, it is both a finely crafted science fiction novel of adventure and character and a sharply observed social commentary on the way the United States was torn apart and radicalized during the late 1960s.

City **by Clifford D. Simak**

Winner of the International Fantasy Award for Best Science Fiction novel, *City* is a work that chronicles in extraordinary terms the very human qualities by which we define civilization. Without elaborate technobabble or farfetched adventure, Hugo and Nebula award winner Clifford D. Simak draws a compelling portrait of the future that will hold readers spellbound.

"A high-water mark in science fiction writing." — *The New York Times Book Review*

Time and Again **by Clifford D. Simak**

This is Simak at the top of his form. It combines the deeply humanistic concerns and fast-paced storytelling of Simak the newspaperman with the inventiveness and far-future vision of Simak the science fictioneer. *Time and Again* rivals Isaac Asimov's Robot series in its treatment of robots as the inheritors of our future.

"To read science fiction is to read Simak."
                                                    —Robert A. Heinlein

Way Station by Clifford D. Simak
This is the story of Enoch Wallace, a simple farmer who just happens to be a keeper of one of the countless stations of a transit system that spans the galaxy. And now, after millennia of quiet isolation, Enoch's lonely outpost on Earth is fated to become the center of a galaxy-wide crisis, all because of a single act of human kindness.

The Steps of the Sun by Walter Tevis
A twenty-first century businessman must bring back a new fuel supply and evade government authorities in order to save an energy-depleted earth.

"Engaging and effortless . . . Tevis's best science fiction since *The Man Who Fell to Earth*."
                                                    —*Publishers Weekly*

Empire of the Atom by A. E. van Vogt
Clane, the mutant heir to the post-holocaust empire of Linn, is one of van Vogt's most beloved and popular characters. Physically weak yet brilliantly resourceful, Clane is endowed with psychic powers that give him an aura of magic. He has to overcome the Machiavellian intrigues and power plays of all those around him before he can claim the throne that he richly deserves.

The Voyage of the Space Beagle by A. E. van Vogt
This classic space adventure created a sensation when first published, and it has continued to do so ever since. A combination of courage, quick thinking and clever tactics help the crew and ship navigate through the terrors of deep space in one of the most exciting space novels ever written.

"A. E. van Vogt is one of the all-time greats!"
                                                    —*The Magazine of Fantasy & Science Fiction*

Ask your bookseller for these and other Collier Nucleus Books, or use the order form to order copies direct.

Other Collier Nucleus titles are available at your local bookstore or by mail. To order directly, return the coupon below to: Macmillan Publishing Company, Special Sales Department, 866 Third Avenue, New York, NY 10022.

Line #	ISBN	Author/Title	Price	Quantity
1	0020160909	ALDISS / *Helliconia Spring*	$12.00	_____
2	0020160917	ALDISS / *Helliconia Summer*	$10.00	_____
3	0020302258	ALDISS / *Man in His Time*	$ 4.95	_____
4	0020315910	DICK / *Eye in the Sky*	$ 9.00	_____
5	0020236212	DICK / *Solar Lottery*	$ 9.00	_____
6	002022348X	LEIBER / *Gather, Darkness!*	$ 9.00	_____
7	0020223471	LEIBER / *A Specter Is Haunting Texas*	$ 9.00	_____
8	0020253915	SIMAK / *City*	$ 5.95	_____
9	0020253958	SIMAK / *Time and Again*	$ 9.00	_____
10	0020248717	SIMAK / *Way Station*	$ 8.00	_____
11	002029865X	TEVIS / *The Steps of the Sun*	$ 4.50	_____
12	0020259913	VAN VOGT / *Empire of the Atom*	$ 8.00	_____
13	0020259905	VAN VOGT / *The Voyage of the Space Beagle*	$ 8.00	_____

Sub-total _____

Please add postage and handling costs—$2.00 for the first book and 75¢ for each additional book _____

Sales tax—if applicable _____

TOTAL _____

Control No. [   ]   Ord. Type [SPCA]   Lines Units [|]

____ Enclosed is my check/money order payable to Macmillan Publishing Company.

____ Bill my ____ AMEX ____ MasterCard ____ Visa   Expiration date _____

Card # _____ Signature _____
Charge orders valid only with signature

Ship to: _____

_____

_____ Zip Code

For charge orders only:

Bill to: _____

_____

_____ Zip Code

For information regarding bulk purchases, please write to Special Sales Director at the above address. Publisher's prices are subject to change without notice. Allow 4–6 weeks for delivery.   FC #1808